A PIRATE'S PASSION

"Tell me something, Captain," Molly said mockingly. "What makes you different from a pirate?"

"Perhaps everything," Bran said softly, his eyes sparkling. His hand cupped her cheek, and she flinched. Something flickered in the depths of his blue gaze, but he didn't remove his hand.

"Or maybe nothing," he said darkly. His fingers tingled across her silken skin; Molly closed her eyes in joy at his touch. "Shall I show you how I plunder?"

He bent his head, and his mouth touched the smooth skin at her throat. Molly sucked in a ragged breath. His lips were gentle even as his hands kept a firm grip on her, sliding up from her waist to her back.

Fire shot through her veins . . . fire and liquid heat. The feeling frightened her, for every part of her cried out for him to touch her, take her . . .

CAPTURE THE GLOW
OF ZEBRA'S HEARTFIRES

AUTUMN ECSTASY   (3133, $4.25)
by Pamela K. Forrest

Philadelphia beauty Linsey McAdams had eluded her kidnappers but was now at the mercy of the ruggedly handsome frontiersman who owned the remote cabin where she had taken refuge. The two were snowbound until spring, and handsome Luc LeClerc soon fancied the green-eyed temptress would keep him warm through the long winter months. He said he would take her home at winter's end, but she knew that with one embrace, she might never want to leave!

BELOVED SAVAGE   (3134, $4.25)
by Sandra Bishop

Susannah Jacobs would do anything to survive—even submit to the bronze-skinned warrior who held her captive. But the beautiful maiden vowed not to let the handsome Tonnewa capture her heart as well. Soon, though, she found herself longing for the scorching kisses and tender caresses of her raven-haired BELOVED SAVAGE.

CANADIAN KISS   (3135, $4.25)
by Christine Carson

Golden-haired Sara Oliver was sent from London to Vancouver to marry a stranger three times her age—only to have her husband-to-be murdered on their wedding day. Sara vowed to track the murderer down, but he ambushed her and left her for dead. When she awoke, wounded and frightened, she was staring into the eyes of the handsome loner Tom Russel. As the rugged stranger nursed her to health, the flames of passion erupted, and their CANADIAN KISS threatened never to end!

Available wherever paperbacks are sold, or order direct from the Publisher. Send cover price plus 50¢ per copy for mailing and handling to Zebra Books, Dept. 3483, 475 Park Avenue South, New York, N.Y. 10016. Residents of New York, New Jersey and Pennsylvania must include sales tax. DO NOT SEND CASH.

CANDACE McCARTHY
SMUGGLER'S WOMAN

ZEBRA BOOKS
KENSINGTON PUBLISHING CORP.

For Keith John

ZEBRA BOOKS

are published by

Kensington Publishing Corp.
475 Park Avenue South
New York, NY 10016

First printing: August, 1991

Printed in the United States of America

Chapter One

Manville, New Jersey; June 24, 1778

"Well, well, if it isn't Molly McCormick . . ."

Molly stiffened at the sound of the hateful male voice. She stepped through the open doorway, squinting to adjust her gaze to the dark interior of the general store.

Reginald Cornsby stood behind the long wooden counter across the room, studying her with beady yellow-gray eyes. A rotund man with a bulbous nose, he wore a white muslin shirt stained with perspiration and had a paunch that hung over the top of his breeches. His white powdered wig was slightly askew, as if he'd recently attempted to set it right. Sensing her hesitation and unease, Cornsby beckoned her closer, a lascivious smile curving his lips.

"Mr. Cornsby," she said, nodding politely at the obese man. "I've brought more baskets." With a shiver of revulsion, she straightened her spine and approached the counter.

"So I see." His eyes took on a calculating gleam as they fastened on the handwoven baskets cradled within her arms. "You've been busy," he commented.

Molly squirmed inwardly as his gaze moved to caress her length, lingering on her breasts. "I've brought ten today," she said briskly, "just like you asked." Carefully she placed the wood-splint scuttles on the counter. These ten were samples of her finest work, painstakingly woven in three sizes. Now if Cornsby would just hand over her money she could be on her way.

"Just like I asked. How nice." His tone suggested he was pleased by the thought. "Let's see now . . . ten baskets at . . ." Cornsby turned to the shelf behind him, taking down a small tin and fumbling inside, ". . . a copper apiece." He extracted several coins before replacing the tin on the shelf.

"A copper apiece!" she gasped without thinking. He faced her, an unholy grin plastered on his flaccid face. With a feeling of foreboding, Molly's heart thumped hard beneath her breast.

Why did the man persist in his attentions toward her? she wondered. The other Manville residents took great pains to avoid her, repulsed by her long matted dark hair, grimy face, and ragged clothing. Why not him? Dressed as she was in greasy buckskins, she was the townspeople's image of a heathen Indian. What was it that kept Cornsby panting after her like a wolf after its mate?

She shivered. The last thing she wanted to do was draw his—or anyone's—attention. Before each visit to town, Molly rubbed her face with dirt and her hair with dried leaves. If playing the role of a heathen Indian kept others from bothering her, then

6

she would so, and gladly! Her ruse worked well; the residents usually avoided her. Only Reginald Cornsby, the Manville storekeeper, wasn't repulsed by her appearance. Which was just as well, she thought. His store was the only one available for her to do business.

Molly sold Cornsby her baskets regularly in order to survive. The man paid a fair price and then sold her work at a hefty profit. The arrangement suited them both, for she knew the residents would refuse to buy from her directly. She relied on the money for food and supplies for herself, her father, and her two half brothers.

She had one problem with dealing with Cornsby. The man lusted after her. She could see it in his eyes, his smile. If she didn't need their arrangement so badly, she'd have promptly and effectively dampened Mr. Cornsby's desire with a good swift kick to his bulging breeches! But with the Rebel uprising, times were tough. And ever since Molly's mother died, when Molly was five, her father was drunk more often than not. Money was precious to the McCormick household, and Cornsby's store was a valuable source. Her brothers made what they could at the iron furnace, but most of their hard-earned money went to paying off their debts at the company store there.

Reginald was studying her from beneath half-lowered lids as Molly extended a hand for the money.

"One." Placing a copper coin in her palm, he reached for one of the baskets. "Very nice," he murmured, caressing the rim with his finger. His pale yellowish eyes glowed hotly as he stroked the weave with a lover's touch.

Molly could sense what was in his thoughts. She

7

felt her flesh crawl at the idea of those fat fingers against her skin. Not in your lifetime, Cornsby! she vowed silently.

"Lovely," he said softly. His eyes rose from the red flower she'd stamped onto the basket side to capture her gaze meaningfully. "So lovely . . . just like its crafts . . . woman."

"Mr. Cornsby—"

"Reginald, my dear." He grinned. "Oh yes, your money."

Molly nodded, relieved. She watched as he returned the basket to its resting place and began to count out the remainder of the coins.

"Two, three, four . . ." He placed the fifth coin into her palm and stepped back, smiling. "There, that should do it—"

"Ten coppers, Mr. Cornsby," she reminded him sharply. "You owe me five more coppers." She needed that money; she'd worked hard for it.

"Oh! Foolish me! I must have left them in the back room." He lifted a hand to his white powdered wig and then gestured toward the door behind him. "Shall we slip into the back? I'm sure we'll find . . . ah . . . ." He cleared his throat. ". . . money in there."

"I'll wait here while you look," Molly replied, her eyes narrowing.

"But my dear, I'm sure you'll be more comfortable sitting down." His pale gaze went to where her breasts pushed against the single layer of her buckskin tunic. "It may take me some time to find it," he warned.

Suddenly Molly felt as if she were suffocating within the store's four walls. If she didn't get her money and get out now, she was liable to do something she'd regret. Her gaze caught the furtive movement of Cornsby's right hand as it groped at something behind the counter. Why the louse! she thought. He's hiding the coins!

"Mr. Cornsby—Reginald." She smiled as she began to edge around the counter. "Perhaps I should rest for a while . . ." The last word trailed off meaningfully, and Cornsby's eyes widened with delight.

"Come, dear, I have just the place where w—you won't be disturbed," he said, his voice rising to a high-pitched squeak. At last! he thought. Beads of perspiration broke out on his forehead at the thought of the girl's naked flesh quivering against his thighs. He'd waited so long to feel those soft breasts in his palms. She was only inches away from him. He was trembling like an untried boy!

"Reginald will see that you're refreshed," he murmured, lifting a shaking hand to run his fingers down the length of her long dark hair. He envisioned how she'd looked that day when he'd spied her bathing in the river. Her black hair had been newly washed, a wet silken mantle about her bare shoulders. Hiding amidst a copse, he'd been able to take his fill of her beauty. Gentle curves and sleek limbs . . . His breath grew harsh with anticipation, and his male member hardened beneath his durant breeches.

"You have my money, don't you, Reginald?"

"What?" He pulled his gaze from her mouth to note the beauty of her dark eyes. "Oh, of course!" He licked his lips once. Again. His beefy hand settled on her shoulder.

Molly endured his touch passively, trying not to display her disgust. Her nose wrinkled; Cornsby

9

stank of sour sweat and cheap whiskey. She fluttered her long eyelashes, and he inhaled sharply, aroused.

If I can just keep him preoccupied, she thought, I'll be able to edge over to where he hid the coins.

"Of course, I have your money." Cornsby nodded vehemently. "Have I ever tried to cheat you?"

"No." She had to admit that he'd never attempted to cheat her — before now. Slowly, so as not to attract his notice, she began easing along the length of the counter.

"You must be weary after your journey. Perhaps you'd like to stay awhile." He ran his hand down her arm, and Molly shuddered. "We can have supper," Cornsby invited. "You can spend the night. I live all alone . . ."

That's because no one would want you! Molly cried silently.

"Thanks for your offer, Mr. . . . ah . . . Reginald, but I really got to go. You see, my brothers are gone, and my sick father's alone." Just a few more inches and then she could reach the money! Carefully she maneuvered her body between Cornsby and the counter, until the wooden table was pressing against her back.

"Your father." Cornsby grimaced with disdain. Meeting her gaze, his expression grew tender. "If you were my daughter, I'd take better care of you."

"I—" Her reply was muffled and became a shriek when Reginald suddenly jerked her close, capturing her lips with his cold fleshy mouth.

Stiffening, Molly struggled to be free, pushing fiercely against him. Her efforts proved futile; Cornsby was too heavy for her to budge. She whimpered, sickened by his smell, his touch, his unwashed body. His hands were rough in his un-leashed ardor. His kiss was wet, sloppy, and she knew the memory of it would forever make her ill. Desperate, she stomped down hard on his big toe.

Howling, he released her instantly, his hands nursing his injured foot. "What did you do that for?" He glared at her with reproach, his yellow-gray eyes bright with pain.

"Don't touch me," she snarled menacingly. Her eyes narrowed as she advanced threateningly, taking him by surprise. "Don't ever touch me again!"

Cornsby blinked, momentarily stunned by her be-havior. "You bitch!" His fat face turned red with rage. "Savage whore! You want it and you know it!" Releasing his foot, he gingerly flexed his sore toe. He moved unexpectedly then, clearing the counter of her baskets with one wide swipe of his fat arm. "Get out!" he ordered. "And see if you can sell your baskets now! Why, I've practically had to force my customers to buy them. The blasted things aren't worth a copper. I've been overpaying you!"

"K' nees' gahk-gay-loon 'en. You nasty liar!" she spat. "You make two coppers on every one of my baskets. I'll sell them—I'll charge only one!" But despite Molly's show of bravado, she had serious doubts about her ability to sell them.

Cornsby looked smug. "You think they'll buy from you, a damn Injun?" His harsh laughter rever-berated about the shop as he kicked a basket with his uninjured foot. "You'd have sold them yourself long ago if you believed you could! You wait, wench! You'll come crawling, begging, back to me with your legs spread! You'll be forced to admit that I was right. You can't get better than Reginald Cornsby! You'll rue the day you denied me!"

11

"In a cool day in hell, Cornsby!" Her dark eyes afire, Molly glared at him while under the counter-. top her groping hand discovered the hidden money. Her fingers closed over the copper coins, and she brought them up against her back. The metal warmed within her tightened fist. How she longed to smash Cornsby's ugly face!

The man's eyes half closed in sudden speculation as he noted Molly's look of triumph. His gaze swung from her to the counter, and cursing, he rushed forward, shoving her aside. "What the hell!" He turned on her in fury. She chuckled and held up the coins. "Why you little—"

He came after her then, and Molly fled as fast as her feet would take her. She heard a thud, and then Cornsby cursed loudly. Giddy with her success, she laughed and ran out the door.

He wouldn't follow her; she was safe. How could he possibly catch up with her? He was too fat to run. She was too fast for him.

Once outside, Molly slowed her gait, lifting up her face to enjoy the sun's warmth. She smiled, unafraid. Cornsby wouldn't want it known that he'd attempted to bed the half-breed savage. No, the worst of it was that now she'd have to travel to Clamtown to sell her baskets. The extra miles would mean an overnight stay.

Damn! she thought. She didn't need Cornsby. She should have dampened his desire months ago!

A commotion rose in the streets behind Molly when Cornsby's voice was heard throughout the village. She glanced back at the gathering crowd. She gasped. They were looking—pointing—at her!

"Stop, thief!" To Molly's horror, Cornsby gestured wildly in her direction. "The savage robbed me," he bellowed to those around him. "She stole my money!"

Liar! she wanted to shout. The money was rightfully hers! She'd earned it! Cornsby had her baskets. The coins belonged to her!

"There she is! Over there!" a man shouted, and Molly started back to defend herself. Facing a sea of angry faces, she paused, changing her mind. *They won't listen to me. Cornsby is one of them and to them, I'm just a savage. How can I prove my innocence?*

"Get her!" The storekeeper's voice rose to incite the crowd. "Take the little heathen. She stole from me!"

"Let's get her!" Several townspeople echoed the man's outcry.

Molly turned heel and ran. Sprinting down the dusty lane, she veered off into the dense woods line. *Some day Cornsby will pay*, she vowed, envisioning the wicked gleam in his pale eyes as he sounded the alarm. She longed to go back, if only to wipe the triumphant smile off his unsightly face.

If there'd been the slightest chance that the villagers would believe her, she would have dug in her heels and faced her accuser. But Molly knew better. Everyone in Manville knew Reginald Cornsby was a lowlife, but to them Molly McCormick was worse. To the people of Manville, Molly was "that filthy half-breed", the bastard spawn of Tully McCormick and his Lenape lover, Shi'ki-Xkwe.

Tears of anger stung her eyes as her feet flew over the uneven ground. She'd never understand their attitude. Why was it a sin to be born a bastard?

Angry voices rallied behind Molly, and she heard the snap of the brush as her pursuers followed.

Heart thumping, breath labored, Molly slipped into the cover of the nearest copse, where she paused to get her bearings.

Her gaze darted wildly about the surrounding landscape, seeking an avenue of escape. Through the next grouping of trees she spied a narrow path, and she raced toward the trail with renewed strength.

Somewhere to the left was her father's cottage. A right turn, several yards, and she could hide amidst the thick foliage.

Dogs! She cursed them silently. I've done nothing wrong! Go away!

Molly stumbled, righted herself, and then turned to the right and off the path. A hundred yards through the brush and bramble she paused to rest, too tired to take another step. Crouching behind a cluster of briars, she listened, her breath still.

The sound of voices receded. Her gaze caught the flash of a bright blue coat on the other side of the distant trail. They were continuing their search toward her father's cabin!

Damn him! Damn them all! When her father found out what had happened, he'd be furious with her. She gave a silent prayer that he wasn't drinking again. Intoxicated, Tully McCormick would punish his daughter first and ask questions afterward.

Molly waited in her hiding place, pondering ways to speak alone to her younger half brother. Shelby would believe her. And he'd make her father believe her too! Unlike Darren, her oldest brother, who made no secret of his hatred of her, Shelby cared for her.

She decided to wait until dark before heading for home. Hopefully by then, Cornsby and his followers would be long gone from the woods and her father's cabin. Perhaps if she waited until it was late, she could wake up Shelby while her father and Darren slept . . .

A twig snapped, and Molly jumped. Her eyes widened as she spied a figure slinking low along the trail toward her. In a sudden decision, she raced toward the cedar swamp. No man would dare follow her there! There were too many ways to die . . .

The forest thickened as Molly entered the swamp. She stepped slowly, carefully. The trees above grew together in a profuse tangle, their entwined leaves blocking out the bright sunlight. A rustling, grinding moan drew her gaze upward to the treetops time and again. Molly's heart pounded as she glanced over her shoulder. There were no signs of her pursuers. *It's just the wind I hear in the trees,* she thought. *I have to get out of this swamp!*

Danger abounded in each step she took, in the creatures that lurked in hidden places. Should she go back the way she came? Or would the man be lying in wait for her?

Ahead, sunlight filtered through the trees, softly illuminating a distant clearing. She immediately changed directions, hoping that the break in the leafy canopy above meant a quick exit from the dismal swamp. The pungent smell of rotting vegetation assailed her nostrils as she cautiously negotiated the unstable ground.

Something made a noise behind her—a crackle, a crunch, like that made by a man clearing marsh grass. The clearing was only a short distance away, and Molly took off in a dead run, praying she'd not get caught in any hidden quagmire. To her relief, she reached the clearing without mishap, rejoicing in the feel of solid ground beneath her feet. She found cover behind a tall cedar, listening, expecting to hear the crash of a man's footsteps, the bellow of a deep voice.

All was blissfully, remarkably silent, and Molly emitted a deep sigh. Smiling with her success at having evaded her pursuers, she turned and then abruptly froze.

She wasn't alone. There were two, no three, men eyeing her steadily. Her gaze fell to the largest fellow, a hideous ruffian with a jagged scar from his forehead to the edge of his scraggly beard. His eyes glimmered with a feral light as they swept Molly from head to toe.

"Oh, sweet Jesus!" Molly swore as she braced herself to fight.

Chapter Two

"What do we 'ave 'ere?" The bearded brute stepped toward her.

"Why, it's a woman!" came another whining voice.

The third ruffian, who was just a youth, spoke up, "Ya calls that a woman? Looks more like a skunk, if ya asks me."

Molly backed away, cursing her new predicament. Her eyes flashed from the man who was slowly advancing on her to his two companions, who appeared less threatening. The men were dressed simply in striped shirts and short, bell-bottomed trousers, their hair worn in queues tied back with hemp. They work black neckerchiefs and black shoes with silver buckles. A knit cap sat on top of Beard-face's sea-weathered head, while his two friends sported hats with wide brims.

"Come 'ere, dearie. Old John won't 'urt ya." Beard-face raised a hand, beckoning her closer. "Oo, yer a right fine thing, if ya ask me. Don't be afeared. Come on now."

"Why won't she say anything?" the youngest of the three asked.

Old John's eyes narrowed. "What's yer name, girlie?"

Clamping her mouth shut, Molly glared at him.

"So that's the way it's to be, is it?" His huge hand hovered near his belt, drawing Molly's glance. Her breath caught as he withdrew a jackknife, flipping it open to wield it dangerously in her direction. He was within ten feet of her now. Molly stepped back and stopped. She knew the ground behind her was unstable; she couldn't risk it.

The middle fellow, who Molly silently dubbed Slim-bones, looked about anxiously, obviously not pleased with the turn of events. "John, I don't think this is a good idea. The captain—"

John shot him a menacing look. "This ain't no concern of the capt'n's. I just wanna to 'ave a little funnin' with the lady 'fore we let 'er go." His voice hardened. "Got any objections?"

"N—no, not me, John," the boy was quick to pipe in.

Slim-bones was slower in agreeing. "Guess not. As long as ya don't hurt her."

Beard-face's eyes gleamed. " 'Urting the fine darlin' is the last thing I wanna do . . ."

Suddenly Old John pounced. Molly screamed as he caught her within his massive fingers. When she struggled wildly to be free, the man laughed, aroused by her spirit, but he dropped his knife.

She stilled her body and hung limply within his grasp, realizing that her fighting actions only incited the bearded man's lust. He shook her. Enraged, she slammed her head up under his chin and heard him grunt with the impact. Her breath com-

18

ing in hard pants, Molly glared up into her captor's face, her dark eyes shooting hot sparks. Old John's teeth flashed as he sneered, and she spat in his eye, renewing her fight.

"Damn it all now, girl!" He gasped and cursed as Molly's foot connected with his right shin. "Get me my knife," he ordered the boy. "Now!"

Old John held tight to Molly's left arm, but she slammed him in his stomach with her right fist. "Damn!" he cursed. "Where's my knife!"

The boy appeared at Old John's side with the weapon, extending it toward the big man. Molly swung, and the boy ducked and withdrew, the open jackknife still clutched tightly within his grasp.

"Jesus, boy!" Old John howled as Molly sank her teeth into his arm. Releasing her, he jerked his arm free, clubbing her in the face. She reeled back under the impact, and stars danced in her eyes.

She had a brief second to gather her senses, but by the time her head cleared it was too late. Old John grabbed her by her hair; Molly felt the point of his knife prick her throat. She flinched as a drop of blood welled to the surface.

"Ya shouldn't 'ave done that," he muttered, his putrid breath hot against her face as he pulled her against him. "A lady oughta behave like one."

"K'ahk-peek'soo ka'wia!" Molly spat. She took great pleasure in calling the man a flea-bitten porcupine.

John's brows lifted and his grip loosened. "A savage! We got ourselves somebody's squaw!" His lips curved upward in a wicked smile, and goosebumps rose on Molly's flesh. "No need to worry 'bout letting this one go. We kin do a little sharing and then be done wi—"

19

"Smithers!" a deep bark rent the air, immediately drawing the attention of the three seamen. "What's going on here?"

Old John let go of Molly as if burned. Molly used the advantage to slip by him, but she was curious enough to stop near the edge of the clearing and glance back. The bearded man cowered beneath the force of the newcomer, who was obviously a superior officer. John's two comrades stood quivering by his side.

"I asked you a question, Smithers!"

"We found us someone snooping about the cove, sir. We was gettin' ready to take 'er in to the capt'n."

There was a moment of charged silence. "See that you do then," the officer said.

Molly's eyes widened, and the rest of what was said was lost as she turned and ran. This time Molly was on firm ground as she headed in the opposite direction. No one was going to take her anywhere! Not if she had anything to say about it!

Heavy footfalls sounded behind her as Molly tore through the brush. Brambles scraped her legs and scratched her bare arms, but she kept on going, ignoring the pain.

She had to get away!

"Hold on there!" a voice cried, and Molly recognized it as belonging to the youth. "I won't hurt ya! We won't hurt ya! Didn't ya heard Mr. Dickon? No one's going to hurt ya! The captain'll want to see ya, that's all."

Before she could utter a sound, she was thrown to the ground by the boy. She fought for all she was worth, but she found the youth surprisingly strong. There was nothing boyish about the stern face glaring down at her or about the callused hands that pinned her to the ground.

"Get up!" His tone held impatience as he yanked her to her feet. "You've got a meeting with the captain."

He caught her hands behind her back and pulled up sharply. She gasped, struggled weakly, and then gave up the battle. The youth grinned at her exhausted expression.

"That's et," he murmured, his eyes gleaming. He squeezed her hands hard, clearly exultant in his display of power. "Just how the captain likes 'em, nice and gentle-like."

"What the hell!" Bran Donovan scowled. "We've been discovered, you say? And by some chit of a female?"

Dickon, the first mate, nodded. "I'm afraid so, Captain."

"Damnation!"

"Take it easy, Bran," his brother urged. "It can't be that bad. What harm could she possibly do?"

Bran scowled. "Harm? I'll tell you what harm she can do. Have you forgotten the shipment of powder? If word gets out and it falls into the wrong hands . . ."

Patrick Donovan signaled to a barmaid across the room. "Agnes, a drink for my brother here!"

Nodding, Agnes brought over a tankard and set it before Bran, who glared at it fiercely.

The men were meeting at the Jug and Barrel Inn, the secret base of Rebel operations. Josiah Morse leaned across the trestle table. "Dickon thinks she stumbled upon the cove by accident. Odds are she'll never be able to find us again. Just take her somewhere and let her go."

Bran thought for a long moment, seriously contemplating the proprietor's advice. Josiah was a short man with a thickening middle and an eternal twinkle in his blue eyes. He had lived in these Pine Barrens since the Donovan brothers were knee-high to a groundhog. Josiah and the boys' father, Marcus Donovan, had been cohorts in smuggling during the years prior to the revolution.

Since Marcus's death five years back, Morse had taken on the role of surrogate father to Marcus's two sons. Following in their father's footsteps, Patrick and Bran became Morse's partners. But where Josiah and Marcus had smuggled for the pure joy of profiteering, the Donovan brothers smuggled to help the Patriot cause. Through their joint privateering and smuggling ventures, they acquired and transported supplies for Washington's Continental Army.

Although Bran respected Morse and didn't take his advice lightly, he still wasn't satisfied. "Need I remind you two that this area is crawling with Redcoats?" When no one commented, he slammed his fist down on the table top. "Damn! We lost three good men last week thanks to those blasted Tories!" He took a hefty swallow of ale before he slammed the mug down and shoved it away empty.

"I don't think you realize the gravity of our situation," Bran continued. "What time is the shipment due?"

"Ten p.m.," Josiah said. "Martin's handling the run. He'll be bringing the *Flying Wench* down river to the *Bloody Mary*, where our men will be waiting to transfer the powder kegs."

22

"Drink up, Bran," Patrick urged, "and relax. I still think you're worrying needlessly. Martin is a wily captain. He can weasel a fly past a frog's nose."

Bran cocked a dark eyebrow. "The girl may have stumbled upon the cove by accident, but I can't chance it. Not only are the lives of my crew at stake, but also those of the men depending on us for supplies." He shook his head, clearly dissatisfied with the decision he'd been forced to make. "The girl will have to be taken care of. In two days we'll put out to sea again, and I want no one interfering in our plans."

"And what are you proposing to do with her? Kill her?" Patrick looked aghast.

Bran looked at his brother with raised eyebrows. "I have no intention of killing the woman. If she is an enemy spy, she'll be more useful to me alive than dead." He became thoughtful, and his blue eyes took on a strange glint. "No, I mean to detain the lady in question until such a time that she no longer poses a threat."

"You're going to keep her prisoner," Josiah said, nodding and smiling.

"Prisoner, guest, call it what you will. The lady is going to be detained on board the *Bloody Mary*. I'll decide what to do with her after we get the powder."

When Bran and his man Dickon had left the inn, Patrick frowned and sipped from his ale. "Do you think he'll hurt her?"

"Damn it all, man, you're talking about your brother!" Morse replied angrily. "Bran may be reckless, but he's not stupid!" The man rose from the table to go about his business.

Yes, but Bran hasn't been himself lately, Patrick thought. *I'm not sure I know him anymore . . .* It was times like this, when the risk was high and lives hung in the balance, that he wanted to strangle his brother, Bran. Bran might be a good sea captain, but he'd become obsessive in his effort to help the cause.

Patrick himself wouldn't have bothered with the Rebel army if it hadn't been for Bran. It was Bran's persuasive manner that had prompted Pat to consider joining forces. And then when Josiah had agreed . . .

Because of Bran and the *Bloody Mary,* the Rebels had a constant supply of confiscated goods. Flintlocks, bayonets, foodstuff, and clothing were just a few of the valuable necessities he was able to provide.

Bran Donovan had a strong sense of honor. What other privateer would be willing to give up his share of the booty, to surrender the cargo seized from British ships? It was that sense of honor that irritated Patrick. What was wrong with keeping some of the profits for themselves?

It was an issue that he and Bran often disagreed on, but Patrick, loyal to his brother, kept faith with the cause.

Pat scowled and straightened in his seat. "Damn that sense of honor," he mumbled beneath his breath. "And damn this war!"

"You're beside yourself for nothing, boy." Josiah had heard Patrick's muttering as he returned to the table. "Your brother's not a cold-blooded killer."

Patrick nodded and raised his mug in a silent salute. It wasn't the girl he was worried about. There were more important things plaguing his thoughts.

24

"Get in there, girl!" The seaman, Will, shoved Molly into a cabin below deck. "And hush your mouth! The captain'll be wit' ya in a minute."

Molly shook the youth's hand from her arm and backed against the far wall. The cabin was spartan. A man's quarters. The captain's, she realized with a jolt of shock. Molly shivered as she imagined the brute needed to control these men.

"Hear me, squaw?" The scowling sailor muttered a harsh oath. "I said yer not to touch any of the captain's things." Then with a word of warning about the dire consequences of such an action, the young man left her alone in the musty cabin.

Pirates! Molly glared at the door, daring it to open again. These men were pirates! "Privateers," Will had insisted when they'd arrived in the cove, and she had disparagingly voiced her thoughts.

Privateers, pirates, it was all the same, wasn't it? These men attacked and plundered helpless or unwary vessels, killing their occupants and taking their loot.

Molly shuddered as she recalled Old John's smug face when young Will brought her back to the clearing. "Yep!" he'd said, "the capt'n will be interested in a piece like you, methinks. Take her in, Will! This one's trouble."

"Trouble," she grated between clenched teeth. "They haven't yet seen just how much trouble I can be!"

How dare they take her prisoner! She'd make them pay, every last one of them. Her thoughts went to Bran Donovan, the man she'd been told she was waiting to see. Molly swallowed hard, wonder-

25

ing if she could prove a match for the brutal ship's captain.

The *Bloody Mary,* this vessel was called. A chill raised the hairs at the back of Molly's neck. She hoped the ship's name was more sinister than her commander.

The schooner rocked slightly in its moorings. She could hear the tread of feet and the rumble of cargo across the deck above. The exchange of male voices as the sailors worked was friendly; she found it hard to picture their camaraderie. Sour-faced and tough, they were salt tars through and through. On the rough seas they'd be in their element, with the wind and downpour lashing their faces, their clothing tarred against the salt spray and rain.

Cutthroats and beggars they were most probably, Molly mused. Eyeing the door warily, she hugged herself. Murderers enjoying their lust for blood. Could she talk the captain into letting her go? If not, how was she to defend herself when she was so at the man's mercy?

Her gaze narrowed thoughtfully on the bunks built into the wall. A man in charge of cutthroats wouldn't be without a store of weapons. She checked the upper and lower berths, the desk against the far wall; all that was left was the chest in the corner.

She heard the heavy thud of feet and the sharp bark of a deep man's voice, then a sailor's respectful reply.

The captain! she realized with horror. She ran to the trunk and fumbled with the latches holding the lid. Damn! It was locked! There was nothing to ward off the man's attentions! Then her eyes caught the glint of steel on the floor behind the chest. Was that a knife?

Molly stretched and struggled until her fingers closed successfully around the pearl handle. She tugged, but the weapon wouldn't budge. Panicking, she tried again, using every last ounce of her strength. The knife pulled free, and she fell back with a thud onto the floor, skinning her arms on the wooden sea chest.

She glanced at the door and then down at herself, experiencing a small flush of relief. She had a knife. A small one, perhaps, but nevertheless, she knew how to use it. Besides, she had nothing to worry about; she was a mess. Surely, the man would be repulsed by her filthy appearance. He'd be anxious to be well rid of her. She stiffened. Like Cornsby was? Or Old John?

"Dickon!" the deep voice boomed from the other side of the thick oaken door, and Molly flinched. "She's in here, you say?"

"Yes, sir!"

The door crashed open, and there stood Captain Bran Donovan of the *Bloody Mary*. Tall, lithe, and with an expression that would intimidate the most wicked of men, he moved into the room, instantly filling it with his presence.

His eyes . . . they were the first thing about him Molly noted. They were blue like the sea. Changeable, she imagined. Right now they appeared cold and stormy, and she squirmed inwardly at the intensity of his gaze.

His hair was black, long, drawn back from his chiseled features and secured at his nape. A white muslin shirt fit snugly across his broad shoulders. Fawn-colored breeches hugged his muscular thighs, then tapered to tuck into polished black boots.

Molly's gaze returned to his face to gauge his expression. His sensual lips curved into an amused smile as he boldly studied her from head to toe.

Feeling violated by that icy blue stare, she stiffened her spine and glared back at him defiantly.

"What do we have here?" His voice was gruff, threatening, as he crossed the cabin to her in three strides.

Heart thumping, Molly backed away, her eyes widening.

The captain smiled grimly; his hand rose as if to touch her, to feel if she was real.

Molly's thoughts raced. *No! I will kill you before I let you touch me!* Their gazes locked as he extended his hand toward her ever so slowly. Her muscles coiled, ready to spring.

"You're not quite what I expected," he murmured. He touched her chin, tilting her face for his inspection.

Her fingers tightened about the pearl handle of the knife.

His expression changed, his eyes narrowed. His hand slid to caress her shoulder. "Easy now—"

With a warlike yell, Molly lunged at him with the razor-sharp knife.

Chapter Three

"What the—!" Bran's exclamation was cut off in a hiss as the girl's knife thrust nicked his arm. She drew back, ready to plunge again. Reacting instinctively, he seized her knife hand.

Molly screeched as she found her arm imprisoned in a steely grip. She kicked his shin hard, but unlike Beard-face, the captain merely grunted and twisted her wrist until she cried out in pain. The knife clattered uselessly to the floor.

With her only weapon gone, Molly fought the captain with a strength born of desperation, kicking and biting any exposed skin.

"Damn it, woman!" Bran boomed when her teeth sank into the soft flesh of his forearm. "Stop this at once!"

She broke loose. The two circled around the cabin, eyeing each other warily, Molly in a half crouch ready to spring.

"Easy now," he murmured, edging toward her. "No one is going to hurt you."

The door behind the captain opened.

"Bran? Good God!" came a startled gasp. The

combatants froze, momentarily caught off guard.

The captain was the first to recover. The new-comer's entrance was all Bran needed to gain the upper hand. With a quick lunge, Bran subdued the girl easily. They stood, captor and captive, each taking the other's measure.

Molly's dark eyes were filled with hate as she stood defiantly before him. Like herself, the captain was breathing hard, she noted with grim satisfaction. *You may have won this time, but the battle wasn't easy for you!*

"What are you doing here, Pat?" Bran's gaze remained fastened on the bedraggled female.

Patrick eyed the woman cautiously as he entered the cabin. "Who is she?"

"You didn't answer my question." Bran flashed him an angry glance before his gaze returned to the girl. Her body appeared slim and fragile, but her stature was deceptive. There was hidden power in her small limbs.

There was something about her, he decided as he inspected her thoroughly. She was a redskin! At least partly. Her deerskin tunic was soiled and torn, her hair tangled, her skin filthy, yet . . . Their eyes locked, and Bran was captivated by the intelligence in the depths of her midnight black eyes.

Bran's lids lowered as his speculation intensified. Could this creature actually be a spy, Tory or otherwise? It was a definite possibility.

One thing was certain, the wildcat wasn't wholly as she appeared. Her hair was tangled, but it wasn't as matted and greasy as he'd first assumed. Despite the surface dirt, she smelled like the forest after a spring rain. The girl was pretending to be something she wasn't, and the deceit intrigued Bran. One way or another, I'll know what she's up to, he decided. Was she Lenni Lenape? Many of the Lenapes had taken sides with King George's men.

Bran's gaze traveled the length of his captive's lithe form . . . over her buckskin tunic shielding her small but well-formed breasts . . . down to her shapely hips and bare calves. Dirty, yet smooth and unblemished . . . He felt his loins stir as he pictured her clean and unclothed like a wood nymph after bathing in a river.

Throughout his study, the girl continued to glare at him. Her hate was tangible; he could feel its strength.

Savage or wildcat? Girl or woman? He cursed as his thoughts took flight. For God's sake, she was only a child. And a heathen one at that! Or was she? an inner voice queried.

"What are you going to do with her?" Patrick asked.

Jolted from his reverie, Bran frowned. There'd already been crude comments from his men about the wench in his cabin. Having her on board ship would be a complication he didn't need.

Patrick? he wondered. Perhaps his brother would take her to that hunting cabin in the woods. A quick glance at Pat and Bran knew it wouldn't work. No match for this heathen hellcat, Patrick would be a poor guard.

No, Bran sighed, trouble or not, he'd have to keep her on the *Bloody Mary* until it was safe to let her go. Bran turned back to her, attempting to intimidate her with his steady gaze.

She didn't flinch; her eyes didn't waver. Suddenly, she gave an ear-curdling screech and broke from his hold.

"Bran, don't hurt her!"

Bran glanced at his brother in exasperation. "I'm not the one doing the hurting. She's taken a chunk out of my arm! Damn it, find me a rope, before she gets away. Hurry!"

Pat stood gaping. Molly had crouched in a stance of attack.

"Pat, I said get a rope!" his brother hollered.

Pat came out of his stupor, stumbling in his haste to get through the hatch.

Bran's breath hissed out when Molly punched him square in the jaw.

"Grab hold of her arm," Bran shouted as his brother returned, rope in hand. "No, not that arm! Yes, that's it! Now give me the blasted rope!"

With one hand free, he took hold of the rope and quickly looped an end around one of Molly's wrists. Exhausted, she slumped against him.

He'd taken on quite a handful, he thought grimly as he tied her hands together and then shoved her onto the bottom rack. He took hold of her dirty bare feet. "I need more rope."

Patrick complied, scowling as he handed it over. "For God's sake, what do you think you're doing? She'd just a kid!"

Molly's ears perked up at the sudden tension between the two men. The man called Pat seemed upset. She watched him through heavy lids. Here was a man who might aid her escape.

She was tired, sore, and hungry. And she'd never felt more miserable or frightened in her entire life. But she wouldn't let them know how she felt—no, never!

How dare they tie her up! How dare they keep her a prisoner!

To her dismay, the captain looked amused as he leaned back against his desk, his arms folded.

A chill ran the length of Molly's spine. This man was ruthless, and she was at his mercy. He was eyeing her with a strange light in his blue eyes. His gaze swept her length, and Molly felt vulnerable, naked.

Then, as if tiring of the game, the captain turned to the other man. "I asked you what you were doing here, Pat." His eyes flashed with anger. "I hope you aren't thinking of playing knight to this damsel in distress," he mocked. "If you are, you can forget it."

"No, well—"

"I said forget it." The captain's lips curved into a slow, wicked smile, and Molly felt a jolt when he glanced at her, his eyes darkening, unreadable.

"I haven't harmed the wench, as much as I've been tempted." Bran paused and then added, "Yet."

Molly glared at him, and he chuckled.

"Go home, Pat," he instructed his brother. "I assure you this lady can take care of herself." He retrieved the knife from the floor and fingered the blade, testing its sharpness.

Spying the pearl handle, Patrick's eyes widened. "Isn't that Father's jackknife?" *Father?* Molly thought with an inward groan. The men were brothers! Her hope for aid dwindled and died.

Bran nodded. "It is." He drew the knife gently along her bare arm, but left no mark. "You, lady, just tried to kill me." His tone was dark and threatening . . . soft, too soft. He towered over her, his expression hard. "Don't ever try it again."

The cabin door opened and Molly looked up,

33

blinking. It had been over two hours since the two men had taken their leave. With each passing moment her fury had mounted as she recalled the captain's parting comment. "You'll be treated as an invited guest if you behave," he'd said. "If not . . ." His words had trailed off ominously.

Damn him! Damn them all! She stiffened as the cabin door opened. Her eyes shot sparks at the tall burly man entering the cabin with a large tray.

"Ah, lass," he crooned, "to be left tied up and all alone." His voice held a Scottish burr, pleasing to the ears, but Molly only glared at him. Undaunted by her hostility, the man set his burden on the captain's chart table.

The appetizing scent of the food on the tray wafted to her nose, making her stomach growl.

The Scotsman fussed with the foodstuff and straightened, apparently satisfied. He clicked his tongue as he caught sight of her bonds. "What could he be thinking to do this to ye, I wonder?" The man smiled.

Molly eyed him warily at first. Then she felt herself responding to the warmth in his brown gaze.

There was no question in her mind who the he might be. It was that bastard, Captain Bran Donovan. This man works for the devil himself, Molly thought. Any softening toward the man instantly vanished.

"Ye must be famished." He reached toward Molly, and she recoiled as if struck. "Now, lass, don't ye be fretting," he murmured. "I'm only wanting to release yer bonds. You canna eat like that."

Molly relaxed. There was truth to his words. She sat passively as he untied her feet with deft fingers.

The Scot stood back, eyeing her thoughtfully. "If

34

I undo yer hands, ye willna try anything stupid?"

They gazed at each other for one long, tense moment. She'd be a fool to think she could outrun this Scotsman. There was power in the stocky limbs, a sharp awareness in his expression. As gentle as he might seem, he would no doubt turn ugly when crossed. If she was to be successful in her escape, she needed to gain his trust. Besides, she didn't want to anger him; he'd been the first person to treat her with any measure of kindness.

She shook her head and held up her hands for him to untie. "I won't do anything stupid."

The man's eyes twinkled, and she had a sudden impression that he was pleased with her. "Ah, the lassie speaks." His pleased tone rankled her.

"Nothing to add, lass?" His voice lowered to a conspiratorial whisper. "Will ye be damning the captain to hell now?" His booming chuckle shook the cabin. She allowed a small smile to surface and was amazed to find that she could like this man.

The Scot held out his hand in introduction. "I'm Angus MacDuff, known as just MacDuff to the laddies here."

"I am hungry, Just MacDuff," she said, flexing her wrists after he'd removed the rope from her hands.

"MacDuff," he corrected. "Only MacDuff." He grinned. "Do ye have a name, lassie?"

She hesitated, wondering if it would be wise to tell him. Could she trust this big, bearded, red-haired man with his soft Scottish burr? "Molly," she said at last.

His gaze flickered with surprise, and her features hardened as she was assailed by unpleasant memories.

"Molly *McCormick*," she added caustically. "What's the matter? Never met an Irish *breed* before?

The man blinked. Then the cabin reverberated with the deep sound of his amusement. "No," he said, sobering. His eyes remained merry. "Can't say as I ever have . . ." He paused and then added mischievously, ". . . met an Irishman."

Molly's lips curved into a rare smile as she acknowledged the kind Scot's sense of humor. She nodded toward the food tray. "That for me?"

He beamed at her. " 'Tis. The captain thought ye'd be hungry."

Mention of the captain caused her expression to tighten, and she considered refusing the meal. The Scot, however, must have sensed her mood, for he quickly came to Donovan's defense. "He means well, lassie. I know ye might not believe this, but he's a fair man."

Molly's eyebrows rose. "Really?"

To her surprise, the big man blushed. "Don't ye be thinking aboot where this came from," he ordered when she stared at the food. "Eat. Ye'll need yer strength."

One look at the warm bread oozing with butter and her mouth watered. He's right, she thought. I'll need my strength if I'm to escape. She reached for a chunk of bread and took a bite. "Thank you," she murmured. It was the best bread she'd ever tasted, far better than her own unappetizing efforts, which more often than not turned out crumbly or hard. "Who made this?"

"Aye, 'tis good." MacDuff smiled. "Cook did, but don't tell him ye like it or ye'll never have it agin."

She nodded in understanding, taking another bite.

The cabin door slammed open unexpectedly, startling Molly and MacDuff both. The bread froze partway to Molly's mouth as Bran Donovan strode into the cabin.

"I see you like my food, if nothing else." His blue eyes mocked her. "Let us hope you enjoy your stay here."

Molly stared at him, refusing to respond. She might be a prisoner of this man, but she wouldn't make things easier for him. A guest—hah! Angered by Donovan's smug expression, she glanced down at the bread in her hand and on impulse threw it at him. The bread glanced off his shoulder. She regretted her actions when she heard the burly Scot scold her with a click of his tongue. And she was still hungry!

Bran felt a surge of annoyance as he picked up the bread, but he only smiled, raised it to his lips, and took a bite of the thick crust. "Thank you."

He made a big show of chewing and was rewarded when she looked longingly at the bread. Bran turned abruptly to his friend. "See that she gets water for a bath." His amused gaze swung to the girl. "Perhaps you'd like to share that, too?"

She made a movement and then checked herself, as if she'd wanted to attack but then thought better of it.

Bran suddenly grew tired of the game; he turned to leave. "Oh, MacDuff, when she's done washing, tie her up again. I don't want her escaping."

The Scot, who'd been stifling a smile, nodded, sobering quickly. "Aye, Captain."

Donovan left, and the room was quiet. MacDuff

studied Molly and grinned.

"You can go to hell, bastard!" she shouted at the closed door. She turned to MacDuff, her eyes blazing. "I'm not going to take a bath!"

The smile left the Scot's mouth. "I'm afraid ye are, lassie." His determined look reminded Molly that MacDuff was the captain's man.

She shivered. Would she escape unharmed? Would they eventually let her go? Why would the captain care if she was clean? Was he planning to . . . to ravish her?

MacDuff read her thoughts. "Yer sharing his cabin, not his bed." His voice was soft.

Molly glanced with foreboding at the bed racks built into the bulkhead. She wouldn't make the same mistake twice. If her virtue was threatened even once by the captain, then as sure as Tully McCormick could drink himself into a whiskey-induced stupor, the blackguard Bran Donovan would die!

Chapter Four

In their search for the savage thief, Reginald Cornsby and his men stumbled onto a cabin in a clearing deep in the forest thicket. Narrowing his gaze, Cornsby held up a fat hand to silence his men. "Anybody home?" he called.

The door opened. A man with chestnut brown hair and a tall, stocky build stepped outside to confront the group. Descending the porch steps, he regarded the band warily before his gaze fastened on Cornsby. "Can I help you?"

"We're looking for an Injun girl by the name of Molly McCormick," Cornsby said. "Do you know of her?"

The young man's eyes flickered. "What do you want with her?"

"She's a thief!" someone in the group cried.

"She stole from Mr. Cornsby!" shouted another.

Cornsby's gaze narrowed as he saw alarm flash in the man's expression. "What's your name?"

The man hesitated. "O'Reilly," he said. "Shelby O'Reilly."

"Liar!" Cornsby accused, and several men behind him rushed forward as if to take the young man by force.

The door slammed back on its hinges as an older man appeared from inside the cabin. "Shelby, what the hell is going on?"

Afraid that Tully McCormick would let loose his tongue, Shelby hurried to his father's side. He grabbed hold of Tully's arm to steady him, grimacing at the foul-liquor odor of his breath.

"Let me be, boy!" Spying Cornsby and his men, Tully resisted his son's efforts to escort him back inside the house. "Is there something I can do fer ye, sir?" He tried to hold himself pridefully erect, and then ruined the effect by stumbling as he approached the group.

Cornsby's lips formed a twisted smile, the only betraying feature of his disgust for the man's condition. "Possibly," he said. "Do you know of an Indian girl named Molly McCormick?"

Shelby closed his eyes, knowing that there'd be no helping his half sister now. To his surprise, he soon found that he had underestimated his father.

"A Molly McCormick, ye say?" Tully asked, appearing thoughtful. "I know of her . . . yes." He blinked bloodshot eyes. "Half-breed, isn't she?"

Cornsby nodded. "And a thief."

Tully raised an eyebrow. "Who'd she steal from — ye?"

Again the obese man inclined his head. He lowered his guard, for it seemed that the young man had told the truth about his identity. He was surprised, though, that he'd never encountered the O'Reillys before.

"Well, I saw her once, but I can't say I've seen

40

her in some time."

"How come I've never seen you O'Reillys at my store?"

Shelby shrugged. "I work at the Benger Furnace."

Reginald nodded, for he was familiar with the company store there. Satisfied, he waved his men on to continue their search. "If you come across the Injun, give us a holler." He named a generous figure as reward for any information. The storekeeper left to join his men.

Scowling, Tully turned to his younger son. "Where's your sister?"

Shelby's face creased with concern. "I don't know, Father. I haven't seen her."

"Damn squaw!" his father muttered, turning back to the house. "Call me when she gets back. Stealing," he mumbled. "As if we didn't have enough troubles."

The younger man's eyes were sad as he watched his father go into the cabin. "Oh, Molly, what have you done now?"

His expression softened. She was a good girl. She did more for the family than any one of them. He himself worked at the furnace, but most of his money went straight to debts owed to the company store, where Tully had managed to spend a fortune on whiskey.

Molly worked hard to keep them clothed and fed. She didn't deserve the way Father treated her. Tully loved her, but the drink made him say things, do things, that he shouldn't. And Shelby couldn't understand Darren's animosity toward their half sister . . . but then Darren had never taken to Molly's mother, Shi'ki-Xkwe, the Indian woman Tully had taken as his lover after the boys' mother died.

Shelby, who had been a just a babe when his real mother died, had found a loving mother in Shi'ki-Xkwe.

Although anxious to hear her side of the story, Shelby hoped his sister kept away from home until their father had slept off his whiskey.

The tub was a hip bath, made of tin, which Mac-Duff easily carried into the captain's cabin and set next to the bed racks. He stood back, his arms folded, his narrowed eyes watching intently as the cabin boy hauled in the water to fill it.

Molly stared at the metal vessel as if it were a hog trough instead of a bathtub. Her eyes widened as steam rose to cloud the small cabin. A hot bath? She'd never before indulged in the luxury! Her family didn't own a tub; Molly bathed in the river, whatever the season. There was a certain secluded spot away from her father's hut . . . and her half brother Darren's prying eyes.

The prospect of bathing on board the pirate ship became almost inviting to Molly. The cabin boy—Tommie, MacDuff called him—finished filling the tub and glanced at her curiously as he left the cabin.

"All right now, lassie," MacDuff said, drawing her gaze. " 'Tis time for yer bath. I'll stand guard outside, so no one'll bother ye."

Molly looked at him gratefully. When the Scot left the room she approached the bath, fingered one of the coarse linen towels that hung over the back of the captain's desk chair, and picked up the cake of soap from the chart table, sniffing its fragrance. To her surprise, the soap had a light floral smell,

42

quite unlike the harsh lye soap she made at home.

She tested the water with a fingertip and found it pleasantly hot. She started to remove her tunic, and then her hands stilled as it occurred to her that she had nothing clean to wear when she was done. She grimaced at the thought of donning her soiled buckskin.

Molly went to the hatch. "MacDuff!" she called.

The Scot answered immediately, frowning when he opened the door and saw her still clad in her tunic. "What are ye waiting fer, lass?"

"I've nothing clean to put on after . . ." She felt heat stain her cheeks.

The man's eyes flickered with understanding. "I'll be right back," he announced abruptly, and left.

Molly edged toward the door, thinking to venture outside. Then she changed her mind, opting for the safety of the captain's cabin. Right now, she had no wish to meet up with Old John, Will, or any of the likes of Donovan's crew.

MacDuff returned with a key in his hand. He crossed the cabin, unlocked the sea chest, and rummaged inside before withdrawing several garments.

"Here ye go, lass." He handed her the clothing: a linen shift, a gown of blue barleycorn, and a white muslin petticoat. He gestured toward the open chest, which was filled with assorted articles of clothing. "The captain said yer to feel free to use any of these garments."

Molly gaped at the woman's apparel. She frowned. She would not wear it! No doubt the clothes had been taken during a pirate raid!

"Don't ye be stubborn, lass," MacDuff said perceptively, closing the chest lid. "No one suffered from the loss."

43

She nodded, feeling relieved. The shift felt soft in her hand; she'd never had occasion to wear such fine clothing. This one time she would swallow her pride and accept something from her captor. She'd be practical, if not free.

The Scot went back outside. Molly pulled off her tunic and gingerly stepped into the heated water. Where on earth did they get hot water? And the water was clean and clear, unlike much of the water in these New Jersey Pine Barrens, where the waterways were a rusty orange color. Iron ore—bog iron ore—lined the rivers, providing an ample supply for the area's iron industry. She knew that the Benger Furnace, where Shelby, and on occasion Darren, worked, produced cannonballs as well as pig iron.

Molly was cramped in the small tub, but she didn't care. She enjoyed the hot water on her tired, bruised limbs. Fear of interruption made her hurry, though, when she would have liked to linger. She soaped up a fine lather, rinsing her body clean, and stepped from the tub. After drying herself, Molly bent over the tub to wash her hair.

She heard the captain's voice as she was dressing. Donovan's deep voice ordered MacDuff away from the door just as Molly finished buttoning the bodice of her gown.

She gasped when the door burst open, and the captain stood framed in the archway, one eyebrow raised sardonically as he scrutinized his captive from head to toe. His bold stare made her feel strange, vulnerable.

"Well, I must say it's an improvement," he said, stepping into the room.

Behind the captain, MacDuff's brown eyes regarded her apologetically. He looked relieved to find

44

her already dressed.

"Now that wasn't all bad, was it?" Bran Donovan asked.

Molly glared at the captain, refusing to respond. She experienced a rush of heat as he continued to study her. Her skin tingled. Her breasts grew taut beneath the linen shift. Shocked at her reaction, Molly allowed anger to conceal her confusion.

"Why won't you let me go?" Her eyes were fierce with her hatred of him.

Ignoring her question, the captain ordered Mac-Duff to remove the bath. He went to the chart table, where he unrolled a piece of parchment, spreading it across the flat surface.

When he didn't answer, she said, "I asked you a question, Captain!"

He looked up, his gaze hardening. "A question I'm not willing to answer . . . yet." His head bent over his charts. "Mr. Dickon!" he called, and to Molly's surprise, a man stepped into the cabin to join his superior.

Fuming at Donovan's rudeness, Molly fidgeted near the cabin door as MacDuff and Tommie removed all traces of her bath. She watched with a sense of unreality as the tin tub and her soiled tunic were carried out of the captain's quarters. One minute she'd been performing the most intimate of ablutions, and the next she was surrounded by a roomful of strange seamen!

Molly stared at Donovan. He and the man Dickon seemed oblivious to her presence, conferring over the charts in hushed tones. It was as if she weren't even in the room! She felt a spark of mischief. *Well, Captain, as I'm here against my will, I'll not let you forget my presence!*

She cleared her throat and moved about the cabin, sighing loudly to disrupt the meeting. Dickon looked at her briefly, before dismissing her to listen to the captain's comments. Donovan, much to Molly's annoyance, didn't even bother to glance up.

"I need a comb," she said at last, fingering her damp tresses.

Neither man looked up.

Molly approached the table. "A comb, Captain? For my hair?"

Bran glanced up, scowling at the distraction. He blinked. "What?" He stared at the girl before him, noting her angry expression and her tangled wet hair, which she was trying to smooth with her fingertips. His gaze dropped briefly to where her breasts swelled against her bodice. His lashes flickered as their eyes met.

"A comb?" he asked. She nodded. He raked her with his piercing blue gaze, and she blushed. He gestured offhandedly toward the sea chest. "In there," he muttered, as if suddenly bored with the exchange. The captain's attention returned to his charts.

Her jaw clenching with anger, Molly opened the sea chest, which had been left unlocked.

She rifled through the trunk and became reluctantly intrigued with its contents. There was a wide variety of apparel in the wooden box; men's as well as women's garments. Some were like those worn by the working people, while others were for the upper class, more elaborate and richer in fabric design. Where did they all come from?

A British ship? She hated the thought that these garments, including the clothes she wore, might be plunder taken during a raid.

46

Molly found a comb, stifling a cry of pleasure as she held up the silver instrument for inspection. It was shiny and detailed with fancy scrollwork. She'd never seen an object this grand. Could it be the captain's comb? she wondered, frowning. More likely it'd been meant for some British lady!

Throwing the captain a surreptitious glance, Molly sat down on the bottom rack and began to comb out her wet tangles. Neither Donovan nor his subordinate wore wigs or had their hair powdered, she noted. Donovan wore his hair pulled back in a queue, and tied with a dark silk ribbon. Dickon's light brown locks were laid up in a four-strand square sinnet, fastened at the bottom with a length of cordage.

Molly combed her hair, enjoying the silken feel of the drying strands that crackled and shone under the light of the lanthorn.

Finally the men finished their discussion. Donovan straightened from the chart table, his expression stern, his hand on his right hip.

"We'll meet again in the wardroom," the captain instructed. "We'll need to go over this with Benson and the others."

Dickon nodded. "How long do you think it'll take her?" he asked, glancing at Molly, who regarded the two with an obvious lack of understanding.

"About two days, if the weather holds," Donovan said.

After a few more words of exchange, the first lieutenant, or mate, quit the cabin, leaving Molly and Bran Donovan alone together.

The girl stiffened and then relaxed as the captain continued to peruse the parchment, seemingly forgetful of her presence.

"So you're Molly," he said, startling her.

She tensed, but pretended she hadn't heard him, ignoring his bold stare as she continued to comb her drying hair. To her amazement, he chuckled as if amused by her ploy, her show of defiance.

He rolled up his charts slowly, and the room resounded with the crinkling sound of parchment. Donovan secured the roll with a piece of string. His gaze held hers as he set it on the table. He approached her, and Molly had to stifle the urge to run for the door.

He is only a man, she reminded herself, averting her gaze from his tall, lithe form. *I will handle him.*

He paused directly before her. She refused to look at him, but she could feel his intense gaze rake her from head to toe. His clean, masculine scent reached out to her, teasing her nose, stirring her blood. He smelled . . . pleasant—a strange but intoxicating combination of sea air, tobacco, and male musk.

She kept her eyes downcast, studying his lower half . . . his long legs and booted feet. His fawn breeches were skin tight, contouring his taut thighs. Molly stared at his black boots, which had been polished to such a high shine that she could see her reflection. The footwear encased his muscled calves to a line just below the knee. Molly wiggled her toes, self-consciously aware of her own bare toes peeking out from under her petticoat.

"Molly," his deep voice boomed from above her. "It would be most wise of you, dear, to be cordial during your stay."

She looked up and caught her breath. There was something captivating about the man's expression, something there that made her heart trip within her chest.

"As I said, I can be easy to get along with or . . ." His voice trailed off meaningfully.

Molly's gaze turned instantly hostile. "Why are you keeping me prisoner?"

Something flashed in his blue eyes. "What were you doing wandering about the cove?"

She refused to answer. What would he say if she told the truth? That she'd stumbled across his men by accident. That she'd been running from a group of angry townspeople who had unjustly branded her a thief . . .

Bran's lips tightened as he studied the girl before him. Why wouldn't she answer his question? Was it true that she was a Tory spy? And if so, how much did she know of their operations?

It was hard for him to believe that such a chit of a female could be the cause of trouble, but he'd seen things in this war that he'd never imagined possible. Loyalties dividing a family's house . . . brothers against brothers . . . fathers fighting sons.

How old was the girl? Fifteen? Sixteen? Not too young to be a Loyalist, but too young to be at the mercy of his men.

His breath caught as he continued to stare at her. She might be older than he'd first thought. She had all the attributes of a full-grown woman. Round breasts, small waist, hips that curved gently outward and invited a man's touch.

Just as he'd first imagined, Molly was lovely beneath the grime. In fact, she was startling!

Her dark eyes radiated hatred with a liquid sheen like—he thought for an apt comparison—like the deep sea gleaming in the moonlight. One could drown in those midnight orbs. He wondered what effect those eyes would have when her face softened with tenderness . . . or grew taut with the fiery passion he knew he could arouse in her if given half the chance.

Bran frowned. He couldn't afford to indulge in such musings. It was too dangerous to become involved with a woman, any woman, but most particularly this spirited heathen.

Molly McCormick. Despite himself, he smiled at the thought of bedding her. Would she respond in bed as wildly as she fought? Not many females possessed her spirit; he couldn't help admiring her for it, even while he was as angry as hell that she'd attacked and tried to kill him with his own blade.

The captain turned away and crossed the room. "Your mother is Indian," he said. "Lenni Lenape?"

Molly stiffened with surprise.

He swung to face her with raised eyebrows. "Well?"

"She was."

His dark gaze softened with compassion. "She died . . ."

"Don't concern yourself, Captain," she said acidly. "It was a long time ago, when I was five years old."

"Such a long time ago," he mocked, but gently. "How long?" His lips tightened and he turned away from her. He hadn't meant to ask. It didn't matter how old she was, or if her mother was Lenni Lenape. What mattered was that she might be a spy, working for the British.

Molly stared at the captain's broad shoulders and muscled back. Why was he curious about her age? Did he have some sense of honor that would keep him from abusing a child? What would he do with her if she confessed she was nearly nineteen?

His hair looked clean within its queue, she noticed. Would it feel as soft and silky as it appeared? She cursed herself for thinking of him as something other than the man who'd cruelly and unfeelingly taken away her freedom.

"Does my age matter, Captain?" she taunted. "Will you let me go free if I tell you?"

She saw his muscled back tense before he turned to regard her through wintry eyes. "I'm afraid that's out of the question, little one," he said softly. Too softly. "I'll release you on my own terms, in my own time."

His cool, dispassionate tone made her furious. "Then you can go to hell, Captain Donovan!" she cried, rising from the rack to stand before him. "I'll not be a willing partner in your game!"

"So you'll try to escape at first chance," he murmured, eyeing her thoughtfully. He went to the hatch. "MacDuff!"

The Scot appeared immediately. "Captain?"

"Miss McCormick has decided to be difficult," Bran said. "Tie her up."

The burly man's eyes flickered, but he obeyed orders. "Put out your hands, lass," he told her gently.

Molly swallowed against a tight throat, her eyes shimmering, as her gaze met the Scotsman's. He seemed genuinely upset by her plight as he looped the cordage about her hands. His brown eyes were dark with concern. "I'm sorry, lass," he murmured for her ears alone. Then he bound her bare ankles.

"Wait," Bran said, and MacDuff glanced up, hopeful. "Her feet are bare. Find her some stockings."

MacDuff found a pair of blue stockings in the

51

sea chest. Molly's hands were bound, so he slipped them on for her.

"Bastard!" she cried, glaring at her captor.

Bran tried not to feel guilty as he watched Mac-Duff lift one dainty foot and then the other, covering each with the silk hose. He glimpsed a bare calf and shapely knee as MacDuff secured the garters. His heart slammed within his breast.

It disturbed Bran to watch MacDuff perform the intimate service for Molly; therefore, his tone was sharp when he finally ordered the Scot to leave.

He studied Molly's face, which was red with embarrassment. "I'm sorry things have to be this way."

Molly glared at him. "Liar!" she accused. "I don't think you're in the bit least sorry, Captain." There was no doubt in her mind that Bran Donovan exalted in power ... even power over a defenseless woman. The man enjoyed having others cower before him. Well, not her! She would never give him the satisfaction! "If you were sorry, you'd let me go."

His lips tightened. She had the satisfaction of seeing his expression darken before he spun on his heels and quit the cabin.

"Captain?" Angus MacDuff hailed Bran as he climbed topside.

Bran sighed. "Yes, Angus, what is it?"

The Scot seemed discomfited. "About the lass—"

"Molly." The captain nodded for him to continue.

"Aye, Molly." MacDuff glanced about the deck to see if anyone was within hearing. "I'm worried aboot her, sir. There's been talk 'mongst the men."

"Talk?" Bran questioned. "What kind of talk?"

But he knew. Each crewmember was hoping for a few minutes' tumble with the fair maid. He thought of what it would be like to have her . . . passionately responsive lips . . . round breasts pressed sweetly against him. "Well?" he said impatiently.

MacDuff looked mildly uncomfortable. "She's just a wee thing, Captain. We must protect her from the likes o' them." He jerked his head toward a couple of crusty seamen scrubbing the main deck.

"The girl is my concern, Mr. MacDuff," Bran snapped irritably. He didn't need to be told how to handle his ship—or the likes of Molly McCormick. "I'll see that she's kept safe."

"Aye, Captain," the embarrassed man said, recognizing the dismissal in Bran's tone.

Molly McCormick must be a witch, Bran thought, for his Scottish friend to be so taken with her. What of the other men? How was her presence going to affect them? Damn! A woman on board ship was a bloody complication. "MacDuff," he called Angus back.

"Aye, Captain?" MacDuff turned back without a smile.

"Would you check on her again?" he said, and his gaze apologized for being testy. "I wouldn't put it past the little heathen to bite her bonds free and try to escape."

Bran and MacDuff exchanged grins in appreciation of their captive's spunk.

Chapter Five

Dusk darkened the sky, throwing shadows across the land. The forest was silent but for the crackle of dry brush under men's feet and the hushed whisper of conversation. The air was fraught with excitement. The Tories had gathered near Manville to discuss plans for their next raid. There were ten men at the meeting, many of them town residents, others from neighboring farms and woods. One auburn-haired man stood apart from the others. Darren McCormick began to address them with bright-eyed fervor, immediately garnering everyone's attention.

"The wagons will be traveling through this section of the pine forest," he said, drawing in the dirt with a stick. "According to our source, they'll be starting here and then following the trail along Keller's Creek to this point." His eyes glowed as he anticipated the confrontation.

"How will we contact the others?" George Merriweather asked. He was an elderly gent, who was known to be the most cautious among the band.

Darren scowled at the older man, for he was afraid that Merriweather's insistent questioning and concerns would rattle the others. He needed the men to trust him implicitly. The success of their raids depended on their ability to stay levelheaded and alert. "James, Matt, and Shelby will go ahead on the day before the scheduled run," he said, stifling his impatience. He smiled reassuringly. "Have I ever led you wrong?"

He spoke to the whole group. "Reginald Cornsby will be keeping an ear open for any change of plans. If any of you hear of something out of the ordinary, I want you to get word to me immediately."

Everyone nodded in agreement as the members of the Tory band prepared to go to their homes.

"Where's Shelby?" someone asked Darren.

Darren stiffened, for his brother's absence this night was a sore point. "He couldn't be here tonight. Don't you worry, he'll be ready when it's time."

"I'm sure he will," Matt Bradford agreed. "Tell him that my Mary was asking after him, will ya? She was wondering when he'd come to supper again."

Shelby's older brother smiled grimly. "I'll tell him," he lied.

Darkness had fallen by the time the band finished their meeting. His thoughts an angry whirl, Darren headed back to the cabin. Where was Shelby? he wondered.

He was cautious as he traversed the forest footpath. The night was alive with the sound of insects and nocturnal animals. His gaze was alert for soldiers as he passed the old pin oak near a small clearing where Shelby and he had played often as young boys. He froze at the sound of snapping twigs, his heart thundering in his chest, his breath coming rapidly. Darren fell into a crouch, waiting, watching, rising when he recognized the man who broke through the underbrush.

"Captain Hoyt," he mumbled, staring.

"McCormick," the young British soldier said by way of greeting. "The general wants a word with you."

Darren cast a wary glance about him. He nodded, and the Briton swept a hand forward to direct the way.

"Do you know what he wants?" It would be the first time Darren had actually met the British commanding officer, and the prospect made him decidedly nervous.

"I'm afraid I'm not at liberty to say," the soldier said.

"How far is he?" Darren asked.

"Not far" was the oblique answer.

The Briton was silent but for an occasional low-murmured directive to the man walking before him. To Darren, it seemed that they walked for miles before they came to the British encampment. Suddenly the captain grabbed Darren by the right shoulder, instructing him to halt. Hoyt took the lead as they entered the sheltered clearing where men sat, checking their muskets and sharpening their bayonets. One soldier flashed Darren a gleaming look that caused him to shiver as he passed by him. The captain ushered Darren before the British general.

"McCormick." The general's expression was inscrutable as he stared at him. "I'm General Robinson. I'm glad you were able to make it this evening."

"Did I have a choice?" Darren asked dryly.

A small, reluctant smile hovered on the British officer's lips. "No." The general paced the ground, his hands clasped behind his back, his head bent forward in concentration. Suddenly he stopped and looked up, his small hazel eyes fixing Darren with an intense stare. "The captain has informed me of your intentions. I wanted to meet the man who'll be stopping the bloody Colonials. You plan to take their wagons?"

Darren's taut frame relaxed as he nodded. He recognized the general's keen interest and sought to profit from it.

"How so?" Robinson asked.

The younger man's eyes narrowed. "Now, general, I'm afraid me methods are me own. I've no intention of telling anyone." Darren glanced about furtively. "No one can be trusted."

The general's lips tightened. "Including me?"

"Now if I believed that, sir, then I wouldn't be here now, would I?"

The officer chuckled and waved Darren to a seat on the trunk of a fallen tree. "Then let's sit and discuss this plan of yours, shall we?" General Robinson turned to the captain. "Captain, see that no one comes near."

Hoyt nodded, flashed Darren an annoyed look, and left.

"Now, Mr. McCormick, shall we get down to brass tacks?"

"Certainly, sir," Darren said. "But first, let's discuss the matter of my compensation . . ."

It was late when Bran went below deck. He was

bone-tired. His only thought was to fling himself across his rack for the few hours' rest he'd need to keep a clear head.

The *Flying Wench* had failed to rendezvous with the *Bloody Mary*. Bran had been forced to sail for open sea, his only option left to return at a later date, prearranged by his cohorts in the event that the sloop got held up due to the weather—or something equally innocuous. Bran didn't want to ponder the likelihood of the *Wench*'s capture by a British vessel.

The cabin was bathed with the golden glow from a burning wall lantern. Entering the stateroom, Bran made a mental note to thank the Scot; Mac-Duff had this uncanny ability to anticipate Bran's every need. Friends since childhood, Bran and Angus hadn't seen each other since they were youngsters . . . until that day, just over a year ago, when Angus had happened by Josiah's inn, the Jug and Barrel, near the mouth of Great Egg Harbor River. Fresh off another privateer, Angus was an experienced seaman who'd already spent most of his earnings from his last stint at sea. He'd been only too glad to take up Bran's offer to join his crew.

Bran pulled off his cocked hat, setting it on his chair. His hands went to the buttons on his shirtfront. A sound behind him caught his attention, and his fingers stilled. His eyes widened as his gaze went to the girl lying on the bottom rack.

Earlier, as he stood on the quarterdeck steering the vessel out to sea, he had found himself thinking about her bravery . . . her spirit . . . wanting her as he'd wanted no woman before her. Damn! She was the last thing he needed! What sort of spell had she cast on him that she continually

58

invaded his thoughts?

He needed to get rid of her, but how could he? The shipment of powder was late. Until he could return for it, until it was safely on board ship, there remained the danger of discovery by British troops.

Even if he could accept Molly's innocence, he couldn't risk letting her go, only to have her stumble by accident upon the British army.

It pained him to have her here in his cabin. She stirred up feelings, desires, better left at rest. Bran had no choice but to put up with her . . . with her nearness. If only he could forget that she was a female . . . a soft, curvaceous, sweet female. And if he admired her for her spirit, well, he'd best forget that, too.

Studying her, he was startled by the difference a bath and change of clothes had made in her appearance. Molly lay on her back, her eyes closed, her dark lashes fanning her silken cheeks. In the soft glow of the lantern, she looked vulnerable — and very desirable.

Her tied hands rested on her flat stomach; her legs stretched out across the bunk. The sight of her bound stocking feet beneath the hem of her white muslin petticoat brought back the image of Mac-Duff handling her dainty feet. He envisioned the lovely length of bare calf . . . the curve of a well-shaped knee . . .

Bran's breath stilled, and he closed his eyes. *He'd* wanted to be the one to touch her legs, to run his fingers down her thighs and calves and cup the sole of her dainty foot in his palm. His loins tightened just thinking of the prospect.

How would she be if she enjoyed his touch? Her dark eyes would be soft with pleasure as he stroked and kissed her; and when he parted her thighs and caressed her more intimately, she'd gasp and arch off the bed. Fool! he scolded himself. Shuddering, he looked away. Damn! What am I doing?

Bran's gaze was drawn back to the bed. She looked so helpless . . . so feminine. There was no reason to feel guilty, he told himself. Nor should he feel sorry for her. After all, her situation was her own fault, wasn't it? If she'd cooperate, then there wouldn't be the need to have her bound.

Was it possible? Was she a spy for King George's men? It was common knowledge that many of the Indians hated the Continentals. And if she was innocent, why did he have this nagging feeling that she was hiding something?

Bran couldn't keep his eyes off her as guilt warred with logic. She looked so uncomfortable lying there. Perhaps he should untie her legs . . .

His chart table also served as his writing desk, where, among other things, he kept the ship's log. Bran turned a key in the center keyhole, unlocking the two desk drawers. After fumbling through the right drawer, he pulled out his knife--the one with the pearl handle, the same weapon Molly had tried to kill him with only that morning. He would cut her legs free so that she could sleep in comfort. Later, if she proved more cooperative, he would free her hands.

Bran approached the bed, his heart softening as he watched the young woman sleep. Despite her predicament, she appeared to be resting. He smiled. All the fight in her must have tired her out. He was overwhelmed by a rare feeling of tenderness.

His gaze caressed her shiny, dark hair, her relaxed features. She apparently suffered no ill effect from her bath, he mused. In fact, it was MacDuff's, and now his decided opinion that Molly McCormick was no stranger to soap and water. His brow furrowed.

How could the young woman before him, dressed in a feminine gown of blue barleycorn, be one and the same with the filthy, knife-wielding savage in buckskins?

Molly sighed in her sleep, drawing his gaze to her pink mouth, so soft, inviting . . . a strong temptation to a man who'd gone too long without a woman. He had an urge to trace her lips with his finger . . . to taste their sweetness with his tongue.

He muttered an imprecation. He was getting fanciful again. Such thoughts must stop, and they must stop immediately! Bran opened the jackknife that had belonged to his father, a smuggler himself, and stared at it for a moment.

Molly awoke to the gleam of a knife blade raised above her. She tensed. Was the captain going to murder her and cut up her body for fish bait?

Pretending to be asleep, she lay clutched in fear, watching him through lowered lids. How was she to avoid this gruesome death? She was startled when the captain merely cut the rope binding her legs together.

Was he going to have his way with her? she wondered. It would be hard for him to rape her with her legs tied together. She didn't know what she feared more: a quick, violent death or the slow torture of being violated by this man.

She closed her eyes at the frightful image. Without moving a muscle, Molly waited with bated breath for Captain Donovan's next move. She sensed that he was staring at her; it unnerved her to be studied so intently. It was difficult, but she managed to maintain the steady breathing of one who is asleep.

How long had the captain been in the cabin? She was shocked that she'd slept through his entry. She wasn't usually a heavy sleeper.

But then it's not every day that you find yourself fleeing for your life, an inner voice reminded her. *And not just once, but twice!*

Bran blinked with dismay as he studied the girl's sleeping form. What a stupid thing to do, he decided. How could he sleep in the top rack when he'd just given her the ability to run? Cursing his fool head, the captain picked up the cut rope, studied its length, and saw that it was too short to tie her up again. For a moment he entertained the idea of calling MacDuff, but then thought better of it. Dickon had the night watch; MacDuff had retired for a few hours' nap. He couldn't disturb the Scot for such a thing, and he dared not leave the girl alone.

Bran thought of his options. He could awaken Molly, and order her to the top rack while he took the bottom one or . . . use the time to go over the plans. His gaze went from Molly to his chart table, and he decided he might as well get some work done. She seemed to be resting more peacefully. How could he disturb her?

He scowled. It worried him that he was concerned with her comfort. He rationalized his decision to let her sleep with the reminder that Molly couldn't be trusted. His ability to work would be restricted when the woman was awake and about.

Bran returned to his desk, withdrawing several papers from inside a wooden box in the drawer.

Moving the lantern to give him better light, he sat down to first study the list of names, routes, and code words for the smugglers.

Why did he cut her legs free? Molly wondered, watching him from beneath lowered lids. Her fear of being raped had been groundless. She felt foolish for thinking he'd attack her in her sleep.

She flexed her leg muscles—carefully, so she wouldn't attract the captain's attention. She had fooled him! Or had she?

Bran Donovan's raven hair glistened under the lantern light, giving the impression that there was a glow about him, like a halo. Molly's jaw tightened. There was nothing angelic about his formidable expression as he perused the papers before him.

The captain sighed, and Molly stiffened as he put away his papers and rose from behind the chart table. He picked up the knife. Molly held her breath and lay rigid, her eyes closed, as he approached the rack. Forcing herself to relax so he wouldn't suspect that she was awake, she braced to fight, her heart pumping fiercely. Her ears picked up the sound of his movements. He was close. Too close, she thought.

He touched her arm; Molly shrieked and spun on the bed to strike out at him with her feet. She gasped with pain. The knife blade had sliced her arm, burning skin and tissue.

"You bloody wench!" he cried. "What are you trying to do? Murder us both?"

Molly's face drained of blood; she felt woozy.

"Are you all right?" he asked gently when she didn't reply.

She shook her head. The cut in her arm was small, but deep and painful, spurting crimson. The room swayed before her eyes. Molly became aware of the captain's concern. His blue eyes shot her frequent, anxious glances while he fumbled about the cabin.

"Molly," he murmured. He placed a hand on her forehead. His touch was tender as he brushed hair away from her cheek. "I'm sorry . . ."

Molly nodded. Tears pricked her eyes as she stared at her injured arm.

Bran was mortified at what he'd done. It was an accident. He hadn't meant to hurt her, only to free her hands! But he felt guilty in spite of himself. He shared in her pain as if it were his own arm instead of hers.

He stared at her arm. Something needed to be done—and done soon. Bran searched her face. "Will you stay still while I cut the rope free?" His tone was soft, almost pleading.

Eyes glistening, she nodded, and he was careful as he sliced through the rope securing her wrists.

Frowning, Bran slipped off his shirt and ripped off a section of the hem, which he used to staunch the flow of blood. Then, using a second strip, he fashioned a tourniquet of sorts above the wound. Next, he made a compress for over the injury itself.

Molly inhaled sharply as he pressed against the cut. Glancing at her with sympathy, Bran stroked her hand and soothed her with soft words.

Bran frowned, studying the girl's pale face with concern. What if infection set into the wound? He didn't like Molly's coloring. He'd done what he could; but was it enough? He didn't think the cut was too serious, but Bran decided to call for Adams, the ship's surgeon, anyway. Adams would know best how to treat Molly's wound.

"Lie down," he ordered, his voice gruff with emotion.

Their eyes met as Bran helped Molly to lie back on the bed rack. Molly winced with the movement. Hearing the captain's sharp intake of breath, Molly glanced up and was surprised to see that he looked pale beneath his tan.

"I'm going for MacDuff," he said. "Will you be all right?"

Swallowing against tears of pain, she nodded, no longer afraid.

"Good girl," she thought she heard him whisper as he turned away. His caring manner inspired her trust.

She heard the hatch open and close. Molly slumped back against the bed, closing her eyes. As she lay in the dimly lit cabin alone, she tried not to think of the burning sensation in her left arm, recalling instead the captain's surprising tenderness and concern as he tended to her hurt arm.

She had a mental image of his pale face and worried blue gaze. Had she been wrong to believe that he meant her harm? She was bemused by his behavior, by the memory of his hand against her cheek.

When she tried to sit up, she fell back gasping. Pain swept through her, making her feel faint. Bran Donovan puzzled her, she thought. She wanted to understand the man—her captor.

He was a Rebel privateer, she knew. She had heard the men talking as they dragged her to the ship. Rebel or Briton, Molly thought, both sides were guilty in this awful war.

So the captain could be kind . . . and gentle. She mustn't forget that she was here against her will, that Bran Donovan's men had kidnapped her.

The Scot burst into the cabin gasping. The captain followed right behind him.

"Ah, lass!" MacDuff cried, spying her on the bed. "What did ye do to yerself?" He rushed over to inspect her arm, confirming what his captain had surmised — that she needed to see the surgeon. The wound needed to be stitched.

Donovan came up behind him, his face grim. "Adams is on his way."

"Adams?" Molly queried hoarsely, fighting back tears.

"The doc." The Scot blanched as he inspected her arm.

Adams entered the cabin just then with a ditty bag. "MacDuff," the man said, "my medicine chest."

The Scot nodded and left, returning within moments with a large wooden medicine chest, which he sat on the floor near Molly's berth. "It'll be all right, lass," MacDuff soothed.

White-faced, she smiled at him weakly. The pain was too great to make comment.

Unable to keep the tears at bay, Molly closed her eyes. The captain mustn't see her cry! No one must see her cry! She heard the scrape of furniture moving across the planked floor. She raised her lashes just long enough to see that MacDuff had drawn up a chair for the surgeon and a table for his equipment. Eyes closed again, Molly listened to the sounds made by Adams readying his tools.

She heard Adams say, "How did it happen?" She felt the tension in the cabin when the captain didn't answer.

A wave of intense, fiery pain made Molly arch off the bed. The doctor had taken off the compress

66

and had untied the makeshift tourniquet, replacing the latter with a screw tourniquet.

"MacDuff, hold her arm," the doctor instructed. "That's it." Then, in a voice that sounded more stern, Adams said, "Captain, I need fresh water and clean bandages."

Surprised that the doctor would use such a commanding tone, Molly flinched as Adams swabbed her wound with a damp cloth. "Now, girl," Adams said. "Molly, isn't it?"

Molly's eyes opened and she managed to nod, her face gray. She was stunned to realize that the surgeon was young man of about twenty-five years, not the old man she'd expected.

"I'm going to stitch your arm, Molly," Adams told her solemnly. "I won't lie to you; it's going to hurt." He smiled at her reassuringly. "MacDuff here is going to fetch you some rum. I want you to drink every bit of it—"

" 'Tis for the pain, lass," MacDuff interrupted.

The captain remained silent behind the two men. MacDuff left to fetch the ration of rum; shortly afterward he returned with it in a pewter tankard.

Accepting the mug, Molly raised it to her lips, glaring at the captain over the metal rim. She took a tentative sip, coughing as the fiery liquid seared her throat on its way, shuddering when it hit bottom.

"Drink all of it, girl," Adams commanded.

Molly made a face but did as she was told. Her eyes watered as the liquor warmed her insides. Her stomach roiled in angry protest.

"You're not going to be sick, lass?" MacDuff questioned anxiously. She shook her head.

"Good," Adams murmured. "Angus, Bran, I'll

need you to hold her arms." He patted her shoulder when she looked alarmed. "You want a neat row of stitches, don't you?"

She sensed the captain kneeling near her head and felt him gently lifting her injured arm. Next to him, MacDuff took hold of her other one.

Molly answered with a weak smile when the doctor asked if she was ready. The first prick of the needle sent shards of pain throughout the length of her arm. Her lips quivered, but she didn't struggle or cry out.

"Hurry up!" Bran exclaimed. "She's hurting, damn it!"

"Relax, Bran," she heard Adams murmur. "She'll be all right."

The rum had begun to make her dizzy. She blinked, trying to focus. Bran? That was the captain's voice? She felt the strangest urge to offer him comfort. *I'm all right,* she wanted to say.

The needle dug in and out of her flesh, burning her skin. She felt lightheaded and queasy. She heard MacDuff's voice; it sounded miles away.

"What's wrong?" a voice said, sounding anxious. The captain's again, Molly realized. "Is she all right?"

"Captain?" she gasped. He wavered in her vision; fire shot from her wrist to her shoulder; and Molly's world went black.

Chapter Six

"She's fainted!" MacDuff exclaimed, his expression alarmed.

"Good," Adams commented. "It'll be easier on her while I finish up."

His throat tight with emotion, Bran observed as the surgeon tied the knot that would keep Molly's stitches. His breath caught. Her arm felt fragile within his grasp, her skin soft and easily bruised. She looked so vulnerable! Below midnight tresses, her face looked pale; there were shadows of suffering beneath her closed eyes.

Bran had seen grown men cry for less than what Molly McCormick had endured. The rum couldn't have done much to dull her pain, yet she'd barely reacted to the doctor's stitches.

He felt himself flush with guilt. It was his fault that she was injured. His only thought had been to cut away her ropes. Why hadn't he foreseen what had happened? With knife in hand, he must have seemed a terrifying menace.

He couldn't help admiring her courage. *And spirit,* he thought. A rare combination in a female.

And there was something more between them. Something physical. He wanted her. His groin ached with desire for her.

"There, that should do it." Adams's comment brought Bran's attention back to Molly's wound. Having bandaged his patient's arm, the surgeon rose to put away his instruments. "She should do fine," he said, flashing Molly a glance.

"Should we wake the lass?" the Scot asked.

The doctor shook his head. "No. Let her rest. She'll come around in her own time." He turned to regard the commander thoughtfully. "I need to see that hand of yours, Captain."

"Hand?" Bran blinked and saw the small cut to the side of his left hand. He'd been so concerned with Molly's injury that it'd never occurred to him that he might have been injured in the fracas. It must have happened, he thought, when he recoiled from the unexpected attack, instinctively shielding himself with his arm.

"It's nothing," Bran mumbled. "Just a scratch."

Adams scowled and grabbed his arm for inspection. "I'll decide if it's nothing or not."

It was little more than nothing, but the surgeon was quick to point out that even a scratch could fester if not properly treated. Bran stood quietly while Adams cleaned the cut and applied a dressing.

"Can we move her to the top berth?" Bran asked, his gaze fastening on the young woman on his bed.

"I wouldn't advise it," Adams said wearily, drawing his officer's glance. The surgeon appeared dead on his feet. His hair was tousled and he wore a

70

sleepy look, as if he'd been roused from his hammock.

Studying the girl through narrowed eyes, Adams ran a hand through his unbound hair, bunching up a handful so that when he released it, it stuck out all over his head like the raised spikes on an angry porcupine. "I suggest you make her more comfortable by removing some of that feminine frippery."

The "feminine frippery" Adams was referring to turned out to be her bodice and petticoats. The three men managed not to disturb the patient while they carefully removed these articles of clothing, taking great pains not to jar the wounded arm. When they were done, Molly was clad in only a linen shift and blue silk stockings.

Bran covered her with a blanket. He was conscious of the thrust of the girl's round breasts against the thin fabric as he tucked the edges of the blanket about her waist.

Averting his glance, he solemnly thanked Adams for his services, his face purposely bland. The captain's heart tripped while desire stirred in his gut.

"You need not fear she'll try to escape, Captain," the Scot said after Adams had left. "The lass'll not stir a bit, I'm thinking." When Bran looked at him darkly, he quickly added, "The rum."

Bran glanced at the girl, unaware of how his expression softened. When he turned back to the Scot, however, he saw that MacDuff watched him closely . . . and looked relieved.

Bran carefully composed his features. "You'd best get back to bed, Angus." He hesitated. "Thanks for . . ." He felt awkward all of a sudden.

MacDuff smiled.

The ship's bell rang eight times, signaling the end

of the night watch.

"I best be off, Bran. I promised Fitzgerald I'd take his morning watch."

Bran nodded and apologized. MacDuff had less than four hours to get some sleep.

The Scot left, and Bran sighed, closing the hatch. He felt a sudden wave of tiredness as he went to the lantern. He left the lamp burning but lowered the flame. Molly might awaken and need care. And he didn't want to have to stumble through darkness should he be called topside.

He decided he would lie down for an hour. It was a rare occasion that let Bran sleep through the night. As captain, he felt it was his duty to be topside as much as possible. His presence on the upper deck was a gentle reminder to his men that as long as they were on board the *Bloody Mary* his word was law.

Bran hated to leave his post for long, so he indulged in catnaps to renew his strength.

He sat down, tugging off one boot, then the other. In the rack, Molly muttered something intelligible, and Bran glanced at her, relieved at this obvious sign of sleep. Molly would be all right, he thought.

No thanks to me. His conscious smote him. What if he'd been wrong about her? What if she was innocent? She didn't look like a spy, Tory or otherwise.

He frowned, his hand settling on his breeches. He unbuttoned the garment, pulled it down his hard flanks, and mentally berated himself, *What does a spy look like, you dolt?*

Whether Molly was or wasn't a spy was immaterial now. She was a woman he'd injured. He would

72

do right by her, see that she received the best care. Bran paused before climbing into the top berth. His gaze was drawn to her face. He inhaled sharply. She was lovely . . . every inch of her. Spying the blue hose beneath the blanket, he smiled.

As long as she was in his custody, he vowed she'd be treated as a guest, not someone guilty of some horrible crime.

With that decision made, Bran's thoughts turned to sleep. This night it would be up to the watch to keep the *Bloody Mary* safe. He was tired . . . damned tired.

Bran climbed into his bed without thought for his nakedness. He usually slept in the buff; he was more comfortable that way.

It was some time, though, before he drifted off to sleep.

"I'm going to find her!" Shelby exclaimed, fighting his brother's hold.

Darren scowled. "Molly can take care of herself."

"She should have been home by now. What if they found her? God knows what they'd do to her! You didn't see their leader!"

"Forget about her," Darren ordered, sitting down at the crude table in their forest cabin. Behind the two brothers, Tully McCormick slept off a full bottle of whiskey. Darren viewed his white-haired father with disgust before addressing his younger brother. "There are things to be discussed," he said, "about the raid."

The younger brother shook his head. "Raid! There's a war out there! How can you talk of raids when our sister could be in danger?" His gaze searched the room, brightening when he spied the flintlock rifle leaning in the far corner. He retrieved the weapon, inspecting it carefully.

"And where do you think you're going with that?" It would be just like his fool brother, Darren thought irritably, to waste shot saving their "precious" little sister.

"I'm going to find Molly and bring her home." His expression was fierce as he shoved his cocked hat on his head. "I don't trust that village storekeeper."

Darren's hand stilled as he reached for his tankard. "Storekeeper?" he said casually, but all his senses had grown alert.

Shelby nodded. "A fat man with yellow eyes."

"Reginald Cornsby," Darren muttered.

"You know him?" His brother was surprised.

"I've had dealings with him, yes . . ." Darren's gaze narrowed. Cornsby was a newcomer to the Tory band, and like Shelby, the man had been absent at their last meeting. Darren had his own doubts about the man's character. If Cornsby couldn't be trusted, then Darren wanted to know.

He sighed, waving his brother into a chair. He had little love for his sister and cared not if she ever returned. Reginald Cornsby was a matter of concern, however. "You'd better tell me what happened, what Cornsby had to say . . ."

Relieved, Shelby took a seat, his face brightening.

Molly awoke to an intense hammering in her head and a burning sensation in her left forearm. She was disoriented at first. Where am I? she wondered and then gasped as she shifted. My

74

arm! What happened to my arm?

Her eyes teared as they attempted to focus. Wherever I am, she thought, it's dark and dank. And it smells musty.

When she moved her head, the world careened dizzily. Everything came back to her in a flash. She was on a ship—a pirate ship! Molly sat up quickly, her body crying out in agony as pain ripped through her wounded limb. She fell back gasping as the room tilted then righted itself again. Closing her eyes, she took great gulps of musty air, waiting until the sharp pain subsided to an ache.

The knife! she thought, her lashes fluttering open. She stared at the bottom of the upper rack. The captain had cut her with a knife!

Molly shuddered. She had a vision of the gleaming steel blade, the captain's stunned face . . . and then oddly, his gentle voice when he asked if she was all right. She quickly banished the last thought. Donovan was her enemy—he'd tried to trick her, to catch her off guard. Lord only knew what he'd have done to her if she'd lain passively instead of fighting.

She quelled the disquieting notion that perhaps he hadn't meant her any harm. He was a pirate who had taken her prisoner. Captain Donovan was Mahz-tan-to—the devil himself with his wicked blue eyes and bold smile. She must never forget that he couldn't be trusted. Evil spirits come in all disguises, she reminded herself. Even that of a handsome sea captain.

Donovan's image was replaced by another . . . of warm brown eyes in a compassionate face . . . of tousled brown hair and gentle hands cleansing her wound. The ship's surgeon, Molly thought. They aren't all cutthroats. The doctor had spoken to her kindly; she had sensed his genuine concern. The man's name was Adams, she remembered.

Clinging to the bulkhead, Molly hauled herself up. She reeled drunkenly from the rum's lingering aftereffects. She felt nauseated; she longed for a gulp of fresh air. The cabin was damp, musty, like a prison cell with the captain as her evil warder.

Moving gingerly, she swung her legs to the floor, inhaling sharply when her surroundings lurched. The pounding in her head intensified, and she blanched, stumbled, and grabbed onto the upper berth.

They'd made her drink rum, she recalled. Lots of it. For the pain — or so they'd claimed . . .

She remembered little else but pain after the first pricks of the surgeon's stitching needle. Staring at her bandaged arm, Molly tried to think. Suddenly she froze, hearing a rustling sound in the rack directly above her. Good God, she wasn't alone!

The captain? she thought. Her gaze confirmed it. Her eyes widened at the sight of his thick, raven mane of hair . . . his broad naked back. Molly swallowed. She could see his bare buttock, the back of his muscled leg . . .

The lantern cast a golden glow over his prone form, making his skin appear burnished. She felt the strongest urge to touch him, to run her fingers over his shoulder, down his back, along his buttocks.

Her eyes flickered, and she experienced desire . . . heat . . . a longing for what could never be. If only things were different and she'd met Donovan at another time, under other circumstances . . .

I'm drunk, she thought. Drink made a person think and do the strangest things. Hadn't her brother Shelby told her so many times? Why else would she feel attracted to her vile captor?

She couldn't see all of Bran Donovan from her position, but she saw enough to know that the captain slept buck bare as a newborn babe. For some reason she was shocked. It wasn't that she'd never seen a naked man before. One didn't share a two-room cabin with three males without accidentally invading each other's privacy—even if she did sleep in the upstairs loft while her brothers and father bedded downstairs.

Bran Donovan isn't father or brother to you, an inner voice reminded her.

No, he wasn't, she thought, her pulse racing.

Molly became aware of the soft rhythmic sound of Donovan's snoring. Why hadn't she heard it before? She stared in fascination. The captain was asleep on his side, facing away from her. It felt strange to be sharing his cabin, stranger yet to be studying him while he slept. It seemed so . . . so *intimate.*

Her senses swam and Molly had to struggle to remain standing. Donovan's grew hazy as her vision blurred. Her hand went to her forehead, moving to massage away the pain. Stumbling, she reached out to steady herself.

Suddenly the captain flipped over, his gaze alert, his muscles coiled to fight. Startled, Molly fell back, hitting her head on the edge of the chair seat.

"My God!" Bran exclaimed, hopping from the upper rack. Molly groaned. His blue gaze studied her anxiously. "Are you all right?"

"Ma'ta!" she gasped. "No!" Bracing herself on her elbows, she tried to rise, but instead she was suddenly gripped firmly and hauled upward. Black-

77

ness threatened to overcome her as she felt anew the excruciating pain in her head.

"You shouldn't sneak up on a man!" The captain caught her by the shoulders and searched her face.

Despite the pain, she glared at him, and just barely managed to contain her shock at seeing his full nakedness.

"Ikuuk — snake!" she spat. "Do you think I can kill you with this arm?" She saw his face whiten when she held up her bandaged limb. Her dark eyes flashed with anger. *"N'win'gi!* I'd do it gladly if I could!"

The captain's lips stiffened for only a second. He seemed unaware of his state of undress or of its strange effect on the girl before him.

"Ever the little wildcat, eh?" His eyes gleamed. In a move that took her totally by surprise, he picked her up under the armpits and hefted her to the upper bunk.

"I suggest you sheathe your claws, little cat," he said with a trace of amusement that surprised her. "You're here, so you might as well learn to make the best of it."

Bran was irritated. Any sympathy, any guilt, was fading as he took in her threat. A muscle ticked along his jaw. She wasn't all light and innocence, he thought with increasing anger. She was the one who'd disrupted his plans! She had ventured into forbidden territory — not he!

The air was thick with tension as they glared at one another, each trying to best the other in a battle of wills that neither could win. Watching the tide of red that swept upward from her neck, Bran suddenly became conscious that he was standing before this heathen woman nude.

Molly was embarrassed, but she refused to look away. It was one thing to study him while he was asleep, but to be caught . . .

She glared at him, pretending that she hadn't noticed his broad, muscled chest, which was smooth and bronzed and without hair. Her eyes fell to his flat stomach . . . the small indentation that was his navel. As if his staff were a magnet, her gaze traveled lower. . . .

She blushed, and her eyes flew to his face, where she held his glance and grew conscious of a faint tingling in her breasts. A sudden warmth invaded her in the juncture of her thighs. A sudden liquid warmth. Leaning on her elbow, Molly shifted on the mattress. Pain shot up her arm, making her gasp.

She was suddenly tired. She wanted to slump back against the bed and lose herself in sleep. Forget all about Bran Donovan.

"Molly McCormick." Bran spoke her name aloud, as if by saying it he would somehow understand the woman it represented. There was a heart-wrenching vulnerability about her, he realized. Bran gazed at her lovely face with its haunting midnight eyes, its lines of pain, and his anger softened. Another more disturbing emotion took its place.

"How's your arm?" he asked quietly, with genuine concern. Her eyes flickered open. He noted her surprise and felt a fresh surge of guilt.

"It hurts," she said. She blinked, and he saw her gaze wander down his full length.

Bran felt awkward. "I'm sorry." To cover his confusion, he casually reached for his breeches, intending to put them on. There'd been something disturbing in the girl's expression. Desire? Had she

79

felt it too? Or was he just imagining it?

Just then Angus MacDuff arrived, hammering on the door with his fist.

"Captain, sir!" The Scot's voice was laced with excitement. "You're wanted up above—there's a brig off the starboard bow!" He burst into the cabin, coming up short, his eyes widening.

The commander muttered a vile oath. "Her colors, Angus—what are her colors?" He hurried to dress, ignoring his friend's startled expression.

"They're flying the red ensign," MacDuff said. The shock vanished from his face, but his eyes sparkled. "She's a brig of at least 150 ton." He grinned at the girl on the upper rack. "A merchant ship— ripe pickings for the *Bloody Mary!*"

Molly's jaw fell open at the sight of the refined captain struggling into his pants, hopping ungracefully from one foot to the other. She was shocked into silence by the sudden invasion of charged excitement, of the sound of feet thundering across the deck above.

Bran shot her a glance. "In no circumstances will you leave this cabin. Do you understand?" His face was grim, his tone formidable. All traces of the kind man were gone.

Scowling, Molly nodded. She was angry, but she was wise enough not to show it. The last thing she wanted was to be tied up again. She'd have a better chance at escape if she pretended to go along with them.

Molly waited until the two men had left before she vented her anger. *Do you understand?* he'd said.

Her lips twisted. "I understand perfectly!" she said to an empty cabin. She cringed when she heard the harsh shrill of a whistle. "But you understand this, Captain Bran Donovan. You are my enemy, and I will escape you!"

Chapter Seven

Shirtless and barefooted, the captain rushed topside, bellowing orders to his men. "Dickon!"

"Here, Captain!" The first mate appeared at Donovan's elbow, handing him his spyglass.

Bran uncapped the three-foot instrument and peered through the lens. It was dawn, the time when daylight hovered on the horizon, turning the vast sea from inky black to murky gray. The target was outlined against the brightening sky—a two-masted, square-rigged vessel with a red pennant flying from her main topgallant masthead.

Studying the prey, Bran calculated the course of the brig as well as the speed both vessels were capable of. He decided in favor of the *Bloody Mary*.

"Mr. Dickon, it appears we've got us a live one." He grinned at his lieutenant as he exchanged the spyglass for his speaking trumpet.

If the brig kept its present course, he thought, the *Bloody Mary* would be chasing to windward. Bran lifted the speaking horn to his lips and called the command that would set the schooner on the same course as the English brig.

"Hoist the ensign!" Bran said, ordering his men to fly the British flag in a tactical maneuver to convince the enemy that they were friends rather than foe.

The ship was a flurry of activity as the red flag was raised up the ensign staff and the Rebel seamen responded smartly to their captain's continuous commands.

The wind tugged at Bran's unbound hair, whipping the dark strands about his face and neck. He stood on the quarterdeck, bare-chested like his men, eyeing the horizon, his expression alight with exhilaration. The two-masted, square-rigged vessel would be a prize worth taking, he thought. His blue gaze held a wild gleam.

Bran was in his element at the helm of the three-masted schooner, with the salt spray in his face and the sea-scented wind in his hair and nostrils. He anticipated the chase with relish. So far the brig's commander didn't suspect a thing, Bran mused, for he'd made no attempt at retreat.

When the brig was off the *Bloody Mary*'s beam, Bran called, "Ready about!" The tension on board increased as the ship silently moved toward its prey.

"Hard alee!" Bran bellowed when it was time. He would give the command to tack again and again each time the British vessel was directly off the schooner's beam. The men knew the routine well, for they had used it before. No matter a change in course of either ship, the two vessels were destined to meet if the *Bloody Mary* maintained this stratagem.

Bran roved an approving eye over his crewmen. The gunners were at the wales, waiting behind closed ports. They had cast off the lashings and hauled their cannon inboard, and were anxiously anticipating the coming fight. Handspikes, rammers, powder horns, and matches lay ready at the gun watches' fingertips. The cartridges had been brought up in their wooden storage boxes and set within reach.

The second gun watch stood at their battle stations, some equipped with cutlasses, ready to board first. The others would wait with pikes for the second wave of boarders.

"She doesn't seem to suspect a thing, Captain," Dickon commented in a satisfied voice.

The captain frowned at the merchant vessel. "All the more reason to be leery of her, Mark."

"Open the gunports!" Bran shouted into his speaking trumpet. The crew waited in suspense, staring as they approached the brig.

"Smithers!" the captain said when they were within four hundred yards of the enemy ship. "Lob off a warning shot. The rest of you hold. I want to show these bloody bastards just what they're up against!"

The ship shuddered and the air resounded with cannon fire as the *Bloody Mary* discharged her first shot. The sea spewed up water and foam where the ball fell short of the English brig.

"Sir! Look!" one of the gunner's mates cried. "It's a trap! They've her gunports covered with canvas!"

"Bloody hell," Bran cursed. He saw with amazement that canvas had been lifted, displaying long guns, quite possibly six-pounders. What had appeared to be a vulnerable merchant ship was actually a heavily armed war vessel, armed for combat.

Suddenly the air exploded and the sea churned beside the Rebel schooner, shaking her hull.

"Captain, they're firing!" yelled one crewman, as if the sound of the blast wasn't telltale enough.

"Engage!" the captain shouted harshly. "Commence firing!"

It was the signal for the gun captain to take control of his gunners and ensure that the brig was bombarded with a continual hail of cannonfire.

"Hanley, shift that blasted muzzle to the right," the gun captain cried. "Byrd! What's the matter, you shit-arsed buzzard? Haven't you got the balls to load her faster?!"

The men moved smartly to Smithers's foul-mouthed commands like well-oiled fighting machines.

The sky thundered with departing volleys. The Rebel ship rocked, and its salty crew swore vengeance as they labored together to fight back.

Down below in the captain's cabin, Molly gasped, bracing herself for the next attack. When the explosion came, her face paled; her hand on the wall grew knuckle-white. She murmured a silent prayer to her father's God and to the Great Spirit of her mother's people.

"*Ekaya'!*" she cried, startled by the thunderous series of eruptions that pitched the ship in the angry sea. "Am I going to die?" She gave little thought to her injured arm as she searched for a better hold. The rolling motion of the vessel made her nauseated. Casting a dismayed glance about the captain's cabin, Molly looked for something—a basin, a mug, anything!—to handle her stomach contents if she should be sick.

She spied a chamber pot on the floor. It was the

same receptacle that she'd been given to relieve herself in. She'd been forced to use the pot only twice, and had been duly embarrassed when the gruff Scotsman had taken it away to be emptied.

She slid toward the end of the bunk, inhaling sharply when the ship jerked with water crashing against its hull. Molly grabbed onto the side to keep from falling. The report that had preceded the movement had been deafening and close . . . too close.

Molly eyed the floor dubiously from the upper berth. She swung her feet over the rack's side until they were dangling off the mattress. The ship pitched and she reeled backward, hitting the mattress and striking her head against the wall.

She sat up, rubbing the back of her head. Three times she'd been hurt now. *"Tay'pee!"* she cried. "That's enough!"

"Captain!" a seaman above deck exclaimed. "They're lowering the red ensign!"

Bran grew alert to a new possibility. Could it be possible that they were fighting their own side? "Benson, hoist the striped flag!" He tensed, his gaze narrowing on the other ship.

"Hoist the stripes!" the marine lieutenant shouted, passing on the word.

Soon the British flag was gone from the ensign mast and the Continental pennant was hoisted. The other ship had done likewise, the captain realized with dismay.

"Cease fire! Shorten her sails!" Bran commanded. "She's one of our own!"

Crewmen hurried to leave off the chase.

"Criminy," the mate breathed with spellbound horror. "We're flying our true colors, but will she believe us, sir?"

Bran hesitated in answering his senior officer, turning instead to issue a brisk command. He faced Dickon with blue eyes that had gone black with concern. "I hope so, mate," he murmured. "I sure as hell hope so."

Then came the sign that Donovan was seeking. It was indeed a Rebel ship, and the brig's captain must have realized the mistake, for the artillery ceased and there came six flashes of light from her starboard bow.

"Answer her!" Bran boomed to the second lieutenant. The man swung a lit lanthorn in a single answering signal flash.

MacDuff, having accepted responsibility for the captain's spyglass, used it now to peer at the other ship. "True enough, Captain," he murmured. "She's one of ours all right."

Bran rubbed his brow as a sudden wave of tiredness overtook him. His shoulders slumped. His keen disappointment mirrored his men's. It was damn embarrassing to have attacked a fellow ship!

"She's leaving us, sir," Dickon said. "What if we're wrong and it's another trick?"

"No, lad," MacDuff answered. "I can read see her stern counter. She's the *Hazard,* from Baltimore."

"Assess the damage, Mr. Dickon," Bran mumbled wearily, before he turned to the hatch. "Report to me in the wardroom."

It wasn't until he was going below that he remembered Molly McCormick. He began to wonder how she'd weathered the raid.

"MacDuff," Bran said, "you'd better check my cabin."

The lass? MacDuff's gaze seemed to inquire. The captain nodded.

"Aye, Captain," the Scot said.

Was it over? Molly wondered, tensing as she anticipated another frightful burst of sound.

The silence seemed as deafening as the cannon-fire. She decided that the battle must be over. The ship's rocking had eased to a gentle bobbing; she could hear water lapping against the great hull, the tread of booted feet across the upper deck.

What are they doing? She envisioned the captain's crew, among them Old John, "Slim-bones," and the boy Will, climbing over the side and onto the British deck. Had the other ship surrendered? Were Donovan's men taking British prisoners this very second?

Molly felt a fierce stab of anger toward the unfeeling Donovan. The man was a monster, she thought. Only a monster could raid the helpless without conscience.

She gave little thought to the rain of return gunfire on the Rebel ship. So the merchant ship hadn't been entirely defenseless, she mused. In the end, the Rebels had won, hadn't they? The *Bloody Mary* remained unscathed, which meant that the English brig must be struggling to stay afloat.

"Damn Donovan!" she cried. How could such a good-looking man be such a black-hearted devil?

The captain handsome? Perhaps, she admitted. A panther was a beautiful animal, but that didn't make one trust it, for all its grace and sleekness of coat! She remembered his heated gaze, his insolent smile . . .

"Molly?" MacDuff's voice inquired at the door. The hatch opened. "Lass," he asked again, "are ye all right now?"

His brown eyes regarded her with concern. She was seated in the captain's chair, her dark eyes huge in her pale face as she cradled the chamber pot in her lap.

"Is it over?" she croaked.

He nodded. MacDuff came to her side, placing a big but gentle hand on her forehead. He smiled as he withdrew his touch. "No fever," he announced. "Good."

Her lips twisted. "I feel sick," she said.

His expression held compassion. " 'Twas a fearful ride for a landlubber." He made a cursory inspection of his surroundings. His gaze grew sharp as he faced her. "Ye didna fall from yer berth?"

"I might as well have," she mumbled, unconsciously rubbing her head where she'd injured it earlier. Her eyes suddenly narrowed. "What happened? Did you capture the ship?"

Molly was surprised to see a tide of red sweep from the Scot's neck upward.

" 'Fraid not, lass."

"Oh?" His manner sparked her interest. "Then the other ship . . . left?"

"In a manner of speaking—"

"MacDuff!" Bran Donovan entered the cabin, drawing the attention of both Molly and the Scot. His jet black hair was in wild disarray, no doubt tossed by the wind as he stood on the quarterdeck.

The captain was still without a shirt. Molly's gaze was drawn to his broad, naked chest, his sinewy arms; she noted the steel and strength in the bare muscles. When she'd fought him, she'd felt the power of those muscled arms. Her throat went dry. She looked away.

Eyeing the Scot, Donovan nodded toward his guest. "She all right?"

"Donovan," Molly burst out angrily, "why are you asking him!" Their gazes locked.

He bowed in acknowledgement, looking amused. "Forgive me, dear lady," he drawled with sardonic pleasure. "Given our past differences, I couldn't be sure you'd respond."

Bran stared at her, again overawed by the savage beauty of Molly McCormick. "Angus," he said huskily, his eyes never leaving the woman before him, "fetch us some grog and victuals. If my guess is right, the lady is hungry."

Bran waited until the Scot had quit the cabin before he turned to her. "I'm sorry," he murmured. "I should have asked. You *are* hungry, aren't you?"

She nodded, albeit reluctant to admit the fact. The scathing retort that had sprung to her lips died at his abrupt turnabout in manner. She started to tremble. His tone had been softly seductive, titillating her nerve endings. His gaze seemed to stroke and caress her.

"What happened?" she asked to cover her confusion. Molly hugged herself with her arms.

His blue eyes dulled and then caught fire. "The brig . . ." he began. He hesitated, his look daring her to make comment. "She was one of our own."

Her eyes widened at his honesty. "You attacked an American ship?" She couldn't keep her surprise hidden.

He inclined his head abruptly, his lips tightening, his expression rueful. "No comment? No laughter?"

Molly shook her head. She didn't feel like laughing. The report of the cannon still rang in her ears. She'd never been this close to battle, and the fighting, such as it had been, had frightened her, changed her.

Bran's face gentled. "You were afraid," he said perceptively. "Are you all right? You weren't hurt?"

She blinked. What trick was he trying now? Why, the captain sounded as if cared!

"I'm fine, Captain." She spoke the truth. Her stomach had settled. Her head had ceased throbbing. Her only pain was a dull ache in her injured arm.

His hearty "Good!" startled her. Before she had time to make heads or tails of his odd manner, MacDuff entered the cabin with a food tray. She smiled at the Scot. The fare wasn't as tempting as her first meal on board, but she was more than grateful for the nourishment. Molly accepted a sea biscuit from MacDuff's large hand and bit into the hardtack without a grimace.

"A drink?" Bran offered, drawing her glance. He stood above the table, pouring a measure of grog into a pewter cup.

She nodded, and he grinned at her, his blue eyes twinkling while she hurriedly took a gulp.

The Scot cleared his throat, drawing their attention to the fact that he was still there, watching the byplay between his commander and the "guest."

Donovan saw MacDuff's gaze settle on his pewter cup. He read hunger in the Scot's eyes. He was suddenly annoyed by the man's presence. "Thank you, Angus," the captain said dryly. "We have everything we need." The last was said in a tone of dismissal.

MacDuff inclined his head, but seemed reluctant to go.

"MacDuff," Bran repeated.

"Aye, Captain." With a furrow across his brow, the Scot left.

"Beans?" Bran asked, spooning some onto a plate from a bowl.

Molly nodded. Eyeing him warily, she accepted the offering from his extended hand. "That bread yesterday," she murmured, studying the rock-solid sea biscuit. She was conscious of the tingle in her fingertips where their hands had brushed by accident.

Donovan's lips twitched. "I'm afraid there'll be no more manna while we're at sea. We didn't get a chance to restock." He handed her some more hardtack. "You'd best eat hearty, sweet. Tomorrow is Saturday—salt fish," he explained. The captain grimaced, but his beautiful sea blue eyes sparkled. "More rum?" he asked her, holding up the bottle.

She stared at her cup, startled to see that she had finished its contents. Ignoring the captain's amused look, she said, "Yes, thank you." Her head had acquired a pleasant buzz. She saw the stark cabin through a golden haze.

With plate in hand, Donovan took a seat across the room on the lower berth, where he began enjoying his meal of hardtack and cold beans.

Molly couldn't take her eyes off him; she was fascinated by the way his sensual lips opened to receive a forkful of beans, the way his jaw flexed as he chewed his food. She experienced a warmth that was strangely new, yet oddly anticipatory. She likened the feeling to being suspended on a precipice, dangling over the edge, excited by the height, yet fearful of falling.

He is just an ordinary man doing a normal thing,

she told herself as she raised her fork to her mouth.

Ah, but is Donovan ordinary? an inner voice queried.

Molly remembered how kind he could be, how gentle. She shivered, wondering how it would be to kiss him.

Flushing at her thoughts, Molly averted her glance from his lean figure. It was crazy to think of kissing her enemy. She bit her lip. He was her captor. A Rebel pirate!

Privateer, her inner voice corrected.

So what? she thought. Pirate . . . privateer . . . they were the same, weren't they? The only reason it was legal was because some piece of paper said it was. That didn't necessarily make it right. At least not to her.

"Ho!" she cried without thinking. "He is still a man without honor!"

"Pardon me?" Bran, who had satisfied his hunger pains, regarded her from the lower berth.

"Tell me something, Captain," she said mockingly. "Do you enjoy killing?"

Without answering, Bran ducked out of the rack and strode to the table where he set down his plate. He stood above her, his blue gaze trained on her uplifted face. Her expression challenged him, yet he seemed neither angry nor impatient as he continued his silent study.

"What makes you different from a pirate?" she asked.

A pirate is one who captures, rapes and plunders for sport as well as profit, she thought. *A privateer captures vessels to keep his enemy from reaching shore. He is a soldier at sea.*

"Perhaps everything," he said softly, his eyes sparkling. His hand cupped her cheek, and she flinched. Something flickered in the depths of his blue gaze, but he didn't remove his hand.

"Or maybe nothing," he said darkly. His fingers tingled across her silken skin; Molly closed her eyes in joy at his touch. "Shall I show you how I plunder?" He withdrew his hand.

Her eyes flew open. His gaze fell to her breasts and then insolently raked her scantily clad form from her raised nipples to her bared calves. She gasped in outrage.

"Stand up." His voice was silky, commanding.

Molly shook her head. She was afraid of the attraction that simmered between them.

"Scared?" He raised an eyebrow.

"No!" she said, rising.

He smiled at her sweetly. "Liar."

Their eyes met, and she inhaled sharply. His blue gaze glittered with triumph. He lifted a lock of her hair, fondling its shiny length carefully, slowly, like a man caresses a woman's skin.

Molly stood passively, her heart thumping within her breast, the blood running hotly through her veins. He let the strands fall through his fingertips, watching the effect under the play of lantern light. Frantic, Molly searched for a weapon, and found one in the fork by her plate. While the captain's attention remained on her hair, she edged her hand toward the utensil.

Donovan's eyes suddenly narrowed. His hand snaked out and grabbed her about the throat. "Ever the savage warrior!" he exclaimed. His fingers fondled the slender column.

Molly stiffened, but only glared at him. He wouldn't have the satisfaction of seeing her fear!

"So slender . . . so fragile," Donovan murmured. He kept a loose hold, his thumb pressed in the hollow against her windpipe, his fingers about her nape. "You're trembling."

Eyes glittering with hate, she shook her head as much as his grasp would allow.

"I can feel it." He eased her toward him, his gaze heated. Donovan appeared fascinated with her lips.

Dry-mouthed, Molly licked her lips without thought, only realizing what she'd done when she heard him catch his breath and saw desire leap into his blue eyes.

"Kiss me, Molly." He released her throat to slide a hand over her shoulder, down her arm. The captain snared her waist, dragged her against him.

"No!" she cried, but he leaned into her. She became vibrantly aware of the heat of his abdomen where it pressed against her, searing her lower half. His warm breath stirred the hairs near her temple. She could feel the moist air on her forehead . . . her cheek . . . her mouth.

He dared to kiss her, drawing away immediately, staring at her with smoldering eyes, only to bend his head again to her cheek . . . her eyelids.

Molly struggled. Her neck tingled. Spasms of pleasure rippled down her spine, making her toes curl.

"You don't want to do this," she said in a quivering voice.

His blue gaze gleamed with the challenge. "Really?"

"Yes, really!" she shouted and jerked away. His hand shot out, grabbing her by the arm, hauling her back against his hard body. She gasped, fighting. He pinned one arm behind her back, the other

95

arm, the injured one, he held at her side . . . gently but firmly. If she struggled, she would hurt herself.

"Sweet," he murmured, and she shuddered with pleasure despite herself. The warmth of his breath caressed her cheek, her lips . . . her neck. Her body arched as desire flowed through her veins like heated quicksilver. It's the rum, she thought. Or was it?

She made one last attempt at resistance, a token move that brought her into more intimate contact with him. She heard his breath catch. His eyes flickered, and she felt him stiffen and clasp her closer. The male scent of him teased her, tantalized her, and she resisted the urge to bury her face in his neck.

Instead she stared at him, stared at his dark tousled hair and passion-darkened face. Something catapulted inside her. Bran Donovan wore the same look she'd seen on Cornsby and Beard-face, only on the captain the expression seemed somehow different.

Molly found herself mesmerized by his gaze. Her brain was neither too befuddled by alcohol nor too weary to recognize a warning in his taut face and hardening body. But she didn't care. It was easy to ignore the danger when her every nerve ending hummed with awareness. Her heart thumped; her pulse raced. She felt her body melt against him, and her eyes softened with desire.

The captain moaned and bent his head. His mouth touched skin, searing her throat. Molly sucked in a ragged breath. His lips were gentle even as his hands kept a firm grip on her, sliding from her waist up her back, tangling in her hair.

Fire shot through her veins as a hand moved to

palm her breast . . . fire and liquid heat. The sensation was new to her. Her nipple hardened beneath her shift, aching and alive. The feeling frightened her, for part of her cried out for him to touch her, take her.

"No!" she sobbed, struggling in earnest now. Taking him by surprise, she broke free, grabbing the fork and brandishing it like a weapon.

The sight of his passion-glazed look made the air hiss from her lungs. She realized with a sense of shame that if he pressed his point, she'd be lost. Enemies they might be, but they were man and woman first. If they didn't stop now, there'd be no turning back for either one of them.

Stunned, Bran Donovan looked from her face to the fork and back again, his face a patchwork of mixed expressions. Laughing, he recaptured her easily, tossing away the utensil. He then took her lips in a rough kiss that stole her breath away and rocked her from the top of her head to the very tips of her bare toes. His head lifted, his features triumphant. Swallowing, Molly closed her eyes to block out the sight of his burning blue gaze.

"Open your eyes," he ordered in a hoarse voice.

She shook her head. *No!* she thought. *This can't happen. I won't let him do this to me!* "You can go to the devil, Captain Donovan!"

Growling in frustration, he released her hands to cup her head, twining his fingers in her long hair. She opened her eyes and glared at him, refusing to be intimidated, refusing to allow him to see just how shaken she was by their bodily contact.

He's no better than Reginald Cornsby! Fight him! "Do you treat all your guests this way, Captain?" she taunted.

His brows lowered as he frowned. "So, you've decided to be a guest."

"In a cold day in hell!" she cried, fighting his hold.

He chuckled, and the warm sound vibrated along Molly's spine, making her shiver. She stared at him in shock, startled by her reaction to his kiss . . . to him.

"I'll be sure to take you with me if I go," he murmured before his head dipped and he kissed her again.

His mouth smothered her reply. Fire shot through her system, making her moan softly in mindless pleasure, and her struggle to be free became a token resistance. Her breasts warmed; her core pulsated with liquid heat. Bran Donovan is your enemy! she reminded herself. But her body refused to listen, for even as she whimpered in protest her uninjured arm rose to stroke the captain's neck, her bandaged limb encircling his waist.

Bran stiffened as the woman in his arms responded. He felt her breasts as she curled against him. Heat invaded his loins at her soft little passionate cries.

She was warm and sweet and soft. He found himself unable or unwilling to tear his lips from her scented skin.

Spy . . . Danger . . . Cove. The thoughts infringed on his enjoyment of her. A harsh, painful sound tore from his throat; he thrust her away from him.

White-faced, Molly gaped at him, shaken.

"You play the game after all, my lady," he said dryly as he struggled for control, "but you play a poor hand."

Molly's gaze darkened with fury. She clenched her hands until her fingernails scored her palms.

"It's my game you're playing, Captain," she said evenly, "and I've yet to play my hand." She lunged at him with a raised fist, angered by his smug expression.

Taken unawares, Bran Donovan's head snapped back under the force of her blow. "Bitch!" Cursing, he captured her wrists in his bruising grip. His expression murderous, he grabbed her, hauling her upward before tossing her onto the bed.

He left her alone then with only his laughter for company, a harsh sound that echoed about the cabin, making her shiver and the tiny hairs at the nape of her neck stand on end.

Chapter Eight

Somewhere off the coast of New Jersey

"You're never going to get away with this, Felter!"

John Felter sneered. "We already have, *Captain* Martin.*" He returned his attention to the papers on his writing desk, the desk that had once belonged to the blond-haired officer now lying on the cabin floor, trussed up like a chicken.

As he ran down the list of goods stashed in the hold of the *Flying Wench,* the former cook's mouth formed a positively evil grin. "There's enough powder kegs to supply several hundred men!" He glanced at Martin. "What, no comment, Captain?"

The captain's green eyes hardened. "You were a lousy cook, Felter."

Felter laughed. "I'd never fixed a crumb until the day you hired me."

"I should have fired you then," Martin retorted. "You made the worst lobscouse I'd ever tasted!"

"I never did learn how long to cook it." Felter grimaced, recalling the unappetizing mess he'd concocted his first day out on the open sea. The dish was made with thin, dried potato slices, soaked salt beef, and dried peas and beans. He'd combined all of the ingredients, cooked it in a single pot as he should, but the result had tasted like salted grit instead of the tasty mush Martin's crew had expected. He grinned. "I make a far better traitor, don't I?"

The hatch to the captain's cabin opened. A gangly youth entered; his eyes flashed to Martin before fastening on the man who was now his superior.

"Gunther, I assume it's all taken care of?" the former cook said. Felter was a short man, painfully thin, whose misshapen lips formed a perpetual pucker.

The young man nodded, his dark eyes huge in his gaunt face. He shuffled his feet nervously.

"The mate?" Felter persisted, his steely gaze narrowing.

Fear flickered across Gunther's face. "Shot. Thrown overboard with the others." He bit his lip. "Just like you ordered, sir."

"Good." Felter sat back in his chair, looking satisfied. His expression turned smug. "Captain, your Mr. Lender is dead. So are those who didn't quite see eye to eye with the rest of us. The way is now clear for me to continue my plans. There's a certain British general who'll be most grateful for the ammunition and supplies." He paused to study his captive's white face. "Still think we won't succeed?"

"You bastard!" Martin cried, struggling with his bonds. "I'll see you hung before this is over!"

Felter's face hardened. "You forget who is the

101

master here, Captain, *sir,*" he taunted. "I'm in charge now. You'd best remember that!" He rose from his seat, his puckered lips grotesque in his grin. "Play your hand right, I might let you live. If not, you'll be lucky to see the light of morning."

June 28, 1778; The Jug and Barrel Inn

"Something's happened," Patrick Donovan said, his face furrowed with concern. "We should have heard from one of them by now."

Josiah nodded. "We could send Nate to the cove again." He took a swig of ale. Setting his tankard down, he wiped a sleeve across his wet chin. "Tell me again, what exactly did Redding say?"

Pat furrowed his brow. "He said, 'The wench didn't come. Mary will return in one week's time.' What do you make of it?" He stared at the froth in his ale.

"The wench is Martin's ship, the *Flying Wench,*" Josiah said. "As for Mary—"

"The *Bloody Mary,* Bran's ship!" Pat exclaimed, his eyes twinkling.

Josiah eyed the younger Donovan brother with fond amusement. "Right."

"So what do we do now? Sit tight and wait?"

The innkeeper nodded. "Bran'll try again in four days. We'll send Nate to the cove then to see if the switch has been executed." Josiah frowned. "I hope to hell the delay is due to those over at Dog Run." Dog Run was the place where Martin was to pick up the powder. The run had been arranged by Benger Furnace's manager, Samuel Foxworth. Fox-

102

worth did his share for the Rebel forces by keeping a sharp eye out for enemy activities often helping in the organization of the smugglers' runs. It was one of Foxworth's men who heard about the recent capture of the British *Jenny* by Andrew Zabriskie's *Pride's Fury,* and the sale of goods and said British brigantine at Payne's Tavern at Chestnut Neck. The *Jenny* was just one of several to be auctioned off this fine June. Unlike the others, she'd gained the attention of the Rebel smugglers with her precious cargo of black powder. A dangerous load, but one valuable to Washington's needy troops.

"Damn!" Josiah's scowl deepened as he pondered the things that could have gone wrong. "What the devil could have happened to the *Wench,* man? Martin's slipperier than an eel! I've never known him to fail."

"This couldn't possibly have anything to do with the girl?" Pat asked, his expression doubtful.

"The one Bran's got prisoner?"

Pat inclined his head. "She's half savage," he murmured thoughtfully.

Josiah raised an eyebrow but didn't comment on that fact. "Bran let her go?"

The younger man shook his head. "No." He shuddered, recalling the tension-filled scene he'd stumbled upon between his brother and the girl in Bran's cabin. "He made up his mind that she'd stay prisoner until the powder was transferred and safely stowed."

"I'd wager she's innocent."

Patrick agreed. "If there's any foul play in Martin's absence, there's one thing we know for certain.

103

Whatever—whoever—it is, the girl is innocent of involvement . . . this time."

Molly grew instantly alert as the hatch swung open and Tommie the cabin boy entered the room with a meal tray. "Tommie," she greeted him. "What time is it?"

Setting a tray on the chart table, he glanced at her warily, refusing to answer her.

Tommie's silence angered her. She was mad that for the last three days she'd been left without company. She was bored and near tears. Her only thoughts were to escape the dim, musty cabin.

It didn't matter that she'd been here only four days. It seemed like weeks. On the first day after the injury to her arm, she'd been too ill to care about her surroundings. But now that she was feeling better . . .

The aftereffects of the rum had worn off. The intense pain in her arm had subsided to a bearable ache.

Four days, she thought, and I still don't know what he's going to do with me! Was he ever going to release her? If so, when? And why had he made her a prisoner at all?

She glared at the scrawny Tommie, her lips tight with frustration. She wanted answers to her questions—and she wanted them *now.*

"I need to talk with Donovan," she said.

Tommie froze in the act of removing the foodstuff from the tray.

"Do you hear me?" she snarled, rising from the bottom rack. She began pacing the floor in agitation. She felt like a caged animal. If she didn't escape soon, she would go crazy! "Get Captain Donovan. I want to talk to him."

With tray in hand, the cabin boy fearfully skittered by her without a word. When time passed and no one appeared, Molly sat down in the captain's chair, closing her eyes.

Stay calm, she thought. Think! There must be some way to get off this ship.

How far out to sea were they? she wondered. A mile? Two? A hundred?

Her throat tightened. Her family must be frantic with worry. Her mouth twisted. Shelby would be worried, she corrected. Her father . . . he'd be too drunk either to know or care about her disappearance. As for Darren . . . Her lashes flickered open and she stared straight ahead. No doubt her eldest half brother was rejoicing in her being gone . . .

How she missed the sun's rays. She gritted her teeth until the muscle along her jaw ached. All her life she'd lived in freedom . . . the freedom of the woods with its wildlife . . . its towering pine trees . . . its ever changing moods. Captain Bran Donovan had taken away her freedom, the very thing he claimed to be fighting for. He had disturbed her peace, churned up a hatred as passionate as his Rebel cause.

Liar, her conscience taunted. Remember the way he kissed you . . . You weren't hating him then.

She was drunk, she rationalized. Scared! What happened would never—ever—happen again!

We'll see.

Shaking her head, Molly gasped for air. The cabin walls pressed in on her, suffocating her. She wanted to scream!

105

She had to escape. Bran Donovan was a tyrant. She couldn't begin to fathom the man with the gaze of stormy blue.

Unbidden came the memory of his mouth on her lips . . . her throat. She felt a tremor of desire. His hands had stroked her, caressed her, tangled in her hair.

Heat flushed her cheeks. Oh, God, I kissed him back! She had clutched at him like a drowning man clutches a lifeline. Her breath quickened as the memory sharpened. Rum might have dulled her brain, but there'd been nothing wrong with her senses. Every one of them had hummed with his nearness . . . his touch . . . his scent.

What strange power did this man possess that he could anger her one moment and make her desire him the next? How could he do this to her?

Molly's mind hardened against him. Her resolve to escape firmed with her expression, her quest for revenge.

You'll pay for this, Captain Donovan, she thought. I swear it!

Pay for what? her mind taunted her. For making you feel like a woman? For liking the way he'd made her feel?

Molly forced the traitorous thoughts away. She concentrated instead on returning to shore. If they were miles out to sea, how would she make land?

She brightened. She had to get to the main deck, she decided. Then she'd be able to determine who — or what — stood in her way of escape.

Molly shivered with cold dread, recalling her encounter with Old John Smithers and the two seamen who'd cornered her in the cedar swamp. How many "Beard-faces" would she have to run from? And if she got free and they came after her, would she be lucky enough to evade their evil clutches?

"I'll have to deal with that when the time comes," she murmured to the empty cabin. First, she somehow had to convince Donovan to allow her topside.

Molly had her first chance to convince the captain that very night. She was shocked speechless when he entered the cabin. It was the first time she'd had occasion to confront him since their last passionately charged exchange.

He barely gave her a glance as he took off his hat, set it on the table, and fumbled to insert a key into the desk lock. He opened a drawer, rummaging inside, looking for something. Satisfaction fluttered across his stern face. Apparently he'd found what he was looking for, what Molly couldn't see, because having found the object, he quickly slammed shut and locked the drawer.

"You wanted to see me?" he said drily. "Well, I'm here. What do you want?"

Molly stared at him. "How long are you going to keep me here?" she said, her voice sharp. She'd meant to speak softly, but she was taken aback by her body's violent reaction to the shock of his blue gaze.

"As long as necessary." He had raised an eyebrow.

"And that is?"

The captain sighed. "I don't know. Three, maybe four more days."

Molly perked up at that. "Then you do plan to let me go?"

He looked surprised by her question. "Of course." Something moved across his features,

107

something Molly thought might be guilt.

"I didn't know," she murmured, looking away. "You never said." She was disturbed by that look of conscience.

"Would it have made a difference?" he challenged.

She shot him a glance. He looked amused . . . and too damned attractive for her peace of mind. For God's sake, stop looking at him, she scolded herself. He kidnapped you, tied you up, and cut you with his knife!

Her lips tightened. Ignoring his last query, she faced him, her dark eyes glittering. "Do you expect me to stay down here for the next four days?"

Bran looked at her, noting her defiant gaze, her pale cheeks, her restless movements. "You're quite comfortable, aren't you? You've been given food to eat, a bed to sleep on. What more could a prisoner ask for?"

"Air!" she cried, startling him with her vehemence. "Fresh air, Captain. Is it too much to ask to feel the sun on my face, the breeze in my hair!

He saw the way her fist clenched at her uninjured side. Molly began pacing the cabin. She was highly agitated, Bran realized. From her behavior, he judged that he'd done her greater harm with her enforced stay in the cabin than with the wound he'd inflicted to her arm. His gaze went to that limb, which hung, still bandaged, at her side.

"How's your arm?" he asked softly. Bran reached for it, running his fingers across the back of her hand, noting with pleasure her skin's softness. Surprised, he felt her tense.

Molly gazed at him in angry bewilderment. "My

108

arm?" she said, her face paling. Her hand clenched; she struggled to withdraw it, but Bran held firm. "Captain," she gasped, "haven't you heard a word I said?"

"I heard y—"

"Damn my arm!" With a cry of frustration, she jerked free of him with a shake of her head, and his attention was drawn to the glorious fall of shiny dark hair. "I need to leave this hellhole!"

"This hellhole you're referring to just happens to be my home," he returned mockingly. Bran saw her swallow, heard her breath rasp in the ensuing quiet as she struggled for composure.

His expression softened at her obvious distress. He felt for her—he honestly did. But what could he do for her when granting her wish meant putting her in proximity with his sorry crew? He wasn't worried about MacDuff, of course. And Tommie? Tommie was too scared of the "savage woman" to harm her or aid in her escape. It was with great trepidation that the boy brought her meals. Since he'd learned of the boy's fear, the knowledge had afforded Bran a great deal of amusement.

"I'm sorry," he offered, meaning it. He didn't apologize often, but she didn't know that.

"Sorry?" Molly gasped. "What does that mean?" She began to feel desperate. She'd go crazy if she had to endure four more days in the cabin.

His lips firmed. "It means I have no choice but to keep you below."

"No!" she cried, moving closer to him. "I don't want to hear it. I don't care about your reasons!"

Molly grabbed onto his shirtfront, pleading him with her eyes. "Take me up for a little while," she said hoarsely. "Just this once."

His hands caught her shoulders. "Molly," he breathed, his face tortured. "I can't . . ."

She blanched, pulling away. "Can't!" she said. "Or won't?"

"My men—"

"Damn you, Donovan! Damn your cold heart and vile soul!" She lunged at him with raised fists, striking him in the chest, hitting his arms. "I hope you rot in a British prison! Then you'll know how I feel!"

"You go too far!" he snapped. His expression darkened like thunder clouds. His eyes were a fierce blue, like a storm-tossed sea. He had captured her wrists, and his fingers tightened before he flung her away from him.

Molly gaped at him, shivering at the force of his anger. It vibrated from his taut frame, searing her.

"You little fool," he muttered. "Don't you understand what's up there? Maybe you'll understand this!" He took her mouth in a brutal kiss.

She whimpered beneath the onslaught. He was rough, cruel, a demon sent to tempt and taunt her. He was hurting her . . . punishing her! And for what? Nothing!

No! her mind cried. Tears burned beneath her closed eyelids as she fought to be free of his marauding mouth. Stop! Leave me alone!

Bran crushed the soft lips with his mouth and felt regret. The feeling began in his belly, uncoiling, spreading, until he grew taut and sick-hearted at the taste of it in his mouth.

He released her, disgusted with himself. It didn't matter that he'd been trying to make her see what

110

his men could do to her. He wasn't a nursemaid He couldn't watch her every minute.

If she thought him a brute, then imagine her horror at his crew! What if one of them assaulted her in a way more severe, more humiliating than the way he'd shown her? He'd kill anyone who tried to touch her, but he knew his men—some of them would try anyway. Must the deed be done before she understood?

His men were cutthroats. They were good fighting men. Bran hired sailors and soldiers, not well-bred gentlemen with fine manners.

From the horrified look on her face, Bran could only surmise that Molly had lumped Bran in the same category as his men. And why not? He'd never claimed to be a gentleman.

He didn't care what she thought, he told himself. She still wasn't exonerated of being an enemy spy. *Liar,* he thought. He cared. He didn't want to, but he cared.

"Did you like that?" he asked, his voice hard.

She shook her head, and his gut wrenched when he saw her tears.

"Well, that's what you could expect from any one of my men!" He paused. "Is that what you want?" he shouted, hoping to instill some sense into her. "Is it?"

She glared at him, but her lips quivered and her midnight eyes still glistened with tears. The sight would probably haunt him for years to come, Bran thought.

"I want you to drop dead, Bran Donovan."

He stiffened with anger. "Well, my lady," he said, his voice laced with sarcasm, "by the time this

bloody war is done, you may just be lucky enough
to have your wish!"

With a grim smile, Bran stalked from the cabin.
White-faced, Molly stared at the closed hatch.

Chapter Nine

"What are you looking at?" Molly said, sniffing. Straightening on the lower berth, she wiped the tears from her cheeks with the back of her hand. She knew her nose was red, and no doubt she looked a sight, but that didn't give the boy the right to gawk at her!

Tommie hesitated near the door, staring at her. "You're crying," he breathed, as if awed by the realization.

"So?" she said, averting her bloodshot eyes. "Haven't you ever seen someone cry before?"

The cabin boy shuffled to the table, where her uneaten midday meal had thickened into a cold jellied mass. "You didn't eat," he commented. His brow furrowed. "Aren't you hungry?"

She flashed him a look, opening her mouth in readiness to snarl her reply, when it suddenly occurred to her that Tommie was no longer shy of her, that he had spoken two — no, three! — entire sentences to her.

"I can't eat," she murmured, searching his face.

"I'm too miserable to eat." She had a mental vision of Bran Donovan's jeering expression, felt again his angry kiss.

Tommie seemed taken aback by the notion that she had feelings.

"Haven't *you* ever felt that way?" she asked. "When your stomach is all tied up in knots 'cause you're unhappy?" The boy nodded slowly, thoughtfully. "Well, that's the way I feel now."

"Why?" To her amazement, Tommie pulled up the captain's chair and sat down.

"Would you like to be down here all the time?" she said. "Below deck . . . without air or sunshine?" He shook his head. "I hate it!" she muttered with a vehemence that made her voice sharp. She bit her lip, wondering if she'd made him frightened of her again. She relaxed upon finding she was the object of his curious gaze.

"How old are you, Tom?"

"Sixteen." He flushed. "Fourteen," he amended, his face beet red. "But I'm just as good as Kenneth Jones, even if he is sixteen and a half!"

Molly stifled a smile. "I have two older brothers," she whispered, as if she and Tommie were fellow conspirators, "I know what you mean."

He grinned at her, displaying broken yellow teeth. His gaze narrowed. "Are you really an Injun?"

She stiffened. "Do I look like one?"

Tommie shrugged. "Never saw one."

"Well, you have now."

His eyes widened. "Really?" He looked like he wanted to touch her, to see if she were real.

"My mother came from among the Delaware."

114

She smiled. "I'm not any different than you or your mother." She regarded the youth with amusement lurking in her dark eyes. Molly sobered. "What's it like outside?" Her tone was wistful.

"Sun's a-shining. Breeze is out of the south."

"Where are we?"

He shrugged again, a careless jerk of his young shoulders. "Somewheres. I dunno."

Molly suppressed a feeling of impatience. She sighed instead — loudly, longingly. "Wish I could go up on deck." She hesitated and then dared, "The captain'd let me, but he's afraid somethin'd happen to me up there . . . what with me not knowing my way around." It wasn't exactly a lie, she thought, although she suspected that her safety wasn't all that concerned Bran Donovan. He was afraid she'd escape.

Tommie's eyes lit up. He puffed out his chest. "I could take you."

"You could?" Molly held her breath.

She wouldn't feel guilty for using the boy. She couldn't afford to!

When the light in the boy's expression died, so too did Molly's hope for escape. "I've got to help in the galley."

"Oh." Her disappointment made her shoulders droop.

Suddenly Tommie smiled. "But I could come back later — after Cook finishes supper. Oh," he said, his face falling. "You wanted to see the sun."

"I want fresh air, Tommie. I need to be free of this musty cabin." She said it with a ferocity that spoke of loathing for her surroundings.

"You don't like the capt'n's cabin?" The youth

115

appeared startled, and Molly realized that to him the captain's cabin represented the most luxurious quarters on board ship. What sort of quarters did the crew sleep in?

"Yes, well," she hedged, shifting uncomfortably. "It's a nice room and all," she lied, "but I've lived most of my life in the woods. I miss being outdoors."

He nodded in understanding. Tommie stood, pushing back the chair. He picked up the tray as if all were settled. Now that Molly saw her chance to escape, she found that she was hungry.

"Tommie?" she said, blushing. "Can you leave that? I'm hungry."

He looked down at the plate filled with the congealed, sticky substance. "You like pudden and beef?" he asked.

"Pudden and beef?" she echoed. So that what it was supposed to be, she thought. Wisely, she inclined her head.

Tommie handed her the plate of pudden and beef, and Molly ate the cold dish with the gusto of one who'd just realized she was starving. The boy left, and Molly grinned at the closed hatch. She was going up above! Soon she would escape!

The captain would no doubt strangle her if he learned of her foray above deck, Molly realized. She set her fork on her plate. He was a horrible man, a brutal man! Her lips still stung from his assault.

A memory infringed on her conscious, denying his meanness . . . visions of his tender concern. Rubbing her bruised lips with her fingertips, she recalled a different kiss . . . a gentle kiss . . .

116

when Bran Donovan had sought not to punish but only to pleasure her.

Her heart fluttered. Her mouth went dry as her breasts tingled with the memory of his palms.

"Who are you, Bran Donovan? Man or beast?"

Molly's features turned hard. She wasn't going to wait to find out. She'd take the first chance to be free of him!

Bran stood on the quarterdeck studying the vista of blue sky and sun-kissed sea. The day was warm, without a cloud to mar the azure canopy. The breeze out of the south freshened, rustling the ship's topgallants, stirring her mainsails.

Below on the main deck, Brett Smith mended a tear in an expanse of sailcloth, and a group of ordinary seamen worked with rigging, greasing and splicing and tying knots. Aloft on the ratlines, a young crewman climbed the mainmast while the boatswain watched him with an eagle eye, bellowing orders from the deck below.

It was a day of calm; not a single vessel dotted the horizon. For a captain with a purpose, the fine weather boded well. The night promised to be as friendly as the afternoon.

In four days' time, the *Bloody Mary* would enter the mouth of the Great Egg Harbor River, Bran mused. If all went well, sometime in the following twenty-four hours the schooner would rendezvous with the *Flying Wench,* and the transfer of munitions would be completed.

Ross Martin, owner of the sloop, was an able captain. A better officer Bran had yet to meet.

The man was sharp as well as wily. Martin wouldn't fail, even if he encountered trouble. It wasn't in his nature to take things lying down. There was no better man for the job, Bran thought.

Why then do I feel unsettled? A raucous cry above drew Bran's gaze to a circling pair of seagulls. He watched one dip to the rippling waters and within seconds, rise again, a fish in its beak. Glancing off the larboard stern, he squinted against the sun's glare, noting the faint outline of the Jersey coast.

He closed his eyes. Unbidden came a vision of a tear-stained face, haunting midnight eyes, quivering pink lips. Molly McCormick. Bran cursed. She'd wormed her way under his skin. She was a she-devil, who tormented him at every turn.

He sighed, his lashes flickering open. She was a woman, a flesh-and-blood woman, who was lonely and miserable within the small confines of his stateroom.

What am I going to do with her? He couldn't let her go, not yet, not until the powder was stashed and the danger of discovery was long past. How many more days must he keep her prisoner? Six? Seven?

Bran realized after their exchange that he couldn't release her in the four days he'd told her. It'd be at least five before the shipment was moved, and another day and a half at best to escape to open sea.

There was also the problem of where to let her go. The cove was out of the question. But if he dropped her off elsewhere along the shore, would she be able to find her way home? Bran scowled. Why should he care whether she did or not? There was a war going on. Men were dying every day. Why should he worry about one female?

Because she's an innocent in this game and you know it! The thought popped out of nowhere. He sighed. Innocent or not, she was no doubt angry enough now to organize the British army against him and anyone else involved with her capture.

"Captain?"

Bran spun to see Dickon's respectful salute as the first mate joined him at the ship's rail. "Mark," he murmured, turning again to stare at the open sea.

"Worried about the *Wench,* sir?"

Bran glanced at him, startled. His lips twisted when it dawned on him that the man meant the sloop and not the woman in his cabin. "You could say that."

"Martin's a good man," Dickon said, and Bran nodded. "What do you suppose happened to him?"

"I prefer not to hazard a´guess, Mark," the captain answered. "I'm sure he'll enlighten us in four days' time."

After a length of silence Dickon stirred, pushing himself from the rail. "About the girl—"

Bran spun to face him. "Yes?" Leaning his back against the rail, he crossed his arms over his broad chest.

"Have you given any thought to her release?"

"I have," Bran said. "I've an idea when, but I haven't a clue to where. Any suggestions?" He gazed at his officer, his eyelids at half mast.

"There's always Brigantine."

Bran cocked his eyebrows. "The island?"

After a moment's hesitation, during which he grew mildly uncomfortable under his superior's stare, Dickon nodded.

"And how is she to get home?" he queried, his voice sharp. He shuddered at the thought of a woman left alone there. Any woman, he told himself. Not just the spirited young woman in his cabin. Brigantine Island was a desolate stretch of sand dunes and tall grasses. Its reefs were treacherous; many a craft had crashed and sunk off the island's shores.

Bran frowned. If a summer storm didn't get Molly, then the isolation would.

"Well, sir . . ."

"No!" Bran's voice boomed like thunder. "Whatever you may think, Mr. Dickon, I'm not a murderer of women!"

Dickon gasped. "Sir, I—"

"She will be released when the time comes," Bran said sternly, "at such a time and at such a place that I deem it advisable. Do I make myself clear?"

Dickon snapped to attention. "Aye, Captain!"

"Good!" His expression softened as some of the tension left Bran's frame. "Relax, Mark. I'm bloody tired, that's all."

The first mate did so with a sigh. "Would you like me to take over, sir?"

Bran shook his head. He had just had a thought, and a longing to spend time with a certain female. Being with her was anything but restful, still . . .

"Tell Cook I'll be dining in my cabin this evening." He'd avoided the cabin these last two days, except to retire for the occasional quick nap long after Molly had gone to sleep.

Bran smiled to himself as Dickon went to obey orders. He felt himself invigorated by the prospects of trading barbs with the lovely savage.

"Freeze!" Shelby commanded. The click of his rifle hammer echoed in the eerie silence of the surrounding woods. "Don't move or I'll blow your head off." He kept his rifle trained on the shadowy figure off the forest trail. His heart thundered beneath his breast. The muzzle wobbled in his line of vision as he fingered the flintlock nervously.

Leaves crunched beneath booted feet. "Son, I —"

"I said, don't move, you bastard!" Shelby saw with amazement that the man kept coming. He was either the bravest fellow alive or the biggest fool. He blinked, astonished, when the man stepped onto the path. "Father!" he gasped. Shelby had his answer. Tully McCormick was a drunken fool.

"Shelby, will ye put that thing down?" Tully grinned. "It makes me a might nervous, it does."

"What are you doing here?" The last person Shelby expected to see in this neck of the woods was his father. Shelby was on his way to visit the Lenni Lenape, the people of Shi'ki-Xkwe. He'd left Manville for Shamong three days past after two days of apprehensive and fruitless searching for his half sister Molly.

Unable to accept that Molly might have been

121

killed, or worse, in the uprising, Shelby had checked all possible avenues of travel. His spirits had plummeted when no clues came to light concerning her disappearance. It was as if Molly had simply left the face of the earth. Then the idea had occurred to him, late at night. If Molly needed a place to hide, a place where she'd feel safe from Reginald Cornsby and his posse, where would she go?

The answer had come to him in an eye-blink. To a place where she'd be accepted without question, loved for being her mother's child. To the Lenni Lenape — Shi'ki-Xkwe's, Pretty Woman's — people.

Shelby stared at his father, wondering how Tully had come this far. He himself had been traveling for days now, dodging British and Rebel troops, keeping away from farms and villages.

"Father?" he asked again.

Tully approached him, a gleam in his Irish brown eyes, a cocky grin on his freckled face. "I've been following you since the day you left."

Shelby blinked. "Why?"

The older man's expression clouded. "Because yer sister must be found. I want to help find her."

Shelby opened his mouth to object, then seeing his father's face, he abruptly closed it again. He checked his surroundings. They were alone. He sighed. No one lurked in the bushes to seize them. He started to walk along the path; his father fell into step beside him.

Not a breeze ruffled the treetops. Not a squirrel scampered across the dead and decaying leaves. If there was troop movement in the area, then it was an army of ghosts, Shelby thought. He'd wager a day's pay at the furnace that at this moment the only two humans who roamed this part of these New Jersey Pine Barrens were the McCormick father and son.

Shelby stopped, placing his hand on his father's arm. "I'm going to see Wood Owl."

Tully stiffened. Anger flashed in his brown gaze. "Tahuun Kukuus," Shelby's father murmured. He jerked his head. "I understand." He sighed and continued down the path. "I thought as much."

Following behind him, Shelby raised an eyebrow. Father must love Molly more than he lets on, he thought. Tahuun Kukuus—Shelby knew him as Wood Owl. The Indian was Molly's grandfather, the father of Shi'ki-Xkwe. There were bad feelings between Tully McCormick and the Delaware Indian chief. Tahuun looked with disfavor on the Irish white man who had charmed Shi'ki-Xkwe away from the Lenapes.

To give Tahuun Kukuus his due, when the old man learned he had a granddaughter, he'd accepted Molly with open arms, bearing no ill will to the innocent child nor any resentment toward Shelby, Tully's younger son. The first meeting between granddaughter and grandfather had been by design—Shi'ki-Xkwe's. Longing for her family, the young Indian woman had taken the two children, Molly and Shelby, for a brief visit to the Delaware settlement where Wood Owl resided.

Shelby had been six at the time, but he still remembered the tension between father and daughter, the heated exchange that had taken place when Shi'ki-Xkwe had refused her father's command that she return to live with the Delaware. He

123

would never forget his stepmother's tear-stained face as they hurried home, nor how his four-year-old half sister had fussed and fidgeted, perhaps sensing, too, her mother's unhappiness. After that day there'd been no more visits to the Indian village. Shelby had been sorry, for he'd been captivated, curious, about the sights and sounds of the Delaware way of life.

A year and a half after that visit, Shi'ki-Xkwe was dead from the fever. She'd never reconciled with her father.

Dusk fell as Shelby and Tully walked along the footpath, deeper and deeper into the virgin woods. They stopped briefly to quench their thirst; the small stream was rust colored, but wet and cool, which was all that mattered to either McCormick.

As night deepened the sky, heightening the sounds of the surrounding brush, Shelby gave thought to a resting place. He saw the droop of his father's shoulders, the way his gait had slowed to a weary lumber. The fact that Tully had been cold sober when he'd been discovered had stunned Shelby. He was amazed that his father remained clearheaded and was without flask or whiskey bottle strapped to his hip for an occasional sip.

Shelby stopped, having spied shelter in the form of a felled pin oak. "Father, we'll rest here for the night." He experienced a painful jolt when he saw his father sink gratefully to his knees. "Are you all right?"

Tully straightened immediately. "Fine, son. Fine." He stared off toward the west. "Tomorrow we go that way," he stated matter-of-factly.

"You know the way?" Shelby shook his head.

Would his father never cease to amaze him this day?

"I've been there." He didn't embellish on that, much to his younger son's disappointment.

Chapter Ten

Molly glanced anxiously at the cabin door and then back at the man who sat across from her. The last thing she'd expected was to share supper with Bran Donovan! Why had he chosen tonight of all nights to seek her company? Why now, when she'd finally discovered a way to the upper deck?

She nearly jumped when Donovan reached for a biscuit. Calm down, she told herself. Tommie isn't due for some time yet. Molly studied the captain from beneath lowered eyelids. There'd be hell to pay if Tommie arrived to take her above deck. Hell and what else? she wondered, shivering at the memory of the captain's last, punishing kiss. She offered a silent prayer that soon Donovan would return to his duties.

"Isn't the food to your liking?" Bran asked gently. A smile crinkled the corners of his blue eyes.

Molly gasped, taken aback by the sudden break in silence. "Oh, it's fine," she answered quickly. She shoved a forkful of meat between her lips, but it tasted like sawdust to her.

The captain was being most charming; it made Molly nervous. She stared down at her plate. He had even arranged to have Cook prepare a special supper for them.

Molly noted the artfully arranged meal of cooked pork and peas over a bed of rice. If she weren't so tense, she thought she might have enjoyed the meal. Bran was not only a gracious host, but his manner was friendly, open. Several times he'd tried drawing her into conversation, but each time Molly responded briefly and then lapsed back into her silent mood.

Sipping from his glass of port, Bran noted his "guest's" strange, fidgety behavior. He regretted his earlier harsh behavior. But she had to understand what could happen if he allowed her to mingle with his men. He set his glass carefully on the tabletop.

The way she was acting made him feel like some kind of monster, he thought as he refilled his glass. The situation on board ship was beyond his control. Couldn't she see that?

"Molly—" he began, and she jerked, startled. "For God's sake, girl! What's the matter with you? I won't bite!"

Her dark eyes flashed; he glimpsed a renewal of the spirit he'd admired in her. "There's nothing the matter, Captain!" When he looked skeptical, she added with heat, "Nothing that wouldn't be cured if you'd let me go!"

His lips tightened. "I've tried to explain things," he growled. And he had, he thought angrily. He'd hoped that if she understood his dilemma, she'd be more inclined to cooperate until her release. No such luck. He scowled. Stubborn female!

The cabin door flew open, and Tommie burst

into the stateroom, startling both occupants. Molly's heart thumped in terror. Would Tommie ruin all her plans?

"Captain," he rasped. "You're wanted above."

She saw her captor frown. "What is it?"

"Sir, ah, they've rent the sail, sir."

"What?" Bran looked like thunder.

Tommie squirmed beneath his commander's angry glance. "That's not all, Captain." He sounded shaken, as if afraid to impart more bad news.

"There's a ship off the starboard stern, sir."

Cursing, Bran Donovan rose from his seat, flashed her a glance that said "stay put", and then grabbed his hat on the way out. "What's her ensign?"

"I don't know, sir," Tommie said.

"What kind of ship?"

Tommie's answer was lost to Molly's ears as the door shut behind them. She heard their muffled voices beyond the door, heard them recede as man and boy climbed to the main deck.

For a long minute Molly stared at the unlocked door. Should she? she wondered. With the captain and crew's attention elsewhere, it would be the perfect time, she decided, to wander topside for a good glimpse of the ship's upper deck. She hesitated for only a moment before hurrying toward Donovan's sea trunk, where she threw open the lid and fumbled inside.

She'd be spied in an instant in this bright feminine garb, she thought. She came across a man's breeches, perhaps the captain's, she judged from the length of leg.

With great haste, Molly unhooked her gown, a low-necked garment made of gold satin with elbow-length sleeves and fine lace trim. She stepped from the frock, taking care not to step on the full skirt, and then draped it over the edge of the sea chest. Reaching between her legs, she pulled up the edge of her shift, tucking the ends up into a ribbon belt. Then she donned the breeches over the shift.

There was no sound from up above, certainly nothing that would alert one of an upcoming battle between enemy ships. She pulled on a white linen shirt. Molly frowned down at herself, tugged off the frilly garment, and rummaged inside the chest until she came up with a striped shirt similar to the ones worn by Old John and the crew. Slipping it over her head, she pulled it down and tucked the ends in her waistband. She felt satisfied that the sleeves hid her injured arm and its thin wrapping. Then with a quick flick of her wrist, she braided her long tresses and tied the end with a silk ribbon.

Her hair was longer than the men's. Would they notice it right off? She tucked the braid into her shirt collar.

Molly frowned. An observant crewman would recognize her as a woman immediately, but if she stayed out of eyesight, then maybe, just maybe, she'd pass for a boy long enough to enjoy a moment of fresh air and get a quick look at the upper deck.

She stared down at her bare toes. Shoes? she wondered, and then decided against them. Surely not every man up above wore shoes, if they did she'd surely have heard more noise!

Swallowing thickly, she went to the door. Placing her ear against the heavy wood, she listened for any sounds of movement and was relieved that the captain had forgotten to post a guard.

Her fingers lifted the latch; the cabin door opened on squeaking hinges. Molly gasped, hearing a rustle. The blood roared through her veins, making her heart thunder beneath her left breast. She waited several tension-filled seconds for her pulse to slow, her heart to quiet. When no danger was evident, when no one came to confront or attack her, Molly stepped from the cabin, her spirits soaring as she hurried up the companionway.

She hesitated before the hatch. What was above her? she wondered. Would Donovan be waiting for her, fire in his eyes, ready to punish her for disobedience?

She cursed softly. Why hadn't she thought of a weapon? Her hands caught hold of wood, squeezing until her knuckles whitened. It's too late to go back, she thought. Besides, I can't attempt an escape now. I wouldn't get very far if I did. She wanted to see topside.

Molly climbed through the open hatch and took a deep breath of the sea-salted air.

"Are you Donovan?" a smartly dressed young man inquired of Patrick outside the Jug and Barrel Inn.

"Who's asking?" Patrick asked, his expression instantly wary.

The man stiffened to attention like a young seamen responds to a commanding officer. "Pete Samuels of the *Flying Wench*."

Some of the tension left Pat's frame. "Captain Martin's ship?" Samuels nodded. "Where is he?" Pat demanded. "What the hell happened that you didn't make the cove!"

"Trouble with the men, Captain Donovan."

"I'm not the captain," Pat murmured without thinking. He saw the young man tense. "Relax, mate. You've the right party." He offered his hand. "I'm his brother—Patrick Ezechiel Donovan—at your service."

"And your brother?" Samuels asked. "Captain Bran Donovan?"

"Gone when the *Wench* didn't show," Pat said in a solemn voice. He grinned suddenly. "But he'll be back."

He led the seaman into the tavern, seeing him seated before ordering a drink for the both of them. With a filled tankard in each hand, Pat returned to where Samuels sat, placing the mugs on the scarred table. "Have a quencher, Pete, and then you can impart the *Wenchman's* news."

Studying the mug, Samuels hesitated and than took a sip. He swallowed the ale and then smiled gratefully at his benefactor.

"Overrun by his own men, the cappie was," Samuels began. "The cook was in charge. Felter—he was a sly one—really a Loyalist, it turns out." He raised his tankard, and Pat, anxious to hear the tale, had to stifle his impatience.

Finally the man continued. "Things looked bad for the *Wench*," Samuels said. "Felter had organized those that had gone too long without coin, you see, and they takes over the ship, ties up the cappie and kills two of the cappie's officers, throws them overboard. The first mate included."

"My God!" Patrick breathed in awe. He was amazed that Martin had stayed alive and finally triumphed over the bloody traitors. "What happened? What did Martin do?"

131

"Do?" Samuels murmured, his gaze reflective. "Well, he waits, the cappie does. Bids his time until he can work free his bonds. When Felter returns to the cabin where the cappie had been tossed, tied up, onto the floor, the cappie jumps the cook, taking him by surprise. After a struggle, which the cappie wins, Felter is lying on the floor, trussed up just like the cappie'd been."

"And when did this all take place?

The young man sighed. "The night befores we were to come to the cove." He paused, his gaze direct. "That's why the cappie sents me — he wanted to make sure all was on for the fifth . . . or if there'd been any change of plans."

Patrick was shaking his head. "All is on, my friend. You tell the captain that the *Bloody Mary* will be at the cove in four days' time. Tell him that the *other* shipment will be ready for him after the transfer. Tell him that we're all bloody glad that he bested that bastard Felter."

Pete Samuels finished his ale and stood. "I'll tell him," he said, his eyes glistening. "Until the fifth, then . . ."

"Aye," Patrick murmured, nodding.

Josiah came to the table after the young seaman had left the inn. "What was all that about?" he asked.

Patrick told him the tale of Martin's capture and return to power.

Upon hearing the end of the story, Josiah whistled. "I told you Martin was slipperier than an eel," he said, grinning.

Patrick returned the grin. "The best man for the job," he said.

"Did you find him?" Felter asked. He grinned wickedly upon seeing Samuel's nod. "Good!" He turned to leer at his silent captive. "You're an impressive commander, Mr. Martin," he sneered. "So impressive, in fact, that it was easy for my man here to convince your people that you've escaped the vicious jaws of an honorable death."

Martin's eyes shot daggers at him. "You're scum, Felter!"

John Felter nodded politely, amusement dancing in his steel gray eyes. "Thank you. Knowing you, I'll consider that a compliment."

"Bastard!" Martin cried, struggling within his ropes. Felter's harsh laughter echoed about the ship's cabin.

"Thank God it's going the other way!" Bran lowered the spyglass and turning a furious blue gaze to the boatswain. "Will you get that fool over here!"

The bosun blanched. "Yes, sir!"

"Dickon," Bran said, turning to the man beside him. "Who tended the halyard?"

The first mate's gaze was on the rent sail. "Jones, sir. Kenneth Jones."

"Well, from now on keep him off those blasted ropes, will you?" His teeth snapped, making his jaw ache. "And find Knots. I need to know what he thinks of this!"

Damn, he thought, why did this have to happen now! Just when Molly was starting to relax with him. Bran's face softened. He wanted to talk with her, learn everything about her. What she liked to eat. What she liked to do. About her mother . . .

her father. Does Molly have any sisters? he wondered.

He looked automatically at the ripped sail, but his thoughts were filled with a vision of sparkling dark eyes, sweet lips, soft, creamy mounds rising from a gold satin bodice.

"Captain?" Dickon said. "I've alerted Knots."

Bran nodded, brought back to the problem of the damaged sail. His eyes scanned the torn foresail. The sail wasn't rent completely, but it had a large enough tear to make Bran question the wisdom of trying to mend the rip. He scowled. It would take five to six hours to bend on a new sail!

"Sir," Dickon murmured, shifting uncomfortably, drawing Bran's attention to the young seaman before him.

Bran took one look at Jones's frightened features and was reminded of fearful dark eyes in a feminine face. His anger drained slightly. "What happened, sailor?" he asked, his voice stern.

Jones blanched. "I lost grip of the rope, sir."

"You lost grip of the rope," the captain echoed, his voice dangerously soft. "Sailor, did you happen to see that vessel out there?"

The youth was shaking. "Aye, Captain," he said hoarsely.

Bran was somewhat appeased by Jones's display of fear. "Just be damn thankful that she's headed away from us," he said, his visage stern. "With us meeting the *Wench* soon, we've no time for chase." He hesitated "And if she were coming our way, seaman, what would our foresail be to us with a blasted three foot hole in it!"

"No good, Captain . . . sir."

The captain nodded. "Exactly." He addressed the

134

sailmaster, who stood waiting patiently behind the young Jones. "You will assist Mr. Knots with whatever he decides to do to right that sail. Do you understand, Mr. Jones?"

Kenneth inclined his head vehemently. "Yes, sir, Sorry, sir."

Bran waved the sailmaster forward. "Dickon," he said to the man next to him. "I want to see Benson in the wardroom."

The first mate nodded and then went for the bosun.

The captain addressed the sailmaster. "Your opinion, Mr. Knots?"

Joseph Knots eyed the sail thoughtfully. "She could be patched, sir, but I'd not guarantee she'd hold. 'Tis best to bend on a new sail. It'll take us four and a half hours at least, Captain."

"That's what I was afraid of," Bran sighed. "Very well, master, a new sail then. But let us pray, Mr. Knots, that for the next five hours at least God keeps the scurvy Briton dogs at bay!"

Turning to go below, Bran froze, his gaze fastening on a small figure leaning against the rail. A small *feminine* figure. He'd known who it was immediately. Molly McCormick. There was no disguising her stature, he thought, his lips twisting.

He shook his head, feeling bemused. He felt torn between anger and admiration. He had to give the woman credit, she had tried to remain unobtrusive . . . and apparently had succeeded to some degree, for his unsuspecting men paid her little heed.

He frowned to see Tommie the cabin boy join Molly at the ship's rail. Bran cursed beneath his breath. "Dickon!" he bellowed.

"Aye, Captain?" The first mate appeared at

135

Bran's elbow.

The captain nodded toward the two figures gazing out over the expanse of sea. "See that *she* gets below deck," he said in a tight voice. Anger curled in the pit of his stomach, making it difficult to breathe. "But first, send the boy to me."

Dickon's surprised look became one of understanding as he spied the smaller of two forms. "Right away, Captain," he said, starting to move away.

Bran captured the man's arm. "On second thought, Mark," he said, his gaze traveling to the rail, "Leave the boy. Alert Benson that I'll deal with him later. As for this little matter, I think it best if I handled it myself."

"Miss Molly!" Tommie exclaimed, recognizing the woman. "What are you doing up here? You got to get below. There might be a battle!" He grabbed hold of Molly's arm as if intending to escort her back. "You got to wait until I come get you."

"Oh, please, Tommie," Molly pleaded. "I don't hear any cannon. Just give me another minute." The cool breeze felt wonderful against her heated skin. She inhaled deeply of the fragrant air, feeling renewed, invigorated. The last thing she wanted to do was to return to the dark, damp cabin.

"Well . . ." Tommie hesitated. She saw him stiffen as he glanced beyond her shoulder. "Here comes the captain!" he breathed nervously.

Molly panicked. She refused to turn his way, sending up a silent prayer that he wouldn't recognize her. She didn't want to go back below! Her fingers clenched the ship's rail.

She felt his presence before she heard him address the cabin boy. "Tommie," he muttered, sounding annoyed. "Are you responsible for this?"

"This?" Tommie stuttered, obviously frightened by the captain's wrath.

"Do you mean me?" Molly swung to Donovan then, her dark eyes glittering.

"I was wondering how long you were going to pretend I wasn't here," Bran drawled. He scowled. "Don't you know it's customary for a seaman to salute his superiors? Even if you had managed to fool me with that absurd attempt to disguise yourself, you would have given yourself away by not showing me the respect due a ship's commander."

"Respect?" Molly said scathingly. *"Kwe!* I have no respect for you, Bran Donovan!" She straightened her back in an attempt to stand taller. "You think you are a great *i'la*—a war captain, but you are not! You're just a *len'o*—a man! You're not even a strong *len'o,* Donovan. You are *shaauise!* And I will escape you!"

The captain's expression resembled a thundercloud. "Tommie," he gritted between clenched teeth, "leave us."

His tone was deadly, his gaze menacing. Molly trembled but held her ground. "What are you going to do, Captain?" she challenged. "Throw me overboard?"

Molly couldn't help wondering what dangers lurked beneath the calm water. What evils would she encounter if he ordered her tossed into the sea? Water monsters?

Donovan laughed, a grating sound that produced gooseflesh along her arms. "And have you swim for shore?" He shook his head. "Not on your life, little

137

one. I've no doubt you'd make land, despite the distance and your injury. You've a stubborn streak a mile wide."

"I'm stubborn?" she uttered with mock disbelief. "What of you? If not for your hard head, we wouldn't be talking!"

Bran chuckled at her feigned outrage. "Touché. I'll agree with you there, cat." He grabbed her arm, his expression sobering. "Now I suggest you sheathe your claws and come with me quietly."

Molly looked as if she wanted to argue. Then her shoulders slumped as she moved from the rail. "Just one last look?" she asked softly.

His eyebrows lowering, Bran gave a nod. Something clutched at his chest in the way she returned to the railing to stare across the rippling sea.

Some of the fine silken hairs had escaped her ribbon; the wind played with the dark strands, tossing them teasingly about her neck and ears. He saw her lashes flutter against her smooth cheeks as he moved to stand beside her. Bran heard her inhale and exhale with a loud sigh.

Her obvious enjoyment in the elements made Bran feel like a brute for ignoring her need to be outdoors. He made a silent vow to bring her back topside. A brief period each day, Bran decided. She'd be safe as long as he himself stood guard. The men wouldn't dare to defy him, their captain.

Bran was loathe to end her freedom, but Molly's presence had attracted the attention of his crew. Glancing toward the nearest gunport, he spied the gun captain, John Smithers, a bearded brute with a hideous-looking scar from cheek to forehead.

Bran flashed Smithers a look of warning. He wondered at the bearded man's interest, and then he remembered that it was Old John Smithers who'd discovered Molly's presence in the cove. He shuddered, envisioning Molly at the gunner's mercy. Old John's ruthlessness made him good at his job, but . . .

No wonder she'd been incensed, he thought. She must have been terrified of the scarred seaman. It'd been Smithers and who else? Bran wondered, searching the deck to stir his memory. Will Peters, he remembered. And Clyde Jamieson.

Bran frowned. He was disturbed by the way his men were studying Molly, although their behavior wasn't unexpected. They were a lusty lot, and except for a few landlubbers, a fierce but experienced crew who'd gone too long without female companionship.

"What are you all looking at?" Bran shouted angrily. "Get back to work!"

"Get back to work!" MacDuff repeated, coming to his commander's aid. A whip cracked in the air. MacDuff raised the lash a second time with the intent to punish any remaining idlers.

At the captain's shout, Molly spun from the rail, her eyes wide and questioning.

"Are you ready to go below?" Donovan asked her gently, his face softening as his attention left his men.

Swallowing, she nodded and was glad when the captain didn't offer her his arm. She was startled by this change in him. One moment the fierce commander and the next a courteous escort. His blue gaze studied her with a gentleness that was disconcerting.

He didn't seem too angry, Molly thought. He's taking this well—too well. Once in his stateroom, would he change again?

The air sizzled with tension. Molly pushed herself away from the rail to walk at his side, her thoughts roiling with confusion.

You have to get away! her mind screamed. *Now, before you find yourself caught in a trap, bound to this man!*

This attraction she felt toward her captor scared her . . . more so than facing his anger. She walked slowly, for she was in no hurry to return below. There they would be alone. Her gaze returning to the ship's side, she began to wonder . . . to plan.

In a split-second decision, Molly suddenly broke away, barreling from Donovan's side, until she caught hold of the ship's rail. Before Donovan could catch her, Molly scrambled over the rail and threw herself overboard. She gasped as she hit the water. She felt the shock of the cold sea as the ocean enveloped her clothed form, sucking her under several feet, before she could bob up for air.

As her head broke surface she heard voices raised in anger, and she envisioned the pandemonium caused by her escape. The captain was shouting curses. There was frenzied movement across deck, and then she dipped below the waterline and kicked out with her feet. The weight of her clothing hampered her, but she continued to swim, oblivious to all but a rush of adrenaline and her desire to be free.

I've no doubt you'd make land, the captain had said. She began a pattern of swimming that she'd learned in the pond near her grandfather's settlement. It was Tahuun Kukuus who'd taught her to skim through the water like a young otter.

Her waterlogged clothing grew heavier and

heavier, dragging her down. The broken skin under her soaked bandage began to sting with the salt water. *I'm not going to make it,* she thought with growing despair. Swimming with so much clothing was nearly impossible. *Yes, I will make it!* she cried silently.

She paused, treading water, and glanced back. Molly was dismayed to see the men lowering a dinghy off the ship's side. She knew there was only one thing to do—if it were possible. She sank below the water, struggling with her breeches. She'd be able to swim faster without the soggy pants that weighed her down like iron. It wasn't easy, in fact, she'd nearly given the battle up when she finally managed to kick free of the cumbersome garment.

With her heaviest burden gone, Molly immediately began swimming. She swam in an established rhythm, just like her Lenape grandfather had taught her. Kick, glide, breathe. Kick, glide, breathe.

Where were the captain's men? Molly didn't stop to check. She swam until her limbs ached and her lungs wanted to burst from the exertion. And then Molly kept on, even after she'd decided that she'd had enough . . . just another few yards . . . and a few more. She couldn't stop now. Freedom was hers if she could grab it.

Chapter Eleven

"Row, you bastards! Row!" Bran shouted. His arm muscles bulging, he pulled on his own set of oars, his visage stern, his mind filled with ghastly images.

When Molly jumped over the ship's side, Bran's breath had slammed in his throat. He'd rushed to the rail with visions of Molly hurtling through the air, striking against the hull to fall limp . . . lifeless . . . into the ocean's depths.

When her head broke water and he saw that she had survived, he secretly rejoiced. Hot on the tail of the emotion had been anger. Anger that she had escaped, anger that she'd made him feel . . . made him care.

He gave up rowing when the men alerted him that they were catching up to her. Again, fear—stark and cold—chilled him to the bone as he saw Molly's tiring form. Any moment he expected to see her go under, sink into the deep, too exhausted to resurface. He saw her falter, her head go under water, and Bran stood and began hurriedly shucking his clothes.

Seconds later he dove neatly into the waves, came up for a quick breath, and then swam toward the girl. His arms cut cleanly through the water; his body shot forward like a bronzed seal gliding through the sea.

She was gasping when he reached her. In her bid to be free, she'd worn herself out, and panic had set in, dragging her downward. Molly flailed out with arms and legs in her futile struggle to stay afloat.

Bran caught her arm, only to have her strike out at him wildly, oblivious to his presence. Her face was wild with terror as she bobbed up after sinking below the surface, gasping, her limbs thrashing. He cursed silently, fumbling for a handhold. Molly was wet and slippery like a fish, and like a fish unwilling to be caught, she fought hard for freedom.

His own limbs were tiring in the battle. With digging fingers, he managed to grip onto her shirt.

"Molly, stop it," he yelled as he tugged her upward. "You're all right. I've got you. You're safe!"

Then she was clutching him, forcing him under, until he too felt the danger of drowning.

After a fight, he finally managed to hold on to her, her one arm trapped at her side, the other between her hip and Bran's groin. "Molly, it's Bran! Relax," he cried, sensing her fear. "It's all right."

She stilled instantly. "Bran?" she choked. Their eyes met, his triumphant, hers full of gratitude for the rescue.

For a time they clung together, buoyed in the salt water, Bran kicking his feet, Molly limp and out of breath. The soaked cloth of her shirt rubbed abrasively against Bran's bare chest. Molly felt cold to

143

the touch, but alive.

Bran closed his eyes. Molly was alive!

He sent up a silent prayer of thanksgiving as he pulled her closer, maneuvering her body so that he could drag her back to the dinghy more easily. He was conscious of their closeness and the sound of her labored breathing as he swam toward the boat. He heard his men cheering at the rescue. Adrenaline saw him back to the dinghy in record time.

"Benson!" Bran called the attention of his lieutenant. Strong hands and arms were extended to accept his burden as Bran encircled Molly's waist and thrust her upward, out of the sea.

Naked, Bran hefted himself onto the boat.

With closed eyes and streaming hair, Molly struggled for air and was glad when she found it. Her chest labored to pull the oxygen into her burning lungs. A buzzing in her brain nearly drowned out the excited exchange of the men on board the small boat.

Bran Donovan, she thought. Bran. Suddenly, she saw him in a different light. Not as captain or captor but as her rescuer . . . and as a *man*.

Shuddering, Molly relived her last moments in the water. She'd been doing so well, until she'd felt her body seize up, unwilling or unable to obey her brain's dictates.

The last thing she'd expected was to feel gladdened by Bran's arrival. That he only rescued her as a matter of anger and pride didn't bother her. She was alive! Better alive than to be dead at the bottom of the Atlantic Ocean!

She sensed when he stood before her. Molly opened her eyes, stunned by the strange light in the piercing blue gaze. He was wet and tired. His queue had come free; he'd lost the ribbon holding his dark locks during his unplanned rescue.

He was naked, but seemed oblivious to the fact. Water streamed from his jet black hair over his shoulders and down his muscled chest to drip in a puddle about his bare feet. His eyes narrowed.

In a strangely tender move, Bran reached out to stroke the hair from her face, his fingers cool fire against her damp skin.

"Are you all right?" he asked hoarsely. She felt the tremor that coursed through him pass through her as well. The sun had set, and the evening air was cool, raising goosebumps along Bran's limbs and torso.

Swallowing against a tight throat, Molly managed to nod.

Bran withdrew his hand from her cheek. She felt the loss of his touch as an ache somewhere in her heart.

"Sir," a voice spoke from behind Bran's shoulder. Benson handed his captain a blanket.

Molly heard Bran's murmur of thanks and was astonished when he turned to her, wrapping her in the dry folds of wool. Then he stood by, no doubt feeling naked and cold, but looking satisfied.

"Thank you," she said in a voice that shook. She blinked and he smiled, a faint curve of his lips that stole her breath away.

Bemused, Molly watched the captain retrieve his clothing from the bottom of the dinghy. He dressed without embarrassment. It was Molly who turned away embarrassed from the sight of his naked buttocks . . . she who in a span of a few quick seconds had memorized every line, every nuance, and every contour of Bran Donovan's powerful, nude form.

Behind closed lids she saw him . . . gleaming eyes in a stern face . . . black hair dripping . . . droplets of water on broad shoulders . . . taut male nipples on a glistening chest . . . and lower . . .

The blood rushed through Molly's veins; desire caught her unawares . . . hard.

"Molly."

She opened her eyes and felt her face flush. Had he read her thoughts? Did he know what she was feeling? Did he feel it too?

His eyes flickered, a blue flame burning a hole into her innermost soul. He held out his hand. Rising, she placed her fingers trustingly within his palm. She felt his heated touch as he helped her out of the dinghy and up the rope that had been extended over the ship's rail.

"Watch yourself," he warned.

He followed behind her closely, his body offering a buffer against the evening breeze, his nearness a comforting shelter.

"Ah, lass," MacDuff exclaimed as he pulled her on board the ship. "Now what did ye do that fer?"

Molly gave him a look that spoke of remorse . . . and something else that made MacDuff gape at her for a long moment. She felt Bran's hand on her arm.

"Dickon!" he hollered. "Get her up and then get *Mary* underway!"

"Aye, Captain!"

Then, when they stood alone, Molly felt Bran's hold tighten, heard his teeth snap as he spun her to face him. Gone was the gentle rescuer of her dreams. The man before her was in a rage.

"You fool!" he grated, his eyes flashing with anger. "You could've drowned!" He forced her toward the hatch. "Go below. Move!"

Had she just imagined his tender concern? Perhaps she'd been dreaming. She must have, for there was no sign of any softening in Bran's wintry blue gaze.

A short time later the cabin door closed behind them with an ominous click that echoed about the stateroom. Bran had just faced the most terrifying moment of his entire life, and this woman before him was responsible.

He wanted to throttle her. He wanted to hug her and hold her close. He wanted to celebrate the fact that she was alive!

"You idiot!" he gasped, grasping her by the shoulders to shake some sense into her. "Are you mad? Have I been so cruel to you?"

Molly's head snapped back as she answered. "No!" she gasped.

Cursing himself, Bran released her abruptly, then caught her arms to steady her. Her midnight eyes were two dark glistening orbs in a face lined with shadows.

"No," she whispered brokenly, her dark eyes rising to meet his.

His gaze flared with passion. "Foolish woman," he muttered affectionately, drawing her close against his breast. "I'm sorry, but you gave me a fright."

Dazed by this new tenderness, Molly allowed him to hold her. The scent of sea water was heavy on his clothes, which were still damp from his wet skin. His hands stroked her back over the woolen blan-

147

ket. Bran Donovan felt warm . . . warm and strong. Molly sighed, unconsciously snuggling closer, causing his hands to still. She heard his sharp inhalation of breath, and she smiled, feeling less frightened of his anger. Despite who he was, despite his occupation, the Rebel sea captain would never hurt her. He'd just proven that.

"Molly," he murmured as he attempted to set her away from him. She refused to budge, for she was quite comfortable in the captain's arms, and even if she hadn't been, she was too tired to move.

A tremor racked her frame, a shudder inspired by the man's nearness as well as by the chill that seeped from her wet garments into her skin. The man holding her grumbled something, and this time he was successful in thrusting her away from him. She didn't fight him, for the same reason she hadn't moved the first time. She was exhausted and felt lethargic.

Bran frowned as he held up the swaying young woman. That she wasn't fighting him worried him. It wasn't like Molly not to fight him. He'd decided from their first meeting that she was a fighter who'd never give up, who would fight and defend herself right to the very end.

He felt a sense of irony that he finally had Molly in his arms, virtually at his mercy, but he was feeling too honorable to give in to his growing lust for her sweet body.

His concern at the moment was to dry and warm her and see that she took a rest.

"Take off your wet clothes," he instructed gently.

Shivering, Molly shook her head. "No, Captain." Her eyes flashing fire, she backed away. The blood began pumping through her veins with renewed life.

"No?" His tone was soft, deadly with intent, as he followed her retreat. He gave Molly a look that gave her gooseflesh; she hugged herself with her arms.

He smiled. A smile of mischief. "I asked nicely, didn't I? Take off your clothes."

"You're crazy!" she gasped, raising her hands to ward him off.

"Me?" he said with a touch of innocence. Then his brow darkened. "I'm not the one who tried swimming to shore!" His hand snaked out, capturing her left wrist. She blanched, expecting his fury, but he regarded her with amusement.

Her gaze fell to his lips, which were sensual and very male. She found herself wanting to know his kiss again . . . not the hard, punishing kiss he'd given to teach a lesson. She wanted a soft, blending of their mouths.

Molly was caught in the web of his magic. Staring into his blue eyes, she swayed toward him slightly, drawn to him like a bee to honey.

His eyes gleamed. "If I ask again nicely, will you be reasonable?" he asked. Without thought, she shook her head. "In that case, I'll say it one more time before I take matters into my own hands."

The threat jerked her to her senses. "You wouldn't dare!" she breathed, horrified.

One corner of his mouth curved upward, mocking her innocence. "Wouldn't I?"

His expression hardening with purpose, he whipped away the blanket, making Molly cry out and shield her breasts protectively with her free arm. She struggled against his hold but couldn't break away.

"Your clothes are wet, Molly." Bran had finally resorted to pleading. "Please take them off before you get sick with cold."

She swallowed. He was right, she thought. If she didn't get out of her wet things she'd become ill. He might have won the battle this time, but she wouldn't make things easy for him.

"You've got my arm, Captain," she reminded him, pointedly looking at her captured wrist. "How am I supposed to undress?" Her smile mocked him, but inside she was a trembling mass of nerves.

His grin was wickedly knowing. "Sorry." He released her, but he kept close.

Molly retreated a few paces, her hands reaching for the wet hem of the striped shirt, her eyes never leaving Bran Donovan's face. "Why are you making me do this?" she asked in a choked voice.

Bran misinterpreted her question. "Because you're wet, you fool!" He had saved the chit's life; how could she still mistrust him?

Brushing aside her fumbling fingers, he took over the chore of removing the striped garment. He was careful not to snag her damp tresses while he tugged the shirt up and over Molly's head. He threw the shirt over the chair.

"Drowning wasn't enough for you!" he mumbled as he reached for her shift belt. He glared at her when she stopped him. "You want to catch your death of fever!"

Desire descended on Bran. He reigned it in, wanting only to see to her physical well-being. Molly's damp shift clung to her, the linen fabric outlining her breasts, affording him a fetching view of the soft mounds with their dark, taut-tipped nipples. The sight of her chilled form reminded Bran of his duty; he grabbed the hem of her only remaining garment. Without ceremony, he divested her of her chemise.

Molly shrieked in outrage. *"Mahz-tan-to!"* she hissed.

Bran Donovan . . . the devil himself, she thought. Come to this earth to torture her with his evil game-playing!

She gulped. He didn't look like someone in the mood for sport, even sport at her expense. She drew in a ragged breath. What if he had more on his mind than teasing her? *Like taking her onto that bed and . . .*

Shivering, she closed her eyes. What if this wasn't a game at all?

"Stop looking at me like that!" Bran boomed. "I'm not a monster." He turned away with a growl of frustration. "For God's sake, if I was going to ravish you, I would have done so by now!"

He faced her again, his features weary. "Even if I had the notion," he said in a tired voice, "you're bloody exhausted. I want a willing partner in my bed, not some lifeless doll."

Bran realized the insult the moment he heard her angry outcry. He reached for her. "Molly—" he began apologetically.

"No!" she cried, backing away. "I believe you! *E'kaliu!* Don't touch me!"

He cocked an eyebrow. A pleased smile touched his lips. "What is it, cat?" he taunted. "Afraid? Afraid you might *like* my touch? My hands burning across your skin . . . ?"

151

She looked glorious in her nakedness. Except for the bandaged arm, every lovely pulsating inch of her was exposed for his appreciation.

Silken skin. Sleek limbs. Bran admired her proud form, the sweet breasts exquisitely adorned with their dusky aureoles and small pert nubs . . . the smooth taut stomach with its tiny indentation of life . . . the dark feminine triangle of curly hair . . .

Bran heard her exhale with a quiver. He saw Molly's confusion, recognized the brief glimmer of naked desire. She feels it too! He gave her a slow, satisfied grin.

"Come here," he commanded.

She shook her head and held her ground.

"Afraid of me, savage?" he purred silkily. "You want me to touch you, don't you?" Was that why she'd run? To escape this physical attraction between them . . . not to return to her friends as he'd first thought?

"Want you?" she spat, her eyes glittering dangerously. *"Kwe!"*

Bran stilled at her hostility. Perhaps I am the crazy one! he thought. How could she want him after the way he'd taken her captive . . . bound her and injured her?

Something catapulted within Bran's chest. Because of her desire to get away, Molly had nearly drowned! He must be an utter fool to think that she might share his feelings.

Too long without a woman, he mused. Too long at sea.

"Get dressed," he said wearily, turning away. "Put on some dry clothes."

Molly grabbed the blanket for quick cover, wrapping the damp folds about her naked body. Studying the captain's dejected form, she experienced a jolt. The man had saved her life, and she felt — what?

Something prompted her to find out. "Captain," she murmured, coming up behind him.

He glanced at her, apparently startled to feel her hand on his shoulder. Their eyes caught, searched, flamed with renewed life. Molly felt the hot rushing flow of blood that caused her to become achingly aware of every tingling nerve ending. Her heart pounded in her ears, nearly drowning out the sound of her quickening breath.

"Captain," she said huskily. Molly saw the captain's blue eyes widen and then darken as passion conquered his surprise.

And then she was in his arms, kissing him back hungrily. Every fiber of her being throbbed with burning heat as the blanket slipped to the floor unheeded.

Chapter Twelve

Molly gasped against Bran's mouth. His hands had cupped her derriere, and he pulled her against him until she could feel the hot hard maleness of him straining his breeches. His mouth left her lips to trail a fiery path along her neck. She arched her throat, shivering as masculine lips glided downward to taste the beating pulse.

She gripped tight to his arms to keep from falling. Bran's caress was like magic that astonished and delighted, that made her head reel dizzily and her knees weak.

"*Lalaheokooen,*" she whispered in ecstasy. "Life," she gasped when Bran caressed her with his gaze, with a look that questioned while it stroked.

Life, she thought. Bran gave life to her body . . . her heart.

She moaned as he played her with skilled fingertips, cupping an aching breast, worrying the taut bud. She jerked when he caught her nipple between this teeth, nipping it gently, licking it with his tongue. Spasms of pleasure rippled along her spine, radiating to all parts of her. In a feverish state she clutched at his dark head, her fingers caught in his silky hair.

When you save a life, it become yours. Her Indian grandfather's words broke through the rapturous haze, banishing Molly's doubts, her lingering fears about making love to Bran.

Bran had given her back life. She would gift him with fire.

Molly became an active partner then, utilizing her own form of sorcery, wanting to please as Bran had pleased her.

His head lifted, and Molly took advantage of the opportunity to slip her hands under his shirt hem, raking her warm fingers across his quickly heating chest. He groaned. Encouraged, Molly plucked at his nipples with soft fingertips. She was untutored, moving only by instinct and the new knowledge of her own pleasure points.

She pushed up his shirt, raising the fine linen up his firm torso. Holding it thus, she leaned forward to rub her bare breasts against his bronzed, muscled chest.

Throwing back his head, Bran closed his eyes and shuddered with pleasure.

Molly continued to press herself against him. Lush breasts swept bare skin in a rhythm that made the hardened sea captain gasp and tremble like a young boy.

Her nipples hummed from the contact; the tilt-tipped swollen mounds pulsed with feeling, a tightening, that spread down to her thighs, invading the most intimate part of her. The sweet ache was heightened by the abrasion of skin against fabric — her stomach against his breeches — and by the deep, convulsive sounds of pleasure that rippled forth from her lover's throat.

"Witch . . ." Bran's murmur became a moan, and for the first time Molly understood a woman's power . . . understood and reveled in it.

Suddenly, as if he'd suffered enough torment, Bran caught her by the hips, stilling her motion, his fingers searing her where they touched. Molly whimpered and gasped and moaned softly. His hands seemed to be moving everywhere!

She drew a sharp breath when he lifted her with powerful arms. He carried her to the lower berth and laid her on the rumpled mattress, where she waited breathless, her lips moist with want, her body anxious for his caress.

Molly's heart quickened as Bran flung off his shirt; his broad muscled chest gleamed copper in the lantern light.

He worked to remove his breeches next, shimmying them down his hard flanks. At the sight of toned muscles, Molly experienced such a burst of feeling that she rose up onto her elbows and reached out to grasp his thigh with the trembling fingers of her right hand.

"*Tshiitunna,*" she whispered. "You are strong, Bran Donovan." She felt the power of muscle and tissue beneath her palm, against her fingertips.

Bran froze, and she felt the tremors instilled by her fondling. He straightened, his eyes smoldering as he faced her. "Molly . . ."

Molly heard his ragged tone, but her attention had moved elsewhere. She was enjoying her first intimate glimpse of male desire. Astonished, fascinated, she moved her hand from his leg to the rigid

156

swollen heat of him. Her fingers burned against his skin.

Bran captured her hand, lifted it from his desire, and with a husky moan leaned down to press her back against the bunk.

The chill of Molly's ocean swim was forgotten as he covered her curves with his steel-corded length.

Hot male skin seared soft feminine curves as Bran kissed her, his mouth fierce and demanding. Soon their bodies were sliding against each other in their search for oneness. Molly spread her legs, inviting the sweet invasion of her lover's power. She stiffened when he gently prodded her, for she was still a virgin and knew not what to expect at Bran's entry. His satin tip touched her moist flesh, making her gasp with pleasure. In a sudden move, she thrust upward in her haste to be joined to him.

Bodies fused. Muscles stretched. Velvet steel pierced swollen softness. She cried out, and Bran stiffened as if afraid to continue. But Molly's pain was only fleeting.

She accepted part and then all of him. He filled her completely, and she closed her eyes, adjusting to the newness and wonder of his strength.

He moved slightly. "Are you all right?"

She opened her eyes to see his concerned face poised above her. She smiled. Pleasure surged through her body when he smiled back and began undulating his hips . . . tentatively at first, then, when she murmured her delight . . . harder.

Gripping his muscled buttocks, Molly bucked against him like a wild thing. He moaned and thrust deeper, clearly delighted with her savage response.

Burying her face in his neck, Molly cried out as she soared on the wings of passion. To her shock, Bran pulled out of her, and she felt the aching loss of his hardened staff.

He began a trail of kisses along her breasts . . . her stomach. Lower and lower, his mouth wound a path until it reached the dark triangle of soft feminine curls. She stiffened at the contact, but he merely crested the mound, turning his loving attention to the area between her navel and thigh, paying particular note to the sensitive, quivering flesh of her abdomen.

Molly was amazed to feel renewed tremors of desire. Bran rose up and covered her with his body just as she neared the breaking point. With a thrust of his hips he plunged into her deeply, joining Molly as she traveled up and over the precipice. They climaxed together. Then, breaths labored, hearts pounding, they floated down from the rapturous pinnacle together.

When two spirits touch, they are bound forever, Molly thought, smiling. More wisdom from her mother's father, Tahuun Kukuus.

"We are one, Bran Donovan," she whispered.

Exhaustion took hold of the clinging lovers. Sated, they slept.

Shelby and Tully McCormick came to the Lenape village, urged on by the smell of the cook fires. Assailed by memories of visits shared in a similar encampment with his half sister, Shelby approached the cluster of thatched domed huts and heard the cry that rent the village as a young Delaware boy spied the two strange men.

"Shu-wun-uk!" the child cried. White men!

Night had come, scattering bright, twinkling stars across a black sky. The Lenape campfires burned orange, casting light on the inhabitants who had gathered in the center of village.

As they entered the illuminated square, Shelby felt the tension of the Delaware Indians, was conscious of the taut frame of his father beside him. But he was not afraid. He had spent too many days and nights with these people to fear them, to believe that they would harm those who would not draw upon them first.

Leaving his father in the shadow of a tall gum tree, Shelby continued toward the great fire of all fires, the one he knew belonged to the leader—Tahuun Kukuus, Wood Owl—Molly's grandfather.

That was *if* the old man was still with them.

Much to his relief, Tahuun Kukuus was. The old man sat out in the open, a testimony of his greatness, for surely at his age brittle bones and aged muscles would ache on a summer night such as this. The air was warm, but it was heavy with a dampness that made light of the temperature. Tahuun Kukuus, however, seemed unaffected by the weather. *And at his age,* Shelby thought with amazement.

Upon recognizing the visitor to his village, the elderly Delaware rose agilely to feet to greet him in his native tongue.

"Mokkee ai-mahx w'," Wood Owl said. *"Ni'tis."*

Shelby blushed, recognizing the name given to him by the Delaware. "Red Bear," the old man had said. "My friend."

159

"Tahuun Kukuus, *ni'tis*." He returned the greeting, understanding enough of the Lenape language to do so without seeming a fool. "It is good to see you again."

"And so it is," Wood Owl murmured, nodding. He gestured for Shelby to sit down.

"Wait," Shelby said. "I have someone with me."

Wood Owl pierced Shelby with his dark gaze. "Siike Aluum?" He spoke of his granddaughter by her Lenape name.

"No." Shelby frowned. "Molly . . . she is not with you?"

The old man shook his head, and then glancing beyond Shelby's shoulder he scowled, his expression hardening. Tully McCormick had stepped into the firelight, making his presence known.

"Shelby—" Tully began.

Wood Owl's frame grew taut, his gaze hostile. "Mokkee ai-mahx w'," the old Indian said, and then he began talking in an angry, long-winded burst of Lenape that Shelby had difficulty understanding. One thing the young McCormick did understand was "What is he doing here? This man who took my daughter from her people! Who killed her!"

"My friend," Shelby replied in Lenape, his tone soothing. "He is *n 'ox*. He is my father."

Wood Owl growled, but once again gestured for them to take a seat at his campfire. A good sign, Shelby thought.

"Aluum—Dove," the old man spoke in English, "she is not with you? You are seeking her?"

Shelby nodded, his gaze worried. "She's been gone for many days. I searched the area near our home, but I couldn't find her."

160

"And you believe she came here?"

Tully spoke up then. "She's yer daughter's daughter as much as she is me own."

Stern-faced, Wood Owl stared at the man he'd grown to hate, the man whom his daughter had chosen above her own people. The two men gazed at one another in a silent battle of wills that spoke of long years of animosity brought on by deep heartache, misunderstanding, and loss. Finally Tully sighed wearily and was the first to look away.

"We must find her," the Irishman said. He hesitated and then shuddered, as if overcome with emotion. "I love her."

The Indian was startled by the simple, sincere declaration of a father's affection for his child. He understood what it was to love and lose a daughter. He frowned, his gaze sharpening as he studied the silver-haired man who sat at his campfire. It had been many years since the Indian had seen Tully McCormick. Age had taken a toll on this white man. Age and years of heartache for the lovely woman he'd lost. Shi'ki-Xkwe. Wood Owl's daughter.

She had loved this man who once had hair like that of the red fox. Wood Owl felt a great sadness for the daughter who had gone before him.

This hatred for his granddaughter's father was a bad thing, she thought. Having decided this, the Indian allowed his features to soften.

"I will help you," Wood Owl said, nodding. "Together we will find our Siike Aluum."

Our Spring Dove. Shelby smiled, noting the "our."

* * *

Bran awoke with a start, experiencing the strange sensation of warm skin and soft curves pressed against him where he lay on his berth. Molly, he thought.

"Fire," he murmured, closing his eyes. She had been all that he'd dreamed of — passionately giving . . . and more.

Fire and spirit, he mused, smiling. A heady combination in a lover. He felt a sudden surge of heat at the memory of her savage passion.

He wanted her. Liquid fire invaded his loins as he shifted to study her, to caress her with his blue gaze as well as his fingertips.

Molly lay on her side, her dark lashes fanning her high smooth cheekbones, her lips moist and parted and begging to be kissed. He gave in to the urge, pressing his mouth lightly against her lips, sighing softly as she responded even in her sleep. Her midnight tresses formed a satiny mantle about her shoulders, entangled about her breasts.

Remembering the feel of those lush curves, Bran swallowed against a dry throat. He brushed the silky midnight strands from a full mound, uncovering a dusky nipple. With trembling fingers, he traced the rose tip, watching with fascination how the nipple became pebble-hard.

With a soft groan, Bran bent his head, drawing the bud into his mouth, bathing it lavishly with his tongue. When he released the nipple, Molly stretched like a contented cat. She arched her back in sleep, thrusting her body toward him in an unconscious offering of firm breasts: one with nipple glistening and moist from his tongue, the other a ripe invitation.

He accepted her invitation, paying homage to both breasts, worshiping each equally. With lips and tongue and skilled fingers, he fondled her soft curves until she was fully awake and gasping and reaching to grasp his head.

He felt her fingers tangle in his hair, felt her jerk, and shudder spasmodically when he trailed kisses down the length of her stomach toward the aching moist part of her that in the early dark morning hours had become a fitted scabbard for his steel sword.

Molly pressed against his shoulders, forcing him to his back. Bran's protest became a harsh moan as she began her own form of sweet torture, kissing him as he'd done her, trailing her mouth from his lips, along his jaw, down his throat, across his chest, and down, down his stomach. She stopped when she reached his abdomen, flashed him a sparkling glance, before her head bent once again. She dipped her tongue in the hollow of his navel. Bran jerked as if shot. His body trembled as she moved her mouth back and forth across his navel, across his taut, quivering stomach muscles.

"Molly!" he growled. Grabbing her by the hair, he tugged her gently but insistently up his long length until he could command her lips in a searing kiss that broke all barriers of restraint, that stole their breaths away.

While Molly shuddered and trembled, he swung her onto her back once more. Mounting her, Bran continued to devour her mouth. When he had sheathed himself inside her warmth, he lifted his head to watch her as he began a slow, steady

163

rhythm of thrust and withdrawal . . . thrust and withdrawal.

Her beautiful dark eyes grew slumberous. Her mouth opened and parted. He could see her little pink tongue, and Bran thrust harder, further aroused, as he remembered how she had used it against his skin.

Molly moaned in pleasure, and Bran plunged into her softness again . . . and again . . . harder and harder . . . faster and faster. Their hips joined, their loins pulsated as they climbed together toward the pinnacle of ecstasy. Reaching the summit, they cried out in unison, straining against each other, their bodies stiffening.

Again they floated downward on the softly flowing tide of love's sweet aftermath. Bran rose up on his elbows, stared into her midnight eyes, and miraculously felt his manhood harden once again, stretching the moist folds of Molly's womanhood.

Her eyes widened at the knowledge of his renewed desire. She opened her mouth as if to ask how, and he kissed her, delving his tongue into her mouth in a hot passionate kiss that surpassed all that had come before it.

How no longer mattered. What mattered was that it was happening again — this wonderful, startling feeling between them. Giving into the power of this physical wonder, Molly and Bran sought release, and found the heaven of each other's arms.

"MacDuff !" The first mate hailed the Scot as he appeared from the lower deck.

The Scotsman came to the man at the helm.

164

"Aye. What be ye wanting, Dickon?"

"The captain." The mate looked uncomfortable. "He's been down there for hours now. Shouldn't we check on him?"

Angus MacDuff grinned as he shook his head. " 'Tis me guess that Bran's fine, laddie," he said. "Sure enough, he'll be up and aboot soon, as bright and cheery as a new copper."

Dickon's startled look changed as the two men exchanged glances.

Chapter Thirteen

The *Bloody Mary* arrived at the cove a day before its scheduled return date. As the schooner entered the murky waters, Bran's narrowed gaze searched the wooded shoreline for any sign of danger. There was no movement amidst the dense foliage. He could see nothing but the lush, verdant growth that grew in abundance over the damp ground and down to the riverbank. The tension within Bran eased as he addressed his first mate. "We'll anchor her where we did before," he said, his voice low.

Dickon nodded. He stood beside Bran on the quarterdeck, his frame as taut and expectant as his commander's. "Do you think he'll come?"

The captain's expression was grim. "If Martin's alive and out there, he'll be here."

Bran's attention was drawn to his men, who went silently about their duties, adjusting riggings and sails to the bosun's commands. This day Percy Weston's "pipe," the sound which usually accompanied the man's orders, was silent. All was an eerie quiet, broken only by the occasional hiss of rope across wood and the gentle lapping sound of water against the ship's hull.

The crew was subdued with the knowledge that danger lurked in these slow-running waters. But despite the grave manner these seamen presented, anticipation simmered behind their solemn expressions . . . a suppressed excitement. Adventure was in the air. Profits were close at hand.

Bran's mind turned to Molly as it had many times in the days following her failed escape. His thoughts filled with her image . . . of her flashing midnight eyes and mysterious smile . . . of her silky dark hair and sleek limbs. He felt like calling her topside, sharing the beauty of the surrounding landscape.

Bran experienced a painful jolt as he thought of the war and the circumstances of their first meeting. *This bloody war,* he thought with grim acceptance. He and Molly might have had a future together if not for the war! Even if she loved—and he was certain of that love—what kind of a life could he give her? Duty called him to sea. Would he even get to see her?

Stark fear for Molly's safety seized him. She was in constant danger as long as she remained on board ship. He knew he should let her go, but how could he? He was being selfish, but he didn't want her to leave!

His heart slammed within his breast as he pictured her as his wife. What would it be like to have such a heathen wife? His mind envisioned their life together . . . sharing a dinner table . . . sharing a bed. His breath caught as he thought of her in the throes of lovemaking—her lips parted, her head

167

thrown back to reveal her slender throat and rose-tipped breasts.

His hands tingled as he recalled the feel of her supple form beneath his fingertips.

Who could have foreseen the course of their relationship? he wondered.

When Molly had been taken prisoner, his only concern had been to detain her until he could be certain her release would not jeopardize his mission or endanger the lives of the men involved.

If anyone had suggested to him that he would become captivated by her spirited soul, her beauty, by her passionately savage response as they loved, Bran would have laughed harshly at such nonsense. He—Bran Donovan, captain of the *Bloody Mary,* a fierce patriot determined to help the cause—besotted with a wild half-breed? Never! he would have told them.

All right, yes! Yes, he was besotted! But in love? Bran scowled.

Lust, love, what did it matter? As long as there was a war, there could be no future for him and Molly. Guts and beauty, he thought wistfully.

As if his yearning for her had conjured her out of air, Molly appeared at his side. She had come up from the captain's stateroom for a breath of air.

"Captain," she murmured softly by way of greeting.

He turned to face her. For a long moment he frowned darkly at her. Doesn't she realize the danger?

"What are you doing up?" he said. It didn't matter to Bran that there were plenty of able-bodied men on board ship. Strong fighting men with weapons and arms to protect her, to protect this ship. He only knew he felt this sudden, irrational, gut-wrenching fear. If anything happened to Molly, he'd expire from the guilt . . . and the loss.

She recoiled from his anger. "I came up for air."

His mission wasn't over, Bran thought. His men needed him. The cause needed him. He couldn't be distracted by this slip of a heathen woman and her sweet savage ways.

"Captain—" she said.

"Who gave you permission?"

"No one—"

"I thought not," he snapped, and she jerked as if slapped.

Molly felt her face drain. Since the day of her escape, since after they'd made love, Bran had been most understanding of her need for air and the freedom of the open deck.

Her stomach churned painfully as she stared at his dark countenance. What had happened to change him? She noted his clenched jaw, his narrowed gaze, and taut frame. Something was wrong. What?

Anger at the injustice of his behavior started in her belly. The painful gnawing like hunger grew and grew until it burned hotly, brightly, to all parts of her.

"Oh, and now I need permission?" she taunted, unable to help it. "Since when? Yesterday—?"

"Yesterday I wasn't worried about the enemy," he muttered beneath his breath.

"What?" Her voice challenged him.

"Tories. British, damn it. Yesterday I wasn't worried!" His harsh exclamation drew the unwanted at-

169

tention of his men. "Be about your business!" he boomed at the unwitting eavesdroppers.

Her eyes stinging with unshed tears, Molly averted her gaze. "Oh," she mumbled. Now she faced him, her expression sullen, her eyes sorrowful pools of liquid midnight. "Why did you have to holler at me? You could have asked nicely, and I would have gone below."

"Really?" His tone mocked her, but his expression was less harsh.

Heart thumping, Molly stared at him. He was so beautiful, she thought. Beautiful and gentle and strong. For her, what they'd shared had transcended the physical.

When two spirits touch . . . They were bound by a force more powerful than physical attraction, a meshing of two inner selves.

Did he understand that?

A muscle twitched along Bran's jawline. His blue eyes glittered with a strange, unfathomable light. "You must go below." He signaled to one of his men. "MacDuff! Would you please take Molly below deck." His tone had become harsh again, and Molly stared at him, hurt.

She was right, wasn't she? What would it have done for him to ask her nicely? Now that she understood the situation, she didn't mind going below.

"Lass," the Scot prompted gently, taking her arm, "It's a dangerous time fer ye to be above."

Nodding, Molly went with him. She turned to the Scot as they were about to descend the ladder to the berth deck. "MacDuff," she began.

"Aye, lass?"

"What's wrong with him? What have I done?"

The Scot gazed at her with compassion. "Ye've done noothin' wrong, Molly." He hesitated. "Noothin' and everythin'," he murmured. " 'Tis the war that's on his mind this night. The war and the bloody Brits."

"Tell me about this war." Having lived her life in a secluded woods cabin, Molly didn't fully understand the American uprising.

"Freedom," MacDuff said, as if sensing her need to know more.

She recalled the moment when she'd been captured by the Rebel seamen, bound, and locked in the captain's cabin. Molly nodded. Freedom she understood.

Damn! Bran felt Molly's pain and wanted to go after her, but this was no time for matters of the heart. He was the captain of this ship; he had his job to do. And by God, woman or not, he would do it!

"Sir?" Benson saluted the captain with respect.

Bran trained his gaze on the marine lieutenant. "Yes, Benson?"

"We're nearing the point."

Mentally cursing his inattentiveness, Bran nodded. "Let go her anchor."

The night's quiet was broken by the sound of the crew releasing the anchor cable and the creak of the rope against wood, and finally by the splash of the anchor as it hit water.

"Captain!" Dickon exclaimed in a hushed whisper. "There! On the shoreline!"

Following the direction of Dickon's gaze, Bran stiffened. A figure moved furtively through the undergrowth. Who? "Alert the men. Tell them to arm

171

themselves, but to continue about their business. If our friend out there is foe, it wouldn't do to caution him of our knowledge. He may be alone, but then again . . ."

Dickon nodded. "Aye, Captain," he said and then went off to do his duty.

Bran signaled to MacDuff, who'd returned from the captain's stateroom.

"Captain?" The Scot frowned, perhaps sensing his commander's concern, the new tension in the air.

"It seems, Angus, that we've got company." He smiled grimly at the Scot's sharp intake of breath.

"How many?" MacDuff's gaze centered on the spot indicated by Bran's oblique gesture.

"Hard to tell. We've spied only one, but—"

"Aye," the burly man whispered with a nod of understanding.

Suddenly a loud cry rent the air, startling the captain and most of the crew.

"Nate!" one of the crewmembers cried enthusiastically.

At that moment the figure broke through the barrier of trees and brush, a splash of white teeth across his familiar face. It was Nate Redding, the crewmember Bran had left behind to alert Patrick.

Bran's tense frame relaxed. MacDuff cursed the vocal crewmember for his stupidity, a sentiment that was shared by the ship's captain. Bran made a mental note to severely reprimand the young sailor who in his excitement might have put them all in jeopardy.

Still, the commander was smiling as the dinghy from aboard ship returned with the grinning seaman.

"Nate!" Bran waved away the sailor's salute, instead slapping Nate on the back in easy camaraderie. "Still alive, I see, you old buzzard!" he exclaimed, his blue eyes crinkling.

"Damn bastards'll never get one on Nate Redding," the man replied cheerfully.

Bran's expression sobered. "How goes it? You reached Pat. Any word on Martin?"

The sailor nodded. "The *Wench*'ll be here. The captain had a tussle with his men." Nate's somber features relaxed into a smile. "Fixed him right he did, though. Slippery as an eel is our wenchman!"

"And the supplies?" Bran asked. Once they'd unloaded the powder from the *Wench's* hold, they'd be reloading both vessels with clothing and foodstuff for the crewmembers.

Nate suddenly scowled. He shook his head. " 'Fraid not, Capt'n. The goods's gone. Both wagons. Damn Tories got 'em!"

Bran felt an uneasy stirring in his gut. "When? Where?" His supplies weren't in danger, but he couldn't be sure of Martin's.

"The day after ya left. Beyond Manville, along the trail near Cutter's Fork."

"Damn!"

"Aye," Nate agreed.

"Any clues?" Bran asked, his eyebrows two dark straight lines above his eyes.

The young sailor grimaced. "Only one, and it's not much to go on." He shuffled his feet in restless fury, his eyes angry gray slits. "They killed four men, wounded two others." He paused. "Your brother, Pat —"

"Pat!" Bran exclaimed. "Pat was hurt?" A sinking feeling settled in his chest at Nate's nod. "How bad?"

"Bayonet wound to his left leg. Just a nick, though. Healing up nicely."

"Bloody bastards!" Bran cursed. Bayonets! There was no doubt whose side the culprits were playing on. Damn Britons! When his anger had cooled somewhat, he inquired, "What clue?"

"Pat and the two others — Walt and Joseph — they saw the leader." The sailor paused as if waiting for more reaction from Bran than a raised eyebrow. Disappointed, Nate continued. "A big bloke with red hair. They heard his name: Darren."

"Darren," Bran muttered thoughtfully. The name was foreign to him. He knew of no one by that name who lived in the area. "No last name?"

Nate shook his head.

"Locals, you say?"

"Josiah thinks so. Said no one else would know enough of these woods."

"Aye." Bran sighed. He looked at Nate then with just a hint of good humor. "You'll be wanting some victuals and a cup of grog, I warrant."

To his surprise, Nate shook his head. "I must be off to the Jug and Barrel. I promised Josiah and your brother." The seaman was clearly disappointed that he couldn't accept.

Bran nodded his understanding. He then gave the sailor a message for his sibling.

"Tomorrow then," the captain said by way of dismissal. "Godspeed." He watched as the man climbed into the small boat that would return him to the night-darkened shore.

174

Molly heard the captain enter the cabin, but because she was still angry with him, she feigned sleep. She had chosen the top rack, because she knew he wouldn't come to her there. The berth, designed for one occupant, was too high off the floor.

Would he wake her and insist that she move to the lower rack? she wondered.

Since their first joining, Bran and Molly had shared the bottom bunk. It was a snug fit for two people, but the space had seemed ample enough for the lovers, whose naked bodies slept closely entwined.

Thinking it odd that a captain's cabin would have two racks instead of one, Molly had asked MacDuff about the subject the last time he'd brought her food. The Scot informed her that the extra bed had been built into the bulkhead for Patrick Donovan, Bran's brother. The young man was a poor seaman, weak in stomach and prone to motion sickness. For those occasions when need forced Patrick to sail with his brother, he remained below in Bran's cabin. Patrick refused to stay in the fo'c'sle and have the crew witness his humiliation.

"And so the captain had the top berth installed," the Scot had told her. "When Patrick comes, the captain sleeps aboove. He's not aboot to sleep under a sickly landlubber!"

At the time, Molly had chuckled at the image of the two brothers, but now the thought didn't amuse her as she listened to the sounds of Bran undressing.

Her imagination went wild. Behind closed eyelids

she envisioned the captain's bronzed, muscled chest and sinewy arms, highlighted lovingly in the soft golden glow of the lamplight. She recalled the rock-hard firmness of his taut thighs, and had to force herself to breathe evenly, as if in sleep. Molly trembled at the remembered brush of a steely masculine form against her soft length.

Fabric rustled against skin in the shadowed darkness. His breath was a barely discernible whisper that nevertheless shivered along Molly's spine. Want—need—ran through her like wildfire. Sensation was alive, rampant throughout her being, quivering along each nerve ending, shuddering along her skin.

Desire, fierce and strong, checked her anger, and she had the strongest urge to climb down from the top bunk, search for him in the darkness, and with caressing lips and hands devour him body and soul. She would bring him to new earth-shattering heights using every bit of her womanly powers.

Two spirits, she thought. Bran Donovan didn't understand that. She loved him. No one had ever treated her like she was someone. Aside from those moments when she wanted to strangle him with her bare hands, Bran had been good to her. He acted as if he cared.

Darren, on the other hand, hated her. And her father? He loved her, she supposed, but he was too often too drunk to even ask her whereabouts, never mind show her love.

Shelby cared about her. And her Indian family did too. But Bran . . . this was different. There was something between her and Bran. A special woman-man bond. Bran not only seemed to care for her,

176

but he desired her. And she liked that. Liked the way he made her feel . . . all soft and mushy one moment, all fire and living flame the next.

They were destined to be together, only Bran didn't know it yet.

A lump rose in Molly's throat. Bran Donovan had been kind to her these last few days, but he was still a stranger. Why wouldn't he open up to her?

A stranger by day, an avid lover at night. She'd felt hope that they'd reach an understanding. Only yesterday she'd caught him staring, saw his blue eyes flame with renewed desire, and she'd begun to believe that he saw the right of their relationship, the specialness of it.

Had she been wrong?

Molly stiffened, sensing the exact second when he rose to stand near her head. She felt his tension, felt his gaze pierce through the shadows to study her.

"Molly." It was the gentlest, most caressing of sounds from his lips.

She didn't move. She was afraid, knowing that if she did, sex between them would be inevitable. But it wouldn't change things. Tomorrow would be as it was before. The captain would be about his business and she'd be in his cabin again, left alone.

Molly heard his growl of dissatisfaction as he climbed onto the lower berth. Silently, she shared his frustration.

At the break of day, The *Flying Wench* sailed silently along the Great Egg Harbor River toward the Rebel hideout in the hidden cove.

Kenneth Jones, aloft on *Mary*'s ratlines, spied the sloop first. With a cry of joy, he clambered down the ropes.

"The *Flying Wench!*" His high excitement gained the bosun's attention, and soon every sailor on board the Rebel schooner was watching the sloop's approach.

Molly heard the cry from the lower deck. Her heart pounding, she swung her legs over the side of the bed and leaped to the floor. The excitement on the main deck was infectious, filtering down to all hands below. Feet scampered across wooden decking. She heard men's voices in the companionway, seeming to echo against all sides of the ship.

She dressed quickly in the closest garments at hand, which belonged to the captain: a pair of breeches that came to her ankles and a white linen shirt that would have hung past her wrists if not for the close-fitted sleeves. For a moment, she glanced down at herself, frowning, longing for her buckskin tunic and its freedom of movement. Then she was out of the cabin and climbing the ladder to see what was about.

The first person she saw was Bran, and her breath stilled while her body responded traitorously. Her pulse beat a wild tempo. She experienced a feeling similar to that of a fever flush.

He didn't see her; he was too involved with his men, several of whom chuckled and cavorted in high spirits. Molly gaped at the startling sight before her gaze found the reason for their good humor. There, approaching from the east, was another vessel. It was but a speck on the horizon, but Molly knew with a certainty stemming from intuition that

this ship was the *Flying Wench* she'd heard a seaman mention. The two vessels and the mission of
the men on board were the reason for her prolonged
captivity, she thought.

Just then Bran turned and saw her standing near
the hatch. Molly felt her hackles rise as she anticipated his anger. He'd been furious at her; no doubt
his wrath would know no bounds this time.

To Molly's amazement, however, the captain
merely murmured something to the man beside him
and headed in her direction, a faint smile touching
his lips.

She brightened. Her heart raced at his approach,
and her mouth curved in an answering smile.

"Molly." She saw his lips move, but her name was
but a soft puff of air. His eyes said things for him.
For a brief second they spoke of regret and apology,
and then he grinned boyishly and Molly was caught
up in his charm.

"The ship . . ." she said, redirecting her gaze toward the advancing sloop. When she looked back,
he was staring at her broodingly. It was if in his
desire to share his joy with her he'd forgotten who
she was, why she was there . . . perhaps the danger
of her being about. His eyes darkened with emotion, some unfathomable but intense emotion that
was gone as swiftly as it came.

Molly was hurt that he mistrusted her still.

"Molly . . ."

She sighed, her shoulders dropping. She couldn't
be angry with him this time, for he had said it with
regret, as if he was genuinely sorry to see her go
below. "I'm going," she muttered.

As she turned he placed his hand on her shoulder. "I'll see you later," he said huskily. And then he did the unexpected. He took her mouth in a brief but hard kiss that spoke volumes of his sincerity.

"Stay below." His tone became commanding then. "There's work to be done." His expression softened. "I don't want you injured." His eyes flickered with guilt as he glanced at her arm.

She found herself wanting to reassure him. "It's nearly healed."

He nodded, a brief jerk of his head.

"Captain!"

Bran stiffened at the mate's call. "Below," he said hoarsely, and then he dismissed her with an abrupt turn of his heels. With a growl of frustration, Molly went below.

"What is it, Dickon?" Bran had recognized something odd in his officer's tone, and his muscles tensed as he approached the helm.

"Look." Dickon gestured to the deck of the Rebel sloop, and Bran immediately understood. Chills caused the hair at the back of Bran's neck to rise. Something seemed out of place; there was a strange stillness about the *Wench*'s crew.

Bran recognized the signs of battle. Martin's men were coiled with tension, waiting, ready to fight.

"Prepare the men for battle," he told Dickon in a low voice. "Move softly. Pistols and swords only." His gaze sharpened as it traversed the other deck. "Tell Smithers no cannon. Make sure he understands." He paused. "I intend to best those bastards and get hold of that powder."

"Aye, Captain," Dickon said, and hurried to speak to the gun captain.

"What the hell is going on?" Bran muttered. He

noticed that one of his seamen waited to speak to him. Percy Weston.

"Captain?" At Bran's nod, the bosun saluted his superior.

"What is it, Weston?"

"Is it true that we're to fight the *Wenchman?*" The man seemed to hesitate before adding, "Me brother's on board."

"We might, yes." Bran fixed him with a concerned look. "But only if it's necessary."

Weston shuddered as he released a breath. "I see."

Bran frowned. "I expect you to do your duty, sailor. You're a Patriot, aren't you?"

The man drew himself up to his full height. "Freedom from tyranny and English rule!" he cried with great feeling.

The captain stifled a smile at the man's enthusiasm. His smile vanished as he turned to study the advancing ship.

Suddenly, pandemonium broke the day's quiet as the men of the *Flying Wench* opened gunfire on the schooner's deck. One hapless victim took a bullet in his side, and he fell to the deck screaming in agony, his face contorted with pain.

"To arms!" Bran bellowed. The call was unnecessary, for the rest of his men had been prepared and had raised their pistols at the sound of the first shot.

The air was charged with the report of gunfire. Smoke filled the air from pistol barrels. Smoke and vile oaths. And as men from the *Flying Wench* boarded the *Bloody Mary,* there came the manly cries of battle and the clash of steel against sword,

181

as the crewmembers threw down their guns in favor of cutlasses, pickaxes, and iron boarding pikes.

Like the rest, Bran had immediately drawn his pistol from his belt, firing off a shot before reloading and firing again. And like his men, he abandoned the flintlock, catching with skill his saber thrown to him by MacDuff, who'd fetched it from his cabin at the first sign of trouble.

Bran fought his first opponent. His arm muscles stretched and strained as he wielded his sword mightily. Steel struck steel. The evil eyes of the sailor gleamed in a hideously scarred face. Sword found flesh — a nick to Bran's arm, below his shoulder.

His enemy laughed, a cruel, blood-curdling sound that rippled along Bran's neck to the base of his spine. Spurred on by anger, Bran attacked anew, thrusting and parrying, backing his opponent until the exhausted seamen got his feet entangled in a coil of rigging. As the man fell backward, he lunged sideways, catching his arm hard across Bran's saber. The sailor screamed as the blade sliced the muscle clear through to bone. The cries of pain, the contest of swords, continued as Bran stared at his felled foe. Believing the skirmish won, the captain switched his attention to his next adversary.

The sounds of war persisted above deck, and Molly, fearing for Bran's life, was no longer able to wait in the cabin. Terror had invaded her heart when MacDuff had come earlier with his suspicions and to retrieve the captain's sword where he'd left it in the corner beyond the trunk. Bran must have put it there late last night while she'd feigned sleep.

She searched for another weapon, something to

182

arm herself with, for it would be foolish to venture above without it. What if Bran Donovan needs her help? What if his men were losing? What would happen to them all? To her?

She found the pearl-handled knife in his chart table, which Bran must have forgotten to lock. She grabbed the knife, flipping it open in readiness and hurrying to the door.

The door opened easily. Just as she'd suspected, MacDuff had neglected to lock the door in his haste to return topside.

The battle sounds were more fierce outside the sheltered cabin. Molly shivered at the wailing scream of an injured seaman. Fear held her momentarily frozen, before concern for the man she loved drove her on, up the ladder and through the hatch.

She gasped at the sight: men engaged in violent battle . . . felled bodies, their crimson life force staining the wooden deck where they lay. Molly nearly swooned. Gulping in air, she turned her head, searching the deck for Bran. At first she couldn't see him, and she reeled dizzily with the thought that he might already be a victim of this vile death dance.

Then her head cleared as she saw him near the helm, battling some hulking foe. Her exhalation of relief became a scream of horror as Bran stumbled and fell, and his enemy raised his cutlass for the death lunge. To Molly, the scene was like a shocking stage play bordering on the macabre. Only the actors were real, and the victim was none other than the man she loved.

"No!" The cry tore from Molly's throat at the

same time the knife left her hand and went hurtling through space. Her aim was true, her target the seaman's heart. The sailor's body jerked before he could bring down his weapon. His eyes widened, his mouth gaping in startled surprise, and then he sank to the floor, his hand still clutching his sword.

Bran scrambled to feet, staring. He turned to flash his savior a look of gratitude, but upon seeing that it was Molly his face whitened, and then his features turned bright red with rage.

Molly's own grin faded. Fear, anger, she experienced a wealth of emotions when Bran shouted at her, commanding her to go below, cussing and shouting until his skin appeared as blue as his stormy gaze.

He was pointing wildly, bellowing in his rage, and she glanced back over his shoulder and saw a pike poised above her, ready to strike.

"No, Jones!" Bran roared.

Molly saw stunned disbelief register on the young seaman's expression. She gasped with relief when Jones lowered his pike and turned his attention elsewhere.

"Get below!" Bran's breath rasped in her ear, and she jumped, flashed him a glance, and was unable to control the burst of gladness that shook her to the core at the realization that he was alive—injured slightly, but alive!

"Damn it, woman!" he boomed, his fingers biting into her arm. *"I said get below!"*

Indecision warred with conscience . . . the desire to be near him should he need her again.

The battle raged on. Amidst the horror of pain and bloodshed, Molly saw the danger of arguing with him, and so she obeyed, and he released her, leaving the imprint of his hand on her flesh.

It was only as she reached the interior of the musty cabin that she realized that the sounds of the fighting had lessened. She detected a jubilant Scottish outcry. MacDuff.

She smiled, the grin spreading across her face, its good humor warming her. The skirmish was over. The crew of the *Bloody Mary* had won.

Chapter Fourteen

Bran glared at the man held by two of his Rebel seaman. "Felter," he spat. His revulsion for the traitor made him sick to his stomach. Felter had been hurt in the fracas, but the captain felt no sympathy for him, not when several of his men were injured and four were dead.

"Dogsbody! I should stab you cleanly and be done with it!" Bran growled, his hand fingering the hilt of his sword. He had the satisfaction of seeing Felter's eyes widen in fear. "Ross Martin—what have you done with him?"

The former cook's gaze flickered. "He's all right," he stammered. "I didn't hurt him! Please, Captain, it was the money. The money! I needed it, I did, for me poor mum."

"Half-witted arse," MacDuff snorted. "Ye've got no mum. Spawned by the divil ye were. Turning on yer comrades, killing innocent lads!"

"Captain!"

With a grimace, Bran glanced up, and then his expression brightened at the sight of his marine lieutenant assisting a man across the *Wench's* deck. "Thank God," he murmured. "Ross Martin, you mangy seadog, you're alive!"

Captain Martin looked tired and much thinner than the last time Bran had seen him, but he was grinning from ear to ear as he was helped onto the *Bloody Mary*. "Donovan! Damn, but I'm glad to see ya." He rubbed his sore wrists where they had been bound.

"No doubt," Bran said. The smile left his face abruptly. His cold blue gaze fastened on John Felter, the wiry man who'd caused all the trouble. "Benson," he commanded. "See that this cur is secured, then throw him into the brig."

"Aye, Captain," Benson replied. He signaled to the two men holding the unfortunate Felter, and the four disappeared below deck.

"Damn, but I'm thirsty, Donovan," Martin said. "Give a poor mate a bit of yer grog?"

Bran laughed. "I'll see that some is brought to your cabin." He eyed Martin's painfully thin form. "Hungry too?" When Martin nodded, Bran ordered his cabin boy to the galley to oblige.

"What's wrong with yer cabin?" the sloop captain asked.

"It's occupied at the moment."

Martin nodded knowingly. "Ah, Patrick is with ya."

"Not exactly." Bran shifted uncomfortably. He issued several brisk commands to see the two vessels situated and prepared for the transference of goods. Then, accompanying Martin onto the *Flying Wench,* Bran told the man of the discovery of Molly and her subsequent stay on board ship.

When Bran was through with his tale, Martin

187

whistled. "So ya think she's a spy."

Bran shook his head. "At first, perhaps. But not now." Martin looked surprised, and Bran added, "My gut feeling is that she's innocent. In fact, I've got a notion that she knows or cares little of this war."

"If she stumbled upon the cove by accident, what was she doing in the swamp?"

"I don't know." It was a question that had begun to nag Bran more and more these past few days. "But I intend to find out." Still, his tone was gentle.

"You're going to let her go," Martin said.

"There was never any question of that," Bran muttered, his spirits plummeting with the knowledge that soon Molly would be gone from the ship . . . and his life. "It was only a matter of when and where." Noting Martin's look, he said, "After we drop off the powder, I'll return her here . . . where we found her."

Darren was seated at the crude table in the McCormick cabin, picking at his thumbnail with the blade of his pocketknife, when Shelby and Tully returned from their journey to the Lenape village. The red-haired man looked up when they entered.

"You're back," he said without feeling. His knife clattered to the table top. He lifted his mug, took a healthy swig, and then slammed it back on the scarred surface. His eyes narrowed. He raised his sleeve to wipe his fleshy lips. "Did you find her?

Without answering, Shelby moved past the table to replace his rifle in the corner of the room. Looking tired, Tully pulled out the chair opposite his eldest son and sat down.

"Well?" Darren said with new impatience.

Tully stared at him. "No."

"As if you care!" Shelby burst out, turning on his brother in angry frustration.

But Darren only chuckled. "Don't get yer hackles up, brother. I've been doing a bit of checking of me own."

That stilled Shelby. "You have?" He pulled out a chair, turned it to straddle. When Darren nodded, Shelby said, "Well?"

"The Rebels got her," Darren lied.

"What?" Both Shelby and their father spoke in unison.

"Who?" Shelby gasped. "Where?"

Darren shrugged. "Don't know fer sure, but I've got men working on it." He had no idea of his half sister's whereabouts, nor did he care, but he saw a golden opportunity to insure Shelby's loyalty to the Tory band, to banish his brother's doubts about the wisdom of their work.

Darren's eyes flashed fire. "Damn it, brother, don't you see? They're an accursed lot who thought nothing of taking an innocent girl!"

Shelby nodded, his expression grim.

"Bloody scum!" Tully cried. His gaze searched the room as if he was looking for something.

" 'Tis time we do something about these damn Patriots," Darren said. "Patriots—bah!" Knowing instinctively what Tully was searching for, he rose from the table, went over to the cupboard, and took out two mugs. Reaching into a crate on the floor, he withdrew a bottle and filled each mug with port.

Neither brother nor father commented on the crate or the liquor, for each was too deep in his

189

thoughts to wonder from where it had come.

Tully took a sip from the mug and started to choke with the unexpected taste. "What the hell is this?" he gasped, shuddering.

Darren grinned. "What do ya think it is?"

Shelby stared at his brother hard. "The raid," he said. "I'd forgotten."

"Obviously." For a brief moment, Darren's features contorted, but then the scowl was gone and he was smiling again. "We got 'em! Two bloody whole wagons full of the Rebels' goods!"

Damn Continentals, Shelby thought. We've got to get Molly back. But until they could rescue her they could at least make the bastards pay! His eyes glowed with a determined light. He sipped his port and felt warmed by the liquor. Understanding flowed between brothers as Shelby met Darren's gaze.

As Tully drank from his mug, losing his troubles in his port, Shelby told Darren of their visit with the Delaware, of Tahuun Kukuus's promise to help look for Molly. Then, the topic turned to the next meeting of the Tory raiders, and the two brothers began to plan.

The door slammed open and Molly bolted upright in her bunk. Bran braced himself against the threshold, a feral gleam in his blue eyes, before he entered the cabin, shutting the door noisily behind him.

"Captain!" Molly's heart pounded in her chest.

"Captain?" he mocked. "And after we've shared a bed." He made a clicking sound with his tongue. "Come, come, my name is Bran." He tottered on his feet.

It was late. Molly had undressed to her shift and was lying in the berth, trying to assimilate the day's events. Rising to her knees, she felt vulnerable under his glittering regard.

She caught her breath. Bran was drunk, she realized. He came toward the berth, cloaked in the scent of rum and tobacco smoke, stumbling over his own feet. Drunk and dangerous, she thought as his gaze raked her scantily clad body.

"Captain," she began, pulling up the blanket to cover herself.

"Bran," he growled, grabbing her arm. His hand burned her flesh; his gaze probed her inner soul.

"Say it," he ordered gruffly. His grip tightened.

She blinked, overwhelmed by his rum-scented breath, his disturbing mood. Molly felt unsure of him, somehow realizing that he'd been pushed past the breaking point. What point and how far she had no idea. "Bran," she said.

"Say it again!" he bellowed, and she jumped. Then Molly's gumption got the better of her. Jerking her arm from his hold, she curled up onto her knees, her dark eyes sparkling defiantly.

"*Kwe!*" she muttered. "I'm not your servant, Captain Donovan. I'll call you what I wish!" Her lips curved into a taunting smile. "Right now I think I'll call you *chax-kal!* You're being ugly like a toad!"

Bran seemed taken aback by her attack. "Damn it, Molly . . ." He felt the room spin and cursed himself for staying too long in Martin's cabin. He wasn't drunk so much as tired. Tired and tipsy.

He shouldn't have had that last mug, he thought. In his mind he saw again the red stain on the main deck. The memory was so sharp that he could smell

191

the blood and the sweat on his opponent's brow.

Bran wanted to forget, but the grog hadn't been potent enough to rid him of a certain memory.

God, he'd almost lost her again! He wanted to clamp her to his breast, lose himself in her softness. She'd make him forget the war and all its horrors . . . for a little while, anyway.

Molly appeared fetching in her chemise, he thought, feeling himself grow taut with desire. The sight of her tempted him. Tantalized him. His manhood hardened, pulsated. More than his physical desire was his need to feel every part of her, to reassure himself that she was all right.

Bran reached for her.

"No!" Recoiling from his touch, Molly glared at him, ignoring his hurt surprise. He looked the picture of injured innocence, like a youth who'd been caught stealing by his mother and reprimanded for his deed.

He is a man. Don't let his face fool you! She'd felt the power of his embrace, felt his rock-hard manhood probing between her legs, filling her completely, making her cry out lustily in mindless pleasure.

He was her enemy, her captor.

I love him. Our lives are bound. Nothing could change that. She could try to change things by reminding herself that he'd abducted her against her will. But it wouldn't work. She loved him beyond all reasoning, all thought.

"I don't understand you," she said with a quaver. "You treat me like a prisoner and then a guest and then . . ." Her voice trailed off as she shivered with the memories of their shared passion. She forced the images away.

"I think I know you," she continued. "And then I don't. You offer me a taste of freedom, and then—" Her voice rose. "You growl like a wounded bear when I take it!"

Bran flushed with guilt. "Mol—"

"No!" She held up her hand to silence him. "I've had enough of you, Captain Donovan!" she said, slapping her hand against her forehead. "I saved your life, but I don't know why I bothered. No matter what I do, you yell at me!" Her eyes were bright with pain.

Bran's expression had changed several times during Molly's tirade, from angry to guilty, from penitent to pleading. But with the mention of her heroics he became furious again, his anger stemming from the fear he'd experienced when he'd spied her on deck.

He was angry, yes, he thought. But damn it, he had a right to be! Didn't the chit know how much danger she'd been in? What if she'd been injured by one of Felter's cutthroats?

My God, what if she'd been killed!

Why should you care, an inner voice queried. Bran ignored it.

"You idiot!" he hissed. He seized her, dragging her from the top bunk. "You could have been killed! Don't you realize that? Killed!" His face was a reflection of his anxiety and concern.

Molly stiffened. She opened her mouth to retort. Staring at him, she abruptly closed it again. Bran Donovan looked the picture of misery; his beautiful blue eyes were agonized and . . . She drew a ragged breath.

Was that love? she wondered. Or desire? Either way, the sight of such intense emotion on her behalf

193

was a heady experience for her. It was more than lust, she was certain.

Feelings spiraled inside her, seeking an outlet. Warmth filled her to overflowing.

"Bran . . ." His name was a soft breath from her lips. Lifting a hand to cup his jaw, Molly caressed him, her gaze full of tenderness, her fingertips light. She felt him stiffen. He closed his eyes, his whole form tensing.

His eyes opened, and he appeared fascinated with her mouth. Molly sensed his inner struggle. Leaning forward, she kissed where she had caressed, teasingly, ever so lightly. Her mouth edged from his jaw to his lips, and she pulled back.

Suddenly Bran groaned as if in pain. With a fierceness that stole her breath away, he pulled her against him, his mouth capturing her lips, parting them with his tongue. He lanced inside the warm, sweet cavern of her mouth, his hot tongue performing the most intimate of mating rituals while his hips ground against her.

Clutching his shoulders, Molly alternately gasped and moaned. She responded wildly, glorying in the hard, warm feel of his male flesh. Her trembling hands slid down his arms, about his waist. She stroked his back.

He's alive, she thought, buoyed by her gladness. She shuddered at the memory of his close brush with death. Her shudder became a shiver of pleasure as he nuzzled her throat . . . the soft swells of her breasts bared above the neckline of her shift. Her caresses became bolder, more frantic.

His head lifted. His blue gaze caressed her face, searing each feature before settling on her lips, which were glisteningly wet from his attention.

"God, woman," he said hoarsely. "Never, never, scare me like that again." He buried his face in her hair, clutching her head to his breast as he'd longed to do. He shook with feeling, clasped her closer, tighter, as if by doing so he could infuse her into his warmth. "You could have been killed!" he said, his voice strangled.

"*You* could have been killed!" she whispered, clinging back.

Bran shivered with pleasure at the way Molly burrowed within his arms, her face against his neck. He swallowed.

"Thank God you're all right."

"We're *both* all right," she pointed out, withdrawing slightly to offer him a tremulous smile.

Bran nodded but was unable to smile back. He felt such aching tenderness that he was ready to explode with it. The feeling was frightening as much as it was exhilarating.

"Molly," he said huskily. With trembling hands he cupped her breast, worrying the nipple until the tip hardened against her chemise. A gleam entered his gaze as he caressed the tiny nub and palmed the lush mound. A look of triumph tempered with affection and desire.

"You're lovely," he gasped before his head dipped once again.

He caught the pebble hardness between his lips, dampening the linen fabric until moisture made it transparent. Molly moaned and arched backward at the sensation of Bran's tongue against her nipple.

When he transferred his attention to its twin, the dark nub he'd abandoned pushed impudently against Molly's shift.

Spasms of pleasure rocked Molly's frame. Want-

195

ing to please him as he pleased her, she caught his head between her palms, lifting him from her breast. Seeing his startled glance, she placed a gentle kiss on his chin, and then, with eyes glowing hotly, she bent again for a long, leisurely exploration down his throat to the pulse at its base, licking and nipping the surrounding area.

Bran gasped and shuddered. Molly tunneled her hand beneath his shirt, sliding her fingers up his chest until she reached a nipple. She plucked at the bud with playful yet precise attention. When the nub grew erect, Molly brushed aside the fabric to bathe the nipple with her tongue.

"Molly—love!" Bran caught her by the shoulders, stared into her eyes. In a sudden move that took Molly's breath away, he swung her up into his arms and was startled when he lowered her feet to the floor again.

When Bran tugged the mattress from the bunk, setting it on the floor, Molly understood. He turned to her then, his hand rising to her hair, stroking its silky softness from her crown past her shoulder to where it clung to her breast.

"*Kaya'*, Bran Donovan," Molly said huskily. "You're beautiful."

He was momentarily overcome by her description. Then Molly tugged the shift from her body and shimmied the fabric up and over her lush breasts. Bran's expression changed. His gaze seared like a blue flame upon her nakedness.

She stopped him when he would have reached for her. "Take off your clothes, Bran Donovan."

Molly sat down upon the mattress, studying him with her heart in her eyes, eyes that had gone slumberous with her desire.

Bran made a strangled sound deep in his throat. A noise that was both a chuckle and a gasp of startled delight. Molly's pulse raced while he undressed quickly. Each newly revealed inch of rock-hard muscle and sinew heightened her anticipation . . . her ardor.

Wul-lut, she thought. Handsome. Both in body and spirit.

And then Molly felt the brush of his hot flesh against her thighs as he stretched out above her and then rolled next to her. They touched tentatively. Kissing, they caressed more intimately, their feelings more intense. A soft sigh of pleasure . . . A deep, full-throated moan . . . They stroked one another feverishly, their bodies joined, his throbbing staff alive inside her moist quivering warmth.

Forgotten was their anger . . . the war . . . their fears of the future and what was to become of them. All that mattered was their driving need to infuse their bodies, their souls, with each other . . .

Bran began thrusting inside Molly with a fierceness born of desperation. He groaned when the woman beneath him responded with all the passion of her nature.

He loved her savage ways. He loved her! A reason for joy that brought him no happiness, he thought, for in a short while Molly would be gone and the war would be his only world. There would be no spirited heathen girl to light up his dark days and nights.

Molly cried out with satisfaction. Holding himself back, Bran intensified his efforts to bring Molly soaring upward once again.

Clasping each other, they crested the peak together and floated down from the starry heavens.

Tomorrow's needs must set his ship and its crew on a course for Philadelphia, Bran thought. But tonight he intended to love Molly as no man had ever loved a woman.

The reality of the war intruded on the lovers' world all too soon afterward. Bran pulled himself from his sleeping woman's arms and dressed quietly. Molly didn't stir at his movements, for which Bran was thankful.

There was much to be done topside. Before he'd come down, he'd seen the deck scrubbed clean of blood and ordered the dead seamen buried on shore in the woods. If they'd been at sea, the fallen sailors would have had a sea burial. But they were too far upriver for that now. Time was of the essence. There was the powder to be transferred from the sloop to the schooner, and subsequently, supplies needed to be found and loaded for Ross Martin and the remainder of the *Flying Wench*'s crew.

Earlier, Bran had sent word to Josiah's tavern for able-bodied Patriots to man the Rebel sloop, which had suffered a terrible loss at Felter's hands. He expected to see Josiah or his brother Patrick at any moment.

He paused at the door for one last glance at the woman he loved, who lay curled up on her side sleeping peacefully. He smiled and felt a feeling akin to pleasure-pain.

Ah, Molly, if not for this war . . . His blue eyes glistened. He blinked as he turned away, and his face assumed a hard mask. Duty, he reminded himself. Honor before happiness.

It was the hour before dawn when Bran climbed

the ladder. The men had already begun to bring up the powder from the *Wench*'s hold; several powder kegs stood on the sloop's deck. Last night, in the calm waters of the cove, Bran had overseen the two vessels grappled together. A gangplank of sorts had been erected between the ships for loading and unloading the powder kegs.

Patrick Donovan waited for his brother near the helm. "Bran!" the younger man looked glad to see him.

The brothers shook hands. Bran's mouth widened into a grin.

"You heard of what happened?" Bran asked, his expression darkening at the sight of the newly scrubbed, still damp, deck. It must have taken several scrubbings to get out all the blood, he thought.

Pat nodded, his gaze grave. "I brought five men. Will that do?"

"It will have to," his brother said. "Time lengthens. Mortimer expected us days ago. And the army—"

"There was a battle at Monmouth!" Patrick burst in with a fervor that garnered Bran's immediate attention. "The army nearly had the British dogs, and would have too if not for Lee!"

Patrick's brown eyes glistened with disgust and anger. Disgust at General Charles Lee's failure in battle. Anger for the escape of the British commander, Sir Henry Clinton, and his troops. Pat quickly explained the circumstances of the battle at Monmouth Courthouse, how Washington, upon learning of Clinton's arrival in the area on the 26th of June, had planned an assault on Clinton's army. General Washington had placed General Charles Lee in charge of the attacking force. Lee, disregarding Washington's direct orders, chose a less aggressive stance in dealing with the Britons, clashing only mildly with Clinton's rear elements before withdrawing in the face of British reinforcements.

"Lee acted the coward!" Pat cried, his disgust evident in his tone. "He retreated when he should have forged on! General Washington had to take over command himself! We hear he's livid with Lee, that Lee faces a court-martial for his cowardice." His features appeared thoughtful. "As you know, Lee was a British prisoner of war for a time. I wonder if he didn't buy his freedom with a promise to help his captors."

Listening to his brother's tale and his subsequent opinion on Lee's actions, Bran's frown had darkened. "I care not to wager." His blue eyes flashed. "Who won, brother?"

"There were many casualties on both sides. It's been so hot! Near a hundred! Men suffered from heat and fatigue as well as injuries in battle."

Patrick looked toward the sloop and the bare-chested men hefting heavy wooden casks. This day would be a hot one, he thought. The men were lathered with sweat and dirt, and this with the sun only a new brightening in the summer sky!

"They need supplies, Bran," he said, turning back to his brother. "Not just powder but food, drink, clothing . . ."

Bran nodded. He was to have delivered the powder to those near Philadelphia. The British and the Continentals were forever trading command of that fair city. The Rebels in the area wanted the city secured in freedom's hands once and for all.

So there would be slight change in plans. "Where is the General now?" Bran asked of his brother.

Patrick thought. Today was July 4th; Washington was supposedly in New Brunswick, where he was to celebrate the second anniversary of the nation's freedom. *Freedom!* he mused with anger. What kind of freedom did they have during these last two years of war!

Patrick told his brother of General Washington's whereabouts and about others of the area's needy troops. "They say the general will be heading northward," he told Bran. "Where, I don't know."

"Great," Bran commented dryly. "I'm only to hope then that the general stays put for a while." Damn! he thought. I'll have to use some of the locals. He'd have to depend on some of these people to keep track of the needy soldiers and to arrange land transport for the supplies.

Women and children in danger . . . Unbidden came Molly's image . . . the memory of her savage sweetness. What was he to do with the lovely witch of his dreams? With this change in plans, he couldn't take her with him. He had to let her go.

Bran cursed. The heathen woman had enslaved his heart as well as his desire. He didn't want to release her . . . ever.

How he hated this blasted war!

Chapter Fifteen

It was late when Bran went below deck. Molly, confined in the stateroom at Bran's request, was feeling restless and closed-in like a caged animal when he appeared at the door, bare-chested, filthy, and looking tired. She glanced up, angry frustration in her dark eyes, when he flashed her a weary smile. His gaze lit up at the sight of her. Her anger fled in the face of his joyful expression. All traces of his tiredness vanished from his expression.

It was as if he'd been gone on a long journey—a dutiful journey, she thought, and had returned home to her arms, finding his comfort for the many trials he'd encountered. In the woman he loved . . .

Molly heard her breath catch. Was it possible? Could he truly care for her as other than a partner to warm his bed? Someone to spill his seed into when he needed release? *She* knew their spirits were one, but did he?

"Bran," she murmured. "You need a bath."

He grinned. "So the tables have turned," he said. "I distinctly remember a time, my sweet heathen, when it was *you* who needed washing."

She blushed, remembering. It seemed a long time ago when she had hated the captain. Hated yet been attracted to him in the same breath. "Mac-Duff—"

"He's as dirty as I and is swimming in the river." His blue gaze gleamed wickedly. "I, on the other hand, prefer a private bath attended by my sweet savage woman."

Sweet savage. She took no offense. His tone stroked her lovingly, promising untold, unexplored delights. My . . . woman, he had said. Molly's cheeks turned a brighter red.

"Captain . . ."

He laughed, a husky sound that vibrated along her spine. "First Bran and now captain." A raised eyebrow in question. "Who am I?"

"You're . . ." Her mouth shut. She didn't know. If only she did . . .

A fist hammered on the stateroom door, drawing Bran's devilish blue gaze away from an embarrassed Molly. He flung open the door. "Ah! Good!" he exclaimed to the newcomers—Tommie, the cabin boy, and Kenneth Jones. "Bring it in."

Molly's eyes widened. Since her first washing on board ship she'd had to make do with a bar of soap, some linen, and a pitcher and bowl of cool water. She gaped as the youths carried in a tub larger than the one she'd first bathed in. The sight of it along with the buckets of steaming water carried by yet another young seaman infused her body with pleasant warmth. She'd found her first and only tub bath delightful.

203

Molly's thoughts were racing as she watched the young sailors fill the tin tub. Of course, Bran would need a bigger tub, she thought. The captain's body was larger than hers . . . much larger . . . She shivered deliciously at the sudden image of Bran naked . . . her sponging him . . . touching the steel-corded frame . . . washing him. She swallowed. Desire made her breasts tingle.

She stole a glance at Bran, only to find him watching her and not the youth who finished pouring the last bucket of water. Her heart leaped when his gaze flamed, his nostrils flared.

Bran looked away then, fixing his glance on the sailor, who lingered for his orders. Bran dismissed the boy. "Thank you, Jones."

Jones nodded and left, shutting the door behind him, closing Bran and Molly off from the outside world.

Without conscious thought, Molly brought her hands to her breasts, touching her hardened nipples. She saw Bran turn from the closed door. He glanced at her, saw the position of her hands, and froze, staring.

Eyelids fluttering closed, Bran groaned. His blue gaze had become a smoldering blue flame when he opened his eyes.

Molly stiffened, mortified at what he'd caught her doing. She dropped her hands and began a wild search for a bar of a soap, a sponge for Bran to wash with.

He wants you to wash him.

"Soap." Her voice cracked with her tension.

Bran's eyes glowed. "Come here."

204

She shook her head. "Where did you get so dirty? Did you have a mud bath?"

"Molly."

Her breath slammed in her throat. "The water is cooling," she said.

"I know," he said softly. "That's why I'd like your help with the string on my breeches!" He grimaced in frustration while he struggled with the knotted strings that looped the front of his pants closed.

"Oh." Disappointment released the tension in Molly's body as she went to Bran's side to help him with the knot. She bent her head and so didn't see the wicked twinkle in his blue gaze, his sensual lips curving with amusement.

She worked at the string, her hands gently bumping against him. Bran's smile left his face as he gazed down at her head, felt her soft touch on his staff. Fire shot through his loins, making his rod rise, straining against the fabric . . . pressing up and against Molly's hand just as she undid the knot.

She gasped and looked up. He grinned at her lasciviously, and then he stepped away and took off his breeches. When he bared his buttocks, Molly's pulse drummed through her veins.

Bran stepped into the tub, sinking into the heated water with a contented sigh. He threw back his head, closing his eyes, shuddering as the bathwater soothed and lapped at his tanned skin.

For a moment he forgot all but the luxury and warmth of the surrounding water. Or so Molly thought. He opened one eye to peek at her. Shutting it again, he stretched like a contented lion. *Or*

205

a panther, she thought again.

His muscles strained as he extended them. His nipples rose proudly from his arched chest, two tight buds surrounded by a softly dark circle.

Molly picked up the sponge and the cake of soap. He wanted a bath, she thought. She wanted to touch him.

Bran felt her presence and sensed her hesitation long before she gathered the courage to dip the sponge into the water and lather it with soap. He didn't move, but kept his eyes closed while he waited, anticipating the heavenly feel of Molly's fingers . . . her hands touching his body.

This new shyness of hers he found amusing. That she could be a savage wildcat in his bed one moment and this shy woman-child the next was amazing to him. What had caused the change in her? Was it the change in him? Had she merely sensed it, responding to it accordingly? He scowled darkly.

She gasped. "Did I hurt you?" She stood behind him, at his left shoulder, probably wondering at his glaring countenance.

Bran inhaled sharply, for in truth he'd only just become aware that she had begun washing him. Her touch was so light, though; it was a wonder that he could feel it at all!

"Molly," he said with a sigh. "I'm tired, and I'm dirty. I won't bite."

"I never thought—"

He reached back and caught her wrist, the hand holding the sponge. Water dripped between them, cascading lightly upon Bran's shoulder.

She trembled, and he asked, "Are you cold?

206

Come, let me warm you."

She shook her head. "I'm not cold."

"No?"

One husky word.

"No." She moved around to the tub side, inhaling sharply when his hand slid along her arm toward her shoulder. His fingers slipped to her armpit, brushed down her side . . . her left breast. His hand left a damp path against the fabric of her gown, the bodice of her simple blue barleycorn frock.

Bran felt Molly's breath quicken; he saw the rise and fall of her delectable breasts. "Bathe with me, Molly."

It was both a command and a request.

"I . . ." Molly could find no excuse not to. After all, they were already lovers. "What if someone comes?"

"They dare not." He leaned back, closed his eyes. "I left specific instructions not to be disturbed."

Still Molly hesitated, studying his relaxed face. Why am I not hurrying to join him? she wondered. She loved him, desired him above all men. He now appeared bored, uncaring, or unaffected by her indecision.

Soon she would be leaving this ship. The thought spurred her to seek another taste of happiness before she returned to her woods and the family, who, except for Shelby, needed her more than loved her.

Her hands went to her bodice buttons.

"Let me," he said thickly, brushing her fingers aside.

He undressed her slowly, lovingly, until Molly was

207

naked and trembling. Like a hot lance, his gaze seared her nude length.

He rose to his full height, sloshing water over the tub's side. "Come here," he ordered, extending his hand.

Molly took his hand and then shrieked when he released her abruptly to grasp her under the armpits and swing her into the tub. Bran turned to face her, his smile golden, his eyes dark liquid pools of desire.

"Molly," he gasped, and he kissed her, thrusting her against his wet sleekness. Bran released her mouth and propelled her downward into the warm water, sliding his frame with hers as she went.

He made himself comfortable and then shifted her to sit close before him, facing him, their legs overlapping. He wet her breasts, her shoulders, cupping the water over the soft golden globes that tingled and pulsated. His expression reverent, he fingered her rigid nipples. Molly, in the face of desire, lost all shyness, and she reached forward to touch him, to handle the swollen male organ.

"Sweet," he murmured, staring at her breasts. He pulled her closer so that he could take a feminine mound inside his mouth. Releasing him, Molly gasped and moaned and then gasped again as he drew the nipple between his lips, sucking and nipping until she arched her body, straining closer to him.

Suddenly she was set back from him and he was handing her the soap and sponge. She gaped at him for only a second, then with a mischievous twinkle lighting her dark eyes, Molly took both items and began to use them, to torment her lover to utter distraction until the bath was forgotten in the pleasure of man and woman touching, kissing, and stroking one another.

Bran's arousal heightened beneath Molly's fondling. Sliding forward and shifting Molly so that she sat on his lap, Bran placed his engorged member between the moist petals of her sex.

When she cried, "Please!" he was lost, and he lifted her above him. Molly's body convulsed with pleasure as he thrust upward.

"Molly," he whispered with feeling. His face grew taut as he sought release in Molly's sweetness. He moaned, a husky sound that was more of a rasping growl, while she moved her hips, riding him, enjoying him as a rider would relish the power of her stallion.

Molly's breasts hung like two moist, plump melons, a bewitching invitation to love. And he did. He palmed the lush mounds. Arching up, he nipped them with his tongue, and felt her shudder, gasp, and her body stiffen in climax. With a guttural cry he fell back and pumped himself inside of her, glorying in that one final burst of sexual fulfillment.

Clasping Molly to his breast, he lay back, feeling utterly sated, stroking the long black satin that cascaded from Molly's head past her shoulders and down her back. Their breaths labored in the stillness, their hearts thundered wildly but as one. The tub water lapped about them.

I love you, Bran thought. He stirred, needing to see her face when it said it aloud.

"Molly," he said, raising her from his chest. He

caught his breath when her eyes opened lazily, the dark orbs slumberous with passion's aftermath. "Molly." His voice grew sharp.

She stiffened, became more alert, attuned. "What? What is it?" Fear flickered across her features.

"I love you."

He wanted to take it back the moment he said it. Not because he didn't care, but because his love made no difference. They had no future together, not with this war . . . this bloody, endless war!

"I shouldn't have said that. Forget it," he said gruffly.

She stared at him, her face paling, her dark eyes huge in her lovely face. "No, don't!" She offered him a smile. "I . . ." A moment of hesitation. ". . . love you, too."

Bran stared. "You can't possibly. I took you prisoner."

She nodded. "I hated you then."

"You saved my life.

"You saved mine."

"And you don't hate me?" His heart increased its tempo.

With a wry smile she shook her head, glancing pointedly toward their joined bodies beneath the water.

His blue eyes flamed. "It cannot be," he said. "There can be no future for us."

Molly opened her mouth to protest. *When two spirits touch,* she thought. It would work — somehow. Someday. She would hold onto that hope. Today she would enjoy their love.

Her smile was radiant. Her eyes glowed. "Love me," she pleaded huskily. She moved her hips against him.

"I will," Bran groaned. "Oh, God, but I do." And he ground and thrust upward in a renewal of shared passion.

The transfer of powder between the two vessels had been executed; the *Bloody Mary* had put out to sea. Bran sat at his desk studying his list of Rebel contacts, routes, and code words. He'd taken the lantern from the wall hook, setting it on the chart table for better light.

Chest bare, clad only in his breeches, Bran looked at his papers with a frown of concentration. He saw the names Woberney and Clamtown before the script blurred as his thoughts wandered. He glanced toward the woman in his bed rack, her face was serene and lovely in her slumber.

His features softened. Molly. He mouthed her name silently. Bran recalled their passion-filled night, the glorious sweet wonder of being in her arms, of losing himself in her softness. He wanted to know everything about her from the moment of her birth until the time of her discovery at the cove.

He frowned. There was no time for learning all. This was no time for love . . .

He fixed his gaze on the papers before him. There was much to be done. He couldn't think of Molly now, not when so much was at risk, so many men depended on him for their lives.

Bran bent his head to his list. The *Bloody Mary*

211

had two stops to make before heading for north Jersey and the Raritan River—one near Clamtown to unload a short stash of powder, the second at Toms Rivers to gather foodstuffs and clothing for the needy troops.

David Hanley. Sam Thoms. He memorized the names of the two best contacts, Hanley, from the Barnegat Bay area, and Thoms, a cooper from New Brunswick on the Raritan River.

What was she doing in the cove? His head snapped up and he stared at the far wall as thoughts of Molly disturbed his concentration. The question continued to nag at him. The more entranced he became with her the more he was bothered by it. Damn! Why couldn't he concentrate on anything but her?

What was she doing in the cedar swamps? Bran glowered at the papers, his list forgotten. He felt in his gut that she was innocent of being a spy, and yet . . .

He knew how dangerous the area was, and if not for a certain well-concealed path, the cove would be useless to him, to anyone. For the past several months it had been the perfect place for the *Bloody Mary* to lay low for a time, for Bran to meet up with his cohorts, to gather information, to load and unload goods.

The cove had outlived its purpose, Bran thought. Molly might be innocent of endangering them, but she did discover their hideout, and he knew that others might stumble upon the area as Molly had done.

Bran gazed at the sleeping Molly, wondering

about her family, her friends. Were her people looking for her? Surely she was missed.

His chest caught painfully. He needed to know more of this woman. She would be leaving soon. He had no choice but to let her go, although he knew in his heart that he would keep her with him if he could.

Tomorrow was soon enough, he thought, and then changed his mind. Perhaps the day after that would be better.

Molly stirred on her berth, reaching across the mattress. Bran felt a wild thrill that even in her sleep she reached for him. When her hand found empty space she frowned and opened her eyes. He saw her search for him, saw her face illuminate when she spied him at his desk. His heart melted when she gifted him with a smile.

"Good morning," she said softly.

He returned her smile. "Did you sleep well?"

She nodded. "What are you doing over there when you could be here?" she asked, and Bran's smile faded. Desire hit him in the gut at her suggestive tone. He was surprised and pleased by the frank invitation in her dark eyes.

Bran frowned and looked down at his desk. He had a job to do; he had to remember that. He couldn't allow this woman to distract him yet again.

"Bran?" Her voice wobbled.

He glanced up. "What were you doing in the cove?" he asked briskly. He heard her inhale sharply. There, I have asked it, he thought with satisfaction. This time he would demand an answer.

Her gaze wavered beneath his stare. Sighing, she

213

rose from the bunk naked. Bran drew a ragged breath at the sight. Molly grabbed her chemise from the top bunk. Slipping the fine linen over her nude body, she wondered how Bran would react when he learned the truth. Would he brand her a thief like the others? Would he believe that her presence in the cove had truly been an accident, and that she was innocent of any wrongdoing?

"Molly . . ." Bran sounded impatient.

She sat on the bunk, stiffened her spine, and folded her hands in her lap. Meeting his gaze, she said, "I was running from someone."

He jerked in surprise. "Who?"

Molly swallowed. "Reginald Cornsby." She paused. "The storekeeper in Manville."

When Bran inclined his head in encouragement, Molly told him what happened. She explained about her arrangement with the storekeeper, the baskets she made and sold to Cornsby, and how until that day their dealings had always been satisfactory for the both of them. She went on to tell how Cornsby had refused to pay her, how she'd simply taken the money that belonged to her, and how he'd rallied the townspeople, calling her a thief. She'd run when they'd chased her, she said, because she was a half-breed bastard and they'd never believe in her innocence.

Bran was frowning when Molly finished, breathless, her heart pumping with anxiety and fear. *This is when he turns against me,* she thought. *This is when he looks at me in disgust because I am a thief and an Indian and . . . a bastard.*

"Cornsby," Bran murmured, his gaze narrowing.

214

"There's something you haven't told me."

Molly blushed and looked away. To her surprise, he hadn't said a word about her parentage.

"Molly," he prompted gently. Bran rose from his chair and approached the bed rack. Seating himself on the bunk, he placed his palm against her cheek.

Molly closed her eyes, rubbing against his hand, enjoying the touch. He withdrew his palm. She gazed at him and looked away. "He wanted me."

"This Cornsby?"

She nodded, and Bran felt the claws of jealousy clamp down on him hard.

"I'm sorry," she whispered, her eyes suspiciously bright.

He blinked. "For what?" Then he realized he'd been scowling, and he forced the ugly feelings away, made his expression less hostile. He found a smile for her.

When she didn't respond, Bran was puzzled. "Molly, love, what's the matter?"

"I'm not a thief."

Enlightened, he placed his finger beneath her chin. He forced her to meet his gaze. "I know you're not."

Her eyes widened. "You do?"

His reply was a thoroughly delightful kiss on her parted lips. When he lifted his head, she was breathless. Her eyes glowed.

"Does that answer your question?" he asked, looking amused.

Molly nodded. "Then it truly doesn't bother you?"

His brow darkened. "Of course it bothers me!"

She reeled in shock, but he apparently didn't see it. "You're mine, Molly. Mine! Cornsby can want you all he desires, but you belong to me."

With a cry of happiness, Molly launched herself into his arms. "Molly, what—?" Bran began, and then gasped when she rained kisses over his face and neck. Her mouth moved lower, grazing his bare chest, tantalizing him, and he groaned at the sweet torment and promptly forgot his question.

Chapter Sixteen

July 7, 1778

Shelby McCormick hunkered down in the brush of the forest, his head bent low. Behind him, past a stand of trees, glistened the waters of Eyren Haven—Little Egg Harbor; before him lay the trail to Clamtown.

Across the path, in the thick of a copse, three other members of the Tory band waited: his brother, Darren; the Manville undertaker's son, Isaac Peabody; and John Keller Adams, the smithy from near Cutter's Point. Like Shelby, they crouched hidden, expectant. Any time now a man would be coming down the footpath, his destination the small clearing at the harbor's edge. The small band lay in wait for Hugh Woberney. Woberney, purported to be a Rebel smuggler, had recently left Falkinburg's Tavern at Clamtown.

Either Woberney has courage to travel alone, Shelby thought, or he's a fool.

A fool, Shelby decided. Only a fool would be so

obvious with his wealth, spending his coin extravagantly, buying drinks for all freely. Only a fool would be so loose with his tongue, and with his life. This night hadn't been the first, Shelby learned, that the man had bragged to the other tavern patrons of his recently acquired riches.

It didn't take an idiot to guess where this Rebel had come by his coin, and Mort Thomas, their Tory man in Clamtown, was by no means an idiot. Two nights past, in a drunken stupor, Woberney had let slip to Thomas about a group of Rebels who paid highly for the use of a man's wagon and a night's stay in his barn. Thomas, putting two and two together, had immediately sent word to Darren McCormick.

Shelby heard Woberney's singing before he saw the man. A soft whistle, like a birdcall, signaled Shelby that the others had heard Woberney too. The singing grew louder. The young man tensed, his gaze riveted on the trail, his heart palpitating within his chest as he spied Hugh Woberney, the man's blond hair making him instantly recognizable. Shelby fingered the handle of his flintlock pistol, gripping and releasing it with clammy hands. A sudden cry rent the air, and Shelby shot up from his hiding place.

"Halt!" he cried.

Woberney froze, saw only a young, innocuous-appearing man, and he blustered, "What is the meaning of this!" He stared at Shelby's gun, apparently unafraid.

"This!" Darren McCormick muttered from behind, before butting the man's head with a wooden club. "Rebel drool!" He grimaced with disgust, shoving the unconscious man with his foot. "Well, that was easy, ya bastard!" He grinned at his co-horts.

"Bejesus, Darren!" Isaac Peabody exclaimed. "You killed the bloke!"

"Good God, McCormick! What good be he to us dead?" Adams stared in horror at the blood welling from the felled man's crown.

"He's not dead," Darren said. He narrowed his gaze on Isaac. "Ye're an ignorant lout, Peabody, for an undertaker's whelp. Look at 'im. The man's breathing."

Shelby shifted, experiencing an uncomfortable feeling in his gut. "Even so, Darren, did you have to hit him so hard?"

For all his brave talk about Rebels and revenge, Shelby had never been one for violence. He was a crack shot with a gun, but his targets had been only the small wild game that inhabited the woods surrounding the cabin. Hunger was a poor substitute for Molly's rabbit or squirrel stew.

Darren, on the other hand, seemed to enjoy the killing as much as the eating, just as he seemed to enjoy knocking the Rebel senseless.

A physical man by nature, Shelby mused, Darren liked to fight — and at the slightest provocation. How many times did Shi'ki-Xkwe have to pull Shelby out from under Darren's fists? With Shelby, Darren's fighting had been for sport, but even so, Shelby had seen the fire in his brother's eyes. And what had started out as a friendly tussle between siblings had once become, for Darren, a dangerous need to impose power over his younger brother.

Still, the brothers were close, despite their childhood altercations, for as the youths grew, Darren's aggression had turned away from his brother. He'd appointed himself Shelby's protector instead. Only one subject remained to cause friction between the two men, and that was Darren's inability to love Molly. Darren had never laid a hand on his half sister, but Shelby had worried a few times that his brother had been tempted.

Shelby didn't like his brother's expression. Trying to banish his unease, he helped Darren lift Hugh Woberney from the ground. He couldn't help noticing, with pride, Darren's strength, the way his brother easily took command of the man's body, tossing the limp form over one shoulder with barely a strain of muscles.

At Darren's order, the other men scurried back through the woods to a clearing, where a fifth Tory band member waited with a horse-drawn cart. If Shelby had wondered about the cart at first, he had no reason to wonder about its need now.

His apprehension intensified, and he lagged behind when Darren followed the others.

"Coming?" his brother asked, turning. Darren's brow creased when Shelby didn't answer immediately. "Shelby!" His tone was sharp.

"I'm coming." He knew he'd been unable to hide his dismay upon seeing Hugh Woberney's blood. "Darren—"

His brother scowled, impatient. "You wanna find yer sister, don't ya?" he growled.

Shelby jerked a nod. Woberney might know of a half-breed woman captured by a band of Rebels, but for what purpose?

"Why do you think they've taken Molly? For

220

what use?"

"Why do you think?" Darren said, his gaze full of meaning.

Shelby's heart stopped momentarily. He had terrible visions of his dear sister being mishandled by a group of ruffians, used and abused by one before being tossed to the next.

Seeing his brother's hardening expression, Darren felt more than a small measure of satisfaction. He didn't know where his half sister was, nor did he care. For the first time, however, he was grateful for his younger brother's attachment to her. One word of reminder to Shelby about Molly's capture by the Rebels was all that was needed to keep Shelby firmly on Darren's side. He stifled a smile. *I loathe you, dear sister, but I've got to admit that for the first time our relationship has proven useful to me.*

"Captain?"

Bran tore his gaze from the shimmering ocean. "What is it, MacDuff?" He was conscious of Molly by his side . . . the warm breeze teasing the silky tendrils of her raven hair, the sparkle of delight in her dark eyes, her joy at being out of the cabin's confines. "Well, Angus?"

To his surprise, the Scot shifted uncomfortably. It suddenly occurred to Bran that he'd never before seen Angus MacDuff at a loss for words. "What is it, Angus?" he said softly.

"I need a word with ye, sir."

MacDuff's gaze flickered to the woman at the rail. Bran frowned at his tone.

"Bran," Molly's soft voice accompanied her gentle

221

touch on his arm. She smiled in understanding. "I'll go below."

"Molly . . ."

She flashed the two men another smile and left.

Bran watched her go, unaware of his soft expression or of the way his mouth curved upward as if he had some fond and gentle memory on his mind.

MacDuff read the captain's look and was disturbed by it.

"Speak up, MacDuff." Bran's voice was brisk. The Scot looked relieved at Molly's parting. The captain's gaze narrowed. "Is something wrong? Out with it! Is there a problem with the men?"

The Scot drew a breath, before saying, "The lads are not happy, sir."

"Oh?" Bran looked stern.

" 'Tis their pay, Captain," his friend said quickly. "Ever since the boot with the *Wench,* they've been a bit restless. And now that we're not goin' to Philadelphia as planned, well, sir, ye can imagine what they be thinkin'."

Bran knew. A trip to Philadelphia meant a visit to Mortimer Vickery, the banker as well as part owner of the *Bloody Mary*. It'd been by Vickery's hand that the schooner had come about, outfitted with cannon, guns, and the like. Vickery's father had had connections with Marcus Donovan in the early days, when smuggling meant evading the duties of the customhouse officials. Mortimer Vickery was a zealous Patriot, who enjoyed the profits of privateering as well as knowledge that he was helping the Rebel force.

The captain firmed his lips. "They've worked long and hard with no rewards," he murmured.

"Exactly!" MacDuff exclaimed with such ferocity that Bran looked at him. At his commander's startled glance, the Scot flushed with embarrassment, mumbling an apology.

"Good God, man, why are you apologizing?" Bran said, scowling. It bothered him that he'd not seen the discontent amongst his crew. Usually there wasn't a move—not even a sailor's grumble—that escaped Bran's keen hearing or eagle's eye.

He ran his gaze over the deck, searching for the something he'd missed . . . the disgruntled idler . . . the sluggish deckhand. But he saw nothing out of the ordinary that confirmed what he now knew to be true. There was trouble about the *Bloody Mary*. In this time of war, the last thing a captain needed was a crew who were not satisfied with their lot.

Bran worried. He knew he'd have to change things. Somehow he didn't think grandiose promises of great rewards would smooth things over, not this time. His men had gone too long without enjoying the fruits of their labors. Bran had been so involved with the right of the cause and what he could do for it—and with the tempting wench who resided in his cabin, if but temporarily—that he'd forgotten for a time the needs and morale of his men. It was something that concerned Bran greatly, more so in his case than with other privateer captains, because those other captains didn't concern themselves with the welfare of Washington's Continental army. They thought only of the riches to be made for themselves and for their men at Britain's expense.

Ross Martin, as wily a commander as he was, was just such a captain, Bran realized. Martin made no bones about the fact that he was in it for the money. Not that Bran didn't trust Martin; he did, for the simple fact was that when Martin took on a job, he did it and did it well. Martin never took back his word once he gave it, and he'd given it to Bran.

Martin believed in the Rebel cause, but his conviction wasn't such that he'd sacrifice his hardearned gain. Profits came first and foremost with Captain Ross Martin; that he was helping the Cause came second in his calculations.

"Sir?"

Bran broke from his thoughts. "I see what you're saying, Angus." He heard his man's sigh of relief; his lips twitched. "Why, Mr. MacDuff!" He cocked an eyebrow. "What did you think I would say?"

Relaxing, the Scot smiled. "It's not me job to tell ye what to think or say, Captain."

The captain stiffened; MacDuff's words had reminded him of his preoccupation with a certain dark-haired, dark-eyed witch.

"If I may be so bold?" the Scot asked. Bran nodded, and MacDuff continued, "There's one other thing I think ye should know. It's aboot—"

"Molly," Bran said with a sigh.

The Scot's gaze held compassion. "Aye."

"Tell me."

" 'Tis not me place to say nay, sir."

"That's right, it's not" was Bran's tight, affirmative answer. Then he quickly waved a hand for MacDuff to continue.

Bran's friend gathered his words carefully. " 'Tis hard fer a lass to be kept inside." Bran nodded impatiently. The Scot hurried on, " 'Tis equally hard fer a man to go too long without a warm bit of

224

feminine flesh between his thighs."

Bran tensed. "What are you saying? That my presence isn't enough to keep Molly safe? The men wouldn't dare defy me!"

"Who knows or doesn't know what's in the minds of these laddies," MacDuff said.

The captain stared and then looked away. "She'll be released," he mumbled.

"Aye." The Scot paused. "Do ye know when?"

Bran glared at him. "Soon!" he boomed, and then turned and stalked off, unwilling to discuss the matter further.

"Well?" It was Dickon, come to MacDuff to learn what had transpired.

MacDuff, watching the captain bark orders to the bosun, tore his gaze away from Bran's lithe form and focused on the first mate. "He's goin' to release her."

Dickon nodded, relieved. "When?"

The Scot shrugged. "Soon."

"Soon?" When MacDuff nodded, the mate grimaced. "It had better be. We've got ourselves a hold full of powder and a captain that's distracted. A dangerous combination, my friend," Dickon commented.

"Aye," MacDuff agreed.

Something was wrong. Molly could feel it. There was tension among the men, a tension, she surmised, that sprang as much from her presence on board as from the demanding duties of men at war. And there was a tautness about the ship's commander. Bran seemed preoccupied of late, unable to

225

relax. His smiles for her vanished. His brow was furrowed with new lines; his eyes were dark, unreadable.

When did this change in Bran take place? she wondered. Since MacDuff had sought him out, she realized.

When next Molly had seen him, Bran had become like a stranger to her again, cool, impersonal, withdrawn.

She frowned. It wasn't that he failed to be solicitous when he escorted her topside each day. He was always quite pleasant, seeing to her needs. Was she cold? Was she thirsty? Did she have enough to eat? But it was as if his declaration of love had erected a barrier between them, an invisible wall that Molly couldn't penetrate. She'd felt it while they stood on the poop deck overlooking the water; she sensed it at the evening meal. Whereas before he was quickwitted, ever challenging her with teasing quips, obviously enjoying her acerbic responses, now there was . . . nothing.

Was it his concerns with the ship?

Shivering, Molly rose from her bunk and paced the room. She hadn't expected the captain to play the lover, not in front of his men, but she did expect an acknowledgement of some sort of what transpired between them in the privacy of the cabin. Perhaps a gleam in his blue gaze when their glances touched? An occasional smile over the dinner table? Something!

She sighed. At least she could take a small measure of comfort in the knowledge that he still found her desirable. She had the memory of last night to prove that. Without it, she would have feared that his admission of love had been merely a figment of her girlish dreams.

She paused in her pacing, a faint smile about her lips as she recalled the moment last night when Bran had drawn her into his arms and she had known once again the glorious fire of his lips, the sweet brand of his masculine touch.

Bran had loved her thoroughly, passionately, with an intensity that had taken her breath away, that had bordered on desperation.

Which made her think of how it would be when she went home. When she finally left him.

Was that what was been bothering him?

Molly worried. She had come to realize that her presence on board ship hurt Bran, endangered his position with his men. She knew instinctively that a preoccupied captain was a danger to both his ship and his crew.

The distraction wasn't his mistrust of her. She knew that because he'd shown his trust in her the day he'd ceased locking his desk. And there was always a weapon within her reach.

Was it the crew? Did he notice the way some of them watched her? Like they were hungry animals and she was a succulent piece of meat?

Old John Smithers — "Beard-face," as she dubbed him — was one such crewman. She'd seen the hot look in his eyes each time she'd happened to glance toward the gunnery crew. Molly had been surprised to learn that Beard-face was the gun captain. But then she recalled her own experience with the man, his deadly determination to get what he wanted that day in the clearing . . . when he'd wanted her.

She shuddered and hugged herself.

Molly realized that the gunner's will to get what he wanted, aided by his rapt attention to detail, no doubt stood him in good stead in his position as gun captain.

Still, that didn't keep Molly from feeling revulsion when his lascivious gaze met hers; in fact, it only served to heighten her apprehension of him. And he was just one of several seamen whom she'd caught eyeing her that way.

A knock resounded on the cabin door, and Molly went to open it. "Mr. Dickon," she acknowledged with a nod.

"Miss." The first mate inclined his head briefly. "Might I have a word with you?"

Molly's gaze flickered with surprise. "By all means," she murmured, and then stepped back to allow him entry, for it was obvious that whatever he had to discuss with her, he felt uncomfortable doing so from outside the door.

Dickon moved into the cabin, maintaining a respectful distance from her. His brow furrowed as he leaned back against the captain's chart table.

"I take it the captain didn't send you?" Molly said.

He swallowed, looking mildly discomfited. "No."

"I see." But she didn't really. She hovered near the door, suddenly recalling the leering glances of some of the other men.

"About the captain," Dickon began.

"Yes?" Molly prompted softly, encouragingly, when he hesitated. All thoughts of danger dissolved in the man's obvious distress. "Just tell me and get it over with. We'll both be the better for it, I'm sure."

He looked relieved at her directness, his eyes lighting with new respect for her. "I don't know who you are, nor does it matter, actually," he added upon seeing her dark look. "What concerns me is that the captain hasn't been himself lately, and I can only think you to be the cause of it!"

Molly gasped, taken aback. "I see."

"Do you?" he answered, his gaze watching her keenly. "Then you know why I'm here."

She shook her head, and told him that, no, she really didn't see. "You want me to do what?" she asked, her expression puzzled.

"Leave this ship," Dickon said. "Tonight. Tomorrow morning. When opportunity avails itself," he explained.

"But Bran—"

"He plans to release you, he told me so himself," he said with a conviction that rang of truth. "However, as I said myself, the captain hasn't been himself lately . . ." The first mate shuffled his feet, his face reddening.

"Are you saying that there is no longer need to keep me prisoner?"

Dickon nodded. "For some reason, he seems to be hesitant about letting you go." He watched Molly's face. His features were solemn, his tone serious, when next he spoke. "It is time for you to leave this ship, Miss. . . . McCormick," he supplied after a few seconds, as if he'd had to think for a time on her name. "You are interfering with the smooth functioning of this vessel."

Something jerked in her belly. It hurt to hear her own fears realized by another's words. And for that someone to be Bran's most trusted officer.

"I understand." Her voice was quiet.

He waited a heartbeat. "And you'll go?"

Silence. Finally, an affirmative jerk of her head. "Yes."

Dickon sighed. "I shall do all I can to aid you." He hesitated and then said almost reluctantly, but sincerely, "I'm sorry."

"Thank you, Mr. Dickon," Molly said, turning away, her heart beating fast.

The officer left then, knowing that his daring had been successful. Dickon silently prayed that Bran Donovan would never learn of his interference. It was for the good of the ship and its commander that he'd taken a hand in this matter, but the good captain might not see eye to eye with him.

Chapter Seventeen

The rebel schooner was nearing her stop at Toms River when her men encountered trouble in the Atlantic waters.

"Captain Donovan!" Benson cried. "Look! Off the starboard beam! 'Tis a English frigate coming our way, sir!"

Bran's face grew stern, his body taut. "Aye, Lieutenant." He squinted against the sun's glare to study the approaching vessel, calculating its distance and speed.

The enemy vessel was approaching fast. Bran saw that the English warship was equipped with at least thirty guns. He had to make a quick decision as to how to handle the situation. With a ship's belly filled with gunpowder, the last thing they needed was to be under fire.

They would attempt to outrun the chase, the captain decided. Studying the New Jersey coastline, Bran felt their best bet would be to head for the inlet near the mouth of the river. If memory served him well, the waters of Cranbury inlet were too shallow for the British vessel. But the Britons wouldn't know that. Cocksure that they were, the bastards would follow *Mary* into the narrow channel. If that happened, the slimy dogs would run themselves aground!

Bran knew that with skillful and careful handling, the crew could handle *Mary* through Cranbury Inlet. The position of both ships, however, called for a daring move on his part. If they didn't increase speed, the enemy would make the Inlet before *Mary* did, blocking off all avenues of escape.

"Sailmaster!" Bran shouted. "Put on more canvas!"

Startled by the command, the man's eyes fairly bulged out. "But, Captain!" he objected. "We'll never turn her with her upper topsails set!"

"Dim-witted arse! The blasted sail is fixed, isn't she?"

"Aye!"

"Are you questioning my orders then, Mr. Knots?"

"No, sir!"

"Then, get to it, damn it!"

The action was hurriedly overseen by a skeptical sailmaster, who feared to disobey his superior officer. The deck came alive as an energetic crew responded to the call for speed.

It was a risky move, Bran knew, turning the schooner with her upper topsails. But then one had no choice but to take risks when your options were limited to saving lives.

The *Bloody Mary* entered the shallow waters just as the English vessel came into cannon range.

"Drop the topsails!" Bran roared.

The topsails were dropped, and the schooner became easier to maneuver through the narrow channel.

"God's teeth!" one observant seaman exclaimed as the air rumbled with a familiar sound. "Hear that! The Brits, they've run aground, sir!"

A wild cheer arose from Bran's crew at the Briton's state of helplessness.

"Dickon," Bran said as a ship came into view, approaching the schooner from the Toms River port, "here comes a friend of ours. John Smith with his *Gambling Lady*. Do you think the captain'd be interested in a fortune's share?"

The *Gambling Lady* was a converted whaleboat; Smith's home base was Sandy Hook off Raritan Bay.

"Signal the *Lady*, bosun!" Bran ordered.

When Benson had done so, Bran allowed himself to relax. The Britons had ceased firing. With their ship aground, they were no doubt arguing about whose fault it was.

"Mark, I'll be glad to rid ourselves of this particular cargo."

Dickon nodded. "I, too, sir." He flashed his friend a grin. "Damn good daring, Captain Donovan."

"It was a fool-arsed maneuver, but it worked," Bran replied. "Thank God."

The battle, such as it was, was over. The *Bloody Mary* was victorious, and with only one shot fired on the British side. *Fortune's Chance* was the British war frigate. What a sad, sorry thing for the Britons to have run aground on the Cranbury Inlet shoals.

After a brief but direct discussion with Captain Smith, Bran gave the command that brought *Mary* under her way again. He watched with grim satisfaction as the helmsman steered the schooner onto Toms River, the *Bloody Mary*'s destination. The deal with Smith had gone better than Bran had thought it would. Bran had offered the commander of the converted whaleboat two thirds of all cargo on board the frigate, and all English prisoners. In return, Smith was expected to extricate the frigate from its predicament and escort the new prize to the nearest accessible Rebel port.

Smith agreed. It was an arrangement that suited both captains.

Bran felt drained after the encounter, a state he later attributed to the strain of knowing Molly was below deck. His stark fear for her safety had convinced him now more than anything that he had to let her go. It would be better for the both of them if she was safe and secure in her own home.

He wanted nothing more than to go below and see how she'd fared, but he couldn't rightly do so, not without raising a few eyebrows or incurring the displeasure of his officers and men.

Scanning the shore, Bran gave the command to anchor, and he prepared to disembark. A quick glance at the group gathering at the Toms River port and his gaze jerked to a standstill, his grin widening. There, accompanied by three other familiar faces, waving his arm frantically and calling his name, was his brother, Patrick.

"Ye gods, if it isna yer brother, Pat!" Angus Mac-

234

Duff said, coming up behind Bran.

Bran barely spared him a glance before fixing his gaze on land again. "I wonder what the hell he's doing here." He turned to his marine lieutenant. "Benson, lower the jolly boats." He then faced the Scot. "MacDuff, coming?"

MacDuff grinned. "Is a baby's arse pink?"

A sudden grin split Bran's face at the Scot's quip. "Dickon!" he shouted, "I'll be taking five men with me. You'll be in charge. Set up a watch and see the rest make shore for a brief respite. Mind you, Mark, we'll be in Toms River but a night or two at most. Keep it in thought when you're arranging leaves. I'll be back in a hour or so; you can have your turn then."

"Aye, Captain," Dickon nodded, smiling at the prospect of a mug of ale and a saucy wench. "Jones! Rogers! Smith! Get yer babe-wet arses over here!" he bellowed. "Unless you've taken upon yerselves the first watch!"

"MacDuff," Bran murmured, his expression grave. "Hasten below to check on Molly, will you? I've got a few things that need seeing to before we go ashore." He paused. "If she's hurt, I want to know immediately."

"Aye, Captain." His brown eyes somber, the Scot nodded and left.

Bran inhaled sharply, releasing his breath with a hiss. Molly. This evening when he returned to the ship, he would discuss with her the subject of her freedom. He would apologize for her captivity. Together they would decide the best place for her release. Then he would send her safely on her way to

235

her family.

The thought of losing her company depressed Bran as he climbed into the dinghy and waited for MacDuff and four other men to join him.

"Aye, yer a fine piece, me dear," Old John Smithers said. "Did ya think I'd forgotten ya?"

Molly glared at the man in the captain's stateroom. How did he get in? she wondered. What had happened to Dickon's guard?

She was alone; Bran had gone ashore again. MacDuff had accompanied Bran. Dickon? He must be somewhere on board the ship. "I'll kill you if you so much as touch me, Beard-face!"

"Beard-face!" He laughed at the nickname, rubbing a hand across his bristly chin. "Well, I like that! Reckon it's an apt name, fer this old whiskers are ma pride, they is."

Smithers crossed the cabin, his eyes full of wicked intent as he approached. Molly shuddered, backing away. The man emitted a sinister glow. His brown queue was greasy as well as tarred; he gave off a noxious odor of unwashed body, grog, and urine.

"Stay back!" she cried, falling into a defensive crouch. "The captain will kill you if you so much as breathe on me!" Molly grabbed the nearest weapon to hand—Bran's spyglass. The three-foot instrument had been propped up against the bulkhead, next to the bed racks.

The man froze, and then a evil smile creased his ugly face, crinkling the puckered scar from beard to brow. "Capt'n will 'ave yer head if you 'urt that glass of 'is." His arm snaked out to capture her.

She spun, eluding his beefy hand. "Get out," she snarled, her eyes flashing.

"Ah, now darlin', why would I wanna do that?" He grinned, displaying broken, tobacco-stained teeth. They circled like wary animals, Molly brandishing the weighty spyglass, Smithers with his hands raised in readiness to grab her.

"Thought ya'd scare me with talk of the capt'n," he said softly. "Everyone knows that 'e can't wait to be rid of ya!" He leered at her, and Molly felt like she'd been stripped naked and defiled.

She felt a snag of pain. Was it true? Had Bran changed? Was he anxious to get rid of her? She knew her presence on board ship caused problems, but . . .

"Liar!" she exclaimed. She recalled that Bran had been in a strange mood last night. He seemed thoughtful, even brooding. When questioned, he'd assured Molly that there was nothing wrong. Drawing her onto his lap, he'd kissed her. They kissed again, and then desire had flamed between them like wildfire as they became almost frantic in their kisses and caresses. Their union had been explosive. They'd climaxed together, and in the aftermath she'd held Bran close and felt him tremble within her arms.

Molly circled about the cabin as she continued to elude the scarred gun captain. *"K'nees gahk-gay-loon'en!"* she spat. "You're a nasty liar, Beard-face!"

"Am I?" Eyes gleaming, the man laughed. "Come here."

Molly scurried about the chart table; Beard-face followed, grinning like he'd already won his prize. Suddenly he lunged at her, and she swung the spyglass at his wrist, hitting him. He gasped at the impact, but caught her healing forearm, pinching her still-tender skin before releasing her to rub his bruised hand.

Beard-face's expression became menacing. He came at her then in anger, his hands raised ready to strike her. "Why, you little—"

"Smithers!" Dickon bellowed from the open door. "What in the hell do you think you're doing?"

Beard-face froze and dropped his hands. "Mr. Dickon, sir," he murmured respectfully, his face pale as he turned to the first mate.

"There are plenty of wenches on shore, Smithers!"

"Aye, sir!"

"Captain Donovan wouldn't take kindly to learning you were in his cabin."

Fear flashed in the seaman's whitened face. "Sir, I—"

"Git! And don't you dare trespass again!"

Old John Smithers bustled from the cabin like a scared rabbit. Molly's mouth twisted as she reflected that she wouldn't have thought such a big man capable of moving so fast. She scowled at the first mate.

"Are you all right?" Dickon asked softly.

"That's all you're goin' to do?" she asked with disbelief. Bran would have been livid at Beard-face's pursuit of her! She shuddered, wondering what would have happened if Dickon hadn't arrived, if

238

she could, in fact, have fought Smithers off.

"I'm sorry. I had a man posted outside the door, but he must have wandered off somewhere. I'll handle them both later," he said. " 'Tis better not to make a fuss." He stared. "Are you ready to go? I've arranged your escape."

Her heart stopped. "Now?"

He nodded. "The captain's gone ashore. He'll be back in about two hours," he said. " 'Tis the best place, I think, Toms River. With help, you'll be long on your way home before Donovan realizes you're gone."

He handed her a cloth sack. "Here. You'd better help yourself to a few things in that trunk. You might need them."

Numb with pain, Molly took the bag and stared at it blankly. *Leave,* she thought. *Leave without saying good-bye?* In her heart, she knew this would be the day, for hadn't Dickon warned her yesterday? Still, it was a shock to realize that she would be with the man she loved no longer.

" 'Tis better this way, girl," Dickon said quietly, as if he'd read her thoughts. "Less painful."

Molly looked up from the bag. "Is it?" she murmured, and Dickon caught his breath at her tear-brightened gaze.

"I'll be back in five minutes," the first mate said. "But hurry. There's a man on shore, a William Sooy. You'll recognize him by his thin build and a red birthmark across his right cheek. Don't let his looks scare you. He'll help you, give you food. He'll be your escort as far as Clamtown. There, another will take his place."

"You arranged all this?" she asked, her dark eyes wide.

"Aye."

Molly nodded, her head reeling. Smithers had come to the cabin while Dickon had gone ashore. "Thank you."

Dickon inclined his head. He glanced at his timepiece, a gold pocket watch he'd pulled from his weskit. "Four minutes—that's all you have." And then he was gone, leaving Molly to move blindly toward Bran's sea trunk.

She was ready when Dickon returned, having haphazardly selected a few garments, stashing them in the cloth sack. While she was rummaging through the chest, Molly had come across something that she'd never seen before—a small, delicately engraved wooden box lined with red velvet. Too big for a lady's jewels, she mused, but too fine to have been made for anything else. On impulse, she grabbed the box, burying it amid her packed, rumpled garments. A memento of her time with Bran.

She stifled the feeling of guilt that she was stealing something that didn't belong to her. Surely Bran wouldn't care that she took such a small, insignificant thing as a wooden box. However lovely the box was, it couldn't be as valuable as the silver comb she'd used or the many other trinkets that graced the bottom of the trunk.

Molly felt her face heat when Dickon glanced briefly at her sack before greeting her. She waited with thumping heart for him to demand to see what was inside, but he merely nodded with satisfaction

240

and then waved for her to follow him from the cabin.

Dickon was right. It was simple enough for her to disembark. If one had looked closely enough, one might have questioned the slight figure garbed in sailor's wear leaving the ship. But with the first mate by her side, no one dared to question or look for more than a heartbeat.

Molly waited near the gangway while Dickon conversed briefly with a subordinate. Then she walked down the plank to the landing without Dickon's aid, although her legs felt unsteady. For Dickon to touch or help her in any way would instantly arouse suspicion in even the most casual observer.

Everything passed in a blur to Molly as Dickon bustled her through the busy Rebel port past the imposing blockhouse. She got a brief glimpse of the log fort with its separate barracks and magazine, a building Dickon hesitantly informed her that housed the munitions and guns for the area's militia.

"The fort was built to protect the saltworks," he told her, and then he urged her to hurry. Molly understood. Salt was a precious commodity in the colonies, for it was used to preserve meat and other foodstuffs. It was one of the key factors in this war.

Molly managed to keep up with Dickon through the town and into the forest. They had traversed the wooded trail several hundred yards when the first mate stopped, placing a hand on her arm.

"I must leave you here," he said. With an abrupt jerk of his head, he nodded toward a narrow footpath that turned off the main trail. "Follow that path until you come to a bend, then take the left trail to the end. There you'll find Sooy's house. He has a passel of young'ins — four boys, I believe. No doubt, they'll be playin' in the yard. Gain one's attention, and tell him, 'The salt is drying, and Mary has meat to fix.'" His expression was grave as he studied her. "Do you understand? Will you remember?"

"The salt is drying, and Mary has meat to fix," Molly echoed dully, her heart constricting with pain.

Dickon looked relieved. "They might reply, 'The salt be ready tomorrow, but ya can sit a spell and visit.'" A grin flashed across his handsome face; Molly was startled from her apathy to compare Dickon's good looks to Bran's. Bran was by the far the more attractive, she thought, and decided it was his rugged features and commanding presence that put the captain in a bolder light.

"Are you all right?" he asked.

Molly felt her chest tighten, recalling the same question and Bran's concern when he'd accidentally injured her arm. She forced herself to smile in reassurance. "I'm fine," she said. "William Sooy, you said?"

Dickon confirmed the name, and turning to leave, Molly thanked him again.

Bran. His name was a painful litany drumming her brain. She didn't want to leave him. There was so much she wanted to say.

Her vision blurring with tears, Molly stumbled along the trail. This was it. She was actually free; she should be rejoicing! She sniffed loudly. Why

242

was she crying instead?

Would she ever see him again? What if something happened to him? What if he got killed in this damn war? She froze, paling, her breath rasping in the peaceful quiet of the woods. And if he survived, how would she find him? Would he care that she was gone? Would he want to see her when the fighting was over?

Suddenly Molly was retracing her steps, running to catch up with Mark Dickon. She would give Dickon a message for Bran, a ray of hope that she might see him again.

She reached the first mate, grabbing his arm as he was nearing the blockhouse. "Dickon!" she gasped.

He looked aghast and then nervous to see her. "For God's teeth, girl, what are you doing in town? Get you gone!"

"I will," she promised. "I will, only please, give Bran a message. Tell him that when the war's over, I'll be in the cove if he wants to meet me. On the first spring mornin'!" She was gasping and out of breath as she hurried to relay the communication.

Dickon's incredulous face softened. "Aye, girl. I'll tell him."

And then Molly was off again, springing on the wings of hope, on feet that no longer felt unstable.

"She what?" Bran shouted, his skin color staining red.

Dickon shifted uncomfortably. "The girl escaped, sir. I don't know how," he lied. His voice lowered.

"I'm sorry, Captain. It must've been when I was down checking the powder."

Bran felt as if he'd been kicked in the stomach. His gut twisted; he found it difficult to breath. Molly gone? Damn! How could she have left him that way? He had told her he'd release her, damn it! He would have taken her home.

My God, he thought. Home for her must be twenty or more miles away!

"Sweet Jesus, what if she gets killed!" Bran paled. "Why couldn't she have waited!"

The first mate cleared his throat. "I believe she hated being below, Captain."

"Aye," Bran murmured. Guilt hit him hard, making him agree. "She hated it all right." He turned blank, blue eyes upon his friend and first mate. "I shouldn't have taken her, Mark."

Dickon disagreed. "It was the only thing you could have done in the circumstances, Captain. She is innocent, but she could just as easily have done us harm."

Knowing Mark was right gave Bran no comfort. Molly was gone. His sweet savage was gone, and without a word, a final kiss to see her off. My God, he thought again, what if something dreadful happens to her?

"If she's hurt because of me," he said quietly, "I'll never forgive myself." He loved her. Damn, he never thought it was possible to love like this!

His friend sought to comfort him. "I may be wrong, Captain, but she seems to me to be a fighting one. She'll do all right. Probably make home in a day or two."

"But the blasted Britons . . ."

"I've heard of no enemy troops in the direct area."

Bran sighed, relaxing slightly. "I suppose that's some comfort, anyway." He tensed. "The Tories . . ."

"Why would they concern themselves over a slip of a heathen girl?"

The captain nodded. "She took her buckskin."

"Well, actually no, but I doubt she wore some feminine frock, either." Dickon placed his hand on Bran's arm. "You said yourself you were going to let her go. Perhaps she simply wanted to save you the trouble. Maybe she hates good-byes."

Bran swallowed. "Aye, maybe she does." He was suddenly overwhelmed by the image of Molly naked beneath him, her face taut with desire as she arched up against him, thrusting her hips. His loins throbbed just thinking about her, but it was his heart and his mind that suffered the most. He would miss her quick wit, miss their verbal fencing.

Would he ever see her again? he wondered as Mark left him to get back to work. "Will I ever again love my Molly?" he whispered.

Bran felt that he would always love her. Someday, perhaps, they'd be reunited. If he survived this war, nothing and no one would stop him from finding Molly, making her legally his. Until then, he had a job to do, and as much as it hurt him, he would see this war through to a victory for the Rebel cause.

In an attempt to ease the pain of his loss, the captain fell into his duties with a vengeance.

Chapter Eighteen

Through the remainder of July and the first weeks of August, 1778, Chestnut Neck on the Little Egg Harbor River was a hive of Rebel privateer activity. Ships came and went, bringing their war prizes, many of them with their captured English vessels in tow. The privateering ships carried a large crew for just such a reason. With British prisoners in leg irons, men were needed to man the ships. The *Bloody Mary*'s crew consisted of more than enough men to crew two ships. And crew them they did, for the Rebel schooner captained by Bran Donovan had been as successful as the rest of the privateers, winning three British ships in one week.

The gunpowder was gone from the schooner's hold. The *Bloody Mary* was on her way back to the open sea. Because it had taken Bran longer to bring his ship into Toms River than was usually warranted, owing to winds and weather and the tangle with the British frigate, Patrick Donovan had arrived at the Rebel port a full day ahead of his older brother. Pat had come to inform Bran that Washington's army had gone north toward Bergen County. In a change of plans, the powder was to be dispensed in the southern New Jersey counties of Burlington, Gloucester, and Cape May, where it was reported to be needed by the local militia. However, the men defending the saltworks at Toms River, Pat had told Bran, would greatly appreciate a cut of the precious powder.

On the day after Molly's escape, Bran had had his men unload several kegs for the defenders of Toms River, and then he'd headed south again, stopping to hand over the powder to Rebel contacts at several points along the Jersey coast. His duty done, Bran was free to pursue vessels in the open seas, and to look to the needs and morale of his motley crew.

Shortly afterward, the *Bloody Mary* made her first attack, winning a cargo of foodstuffs, rum barrels, fabrics, and other prized goods. Buoyed by their success and by the newfound riches they shared after most of the goods were auctioned at a tavern at Chestnut Neck, the men were ready and eager to conquer anything or anyone that happened to sail within the schooner's range.

It was a cloudless, sunny August day. The breeze was a southwester, perfect for sailing. Captain Donovan leaned against the bulwark, his gaze on the shimmering ripples of the Atlantic Ocean, reflecting on his ship's last battle at sea. A triumphant smile tugged at his lips as he recalled the exact moment in which he'd known they'd won. The prize was *Fortune's Chance*, a British two-decker that had become the scourge of the New Jersey coast for the past several weeks.

247

The *Bloody Mary*'s hold was empty, but her hands were richer than ever before. With fresh supplies in her storeroom, they were good shape, Bran thought, thinking of the barrels of fresh water, salt pork, and other goods necessary to a seaman's survival. Items such an lime juice to prevent illness.

Mary had suffered little damage during her last fight, Bran mused. Nothing that Matt Beatty, the ship's carpenter, hadn't been able to handle within a few hours. As for her yardage, the topmen had already hung the sheets mended by the sailmaker. The seamen were ready and anxious for more action.

"You, sailor," Bran addressed a petty officer crossing the gun deck.

"Captain." The boatswain's mate came to attention, giving his commander a respectful salute.

Bran eyed the young eager seaman with amusement. The lad was a new recruit who'd signed on only two weeks before the battle with *Fortune's Chance*. "I saw you during the fighting, Talbot," he said. "Good show."

Talbot beamed. "Thank you, sir!"

"A ship needs able men like you." He stifled a smile. Having been likened to a man, the youth had drawn himself more pridefully erect. "I reckon it feels good to have coin in your pocket."

"Aye, Captain, indeed it does."

"Things won't always come that easy, sailor." Bran's gaze narrowed, and his expression became grave. "The test is yet to come. Do you understand, son?"

The smile fell from the seaman's face as he nodded solemnly.

Suddenly Bran grinned. "Git back to work, sailor.

248

You're dismissed."

His face brightening, Michael Talbot obeyed.

"He's a good boy," Dickon observed quietly. He had come up silently to stand beside his captain on the quarterdeck.

"He's young," Bran murmured with the sudden realization that Talbot must be all of seventeen. His face sober, he watched Talbot confer with the bosun. "Too damn young and too bloody eager, if you ask me."

The first mate noted a flash of pain cross Bran's features.

Bran looked at him with tightened lips. "When will this all end, Mark? We're fighting not only with seasoned men but with children manning our ships. They're the future of our nation. What good is freedom if there remains no one to enjoy it?"

Dickon experienced dismay. Surely Donovan wasn't wavering in his convictions? "Captain, perhaps you're driving yourself too hard."

"And my men?" The captain's tone was laced with dry humor.

Dickon denied that, but his red face suggested otherwise.

"Perhaps I have been pushing it a bit." Unbidden came a mental image of Molly McCormick. He'd pushed himself relentlessly since the day of her escape, hoping to banish the ache caused by her absence. But no matter how hard he drove himself there wasn't a day gone by that he'd not wanted to turn back time and have Molly with him again. What he wouldn't give to see her smile. His fingers itched to touch her hair . . . caress her satin skin.

Where was she now? Did she arrive home safely?

Damn, if he could only forget her! Even absent she was a distraction!

"It's that girl, isn't it?" Dickon commented, watching the emotion flicker across his commander's features.

Bran flashed him an angry look before softening his expression in self-reproach. "Is it so obvious?"

"Only to me, Captain," his friend said softly. "And only because I know you so well."

"You do, do you?" Bran's gaze had narrowed on the open sea, where he spotted a shadowy outline against the horizon. He sounded distracted to Dickon, who became instantly aware that his commander had stiffened with sudden tension.

"Tell me," Bran drawled, turning to his officer. "What am I thinking?"

Mark Dickon frowned. Following the direction of Bran's gaze, his brow cleared as he noted the approaching ship. "That you're in a fighting mood?"

Bran laughed, and Dickon felt relief at the sound. "Close."

The captain raised his spyglass, training it to better see the other vessel. "Good. She's coming our way at a fast clip." He lowered the instrument, his blue eyes glowing with the fire of anticipation. The flag, Bran had seen, was the English ensign.

His eyes again lighted on the first mate. "Actually, I'm thinking of what her cargo will bring us."

Face firm with concentration, he became the commanding officer his men had come both to fear and respect in recent weeks. His mouth was a tight line; his dark brows lowered to make him appear stern, forbidding. A pulse throbbed wildly at his left temple.

"Give the call for all hands, Mr. Dickon," Bran said. "If luck be with us, she'll be our fourth prize this week." His features mirrored his satisfaction when Mark immediately turned to obey the order.

"Benson, all hands on deck!" Dickon's voice boomed across the top deck.

"All hands on deck! All hands on deck!" The cry echoed about and below the main deck, spreading to all seamen. Abler or idler, all members of the schooner's crew were to present and prepare themselves for possible battle.

In a cacophony of sound made by feet across floorboards, the deck filled with hands running for their stations. Above the din, their commander called everyone to arms.

As the men assumed their positions and the din quieted in anticipation of the fight and the captain's next order, Bran was suddenly glad that Molly was absent. He only hoped that she'd made it safely home, and that home was far out of reach of danger and the British troops.

"All right, you bastards," Bran muttered after he'd given the commands to switch flags.

He issued the order to give chase. "Let's get this bloody war over with. Gun captain!" he shouted. "When we're close enough, aim for their tops. Who gives a devil if we damage her sails; 'tis the cargo we want! Benson, ready your boarding parties! Damn it to hell, sailor! Yes, you, over there! Where's your cutlass? For God's sake, man, have you no weapons? Well, then, how in the hell do you plan to fight?"

The captain searched the deck, looking for Michael Talbot. "Talbot! Take care of this kid! See

251

that he lives long enough to spend his money."

The captain barked orders left and right, while all scurried to do his bidding. And the *Bloody Mary* homed in skillfully, swiftly, on target.

The scent of fish broiling over an open fire permeated the Lenape village, filtering into the wigwam where Molly slept. Dawn had come and gone. The Lenape men had returned from their morning hunt, and the lingering scents of roast rabbit, muskrat, and venison joined the odor of cooking fish, the mouth-watering aroma urging Molly from the depths of a deep morning sleep induced by a fitful night.

She woke slowly, blinking into the muted light. For a horrifying moment Molly was trapped in the memory of her nightmare. Last night, and almost every night since she'd left the *Bloody Mary,* she'd dreamed of seeing Bran, of kissing him, caressing him . . . making love. In the midst of such heaven, Bran was suddenly wrenched from her arms. Molly heard the crack of a rifle shot, saw Bran fall to the ground, a red-coated figure bending over his lifeless body. She struggled to get to him, but she was held captive by her half brother Darren. Darren laughed cruelly, chanting, "He's dead. Your lover's dead!"

She was screaming, screaming but making no sound. She fought to be free of Darren's hold . . . And then she'd wake up as she thrashed above the bed covers. Her heart would be pounding, her body drenched with sweat.

Her pulse raced now, remembering. And she was soothed by the everyday sounds of the Indian village.

Molly sprang from her sleeping platform and was aware that the Delaware had been up for hours. After slipping a soft doeskin tunic over her naked form, she straightened her sleeping mat and then ventured outside Basket Woman's wigwam.

Basket Woman, Molly's aunt, sat on a mat near her cook fire, her nimble fingers deftly weaving thin moistened strips of wood into a basket. It was from Basket Woman that Molly learned the craft. Molly's baskets were objects that even the white ladies thought beautiful. Reginald Cornsby had known the quality of Molly's merchandise. Despite his claim to the contrary, Molly knew Cornsby had enjoyed a good profit for every basket sold at the general store.

Molly scowled. Just thinking of the lascivious, obese storekeeper brought her ire up!

"Aluum," her aunt greeted Molly, using the abbreviated form of her Indian name. Molly's full Lenape name was Siike Aluum. Spring Dove.

Offering her grandfather's younger sister a brief smile, Molly approached the old woman.

"Onna." Molly had murmured as she bent to give Basket Woman a kiss. The term was one of endearment, meant to give the older relative her rightful respect. Basket Woman and Molly were of the Turtle Clan of the Delaware, the right of sect being passed down through the female line. Tahuun Kukuus was Basket Woman's brother, and he too belonged to the Turtle Clan.

Basket Woman waited for Molly to sit down before she silently handed her the beginnings of a basket. Without conscious thought, the younger woman began to fashion the wooden splints into a sieve, her fingers bending, shaping, weaving the wood skillfully.

Molly liked life in the Lenape village. If not for her father and two brothers, she might have stayed with the Delaware. There were no bastards among the Indians. All children belonged to all members of the tribe. And all members of the same clan — like the Pokoun'go or Turtle Band of the Lenape Indians — were regarded as family.

She thought of how different life was in the woods cabin with her father and half brothers. It had been hard enough before, when her main worry was to keep food on the table and clothes on her father's back. Life there seemed especially painful to Molly after those last precious days spent with Bran Donovan.

She'd tried keeping herself busy, cleaning the spartan cabin, working to salvage the small vegetable garden that her family had left to weeds. The McCormicks had come into money while she was gone. From both brothers working extra hours at the furnace, Darren had claimed. But Molly had her doubts.

There were no longer debts at the Benger store; Molly realized she probably should feel relieved, happy. But she wasn't. She'd never felt particularly loved, but at least she'd felt needed. Now she felt neither loved nor needed.

Molly's tears made it difficult for her to work her basket. She missed Bran. If only she could see him one more time . . .

Did Dickon give him her message? she wondered. Was Bran angry that she'd left?

Too angry to come meet her at war's end?

She hoped not.

"Aluum," Basket Woman said. "You are silent. What is it, child?"

"It is nothing, *Onna.* I am tired, that's all."

"You have been tired for many days now. Something is troubling you. Is it Running Deer?"

Molly shook her head. Running Deer was a Lenape brave who had been placing gifts at the door of the wigwam Molly shared with Basket Woman. Running Deer was courting Molly. While it disturbed her that Running Deer had shown an interest, she wasn't overly concerned. She left the gifts where they lay, in the hope that Running Deer's attention would move elsewhere.

If only she could love the strong Lenape brave, she thought. But how could she when her heart belonged to a raven-haired sea captain?

"Your grandfather worries, Aluum," Basket Woman said. "Since your journey on a . . . what was it?"

A smile touched Molly's lips. "A schooner, *Onna.* It is a boat, a big *mux hole.* It has big cloth sheets that catch the wind's power."

Basket Woman's wrinkled face mirrored her wonder of such a boat. *"Kaya!"* she exclaimed. "It is hard to imagine such a large *mux hole.*" She paused in her basket-making to regard her niece with piercing dark eyes. "This *len'o*—this Don-o-van. He is a brave warrior, you say?"

"Kihiila, Onna, Molly grumbled, averting her gaze from Basket Woman's all-too-knowing glance. "Yes, Mother," she'd said.

"Aki'," her great-aunt breathed with a sigh. "Oh,

255

dear!"

Molly stared at her then. "It is not what you think, *Onna.*"

Basket Woman held her gaze steadily. "It is exactly as I think, Siike Aluum. You love this *i'la.* I can see it in your eyes." Shaking her head sadly, she clucked her tongue. "Aka'kwi! Shu wun uka—these white men, they like to fight. A warrior thinks little of love while he wields his spear."

Molly sighed sadly. "I know, Basket Woman. That is why I am sad."

The old woman nodded. *"Kihiila."* Yes, it is as I thought, she mused.

Setting her basket aside, Molly rose to poke a stick into the fish broiling over the fire. The stick entered the meat easily. The *num ai is* was cooked. "Mother, do you want some?"

Basket Woman shook her head. "I have eaten. The fish is for you." She paused. "You missed breakfast."

Nodding her thanks, Molly carefully placed the broiled fish into a wooden bowl. After returning to her seat beside her great-aunt, she poked open the steaming trout with the stick. When the fish had cooled some, she began to eat the white flaky meat with her fingers. "This *num ai is* is delicious, *Onna,*" she commented, pausing in her chewing to flash her aunt a grin.

The old woman's nod was abrupt, but Molly could tell Basket Woman was pleased. Her next words confirmed it. "Red Bear was right to bring you home to us."

Molly grinned. "Red Bear wanted to stay, too, but he had work to do." The smile faded from her face as she thought of her brother's recent strange behavior, of the newly acquired riches in the McCormick household. What were her brothers doing? Where did all that money come from?

Basket Woman interrupted Molly's train of thoughts. "I will miss you when he comes back for you." Her voice was gruff.

"And I will miss you, *N gax ais,*" Molly whispered. She loved Basket Woman. She would always be grateful for the day long ago when she returned to the Lenapes, brought back by her uncle, Midnight Hawk. The woman had opened up her wigwam—and her heart—to the motherless child.

Molly smiled, remembering. That day she'd left the cabin after arguing with her two brothers. She'd wandered toward the Shamong and become lost. It was her uncle, Midnight Hawk, who'd found her. Immediately recognizing the frightened little girl as the child of his dead sister, Hawk had taken her to the village. To see his father. Her grandfather.

It'd been two years since Shi'ki-Xkwe had visited the village, one year since her death. Tahuun Kukuus had taken a hard look at his granddaughter, and then with tears in his eyes he'd embraced her. Molly had basked in the attention. While she was fawned and fussed over by the village women, Wood Owl sent a messenger to Tully McCormick to inform him of his daughter's whereabouts. The next day Tully came for her, his face full of anger, his eyes shadowed with worry. Molly had noted the instant tension between her father and grandfather. The two men had gone into Wood Owl's wigwam for a lengthy discussion. When they finally emerged, the hostility and anger had eased between the two men. Molly realized that, for her sake, they'd reached an understanding.

From that time on Molly was allowed to return to the Lenape village. During the years that followed, Molly had come to love her grandfather, her aunt, and everyone within the close-knit Lenape community. Shelby understood this. When Molly seemed unhappy after her return, it was Shelby who suggested she visit the village.

"And Shelby was right," she murmured. "I have found a certain measure of peace here." She still missed Bran, missed him with a passion bordering on obsession. But here things were bearable. Here they all loved her.

When she'd finished eating, Molly wiped out the wooden bowl with a handful of grass. She returned the bowl to its rightful place in the wigwam, under her sleeping platform, where baskets, bowls, and other utensils were stored.

"Red Bear will come tomorrow?" Basket Woman asked when Molly resumed both her seat and her weaving.

Tomorrow. Had it been two weeks already? "Yes," she said. "Tomorrow my brother will come." And she sighed, for the future loomed ahead . . . dully . . . without Bran's love.

Chapter Nineteen

August 12, 1778

The cart traveled over a road darkened by night. The forest was silent but for the distant *hoo-hoo-hoot* of an owl and an occasional rustling where raccoons, opossums, and other creatures of the darkness foraged for food in the undergrowth. The driver of the horse-drawn vehicle, an old man with stooped shoulders and dusty beaver-felt hat, maneuvered the conveyance skillfully over the rutted byway. His elderly female companion sat silently beside him, mobcap on head, a loosely woven shawl wrapped about bony shoulders.

The couple's journey had begun that afternoon from The Forks of Little Egg Harbor River. In the lengthening shadows of the approaching night, they'd openly traversed westward on the main thoroughfare that ran from The Forks toward Blue Anchor, leaving the road before reaching Long-A-Coming to travel north. Their cart appeared to be laden with grain and enough goods to see the farmer and his wife through their two-day journey. Beneath the grain lay precious cargo: three crates of pistols and rifles, one of black powder, and another with shot. The two figures were Rebel smugglers making a run.

Neither spoke. As the sky had blackened, their situation had become more dangerous. While no one would question the sight of a couple traveling by daylight, a journey so late would arouse suspicions. But blackness or not, it didn't matter. They kept on, for there was much ground to be covered, and on a route the Rebel compatriots had never used before. Should they be stopped and questioned, they had their excuses ready. *We are not far from home and are anxious to get there. Why should we stay at a strange inn when we can enjoy the comfort of our own beds?*

The Rebels had been warned of the risks, risks that increased as the hours of night passed into early morning. Where one excuse would sound implausible, they had another ready to take its place, and several more after that one should the need arise.

The wheels rumbled over the dirt track, bobbing the cart's passengers, shifting the cargo in back. The stillness of the night grew eerie, unnatural. The man stiffened, his tenseness transmitting itself to the woman by his side. If one were to scrutinize the man, one might question the youthful brightness of his hazel eyes, his unusually smooth hands and wrinkle-free face. His companion's visage, too, would raise eyebrows, for the seemingly old woman wore a fine stubble of blond whiskers on her chin.

The man's fingers tightened about the reins. He

glanced down to where his rifle leaned on the seat next to him, and feeling somewhat reassured, looked forward again. The figure beside him encircled large masculine hands about the handle of the flintlock pistol hidden beneath her dark skirts.

Suddenly a loud cry rent the air, and the path ahead filled with armed men, their guns raised, their voices shouting at them to halt the cart. The old woman brought out the pistol, fired it into the Tory band, and was unexpectedly dragged from her seat by an angry Pine Robber, who threw her on the ground with knife raised, ready to strike.

The driver was shot twice as he reached for his rifle. Eyes bulging, he fell from the wagon to lie dead, his eyes open in a death stare. The Pine Robber on the cart's opposite side brought his knife downward until a deep-throated command stopped the kill.

"Quick, check those barrels. Open those boxes!" Darren McCormick ordered. "And bring that prisoner to me." His eyes gleamed with a wicked light; his lips curved into a slow, malicious smile.

When the "woman" had been brought before him, the leader tore off her mobcap, gave a harsh grunt of pleasure, and ordered the Rebel bound hand and foot. "Throw him into the back of the cart," Darren ordered.

Shelby had gone to the driver's side and was surveying the blood-splattered clothes with stupefied horror. He turned white-faced to see his brother eyeing the gory scene with satisfaction. He shuddered and wondered again what drove Darren to delight in such evildoings. Controlling the Rebels was one thing; murdering and stealing for sport was quite another. Molly was home safe; the desire for vengeance in Shelby was gone. He'd come to abhor his brother's nature, the fanatical fervor with which he attacked his victims. For not the first time in recent weeks, Shelby questioned not only his brother's methods but his motives as well.

"Guns!" One of the men yelled.

Shelby frowned. The Tory raid was a success.

August 19, 1778

"Damn it, Bran!" Patrick exclaimed, pacing the room. "How could they have found out about our alternate route?"

Bran shook his head, frowning. "By God, if I only knew!"

The raid on the smugglers' transport wagons yesterday was the fourth in two weeks. Neither Bran, Pat, nor Josiah Morse had been able to figure out where the Tories had received their information, especially on those last two runs. The first raid, Bran might have deemed a coincidence, the Tories simply stumbling by accident across the Rebel wagon of British muskets, flintlocks, and other stolen goods. But a second time? Bran hardly thought that luck would be so kind to the blasted Tories twice in two days. Someone among the Rebels was a traitor. But who?

"There's only one thing to do," Josiah said, his face grave. "Bran, I'll need your lists of contacts, routes, and code words. We must sit down together and go over each one, one by one. Maybe between the three of us, we'll come up with a clue as to who betrayed us. Bran, you've dealt with most of the men. When it comes down to it, the final clue will probably be from you." He frowned. "We'll have to revise our plans yet again."

Wood scraped against wood as Bran pushed his chair back from the table. "I haven't had call to look at those lists in over a month. We've used the same people since that time." He leaned forward, his hands braced on the table, his expression thoughtful. "I'd swear on a stack of Bibles that neither Hanley nor Thoms is our traitor. Both have been of tremendous help."

"Well, who then?" Pat asked. "Who could have had access to that information?"

"As far as I know," Bran murmured, straightening, "no one but the three of us and, of course, the drivers, but they didn't know the route they'd be taking until they were told at the very last moment." He shook his head. "Frankly, I'm stumped."

Bran then addressed his brother, "Where are your lists, Pat?"

"Destroyed. I burned every one right after I memorized all the contacts."

"Josiah?"

"I buried two in the rock pile outside the tavern. A man digging for hours wouldn't be able to find them. Besides, Bran," Josiah said, "I didn't have the list of alternate routes. Just our first choices, and those roads I know so well that, like Pat, I burned the road list."

"So that means only mine are readily available," Bran thought aloud, "and those are locked up in my desk." He dipped his hand into his waistcoat pocket. "*And* I've kept this on me at all times," he

263

said, holding up the key.

The other two men grunted their frustration.

"Well, someone is giving the murderers information!" Pat exclaimed. "One way or another, we'll find out!"

"Aye," Bran said. He sighed and rubbed the back of his neck, two telltale signs of his weariness and concern. "I'll retrieve those lists from the *Bloody Mary* and we'll meet back here tomorrow morning at eight."

August 20, 1778; 1:00 a.m.

Molly woke up with a start, her face flushed, her body pulsating with heat. She had had the dream . . . of Bran touching her . . . kissing her breasts . . . their naked bodies brushing against each other. But this time she wasn't frightened. She'd been roused from her sleep before the awful ending when Bran fell dead in a pool of blood, shot by some British soldier. No, it wasn't fear that Molly felt now, it was desire, unfulfilled, hot, intense, and insatiable. Her body ached and throbbed with it. A month and a half had passed since she'd last seen Bran, and she still yearned for him with every passionate fiber of her being.

Why was tonight different from all the other nights of her dream? she wondered. What had awakened her?

Voices. She heard voices out in the yard. Rising from her mattress, she went to peer through an opening in the loft toward the front of the cabin. The crack in the wood was too small for Molly to see outside. She moved to the other end of her sleeping room, and it was here that she could see out.

Moonlight splashed over the forest clearing, bathing the two male figures in the yard. Her brothers. They were arguing. Frowning, wondering what the argument was about, Molly climbed down to the main floor, creeping past her father's snoring form to the door, which had been left slightly ajar. Pressing her ear to the opening, she listened but heard nothing. Her brothers were on the other side of the house. Molly pushed the door outward and slipped into the shadow of the front porch.

"You've gone too far, Darren!" she heard Shelby exclaim to their brother as she came to the side of the house. Curious, Molly hung back, eavesdropping.

"And I say I know what I'm doing," Darren hissed in reply. "What's the matter, little brother? Haven't you got the stomach for it? We've got a job to do, damn it! And I intend to do it right."

"By killing innocent people?" Shelby sounded incredulous, and Molly gasped, stepping back.

"Those men weren't innocent and you know it! For God's sake, Shel, you saw their weapons. They had a bloody arsenal in their wagon! Do you think those rifles are for hunting game?" Darren snorted. "Grow up. If ye're not man enough to stay with us, then fine! Stay home. Whittle yer sticks and weed your sister's vegetable garden."

Molly inhaled sharply at her half brother's savage tone when he'd said *sister.* She heard Darren exhale a weary sigh. "I can't say I'm not disappointed in you, Shel. But if that's the way you want

265

things . . ." After a moment's pause his voice became a menacing growl, "Just keep yer yap shut and stay out of our way. We'll stop the Rebel bastards one way or another. The sooner the better, if you ask me!"

Molly peered around the corner of the house in time to see Darren stalk off into the woods, Shelby hesitated before following him. Not understanding, but disturbed by what she'd heard, she crept after her two half brothers, determined to find out what the argument was all about. She had the feeling that it had something to do with their strange behavior of late and the sudden, inexplicable funds they'd accumulated. The same funds that had been used to pay off the debt at the Benger store and that had brought a wealth of foodstuffs and liquor into the McCormick household.

She followed the path Shelby and Darren had taken to a secluded clearing near a stream. To her surprise, there were several men waiting for her brothers. She watched Darren join the group first, saw the men part to include him in their midst. Shelby was slower in his approach. Molly saw Darren turn at Shelby's entrance. Darren's smile flashed in the moonlight as he waved his younger brother to join the gathering.

The men went into instant discussion. Their hushed, intense tones drifted back to Molly, where she crouched behind a cluster of pines and cedar trees, their lower branches thick with evergreen foliage.

Words filtered to Molly's ears: "Rebel scum . . . smuggler bastards . . ." And then laughter and congratulations accompanied with much backslapping.

My God, she thought. Were her brothers involved with the infamous Tories raiders? The ones called the Pine Robbers? A shiver ran down her spine. The Pine Robbers were a band of ruthless men who'd acquired a reputation for murdering and plundering in these New Jersey Pine Barrens. No, she denied, Shelby couldn't be a heartless killer! Darren? Darren was capable of anything, she realized with a shudder.

When the name Donovan reached her from the men's discussion, Molly froze, then leaned closer. What were they saying? Was their Donovan and *her* Donovan one and the same?

With a suddenness that made her gasp, nearly giving herself away, the group broke up, the men moving to points unknown. Darren and Shelby headed for home on a path that would pass Molly, who remained hidden, wondering what to do.

Her heart thumped hard. If she didn't get abed before her brothers then they would know that she'd been spying on them. Shelby's reaction didn't concern her, but Darren's . . .

Someone from the departing group called Darren's name, and he and Shelby paused, turning back to talk briefly with a huge man with a white-powdered wig.

Molly blinked and cursed, recognizing the horrible man as he came from the shadows into the light. Reginald Cornsby! What on earth was he doing here? What terrible thing were her brothers involved in with the fat, slimy, wicked storekeeper?

Did Cornsby know that Darren and Shelby were her brothers?

The discussion was nearing an end. Molly sprang

from her hiding place, hightailing it back to the house. Her time with her Lenape family had taught her how to move about easily on silent feet. Her thoughts roiling inside her brain, her pulse racing furiously, she hurried up the ladder to the loft past her snoozing father. Once safely in her sleeping room, she flung herself on her bed, trying to make sense of the scene she'd witnessed.

Pine Robbers! she thought, her hands clenching against the mattress. What are they planning? And where did Donovan enter into things?

Molly vowed to find out. If her brothers were indeed Pine Robbers, then they were up to no good. She needed to know their plans. And if Bran and his brother Pat were in any way involved, endangered, then she had to formulate a plan of her own to help the Donovans without hurting her brothers.

"Shit!" Bran's face whitened as he stared into his empty desk drawer. The papers were gone. The papers, the wooden box, everything!

"What's wrong?" Dickon asked with concern.

"I'm missing some important papers, very important papers." Bran scowled. "Who the hell could have taken them? I was so sure I'd locked them in my desk when I finished with them last . . ." The image of Molly invaded his thoughts; he thrust it away. "Have you seen the box, my wooden box?" He described it in detail to his most trusted officer.

Dickon shook his head. "I'm afraid not." He paused. "Just how important were those papers?"

"How vital is a man's mind to his body?"

The first mate cursed, sharing his commander's

dismay. "The raids?"

Bran nodded. "We think so. Damn!" He slammed his fist on his chart table. "When I find out who stole that box I'm going to kill him with my bare hands! Do you know how many men have died because of the betrayal?" His blue eyes dimmed with sadness. "Yesterday it was Elijah Hempstead and James Hanley, Dave's brother. Who will it be tomorrow?"

"Perhaps you've simply misplaced those papers, Bran."

"Or perhaps a certain vicious bitch stole them to get back at me for holding her captive." He heard Dickon's sharp inhalation of breath. Raising his eyebrows, he said, "Oh, you don't think her capable?"

Dickon shifted uncomfortably, for if Molly was the one who'd taken Bran's papers, then he himself shared Rebel blood on his hands. He had helped her escape; he was responsible for a traitor supplying the enemy with enough ammunition to ruin the entire Rebel smuggling ring! The first mate groaned, put his hand to his head. "Surely you don't think she is the guilty one," he said hoarsely.

Bran's gaze shot sparks like blue lightning. "It's possible." He thought of those times he and Molly had fallen asleep together after making love. He knew with certainty that she'd had occasion enough to steal his desk key. Had she snatched it from the pocket of his breeches while he'd slept, exhausted from their savage joining? The notion afforded him great pain. After the passion they'd shared, would she—could she—have sunk so low? Did she hate him that much? She'd told him she loved him. Had her responses to his caresses been skillfully staged to lower his guard?

"I was a fool not to have gone after her," Bran said, his brow furrowed into dark, deadly lines.

"Don't condemn her so hastily. The girl seemed . . ." Dickon strove for the right word to describe Molly's attitude toward the captain, "smitten with you."

Bran's expression softened for only a moment. "I hope you're right about her innocence, because if I find out that she seduced me into trusting her, I'll track her down, and by God, I'll see her pay for the loss of American lives!"

Chapter Twenty

A man's harsh laughter filtered out of the general store in Manville to where Molly crouched below the window. It had been a week since she'd first discovered the existence of the Tory band, a long, danger-filled week during which she'd left her bed nightly to trail her brothers and to spy on the group. This night had proved to be the most risky to Molly, for she'd already been branded a thief in Manville. What would they do if they found that she was spying on them?

Something was in the making. Molly had sensed it two nights ago, and her feeling of foreboding had intensified as she strained to hear the discussion of the men inside. She pressed her ear tightly against the back wall of the building. The thick guttural tones of the man she'd come to know as Bad Jack was arguing the finer points of weaponry.

Apparently, Bad Jack—John Jacob Iden—was for attacking silently with honed knives or bayonets, while Molly's brother Darren saw no reason not to stage a show. A colorful, noisy show. Rifles and pistols, Darren insisted, was the proper way of precision attack. Men could be cut down at several paces; why dirty their hands with the bloody bastards' blood? Thanks to a previous successful raid, Darren pointed out, there was plenty of guns and shot. Why not use them? Why leave them about when the possibility existed, however slim, that the Rebels would find out where the weapons were hidden? The Rebels could steal the guns back to use against them.

There was much heated discussion on the subject, until all came to agree with Darren. Even Big Jack, Molly noted, had changed his mind. Her week of spying had brought her some startling facts about her oldest brother. Darren was the leader of the group. The power he wielded was terrible—everyone in the band ultimately went along with his decisions. Molly had been most disturbed to realize that Darren's hatred for the Rebels bordered on obsessive. His hatred combined with his power made him a deadly enemy not only to the Rebels but to any innocent bystander who got in his way.

The talk turned to the subject of Rebel privateering, and Molly's ears perked up.

"General Robinson says the Britons are damned plagued by the nest of Rebel privateers," Darren was saying. "They want the hive destroyed. Britain's suffering greatly from her losses at sea. He's promised us men and riches if we give him information and help corner the Rebels in their hiding places."

"Corner the sonuvabitches!" one man exclaimed. "Deuce! We've got no ships, no cannon! And these coastal waters cover miles, damn it! What 'e wants is for us to make bloody miracles!"

"Obviously," another man drawled in a dry, cultured tone, "Darren here believes it's possible, or else he wouldn't have brought up the issue."

"Darren? Is it true? Do you have a plan?" said a voice Molly had come to recognize as belonging to George Weatherby, the most cautious of the group.

"Of course." Molly gasped at her brother's confidence. "Do any of you recall the name Woberney? The Rebel we took near Clamtown?" Several acknowledged the incident. "Well, Mr. Woberney agreed to give us aid."

Darren seemed to pause for effect. "The man admitted—after a thorough and lengthy period of persuasion," he added with a snicker, "that he was more than just a worthless pawn in the smugglers' game. In fact . . ." It was here that Darren's voice dropped to a whisper, and Molly grimaced with angry frustration that his explanation was lost to her ears.

"So you see, gentlemen," Darren said, his voice back to normal, "it's simply a matter of laying a trap for the Donovan scum. Bran Donovan and his brother Patrick are said to be the leading suppliers of the militia, damn them! But," Molly could have sworn now that Darren was smiling as he went on. "they hadn't reckoned with a traitor in their midst. And I'm not talking of Hugh Woberney, I'm talking of someone in the very heart of the Rebel bosom. Ah, but then I've promised to keep his identity a secret, so . . ."

A traitor! Molly gasped. Who on the *Bloody Mary* would dare to defy his captain? She had a mental picture of Old John's evil leer. Beard-Face?

"So the Rebels harbor a snake and they don't

even know it, eh, McCormick?" a man snickered. It was Reginald Cornsby. Molly wished the wicked man to be the first one Bran brought down.

Wildly, Molly pondered the question of betrayal. Who? Who hated enough to act turncoat? Surely it wasn't Tommie, the cabin boy. She bit her lip. Or any other young member of the crew. Hadn't she seen for herself the respect, bordering on idolatry, the sailors had for their impressive commander?

But what of the seasoned men? Could one of them be hateful enough to want to see the captain destroyed? To relish seeing the Rebel cause turning into a dying ember, readily snuffed out by Tory boot heels?

She listened again, her cheek pressed against the wall. If she could just hear something that might identify the traitor!

Molly determined to find Bran and tell him what she'd learned.

Only when she was certain that her beloved captain was safe would she be able to rest easy.

When the conversation inside the general store turned to refreshments, Molly knew that the business of the meeting was at a close for the night. She'd heard all she was going to.

Rising carefully, she ran toward the forest trail that offered a shortcut home. She had no fear of discovery; her deerskin tunic blended easily with the darkness of the woods.

"I've done it!" she whispered, her feet flying on joyful wings. She knew enough to help Bran. Perhaps she didn't know the traitor, but she did hear the name Woberney. That information, along with a warning of the traitor's existence, would be all Bran needed to begin a hunt for the villain's identity.

As her feet flew across the worn ground, Molly thought ahead to her meeting with Bran. Her spirits soared at the prospect of seeing her love again, then sank as she considered his anger at the fact that she'd snuck off the ship.

It doesn't matter, she thought. When Bran realizes that I've come to help him, he'll forgive me for leaving. He'll take me into his arms and thank me properly . . . with his kisses. Besides, Dickon must have given Bran her message. Her love would be only too happy to see her again!

Molly shivered deliciously with anticipation. Her fingers itched to stroke his hard, muscled flesh; her tongue longed to dart into his mouth in rapturous joining. She loved Bran. God, how she loved him! And she would tell him so, over and over, not only in English but in the musical Lenape language as well. She would touch his cheek, kiss his lips, love him until he cried out in mindless ecstasy. When the war with Britain was finally over, Bran and she would be together again; there would be no question of that by the time she was done convincing him of the rightness of their love.

When two spirits touch, she thought, her lips curving into a faint smile as she ran home, *they are bound forever.*

"C-captain s-sir?" Tommie stuttered nervously as he came into Bran's stateroom. "You w-wanted to see me?"

"Aye, Tommie." Bran gestured for the youth to pull up a chair and sit down.

Tommie obeyed, placing the chair before the chart table. He took a seat and regarded his superior with apprehension.

"What's wrong, sailor?" Bran said softly. "Did Mr. Dickon tell you why you're here?"

Swallowing, the boy shook his head.

"If Dickon didn't tell you, boy, then what the hell are you afraid of!"

Tommie gasped, and Bran cursed himself for his approach.

"Tommie," Bran began again, more quictly, "I'm missing some papers. Papers vital to the cause." He watched the boy's features for some sort of reaction and was disappointed when Tommie looked blank. Before he'd been able to unearth his papers, Bran had been forced to make sail again, this time on a return call for aid from the Rebel men at Toms River. The messenger had come to the Jug and Barrel the day after the schooner's arrival at the cove.

Studying the young seaman, Bran tried another tactic. "You clean my cabin on occasion, don't you?"

"Yes, sir," Tommie whispered.

The captain smiled encouragingly. "You do a fine job of it, too, sailor."

The youth relaxed. Bran allowed a slight smile.

"Tommie, I'm going to ask you something, and I want you to think, son. Your answer is very important." Bran waited to see Tommie's nod. "Good. Now, tell me, while you were here in my cabin, did you ever come across a small wooden box about so big?" He spanned a distance with his hands, and then went into a detailed description of the missing box.

"Why, yes, sir. I've seen it. Found it lying on the bottom bunk over there. Figured the w—Miss Molly must have taken it out of yer chest. She and you, sir, were topside, I remember." He suddenly grinned. "Thought I'd do her a favor and put the box away fer her, so I tossed it in yer trunk." He paused, looking worried. "Did I do wrong? Did ya look there, Captain? It's probably still in there."

Bran's pulse pounded rapidly at his temples. "In the chest, you say?" In the chest! Why hadn't he thought to check there! Relief made him giddy. He cleared his throat. "Thank you, Tommie. I suspect you're right. The box is probably in the trunk. I must've have missed it." He dismissed the boy, who headed for the door.

Tommie paused at the threshold. "Sir? Those papers, are they in the box?"

The captain's gaze sharpened. The young seaman's face was the picture of innocence, however, and the hardened look left Bran's rugged features. He allowed a slight smile. "Aye, Tommie. The papers are in the box."

The boy beamed. "Then it was good that I could he'p ya, Captain?"

Bran nodded. "Good work, sailor." Thus having been properly commended for doing his duty, Tommie left. Bran heard him race up the companionway to the deck above.

After carefully locking the cabin door, Bran went to the trunk to check its contents. A quick turn of the lock key, and he was raising the heavy wooden lid. Peering inside, he grumbled at the lack of organization. Bran searched through garments, blankets, and other items. He found no sign of the

277

engraved box.

Cursing himself for not going through the chest to rid it of the garments he'd procured from the English for his mother and cousin, Mary Catherine, Bran began to pull items from the trunk, tossing them on the stateroom floor. As the messy heap grew, so did Bran's impatience. He was halfway through the trunk's contents, when his impatience turned to worry, his worry to fear. The box wasn't in the trunk. *Someone must have taken it.*

He himself had questioned all of his officers. Bran had to believe those who said they'd never seen the box or the papers. What about his most trusted men — MacDuff, Dickon, Benson, and a few others — those who'd known of the box's existence? None of them knew of its whereabouts.

Bran ran a hand along the back of his neck as he straightened. If none of his crew had taken the box, that left two others who'd had access to his cabin, who could possibly have stolen the precious documents. His brother Patrick. And Molly McCormick. Patrick, of course, had had his own copy of the lists. Therefore, that left only one suspected guilty party — Molly. Tommie said the box was on their bunk . . .

Closing his eyes, he shook his head. Molly didn't do it. Surely, she didn't hate him enough to betray him!

You took her prisoner, an inner voice taunted, *locked her in your cabin. You injured her, ravished her. She nearly drowned trying to escape you. And you ask yourself if she could betray you?*

"Oh, God!" he whispered, ridden with pain. His hurt became anger. "The vicious witch! Men died

278

because of her treachery!"

Bran strode to the door, opened the hatch, and bellowed for his first mate. When Dickon appeared moments later, the captain resembled the devil incarnate, his demeanor frightening, his thoughts on revenge.

"Set the *Bloody Mary* on a course for the cove," he said evenly. "The heathen has betrayed me—it's the only answer." His mind worked quickly, formulating a plan that would minimize the hunt to track down the half-breed traitor.

When he quit the captain's presence, Dickon was white-faced, nervous, feeling guilty as all hell. Bran, on the other hand, had become red with rage. Fist clenching about his clay pipe, he paced his stateroom, his mind full of images of what he'd do to the lying Molly when he got his bare hands on her. The pipe within his fingers snapped in two. His hand rose and the clay pieces flew across the room as Bran's temper snapped.

"Damn her!" he roared. I loved you, Molly. Damn, but I loved you! And he felt the gut-wrenching pain that came of betrayal.

"But you and I, Molly McCormick, we're not finished!" He firmed with purpose. "You, my sweet savage, are going to lure the Tory bastards to their deaths. And then, my silken heathen, you'll feel the dark side of justice firsthand."

Chapter Twenty-one

Molly stared at the water lapping against the shoreline. It hadn't been easy for her to find the hidden cove again. Her first visit had been the result of her flight from Reginald Cornsby, the Manville storekeeper. Considering the circumstances, it would hardly be a path one would remember!

But she was here now. Not that finding the old Rebel hideout had brought her any closer to finding Bran. The area had become overgrown, a true indication that the Rebels had abandoned the docking point. She might have questioned whether she was at the right place, but she had already seen signs of past activity in the dense undergrowth. A piece of wood from a broken cask, a discarded length of rotting rope.

Now what? she wondered. Where should she go next? Molly worried. What if she didn't reach Bran in time to warn him? What if Woberney's involvement with the Tory band was the key to the Rebels' downfall?

Shivering, Molly hugged herself with her arms.

Think! Who would know Bran's whereabouts? She dropped her arms; her expression brightened. William Sooy! The man who'd escorted her to Clamtown.

No, she thought, changing her mind. That other man, the one who was to have brought her from Clamtown to Manville! Damn, what was his name?

Cursing, Molly headed for home. She had never actually met her second escort. She and Sooy had encountered members of her Lenape family just before Clamtown. Molly had gone the rest of the way home with Midnight Hawk, Running Deer, and a number of other Lenni Lenape braves who had joined in Shelby's search for her. Sooy had been reluctant to leave Molly in the Indians' hands, but after assuring the worried man that these people were her kinfolk, he acquiesced and seemed almost relieved to be free of his charge.

Molly's discovery of the path that had obviously been used by the privateers made it extremely easy for her to leave the cove without the danger of crossing the cedar swamp. Easy enough to return someday, she thought.

Frantically she searched her brain for the name of the Clamtown resident that was to have been her next escort. Hugh? Henry? Hanley?

Hanley! she thought with excitement. That was his name, Stephen Hanley!

"You can trust the boy," Sooy had told her gruffly. "He and his brothers are true supporters of the Patriot cause."

Molly grinned at the memory of Sooy's solemn face. As if his statement that the Hanleys were

Rebels would reassure her that they were good, trustworthy men! Beard-face was a Rebel, and he was the worst spittle she'd ever had the misfortune to come across!

Ah, but what of Dickon? she reminded herself. And MacDuff? And Bran . . . She sighed wistfully. Bran. How she missed her lover! His soft touch and teasing voice . . . his commanding presence . . . even his tendency to be high-handed!

There were good men on both sides, she realized. But after what she'd learned of Darren's Pine Robbers, Molly decided that perhaps the Patriots had more good men than their Loyalist counterparts.

The next day, Molly informed Shelby of her journey. Knowing that he would try to stop her if he knew her true destination, the real reason for her journey, she'd lied to her brother, telling him that she was returning to the Shamong to see her grandfather. She was surprised when Shelby didn't insist upon accompanying her. His easy acceptance of her plans was an indication of just how preoccupied and troubled her brother was, and Molly was filled with dread.

She set out to find Stephen Hanley of Clamtown with a satchel containing provisions and the wooden box she'd taken from Bran's ship, which she'd come to regard as a talisman against evil. Something was to happen soon, she realized. Her sense of urgency increased, and she hurried along the trail, anxious to find the man she loved.

If only she knew what her brothers were up to! she thought. Yet Molly knew that if she lingered to find out, she'd reach Bran too late to help him and his men.

Preoccupied with her concerns, Molly never saw the soldier slinking low off the forest trail signal to his armed comrades. Her first awareness that she was no longer alone came when she was suddenly surrounded by several men muttering in a harsh, guttural tongue that was unfamiliar to her. She crouched, her hand hovering at her side, her thoughts on the knife strapped to her right leg beneath her tunic.

"What do you want?" she asked in English. Her dark eyes flashed defiantly. "I'm going to Clamtown. Let me through!" Some instinct told her that now was not the time to reach for the hidden knife.

The Hessians stared at her silently. She realized they were German soldiers, not only by their strange speech but by the color of their tattered uniforms. Greencoats, some called them, she remembered.

"Please," she said, starting to press forward in the hopes that they would part and let her pass.

The soldiers before her refused to move. One man jostled another, murmuring in his ear, and the pock-faced listener laughed raucously with great amusement.

Molly felt chills of apprehension. She'd suddenly become the focus of leering eyes. There were seven men in all, she noticed as she checked behind her. Her mind searched wildly for a method of escape.

A man stepped forward, his pistol trained on her heart. The commander, Molly thought, judging from his air of authority. "Fraulein, you vill come vit us!" He then rattled off a rapid spate of German to his comrades.

Molly sighed with relief when many of the Germans moved off into the woods. Most probably they were returning to camp, she thought. She was grateful that at least one of them spoke English.

"Fraulein, come!" the commander ordered, grabbing hold of her arm. He prodded her with his flintlock.

"Where're you taking me? Why can't you let me go?" she demanded, attempting to break away.

"Because, my dear," the captain said with his thick German accent, "you are a bea-u-ti-ful voman, and it has been a long time for us."

The warm assessing gleam in the Hessian leader's light eyes brought the little hairs up at the back of Molly's neck.

"Now move!" he ordered, and with a sinking heart, Molly had no choice but to obey him.

Bran stared at his friend with mixed feelings. "Mr. Dickon, in light of what you've just confessed, you realize that I must relieve you of your post?"

The first mate nodded. "Aye, sir," he said quietly.

The captain rose silently from behind his desk. He paced the length of his cabin, returning to the table where he paused to slam his fist down on the wooden surface. "For God's sake, man, what possessed you to help her escape!" Bran glared at him. "Tell me, damn it! Do you realize the consequences of your actions? Thanks to you, important documents are in the hands of our enemy!"

Dickon shifted uncomfortably.

"Mark!"

"The truth, Bran?" Mark said softly.

Bran nodded abruptly. "Aye, the truth."

"You were bewitched by her."

The captain flushed. "I wasn't . . ."

Dickon raised an eyebrow. "Then captivated perhaps." He leaned across the table, bracing himself with his hands. "You were distracted," he went on. "We . . . I," he amended quickly, "was afraid she'd interfere with our work."

"You felt I wasn't doing my job."

His friend was quick to defend him. "Not exactly, Bran. But, we . . . I saw that the men were unhappy. We had a cargo hold of gunpowder and a disgruntled crew. The last we needed was a woman on board. And you said yourself that you were going to let her go. I merely hastened things along a bit."

"We . . ." Bran murmured thoughtfully. He sat down, his face white, staring off into space. "Angus—he tried to tell me, but I didn't listen . . ." He glanced up at his friend. "He felt it too, didn't he?" His fingers clenched into fists.

Dickon's expression was an answer in itself. "Aye."

"Then I'm as guilty as you." Bran's thoughts churned with the awful discovery.

"Bran—Captain," Dickon said. "Let me bring her back. If you're right and she stole those papers, she has a great deal to answer for. I arranged her escort home. I'll bring her back myself."

"She's guilty all right," Bran said. "She stole the papers along with the box they were kept in. No

285

doubt she's glorying in the knowledge that she bested the lot of us—me, in particular." He told himself he wasn't glad that Molly had made it home safely. She had betrayed him. He no longer cared if she came to harm. "I appreciate the offer, Mark, but I have to do this myself. I have a personal bone to pick with the dear lady." His face became unreadable. "If you'd a mind to accompany me, however, I could use your help."

Dickon nodded. "Clamtown and Stephen Hanley first."

Bran's smile was grim as he agreed. *Molly, my love, you may think we're done,* he thought, *but we're not . . . not by a long shot!*

Molly sat on the ground, her hands and feet tied, her back against a gnarled tree trunk. Her eyes trained on her Hessian captors, she struggled to free her bonds. She leaned forward ever so slightly to keep her knuckles from scraping against the rough bark. But no matter how much she fought her ropes, she was unable to break free.

It was late, and the German soldiers had built a fire to roast the squirrel one of them had shot only an hour earlier, just before dark. The men were in a temper, for their food provisions were low and one small squirrel was hardly enough to feed seven men. The captain had taken Molly's satchel, and the men had quickly devoured every last crumb of her hard baked bread, every last mouthful of her dried venison. Molly had hated to see the ruffians attack her precious food supply, but when the captain had promptly claimed for his own her wooden box, she had protested loudly and fiercely, fighting the hold of the two Germans who held her by her arms.

When one young Hessian glanced her way, Molly froze and then casually leaned back against the tree so he wouldn't guess what she was doing. With a gleam in his eyes, the soldier rose to his feet and approached her. She stiffened and wished all sorts of horrible deaths for him as he came to within a few feet of her, staring down at her.

Green-backed horse-piss! she thought, glaring at the youth as he squatted before her.

The soldier bent forward to stroke Molly's cheek. "Gie werden heute abend zu mir fommen, oder ich tomme ze Thnen," he murmured.

Molly shrank back, staring at him in the shadows. She had no idea what he'd said to her, but his meaning was clear by his expression. His glittering gaze raked her from head to tied feet; he looked as if he were mentally undressing her.

She straightened, her glare mean enough to kill. "Go away," she hissed. "Leave me alone."

But instead of being deterred, the Hessian grinned, looking pleased. "Ah, a spirited one," he said in German, then in English, "Vhat I said vas, 'You vill come to me or I vill come to you.'" His voice became thick with desire. "When the others are asleep, you and I—ve vill go to another clearing, vhere I vill show you vhat it is to know a real man."

"Ha!" she spat. "You don't know what a real man is. Must a real man resort to this?" She nodded toward her bound feet, and then leaning forward, she wiggled her hands to display more rope.

"A man's power is stronger than ropes," he said huskily, bending close to breathe into her ear. He touched her hair, running his fingers down the side of her face to her throat, farther still to where the open neck of her tunic just brushed the soft upper swells of her breasts.

Gasping, she jerked away, and then grimaced when she abraded her tied hands on the tree bark.

"Soldier!" the commander called in German to Molly's admirer. "Get away from the prisoner."

"Yes, Captain," the youth replied. "I was just checking her bonds." Staring at Molly, the soldier chuckled softly, meaningfully, as he unfolded his length. "Tonight, Fraulein," he promised, his eyes gleaming wickedly. "Ve shall be alone together . . ."

Molly swallowed her fear and summed up anger instead. Anger would help her to plan her escape route logically. Fear fogged the mind; fear and panic blinded a person, getting her nowhere. Her gaze spanned the distance to the fire, encountering the captain's stare. The man's eyes narrowed and he frowned before one of his men drew his attention elsewhere.

Should she tell him of the soldier's threats? Molly wondered. Or would she merely be putting an idea in the commander's head, making matters worse for herself by doing so? What if the captain thought the youth's idea a good one? What if he decided to allow the soldier to have her, but adding himself as a party to the boy's lecherous games?

On that thought, Molly decided to keep her mouth shut. Her only chance was to continue to work at her ropes. Maybe she could rub the cord thin against the rough bark so that the hemp snapped with little pressure. Her hands might get cut in the process, she thought, but better a few minor injuries than to suffer the vile touch of her German captors.

Molly released a shaky breath as not just one, but several of the men glanced her way. What if they *all* decided they wanted her this night? She shuddered with the image. What if they surrounded her, each soldier taking his lusty time before sharing her with the next?

Swallowing against her terror, Molly began frantically rubbing the rope against the rough bark at her back.

"We've found her, Captain." Nate Redding crouched beside his commanding officer in the thick brush a few miles out of Clamtown.

Bran felt a jolt. At last! he thought. They'd finally found her. Thanks to Mark Dickon's confession, it had been a simple enough feat. "Where is she? Why didn't you make her captive?"

"She's already someone's prisoner, sir." He hesitated, looking unsure. "Hessians, Captain. The girl's in their camp, tied up under some old tree."

Fear pierced Bran's breast. Not fear, he told himself. Anger and frustration that someone else had gotten to the little lying seducer before he did.

Now who's doing the lying? an inner voice mocked him. Forcing the voice away, he shifted against the ground and wondered how best to proceed.

"It doesn't make sense, does it, Bran?" Mark said. "If she's an enemy spy, why would they be holding her prisoner?"

Bran scowled at his friend. "Hessians aren't Tories. They're German soldiers, Mark. 'Tis my wager that they've no idea whom they have within their grasp."

"Shall we just leave her there then?" Nate queried, as if it were the most natural thing in the world to travel miles in their hunt for an Indian half-breed, only to leave their quarry in the hands of the enemy.

"Absolutely not," Bran said sharply. "We're going to rescue her for ourselves. I want to see her face when she realizes that instead of being saved she's merely gone from one pair of dangerous hands to another." He paused and then added with great feeling, *"Mine."*

Molly awoke with a start. She turned her gaze to the campfire, believing the sound that had awakened her was the snap and hiss from burning twigs. But the fire had nearly burned itself out; there remained only a lingering smoke scent and the muted red glow of a dying ember in the darkness. Then what, or who, had disturbed her sleep? she wondered, her heart thumping.

Her gaze sought out the young soldier in the place where he'd bunked down earlier. To her horror, she found that the ground there was empty. The other Hessians slept on without a care while she sat dreading the moment when the young soldier hunkered before her, dragging her to her feet and then off into the woods to have his way with her.

Fortunately, she still had her knife. Unfortunately, as long as her hands were encumbered, she'd be unable to use it to defend herself. Molly searched her mind wildly, and then she smiled into the darkness. She had a plan.

A twig snapped off to her right, and Molly glanced that way, expecting the soldier to come out of the bushes in his approach.

"Fraulein," the youth whispered, and she gasped when he stooped before her, coming not from the brush as she'd expected but from the other direction, where a stream meandered not far from the German camp.

The soldier held a finger to her lips in warning before he touched her shoulder. Pressing her to bend forward, the Hessian ran his fingers down the length of her arm until he grabbed hold of the rope binding her hands. He tested the tightness of her bonds. Leaning back, he fixed her in his gaze.

"Very clever, Fraulein," he breathed, a soft chilling whisper in the night. "Clever . . . rubbing your rope against the tree, but done futilely, I can assure you." He reached behind her, jerking the rope to show its remaining strength, making Molly gasp at the sudden painful wrenching of her sore arms.

He grabbed hold of her feet with one hand, his fingers playing softly against her bare ankle. "Now, *meine Liebe,* I vill release your feet if you promise to be a good *Fraulein* and keep silent." His eyes gleamed wickedly in the night. "I can assure you that should the others avaken they vill vish to join in the fun. My touch can be gentle, *Fraulein,* but I'm sorry to say I cannot promise you the same from my comrades."

He stared at her, his hand settling about one ankle. "Vhat vill it be, *meine Liebe?* Me . . . or all of us?" His voice insinuated that he would be the better choice.

"I'll not make a sound," she promised lightly, and her jaw clenched when he smiled at her in smug satisfaction.

"Good." Withdrawing a knife from the pocket of his green coat, he cut her rope and then dragged her to stand on unsteady legs. His arm encircled her shoulders, pulling her flush against his side. "This way," he rasped into her ear, his breath increasing with the heightening of his desire.

The Hessian pulled her, and Molly stumbled along with him.

"What's your name?" she asked, making her voice sound interested and softly seductive.

"Heinrich," he murmured, sounding pleased. "I shall enjoy hearing my name on your lips vhen I spear you with my sword!" He gave a chuckle, and it took all of Molly's strength not to stiffen in revulsion.

Stars dotted the dark sky, but without the brightness of a full moon, their path was made difficult by the surrounding night. Heinrich stumbled once, nearly bringing Molly down with him in a clump of briars. Cursing, he firmed his hold on her and changed directions.

Molly's hands remained tied at her back. She was

helpless, but for her two unbound feet and the knowledge of a knife that would be discovered by the soldier if she didn't find a way to make use of it first.

"Heinrich," she said in a soft, sweet voice. "My arms—you are hurting me." She stopped to flash him a beseeching glance. "Will you untie me that I might pleasure you with my hands as well as with my . . . *lips*." Her words trailed off, thick with meaning.

Heinrich halted abruptly. She heard him swallow, saw him stiffen with renewed desire as he turned to face her. "You vould," he said in a choked, rasping voice, "pleasure me villingly?"

Oh, Bran, she thought, *where are you when I most need you?* Molly nodded. "Yes," she whispered, pressing against him. *Forgive me, Bran. I will escape soon and come to you.*

With a growl of satisfaction, the soldier led Molly farther away from the remains of the campfire. "Vhen ve get there," he promised.

"There" was a small secluded clearing several hundred yards away from the German encampment. Molly was glad for the distance; she wanted no one to hear Heinrich's cry when she finally buried her knife between the soldier's ribs.

Heinrich shoved her gently to the ground and then proceeded to cut her rope free, yet retaining a firm hold on her hands, which tingled and ached with the surge of blood to her fingertips. Molly dared not make her move yet. Her knife was still in a place beyond her reach.

"Now," Heinrich said, his breath warm in her

293

face as he changed his hold on her arms. Drawing them up and over her head, he pressed Molly's back against the hard, uncushioned ground. He shifted to cover her length, and Molly tried not to cry out as his mouth settled on her lips, gently at first, then more roughly as his desire spurred him on.

Tears came to Molly's eyes as she thought of Bran, thought of what he'd think of her if he'd ever found out to what lengths she'd gone to get free. After Bran, Heinrich's kiss was like a vile invasion of her mouth. He kept trying to force entry between her lips, but determined to deny him that pleasure, she moaned softly and turned her face away, hoping he'd be fooled by her skillfully staged response.

The soldier *was* fooled. He lifted himself away from her, his dark eyes glazed with passion, his mouth curved in a triumphant smile. "You like my kisses, *Fraulein*."

Molly swallowed the words at the tip of her tongue. Not trusting herself to speak, she nodded and was rewarded when he released her hands to cradle her face with trembling fingers.

"You have such a lovely mouth, *meine Liebe*." He kissed her, and then shuddering with desire, he gasped, "You may do vith it vhat you vill."

To her surprise, he released her to roll onto his back, obviously believing that she had become so enthralled with his manhood that she wouldn't think of doing anything but making him happy.

Molly moved slowly to her knees. He opened his eyes, and she gave him her most provocative smile. Satisfied, he closed his eyes again, and Molly shifted closer to him, reaching for the knife under her tunic at the same time.

Something must have alerted Heinrich to her actions, because suddenly she was knocked to the ground, pinned beneath Heinrich's weight. The German soldier leered at her cruelly while he held her only weapon—her last hope—in his right hand. He clicked open the blade, bringing it to where the pulse beat at the base of her throat.

"You must think me an utter fool, Fraulein," he grated, scrapping the edge of the knife against her tender skin. She flinched as the contact.

"Maggot-brain!" she derided him.

His face hardened with fury. "Slut. I vill show you vhat a man does to get even!"

He moved unexpectedly then, throwing the knife aside, capturing her lips in a brutal assault that made Molly cry out at the humiliation of it.

In defending herself, Molly became like a wild thing, kicking and hitting, struggling and biting, but Heinrich used brute strength to keep her beneath him.

Molly's tears were flowing freely now. She wouldn't let him rape her, she vowed silently as she fought against his kiss. *Oh, Bran! Love! Please . . . I need you.*

Suddenly she was free of Heinrich's weight. Gasping, shuddering, she opened her eyes and was astonished to see that the German soldier, who had been knocked senseless, was being held by two men—Mark Dickon and another man she'd seen working on Bran's ship.

"Mark!" she gasped, and was taken aback when

he glared at her hatefully.

"Well, little savage," drawled a familiar, beloved voice from behind her, "it seems you and I were destined to be reunited."

"Bran!" She shot to her feet and barreled across the clearing to launch herself at the man she loved. Hugging him was like hitting a brick wall, she noted with numb disbelief. She released him abruptly, surprised that instead of embracing her, he set her away. His expression held no fondness, no welcome for her.

Bran's eyes resembled chips of blue ice. "And to think that I believed I'd be your only lover," he drawled cuttingly.

Chapter Twenty-two

"No, Bran, it's not what you think!" Molly cried, her eyes brimming with tears. She placed her hand on Bran's arm and felt his muscles tense. "He was trying to rape me!"

The captain shrugged away from her touch. "Aye, a classic case of ravished captive." His mouth twisted. "You've played it before, I believe."

Pain lanced through her breast. "Please—"

"Dickon!" he commanded, ignoring her, shaming her before his men. "Get rid of the German's body." His blue eyes captured and held Molly's gaze. "Tie her up," he growled, turning away. His disgust for her was obvious.

Molly was too numb with pain to move, to even think of escaping. This was Bran, her beloved, who'd claimed undying love for her. What had happened to change his mind? Was it simply because she'd escaped?

Heinrich is dead, she thought, shuddering, seeing

it was true. She saw the red stain on the Hessian's back as Bran's men moved the man's lifeless body. Oh, God, when will the killing end?

A lump formed in her throat as she stared at her ex-lover, wanting to go to him, plead with him to listen and understand.

She felt someone grasp her arm. "Molly."

Swallowing against the lump, she glanced blindly at the man who held her, her dark eyes awash with tears. She heard a muttered imprecation. Blinking, she saw that it was the first mate.

"Mark," she said, her voice pleading, "what have I done?"

Dickon's fingers tightened painfully about her forearm. "You can ask such a thing without shame?" he said, sounding disbelieving.

Dumbly, she followed where Dickon led her, farther away from the threat of the Hessians. They joined the others where they'd set up camp. The mate pushed her to the ground, releasing her to unhook the ropes at his belt loop. She saw the ropes and fear struck her breast.

Molly reached up to clutch Dickon's arm. "Please," she begged, "what did I do?"

Dickon refused to answer. She played her innocence superbly, he thought. Grabbing her hands, Mark frowned upon seeing the condition of her wrists. Even in the night's muted light he could see the red rawness of her skin. He felt vaguely uneasy as he looped the rope further up her arms so that he wouldn't hurt her any more than necessary.

"Why did you take the box?" he asked, studying her face carefully.

"The box," she echoed blankly, then she flushed

298

guiltily and looked away.

"I didn't think he'd miss it," she murmured. All this over the stupid box! So she was a sentimental fool who'd wanted something belonging to the man she loved! What was so horrible about that!

"Didn't think he'd m—!" Dickon stopped, seized by anger.

Molly was taken aback by the depth of the first mate's fury. "What's so damn important about a wooden box!" she burst out, her own temper rising.

Dickon's hands settled on her ankles.

"Don't," she pleaded. "Please, I won't try to escape." She loved Bran too much to run from him. If she'd done something terribly wrong, she wanted to know what it was. And she wanted to right that wrong between them. She thought quickly. The box was now in the German captain's hands, but what if she could get it back?

Dickon studied her with cold eyes and tight lips. His head bent; his hands moved. She felt the rope about her ankle. "I beg you, not again," she said.

The first mate seemed unsympathetic to her plight. "Captain's orders," he said gruffly, and then quickly tied up her feet.

"Tell Br—the captain—I want to talk with him." Molly raised her chin with proud dignity. She wouldn't let them know how much they'd hurt her!

"I'm afraid the captain isn't in the best of moods" another voice said. A stranger stepped into Molly's line of vision. "He'll not speak with you." The face was unfamiliar to Molly, but sympathetic.

"Nate," Dickon warned.

"Just stating a fact," the newcomer said without concern. Nate left them with a casual shrug of his broad shoulders, and Molly decided that she must have imagined the man's compassionate look.

Dickon rose to his feet, his narrowed gaze observing her silently for a moment before he too turned and left her.

"I wanted something of his," she whispered, bowing her head to hide her distress. "If I've done wrong, I'm sorry." She blinked against tears. "But surely I don't deserve this!"

Sniffing, Molly studied Bran across the Rebel camp. His expression looked stern as he conversed with his men. Closing her eyes, she tried to picture a better time, a time when there was tenderness in his smile, love for her in his fiery touch.

Her heart longed for him. Her body yearned for him. But in light of his recent treatment, her mind had begun to harden itself against him.

The night lengthened and the Rebels slept, each taking a turn at keeping watch. Just before dawn, Bran rose from his circle of sleeping men and moved to where Molly lay napping on the fringe of the clearing. He stood above her, scrutinizing her pale features. The moon afforded enough light for him to see her clearly. Her hair was unbound, a wild tangle of raven silk about her face and neck, cascading over her shoulders to drape her breasts. Bran swallowed, remembering the raven strands against her dusky-nipples.

He stared, forcing the memory away. Dark lashes feathered her smooth cheeks. Her lips, which looked pink and perfect for a man's kisses, appeared softly relaxed in her state of sleep.

Why in bloody hell did she have to be so beautiful?

Something twisted in his belly as his gaze moved from her chin to her breasts, gliding farther to her waist and thighs. He had a sharp vision of her naked form. He could almost feel the satin texture of her taut stomach against his hard belly, the subtle curve of her hips beneath his hands as he held her firmly while he thrust himself deep within her.

Bran inhaled sharply, closing his eyes. God, how perfect her breasts had fit his hands! As if she'd been created and designed especially for him!

His staff hardened within his breeches as he recalled how she'd bucked against him in the throes of their lovemaking, writhing savagely, responding passionately to his demands.

She was a consummate actress.

Opening his eyes, he glared at her. *Why, Molly? Why did you betray me?* He'd loved her, for God's sake! And she'd used that love to further her own ends!

Drawn to her despite himself, Bran reached out as if to touch her, his fingers aching to cup her face, his mouth longing to kiss every intimate inch of her. She was a lying, conniving bitch, whose only thought had been to seduce him in order to gain information. How excited she must have been to have found important Rebel documents!

His hand fell to his side, his fingers like white-knuckled claws that itched to grab hold of her pretty neck and tighten and squeeze until she ceased to torment him.

Molly stirred in her sleep, frowning as if protesting her bonds even in her dream state. Suddenly her eyes flew open to meet Bran's gaze.

"Bran," she murmured, smiling at him seduc-

301

tively. He saw her face transform with awareness of his presence. Her joyful expression vanished as she attempted to sit up.

"Heathen," he said, feeling strangely disappointed at the change in her features.

"Have you come to do your vilest, *Kuinishkuun?*" she said coldly.

Bran's smile was grim. Despite what she'd done, despite her betrayal, he had to admire the woman's show of spirit.

"Kuin-ish-kuun?" he asked, as if she'd willingly tell him what the word meant. If there was one thing he'd learned about Molly McCormick it was that she spoke words of Lenape only when she was agitated or deeply moved . . . or sexually aroused.

"Pig trotter!" she taunted. "Twice you have taken me prisoner for some imagined crime! Twice!"

The captain raised an eyebrow. "And the box? Are you saying that you didn't steal it?"

"And if I did?" Molly challenged.

Bran looked like thunder. "Then you are as guilty as sin, my sweet savage." He thought of the Hessian. "You can forget the act of outraged innocence, for I of all people know that you lie!"

Molly struggled to rise, but the ropes about her ankles hindered her, and she fell back with a cry of pain, glaring at him and breathing hard. "What is so damned important about a stupid wooden box?"

The captain's eyes flashed. "As if you didn't know!"

"I don't know," she said, trying again to stand before him. She wouldn't allow him to look down at her! She would stand before him on equal footing, hold up her head, straighten her spine. She'd

302

done nothing wrong! The ropes burned her ankles, and she toppled back again, tears of frustration and pain filling her eyes.

"I could get the box back for you, she said.

Bran perked up at that. "You'd get it back?" His voice held suspicion.

Molly nodded, confused by his odd fascination with an engraved wooden box. "The Greencoats—the captain—he took it away. But if you'd let me go, I could sneak into their camp and steal it back."

Steal. The word hung tensely in the air between them. Staring at Bran's changing features, Molly recalled a time when she'd feared telling him of her flight from Reginald Cornsby, feared that he'd believe her to be the thief the storekeeper had accused her of being.

Molly's heart tripped. And now she'd just told him that she would steal for him.

"I won't release you," he said, his brows forming a dark, angry line. Even now she tried to trick him, he thought furiously. Did she think him so enamored of her charms that he'd forgive her so easily? "You expect much if you think I'd accept your word."

"My God!" she cried. "What have I done? Take a stupid box? It's not as if it were anything of importance!"

Bran reached down, grabbing her by her tunic, dragging her to her feet to crush her against him. "You pretend those papers don't exist? How dare you!"

Molly felt the angry heat of him sear her flesh through her deerskin tunic. "What papers?" she choked as he caught her by the hair, bending her head back to pin her with his icy gaze. "I know of no papers! The box was empty!"

"Liar!" he accused. Disgusted, he dropped her like a sack of potatoes. The thud made by her fall seemed to echo about the quiet night.

"Please . . ." she said when his eyes suddenly took on a strange gleam, ". . . the Greencoats."

"They're dead. My men killed every last one of them." His lips curled. "This is war. Did you think we'd camp near the enemy?"

Molly paled. "While they slept," she said.

Bran acknowledged her perception with a nod. His eyes flamed with desire as his gaze traveled her length, lingering on her breasts. Molly shrank back as she saw his intent.

"No, Bran," she protested wildly. "Not like this! Your men —"

"They sleep soundly. They'll not disturb us."

Molly's breath caught. Lust had transformed his features. Lust, she thought, hating the look, and his desire to punish me for a wrong I didn't commit.

"I've taken no papers. There were none!" she cried. In her pain, she wanted to hit him, scream at him! He wouldn't touch her in anger, she vowed. She fought to be free of her ropes.

Rage made her face red. Pain seared her breast. She vented her spleen in an angry, highly imaginative spate of Lenni Lenape. She was breathing hard when she was done. Her midnight eyes flashed with fire; her nose flared angrily.

"What are these papers?" she snarled, glaring up at him. "You won't tell me? You won't listen? I've done nothing wrong, but nothing I say will make you believe that."

Something moved in Bran's expression. He was shocked at the depth of Molly's fury. Would a guilty one rage so? The box he got back from the Germans was empty . . .

His eyes narrowed. "This is some new kind of trick," he decided aloud. "I was wrong. You're a better player at games than I. If only I'd realized it sooner, I could have saved lives."

"You believe I . . . ?" She couldn't say it. Her pain was beyond imagination. Bran believed her responsible for death! Did he believe, too, that she'd faked her love for him? That everything they'd shared had been a lie?

The thought saddened her. He believed she'd seduced him so she could steal his precious box! She cursed. She didn't even know the box existed until she'd happened upon it in Bran's sea chest!

Molly grew weary of fighting him. "I swear on my dead mother's soul that I know nothing of your papers," she whispered.

Bran stiffened. "On your mother's soul . . ." He hunkered down beside her, capturing her face within his large hands. "You would defile your parent's spirit with your lies?"

The captain pierced her with his blue gaze, as if he were trying to read her mind. She met his gaze unflinchingly, hoping, praying that he'd realize the truth. His eyes narrowed. His lips firmed, as did his grip on her chip.

"No. No, I don't think you would," he said finally. He released her chin. "Perhaps you're telling the truth." He sounded relieved.

305

Molly sighed, closing her eyes. Her lips trembled; her heart beat wildly, joyfully, for Bran had begun to unbend.

"Molly."

Her eyes opened. Bran's voice had grown husky. His blue eyes glowed hotly, searing her. There was desire in his look, but it had mellowed; there was no more look of punishment.

He touched her face. His fingers tingled against her cheekbone, gliding upward to tangle in her hair.

"Bran," she murmured. He believed her. She had something she had to say to him, she thought, frowning. What?

The warmth of his nearness enveloped her, rushing blood to all parts of her.

Woberney. The name came to her. *Hugh Woberney is a traitor.*

"Bran—" she began, but then Bran shifted closer to her, and Molly's mind went blank as he kissed her. Her body hummed with life. Her heart echoed her thoughts: Bran, I love you!

Whimpering, wanting only to be closer to him, Molly leaned into his kiss, and then gasped as her movement tightened her bonds. The hemp cut into her flesh. She winced, not wanting to end the contact with Bran's mouth, but the pain invaded her pleasure, and Molly fell back, her eyes alight with passion and pain.

"Please," she said, not knowing exactly what it was she was asking of him.

He moved away, and she wanted to cry out. He untied her feet and then his fingers were at her arms.

Bran cursed himself for wanting to believe her,

for the hot flame of desire that had invaded his groin and filled his manhood to erection. He found he was unable to keep himself from lifting her wrists to study the abraded skin, from bending to kiss the damage. He heard Molly gasp, and he raised his head. His eyes glowed as he assessed her features, pleased but not entirely taken in by the soft yearning he saw there.

"Please, there's something I must tell you," she whispered, and Molly knew what it was she wanted from him. She wanted to heal the hurt between them, bridge the gap that mistrust, misunderstanding, and incriminating circumstance had created. She wanted to tell him of Rebel treachery and then to feel his fire. Molly licked her lips. "Woberney—"

Bran's lips stopped her words. Closing her eyes, Molly gave into the feelings. Woberney could wait, she decided, opening her mouth for Bran's tongue.

Bran groaned and helped her to rise. They moved farther off into the woods where they could be alone, where their cries of passion couldn't be heard. They stopped in a shelter of short pines in a clearing hidden from all who might pass it. There Molly felt Bran's arms surround her. Embracing him, she trembled. She knew the sweet-scented warmth of his breath as he recaptured her lips.

A sense of urgency invaded Molly's limbs; tears of joy washed away the sting of heartbreak.

"Molly," he murmured when his head rose. Doubt had invaded his thoughts. His hands fastened on her arms like silken steel. "Why did you take the box? How did you find it?" His voice was a satin caress, bent on seducing answers from her.

Before Molly could gather her wits, he quickly

recaptured her lips again, wringing from her a soft moan of pleasure. He worked his magic, teasing her lips apart, darting his tongue inside her mouth to deepen the intimacy and the pleasure. He felt his flesh respond, allowing passion free reign for only a brief moment before he pulled it under control.

Bran pulled back to stare at her flushed features, her passion-glazed eyes, her quivering mouth.

The haze disappeared and Molly could see Bran's face. Coldness invaded her warmth as she studied him, seeing his look of purpose and hard intent. Then she realized what he'd asked, and she wondered if he was merely using her to gain information. The thought enveloped her like a dash of frigid water. It chilled her to the core, invading her soul.

But then Molly thought she must have been imagining things, for Bran had tenderly drawn her to his breast once again. He kissed her, running his hands over her with reverence. He sipped from her lips and dipped to taste her sweet nectar. Groaning, she felt him shudder beneath her hands, which had moved to his muscled chest.

He was both gentle and forceful as he kissed and caressed her and lowered her to the soft bed of pine needles. He was the man she loved as he lifted her tunic, sliding his hands up her thighs, over her hips, and along her stomach as he did so. Then Bran paid homage to her breasts—moist, loving homage with lips and tongue and teeth and fingertips. And Molly gasped and clutched at his dark head. Tears of joy spilled from her eyes and trickled down her cheeks. She'd thought she'd lost him; now he was hers.

Bran tasted her tears and grew inflamed with a passion that blocked out all worries, all concerns of betrayal, until his thoughts centered on making love to the woman who gave to him freely, who responded wildly to his every touch.

She was like a woman possessed as he pulled off her tunic. She touched him wherever she could, kissed him wherever she could reach. Her frenzied display of passion raised the heat in Bran's loins until he was as wildly aroused as she.

While he fought to undress her, she tore at his clothes. He heard her growl of frustration, when their limbs tangled in the process, felt her hands slip under his shirt to caress his chest. He laughed huskily and removed her hands. Only when she was naked with only the moonlight to cloak her did he allow her to pull at his clothes. She rose to her knees as she tugged the shirt up and over his head.

Bran stared at the golden, rose-tipped globes that hung temptingly before him as she tossed the shirt aside. He reached out to cup one delicious mound, sampling the fruit with moistened lips.

Molly gasped, clutching at his shoulders. He suckled the tip until she shook and whimpered and arched her neck. He pressed her to lie back, then he stood, shucked his breeches, and joined her again on the soft bed of fragrant pine needles. He began a thorough, leisurely exploration of Molly's naked curves . . . down her throat . . . over satin breasts . . . along taut stomach—pausing a moment to dip his tongue in her navel . . . down, down, down until he came to the dark curly triangle that shielded her femininity.

As Bran's lips brushed magic across her sensitive

309

flesh, Molly closed her eyes, feeling lethargic, glorying in the warm sensation of being loved. When Bran cupped her mound, she stiffened, but then she relaxed, for his fingers were gentle, feather-light. She jerked with startled surprise as he kissed her there—in that most secret part of her.

"It's all right, love," Bran soothed as she froze and tried to get up with fear of the unknown. "I only wish to love you a little with my mouth."

Molly tried to relax. Bran helped by stroking her legs, her belly, everywhere but *there*. Then, when she felt as if she were floating on air, he bent his head. Molly's eyes widened and then closed as he kissed her intimately. Sensations curled and spiraled and radiated and pulsated from the point of his attention outward. She felt his mouth between her thighs, experienced the feeling in her nipples . . . her toes . . . her fingertips . . . *everywhere* . . .

"Please," she choked out when she knew she was about to shatter into shards of sensation.

Bran rose, smiling at her. His blue eyes were tender and hot and alive. Molly reached for him. He obliged her by covering her with his hard length. She was ready for him when he entered her. His first thrust was gentle, the second harder, and those that followed were fierce and fast and deep.

"Bran," she gasped. "Love!" She wrapped her arms and legs about him tightly.

"Molly!" he said with a husky groan. Molly was so soft, so wild—she wasn't acting, he knew it now. No one could love with such abandon, with such depth, and not be sincere. He increased his movements, kissing her, murmuring love words, driving Molly and himself up to the peak.

She didn't betray me! She told the truth! The realization was enough to drive Bran over the edge, and he took his love with him as he soared to new heights.

Chapter Twenty-three

"I don't want to leave you." Molly's gaze memorized every facet of her beloved's features: his dark, masculine eyebrows, his eyes of bright blue, his sensual lips, his firm jaw. He was bare-chested but for a dark blue waistcoat, left unbuttoned to combat the late August heat. His thigh muscles stretched his knee breeches, made of buff-colored linen that was dirt-stained and travel-worn. Bran sported no hose, but was bare-foot; his calves appeared rock-hard and bronzed beneath the gathering about his knees. He presented a virile, sensual picture.

"I know," Bran murmured for her ears alone. His smile was tender. "I hate to see you go. I'll miss you, my sweet savage."

"When will I see you again?" she asked, her heart already aching with her impending departure. *I love everything about him,* she thought. She loved the way his raven hair looked unbound, hanging about his broad shoulders . . . and those times he wore it bound back in his ribbon-tied queue—like it was now. When he didn't immediately answer, she suggested, "In the cove? Dickon gave you my message, didn't he? About meeting at the cove after the war . . . on the first spring morning?"

Bran's lips firmed as he glanced over at his former first mate. "Lovely idea, sweet," he said. When he faced Molly again his expression was clear of any anger he felt for Mark Dickon. "But let's change that, shall we? Let's make it the second morning after the war, whatever the season."

Molly beamed, nodding. But Bran already regretted his words of promise. Would he be able to keep it? What if when the war ended his ship was more than two days' journey away?

His gaze caressing the woman he loved, he made a silent vow that he would keep that promise . . . if he had to sprout wings and fly to do so! "Molly, two of my men will see you home."

"You will remember what I told you?" she asked, her eyes bright with anxiety. "About Woberney?"

That morning after they'd made love, Molly had confessed what she'd learned in Manville. When asked, she told Bran that she'd heard it as she stood outside the general store. She implied that her eavesdropping had been accidental; concern for her brothers kept her from telling Bran the whole truth.

She lowered her voice. "Beware of that other traitor! The one who is close to you. You will be careful?"

Bran kissed her sweet lips. "Aye, little heathen," he said with affection. "I'll be careful."

313

Her whole body seemed to sigh with her relief. She touched his cheek with light fingertips.

"I love you," she whispered, her eyes filling with tears. "I will miss you, Taande Wee-lan-o." Bran raised his eyebrow in question. Molly smiled and then caught her breath at a certain memory. She shivered and closed her eyes briefly. "You are Taande Wee-lan-o." She paused and then explained, "Fire Mouth."

Surprise transformed Bran's features. Surprise and pleasure at her choice of a name for him.

He felt like he was drowning as he gazed into her eyes, two dark, shimmering orbs. He saw the bright red coloring of Molly's cheeks. His gaze flamed with renewed passion.

"Bran." Nate Redding approached the couple. "We're ready to go."

Bran nodded. "Molly," he said gently, "Nate here is one of the men who will be taking you home. Nate Redding," he introduced him. "Nate, Molly McCormick." Molly was thrilled by Bran's look and possessive tone.

Nate's eyes narrowed at the captain's implied warning. Then he smiled at his charge. "Manville? It should take us but a day to get there."

Molly inclined her head. "I live a mile or two outside the village. The journey shouldn't take long." She turned to the man she loved, knowing the time had come to say good-bye. "Bran, I —"

"Mr. Redding," Bran drawled drily, "if you would wait by Kenneth Jones?" The man shrugged and moved off to leave the lovers alone.

"Molly, I . . ." Bran studied her pale face, her

tear-bright eyes, and felt that he'd never before experienced such agony. That's not true, he told himself. Believing she'd betrayed him had been an agony just short of a slow, torturous death.

Heedless of the other Rebel seamen, Molly didn't wait for Bran to finish. She threw herself into his arms, kissing him with all the fervor, all the desperation she felt at having to leave him.

"Godspeed, Bran!" she choked out as she pulled away. Then Molly turned from him abruptly. "Mr. Redding!" she called, waving a hand to signal her escort. "I'm ready to go home."

Bran watched her leave him without a backward glance. "Mr. Dickon," he said briskly, forcing the pain away that had lodged in his chest. "To Clamtown!"

Shelby stared at his brother across the crude tabletop. "Molly's gone to the Lenape."

"She lied to you, little brother," Darren said. "I saw her direction; she went toward Clamtown." He hid his satisfaction at seeing Shelby's anger. Anger directed at their dear half sister.

"Why?" Shelby asked, sounding unconvinced. "Why would she lie?"

"To return to her Rebel friends?" Darren stood abruptly, not bothering to hide his fury at the thought of Molly's involvement with the enemy.

"No!" Shelby shook his head. "She was kidnapped, you heard her say so. Just because they didn't hurt her doesn't mean she's sided with them."

"Think, brother!" Darren growled. "How do you think she escaped unharmed? Perhaps one took her for his doxy, perhaps she's convinced herself she's in love with him." He paused. "A woman in love will risk much for her man."

Silence hung heavily in the McCormick cabin as both brothers remembered their father and Shi'ki-Xkwe. Molly's mother had given up much to be with the man she loved: life with her people, her father's love.

"You don't know this to be true!" Shelby insisted. "She wouldn't hurt us."

"You, perhaps," Darren said. His lips curling, he bent forward, his hands on the back of his chair. "My sister has as much love for me as I do for her."

"She would not betray you!"

"No?" Darren looked skeptically. "What if she believes we mean danger to her lover?"

"She has no lover!"

"Bran Donovan." Darren spoke with the surety of knowing it to be true.

Shelby gasped. His hands clenched. "How do you know this?"

"I heard her call his name while she slept."

Bran and his men made Clamtown within hours. They headed to Falkinburg's Tavern first. *If Hugh Woberney is there,* Bran thought, *so much to our advantage.*

A chance meeting of men in a local tavern would not arouse Woberney's suspicions, as would confronting the man in his own home. If Molly was right, and Hugh Woberney was a traitor to the Rebel smugglers, then Bran wanted the man to gain a false sense of security. Only then could Bran learn more of the enemy—the Pine Robbers led by a man called Darren. In the course of events Hugh Woberney would condemn himself, Bran believed. The captain would not kill a man without evidence of his betrayal—not on the basis of a few overheard words.

The *Bloody Mary* was moored off the Jersey coast, not far from Clamtown. Bran discharged two of his four remaining men, Mark Dickon and Terence Walden, to return to the ship. The captain had reinstated Dickon as first mate. Despite what Mark had done, Bran found that he still trusted the man. Dickon had been wrong to let Molly go, but Bran realized that the first mate had firmly believed he'd been acting in the best interest of all concerned. In the best interests of the ship.

Bran told Dickon of Molly's warning. Dickon would inform only Bran's brother, Pat, who was to come to the ship later that day; Josiah Morse, who was to accompany Pat; and Angus MacDuff, Bran's trusted friend, of the traitor. Bran decided to keep Molly's other warning—of a possible traitor on board the ship—to himself. He alone would watch and wait and discern who it might be.

Dickon and Walden left. Bran ordered the two men to wait outside, and then the captain entered the tavern alone.

Falkinburg's Tavern was filled with patrons, imbibing freely. The sound of their raucous laughter filtered out through the open windows, as did the smell of stale liquor and men's sweat. As Bran entered through the scarred painted door, a man called to him from across the room. Bran's eyes widened. It was Josiah Morse.

Josiah rose as Bran made his way casually to his friend's table. The keeper of the Jug and Barrel smiled as Bran pulled out a chair and sat down.

"What's up?" Bran asked, his brow furrowing.

Josiah held up his hand to silence further talk. A comely looking wench had come up to their table and was giving Bran a thorough once-over.

"Your pleasure?" Her gaze and her tone were an open invitation.

Bran was amused. "Any suggestions?" His voice was thick with meaning.

Smiling, the girl cupped and lifted her voluptuous breasts.

The captain arched an eyebrow. "Tempting," he murmured, "but I'm afraid, my sweet, that this night my thirst seeks something wet." He paused for effect. "And cold."

The wench grinned without disappointment, for Bran's rejection of her charms had been tempered with a hint of regret. "Ale?"

"A *cold* one," he emphasized. She left with an exaggerated sway of her heavy hips. The practiced smile vanished from Bran's expression as he turned back to his friend.

Josiah chuckled. "I have to hand it to you, son. When it comes to women, you're the master. You sure know how to handle them!"

Bran relaxed. "Hardly!" he said, thinking of

318

Molly McCormick. He grinned. If Morse could laugh about the way Bran handled the wench, then the news couldn't be too terrible.

"Right!" Josiah agreed.

Understanding his friend's hidden meaning, Bran felt himself redden. "What brings you here? We didn't expect to see you."

"We?"

"Smith and Talbot are outside," Bran said.

Josiah nodded. His face darkened. "The bastards—they've done it again!"

Bran inhaled sharply. "Sam Thoms's run?"

"I'm afraid so." Glancing behind Bran, Josiah shifted his seat.

Bran looked up to find the tavern maid's smiling eyes on him. The woman set down a tankard of ale, and the captain thanked her most graciously. He then dismissed her with a polite nod. "All dead?" he asked.

"Two of three. Hanley, the youngest boy, suffered a gunshot wound, but he's all right. Pretended to be dead, and the Tories left him, thank God!"

Bran murmured his agreement. "What of the boy? Where is he now?"

Josiah smiled. "That's why I'm here. Bless the boy, but he heard the men talking." He reached out across the tabletop, but Bran had raised his right arm to take a sip of the cool ale. "Darren McCormick," he said.

Bran's arm froze on its way down. "What?"

"Darren McCormick," Josiah repeated, oblivious to the new tension in his young friend. "John heard the name of the Tory bastards' leader. We

319

knew of Darren. Now we have a surname. It should be easy enough to find him."

"And that's why you're here." A hard cold lump had settled within Bran's chest. McCormick. As in Molly McCormick. Could Darren McCormick be her father? Her brother? He told himself to calm down. There was no evidence that his McCormick and the Tory McCormick had any connection at all.

"Yes. We've traced the name to a family near Manville. An odd family, actually. An old drunk and his three children. Our man Darren is a son. Apparently he has a brother . . ." Josiah's expression changed as he saw Bran's face.

"And a sister?" Bran inquired drily. When Josiah nodded, it took all the captain had in him to conceal his inner turmoil. "When did this happen?"

"Day before yesterday." Josiah stared at the younger man. "Bran, that girl, Molly—"

"Molly McCormick," Bran confirmed.

"Shit!" the innkeeper swore.

Bran's thoughts ran along the same line. Biting back the fierce anger that threatened to erupt with violence, Bran excused himself for a moment and went outside to speak with his men.

"Talbot," he addressed the younger of the two, "do you know Manville?" The boy nodded. "I want you and Smith here to find Redding and Jones. Tell them to stay behind to watch the girl. Her brother's name is Darren." He paused. "The Tory robber."

He saw Talbot's eyes widen before he and Smith exchanged a look of understanding. Bran gave his men further orders, including the command that they send word of anything they witnessed that was unusual. He went back inside the tavern, wondering about Hugh Woberney. Now that he knew Molly's game, should he bother with Woberney? Most likely she'd taken his name from the stolen lists.

Rejoining Josiah, Bran told his friend of Molly and the warning she'd given to mislead them. Then he and Josiah began to discuss a plan for capturing the Tory raiders.

Molly stopped her two escorts when she was within a half mile of home. "It's best if I go the rest of the way alone."

Nate Redding frowned, but it was Kenneth Jones who spoke up, "But, miss, the captain said . . ."

She turned to the young seaman. "I know what Bran said." Her smile was warm. "My father's cabin is just beyond those trees. I'll be fine."

"Donovan isn't going to be happy," Nate said, his eyes following the path of her pointing finger.

"Then don't tell him, and he won't be." Molly chuckled softly at the horror on the sailors' faces. She felt warmed by the men's loyalty and respect for their commander, the man she loved. "Tell Bran that I wanted it this way. My father . . ." her smile faded. ". . . he drinks heavily. If he sees me with you, he may think . . ." She stopped and sighed heavily before going on, "I can't be responsible for his actions."

Nate's gaze flickered with understanding. "Jones, let's go. I'm sure Miss McCormick is anxious to be home." His last statement posed a question.

Molly nodded. "I am anxious to get home. My brothers worry."

Seeming satisfied with her response, Nate captured her hand and bowed over it with flourish. "It was a pleasure traveling with you, my lady," he said, his tone teasing.

Molly dipped her head. "Thank you, kind sir. May your return journey be a safe one."

And then Bran's men were gone. Molly continued home alone, a faint smile lingering on her lips.

Molly's smile faded the instant she opened the cabin door.

"So the prodigal sister returns," Darren said sarcastically. He rose from his chair.

The sound of their father's snoring filled the room. Molly glanced toward Tully's bed and saw him sprawled out across the mattress in the throes of a drunken sleep, his eyes closed, his mouth open.

"Did you see your lover?" Darren asked.

Molly paled as her gaze met his. "What lover? What are you talking about? I went to see Wood Owl."

"Liar," Darren accused. "You went to Clamtown."

He circled the table, coming up to his half sister's right side. Grabbing her arm, he leaned close. "Tell me, how is Bran Donovan?"

She gasped and tried to pull free. Her brother's hold tightened until she winced with pain. "I tell you—"

"And I tell you that I know where you went. I

saw where you went." Darren's eyes flashed. "To Clamtown." He pulled her across the room, forcing her to sit on the chair he'd vacated.

The snoring sounded loud in the ensuing silence, reverberating about the small room.

Darren glared at his sister. "I know about your lover. You have lain with him; I have a witness."

"Witness?" she exclaiming, rising. "Traitor, you mean!" Darren put his hand on her shoulder and slammed her down hard.

"You're the traitor! You would betray your family!"

"I've betrayed no one!"

"You deny that you love Donovan?" When she didn't answer immediately, Darren's lips twisted into a cruel smile. "I didn't think so."

"All right, so I love him! He's good and kind and he doesn't enjoy killing!"

Darren's face went red. "Ah, well, then I guess he has me there, dear sister, because I do, you see. And now that I have the lure, I'll enjoy killing Bran Donovan." He paused. "And enjoy watching his lover's torment as he suffers a slow, agonizing death!"

Molly's blood turned cold. "You wouldn't," she whispered.

His harsh, maniacal laughter drowned out Tully McCormick's snores. "Oh, I would, dear sister. I most definitely would!"

She struggled to rise. "Shelby—"

Darren stopped her. "You'll find no quarter from Shelby, Molly. Not when he learns the truth of your Rebel love!"

323

"Father!"

Her brother snorted. "You'll get no help there," he said with disgust. "He's drunk, as usual."

Darren jerked her up by grabbing hold of her tunic. "Come, dear sister." Darren pulled her toward the door. "You and I, well, we're goin' to take a little trip."

"A trip?" Molly gasped. "Where?"

"You'll see," was all he said. But Molly didn't care for his tone or the evil glint in his green eyes.

"Shelby . . ."

Darren's smile was wicked. "Oh, he'll join us soon enough, I imagine." His face transformed, and he looked angry. "Let's go," he ordered. And he shoved Molly outside the cabin.

Chapter Twenty-four

Hugh Woberney couldn't be found anywhere. Bran had questioned the town residents, searched the man's home, but there was no sign of the Rebel smuggler. No one had seen him in days. Woberney hadn't visited Falkinburg's Tavern for the past two weeks.

Seated behind his chart table, Bran frowned. *Where in the hell is Woberney? Is Molly right? Is he a traitor to the Rebel cause?*

Patrick Donovan rose from the bottom bed rack. Josiah Morse sat on the only other chair in the captain's stateroom, his dark thoughts reflected on his aging face.

"What do we do now?" Pat asked.

Bran looked up from a map of the area. "What can we do?" His brow furrowing, he ran a finger along the mark that represented the Little Egg Harbor River. "We wait," he said, "until we hear from Redding and the others."

The others included a man stationed at Falkinburg's Tavern, two Rebels farther inland at the

Forks in the house of Richard Wescoat, and Mark Dickon, who was well on his way to Long-A-Coming to keep his ears open at the inn there.

The *Bloody Mary* remained moored off the coast at Little Egg Harbor.

"How long do we have to wait?" Pat cried. He rubbed his leg, which still pained him from the bayonet wound he'd received several weeks ago at Cutter's Point. "I say we should take the girl. If she's a member of the robbing bastards, then we can use her as bait. Especially if she's Darren's sister."

"Do you honestly think that they'd send every man to rescue her?" Bran scowled at his younger brother. "Not bloody likely! Better she stays free so we can watch her."

"Bran's right," Josiah said quietly. " 'Tis better to keep an eye on the girl. As long as she doesn't realize she's being watched, there's a good chance she'll led us straight to their headquarters. Somehow, I doubt that even Darren would attempt a rescue, even if Molly is his sister. He'd send his underlings, but he'd dare not risk his own self, not when he's the brain behind all their plans."

Bran didn't want to think of Molly's involvement in all this. He kept remembering the sweet, abandoned way she'd given herself to him. Her soft breasts, her wet kisses . . . No one could fake that kind of response, he told himself. No one. He forced his thoughts elsewhere. "What in God's name are they doing with all the goods?"

Josiah gave him an even smile. "They use what they need and sell the rest. I've heard there's a lucrative market in New York. A successful one, thanks to the damn Britons."

A knock resounded on the cabin hatch, and three sets of eyes glanced toward the door. "Come in!" Bran called.

The young petty officer saluted. "Captain," Michael Talbot said. "We found Redding, sir, just like you wanted."

Gaze narrowing, Bran stood. He thought the boy seemed anxious for some reason. "And?"

"We went to her house, sir. It wasn't far, you see, not by the time we reached them." The boy sounded worried; his words gushed forth. "We came to the cabin, and she—Miss Molly—we saw her being dragged out of the cabin by a man, Captain. We think it was he, their leader, Darren. A big man with red hair and a mean gaze."

Bran felt his breath catch painfully. "The girl—was she being mistreated?"

Talbot swallowed, nodding. "He struck her, sir. He looked awful mad. Jones, he wanted to go to her, but Nate wouldn't let him." He paused. "The man—he had a gun to her head."

Bran's thought whirled angrily with fear. What kind of man would strike and threaten his own sister? A desperate one, he thought. *A man who believed he'd been betrayed.*

"Where are the others?" Pat asked, coming to stand beside his older brother.

"They stayed behind to follow them," Talbot said.

"Good!" It was Josiah who'd spoken Bran's very thought.

"I must go after her," Bran muttered. "If he dares to hurt one hair on Molly's head—"

"I'll go," Pat said. "What if it's a trap? What if they realized she was being followed? Besides, Bran, you're needed here on board ship. At least until we hear from Dickon and those other two near the Forks. Who are they? Percy Weston and—"

Bran's response was automatic. "Weston and Smithers. John Smithers."

His brother nodded, his eyes gleaming.

The captain, however, was filled with the urgent need to see Molly again, to assure himself that she was all right.

Patrick stared at his brother, perhaps reading Bran's thoughts. "I know the area well," he said, defending his position. His gaze never left Bran's face. "Much better than you."

"And who would oversee the ship in your absence, Bran?" Josiah asked.

MacDuff, Bran thought. And then he realized that Angus had left the ship, the Scot having volunteered to be the emissary between their men afield and Bran.

MacDuff wasn't due back for hours. Too long a wait to send help to Redding's party of three men.

As much as he abhorred the thought of remaining behind, he realized it was for the best, even when every fiber of his being cried out to join the rescue of Molly, the woman he loved.

The cabin was silent; the air was tense as the three men waited for Bran's decision.

"Go!" Bran's expression was fierce, his jaw clenching. "Go and keep her safe." His voice was husky, raw with emotion.

"If she's innocent, I'll bring her back," Patrick

328

vowed, meeting his brother's vibrant blue gaze. "But if she's not . . ."

A shutter dropped over Bran's rugged features. "Do what you have to do," he rasped.

Molly glared at Reginald Cornsby. "Tut-mouthed leech!" she hissed. She struggled against her ropes. She was in a tent deep in the New Jersey Pines, a prisoner of the notorious Tory Pine Robbers. And she was at the mercy of the lecherous storekeeper.

"I knew we would meet again, but I didn't dare hope that it would be under such . . ." he paused, ". . . delightful circumstances." Cornsby's eyes gleamed with lascivious delight. He had the girl right where he wanted her.

"My brother—" she began.

"Your brother," he said, "has made me your official keeper." He paused, his smile one of malicious triumph. "You're mine to handle as I see fit." He laughed, a sound that slithered down Molly's spine like chilled oil.

She inhaled sharply. "You're lying. Shelby won't allow—"

"Ah!" Cornsby's features turned hard. "The other brother. The O'Reilly."

Molly looked at him as if he'd taken leave of his senses, and the storekeeper squatted beside her, his fat belly making his movements difficult. "He lied that day," Cornsby said. "To keep me off your trail." He didn't seem angry as he leaned close. The man was apparently too fascinated with Molly's physical charms.

"Your brother Shelby would risk much for you,"

329

he murmured, his hand reaching to lift and finger Molly's hair. She recoiled from his nearness, and he tugged on the dark strands until the pain brought tears to Molly's eyes. "Yes, dear Shelby would do much for his little sister." He jerked her hair hard. "Even lie!"

"My brother loves me!" She faced him bravely despite the pain, despite the tears.

"One of your brothers loves you," Cornsby pointed out. He stared, mesmerized by her smooth satin skin. She felt his hot and sour breath upon her face and was repulsed.

His hand moved to caress her cheek. Molly spun her head, biting a fleshy finger. The man pulled back, gasping with pain. "Bitch!" he snarled, and backhanded her across the face.

Molly's head snapped back under the impact. Pain made her dizzy, but she regained her wits to face her tormentor defiantly. "Don't touch me!"

The man's face went red with rage. "Oh, I'll touch you," he said softly, too softly. "As often and . . ." His hand grabbed her breast, squeezing hard, making Molly wince, ". . . as intimately as I want!"

"I'll kill you, you dub-snouted pig-licker!" Molly spat. "I'll kill you in the night!" Her gaze hardened; an air of cool control settled about her. "Beware of sleeping, Reginald Cornsby. For I've called down evil spirits to lift your scalp."

She managed to shift away from him, closer to a wooden crate, which was one of several boxes that were stored in the crudely constructed shelter. Cornsby watched her, but didn't attempt to touch her again.

"Beware," Molly continued in a low, even voice. "They come in the night to cut me free. The *chi-'paiuk* will be of the Iroquois," she said, a chilling look in her dark eyes. "Do you know of the *men'gwe*, storekeeper? Do you know what they do to their men captives?"

She stared, waiting. Reginald Cornsby had leaned back. He looked pale, more than a little nervous, and Molly stifled a smile. Indians, she thought. It was easy to frighten white men like Cornsby, who didn't understand them.

"First they tie you up between two great stakes, spread like an eagle." Her voice lowered as she went on, "Next they build a *taande*—a fire. A big smoking flame with lots of sticks and many logs."

Molly tossed back her hair with a jerk of her head, her level gaze holding the man's. "The *men'gwe* like to feast on their captives, Reginald Cornsby. They cut you open while you watch. Laughing, they pull out your entrails and skewer them to cook over the big fire. Then," she growled, "they rip into your flesh with their teeth."

The storekeeper swallowed. "You're just trying to scare me!"

Molly stared at him. "Am I?"

A loud commotion outside the tent drew the nervous man's attention. He struggled to rise. Pausing by the tent flap, he glanced at her, his features hardening as he glimpsed triumph in Molly's gaze.

Molly quickly steeled her expression but it was too late. Reginald saw through her little act, and his look promised retribution.

His gaze fell to her breasts, slid down to the buckskin-covered juncture of her thighs. When their eyes finally met, there was no mistaking Reginald's intent, or the flicker of desire that contorted his flaccid features. "I'll be back," he told her. He grinned. "I told you that in the end you'd have me. By the time I'm done, you'll beg for me to take you. You'll be down on your hands and knees!"

His eyes glittered hotly; he licked his lips with anticipation. "A real man," he murmured, and then he was gone.

Closing her eyes, Molly sighed with relief that she'd escaped the man's attentions. *For now,* she thought. She remembered his evil promise, his glittering yellow gaze, and she shuddered, a sensation that encompassed her entire body.

Beg for his touch? "In a cool day in hell," she vowed softly.

"What's this?" Darren asked his brother about the three men taken captive by Shelby and several others of the Tory band.

"We found them in the woods not far from our cabin," Shelby said. His eyes narrowed upon the three Rebels.

Darren's mouth curved into a slow smile. "Good work, little brother. Who are you?" He shoved the nearest man.

"It's Donovan," one of the Tories said.

Shelby tensed, raising his rifle. "The bastard who kidnapped Molly?" A click resounded as he drew back the gun hammer. "Lemme kill the scum!" he grated out through clenched teeth.

Darren grabbed hold of the gun muzzle, forcing it down. "Relax. He can't be the one." He studied his captive, amusement in his green gaze. "But he's the captain's brother." His gaze went to Shelby. "Added bait."

Shelby frowned. "Added?" he asked, watching the changes in Darren's face. "Who?" He was interrupted by Cornsby's arrival on the scene.

"Well, well, so the O'Reilly has finally returned," the storekeeper drawled. His eyes flickered to the three captives. "And with company, too!"

Shelby scowled at his brother. "What is *he* doing here?" he hissed.

"He's one of us," Darren said. "What do you think he's doing here?"

Cornsby smiled. It hadn't taken him long to accurately sum up the relationship between the three McCormick siblings. When Reginald had made clear his desire for the savage Molly, Darren had had no compunction about surrendering his half sister into the lecherous man's care.

"Easy, O'Reilly," the obese man said. "I'm just visiting your sweet sister." His tone was meaningful.

Shelby started. "My sister?"

"She came home," Darren said quietly. "I brought her here for her protection."

Shelby pulled his brother away from the prisoners. "She went to Clamtown?" He looked disbelieving.

Darren nodded. "To her Rebel lover," he said with such venom in his voice that Shelby's eyes widened. Seeing his mistake, Darren cleared his face of all expression.

Shelby blinked. "Where is she?" He sounded anxious to see his sister, a fact that irritated his

333

brother.

Cornsby had come up behind them. He swept a hand to point the way. "Over there. In the tent."

Shelby started forward, stopped, and turned back. "What of them?" He eyed the prisoners, who were glaring but silent.

Darren smiled. "I'll see that they're . . . taken care of," he said, his eyes glowing with that strange light that always gave Shelby gooseflesh.

The younger brother hesitated for only a moment before concern for his sister drew him to the crudely constructed storage tent.

The tent flap lifted and Molly looked up. "Shelby!" she gasped, relieved to see him.

Shelby's cry of gladness became a sound of horror as he saw that Molly was tied. "My God, what could he be thinking!"

"Shelby," Molly begged, "untie me. Help me escape! You don't understand what they're planning."

Her brother's hand froze on its way to her ropes. "What do you mean? Why have they tied you?" His voice rose a octave. "What have you done?"

"What have *I* done?" she gasped. "It's not me! It's Darren. He's going to capture Bran. Kill him!"

"Bran," Shelby echoed. "Bran Donovan?" His face turned hard. "Darren was right, wasn't he? You didn't go to the Shamong at all. You went to your Rebel lover. You lied to me!"

Molly's breath caught as she felt her brother's pain. "You don't understand. I didn't want—"

"No!" Shelby exclaimed, rising. "*You* don't understand!" He eyed his sister like he'd never seen her before, like she was something ugly and grotesque that had crawled out from under a rock.

334

"Bran Donovan is one of them! He's a damn Rebel. My God, he raped you!"

"He didn't rape me," Molly said, her soft tone making an impact, more so than if she'd gone into hysterics. "We . . . I did it willingly."

Shelby's harsh inhalation of breath filled the ensuing quiet. "Jade!" he cried, backing away. "Rebel whore!"

Pain lanced Molly's breast; tears filled her eyes. Her brother Shelby—the only one who ever loved her, understood her—hated her now. *Oh, God, Shelby, not you, too!*

"Please, Shelby, help me. It's me, Molly. Remember? I love him. Surely you can understand love? For God's sake, I'm your sister!"

Shelby stared at her as he raised the tent flap. "Sister?" he repeated. "Yes, yes, Molly must be protected." His eyes were glazed, unfocused. He appeared dazed, his thoughts turned inward. "God," he said in a ravaged whisper, "I can't let the Rebel bastards hurt her! No! No!" He gasped and seemed to come to his senses.

Shelby stared at her, his gaze clear and direct. "Darren was right to tie you up. It's for your own protection." Then he left.

Molly released a loud sob. "No!" She blinked away tears. "Bran and I, we are one. I must get free. I must save him!"

She fought her ropes but only succeeded in reopening the wounds inflicted by the Hessians.

Defeated, Molly hung her head until she perked up at the sound of a familiar voice.

"An ingenious operation!" she heard the man say casually. "How many men?"

Bran? Molly thought, and knew immediately that she was wrong. Her love for him must have made her imagine a similarity in the voices. She listened carefully. Men were talking. Footsteps crunched past the tent on dry twigs and dead leaves. She heard a muttered imprecation, then laughter.

Straining, she heard a few words that sounded again like Bran's voice, words that included *Rebel* and *wagons* and finally *Mary*.

Mary? Molly froze.

"My brother," she heard the voice say.

She gasped. "Patrick?" She stiffened in anger. It was Patrick! It had to be. Bran's brother is the other traitor!

Molly hurt for Bran. The pain of betrayal was great. She thought of Shelby and the way he'd turned from her when she most needed him.

Betrayal was worst when it was someone you loved.

She released a shaky breath. Suddenly she understood Bran's anger, his cold contempt toward her after his rescue of her from the Hessians. The pain must have been unbearable . . . if he loved her. And so he did, she realized with joy in her heart.

The joy dimmed. If she didn't get free to help him, then Bran would die! Led to his death by his own brother!

"We must move," Darren told his men. "Pack up and we'll move west." He looked to his brother. "Shelby, you know the Shamong better than any of us."

"The Shamong? You want to enter the Shamong?" Shelby frowned. "But the Lenape . . ."

Darren scowled. "Won't bother us if we don't them." He eyed the camp. Men were gathering their few belongings. Someone had fetched a horse-drawn wagon. They would need to take the supplies stored in their makeshift tent.

"I don't know. Tahuun Kukuus—"

"Is Molly's grandfather," Darren finished for him. His lips firmed. "No problem. As long as you keep away from the village, and we keep *her* out of sight."

Shelby looked skeptical as his brother turned away. He knew there'd be no arguing with Darren, and so he didn't point out that the Indians wandered freely about the Shamong to hunt and fish and gather food. He hated the idea of going to the Shamong, not when he'd be bringing the war into the territory of the peaceful Lenapes. Some of the Indians had become involved in the fighting, but not this group of the Delaware. Not Wood Owl, Molly's grandfather, Shelby's friend.

Could he lead them elsewhere? Would his brother realize if he headed southwest instead of west-northwest?

"O'Reilly?" Cornsby called mockingly. "What's happening?" The man's eyes appeared more yellow, more beady than usual. Shelby saw Cornsby glance toward the tent, and he felt rage that Darren would have entrusted their sister to this fat, slimy pig of a man.

"We're moving out." Shelby moved toward the tent. "I'll handle Molly."

"Not so fast." Fleshy fingers engulfed Shelby's arm. "Your sister belongs to me."

337

Shelby's eyes flashed. "In a pig's eye! You were posted guard for a while, that's all!"

The storekeeper smiled. "And what I guard I keep." He jerked his head in Darren's direction. "Ask him. Go ahead, ask your brother. We have a deal, him and me."

Shelby stared. Cornsby was minus his white-powdered wig, and his gray locks were straggly and greasy. His clothes were filthy, sweat-stained, and torn. His body odor was strong, malodorous, so strong it made Shelby's eyes tear.

His stomach churning, Shelby glanced at his brother. "You're not to touch her," he rasped, turning back to Cornsby. "I'll speak to Darren, all right, but until I do you're not to touch her, do you understand? If you do, I'll kill you. I'll kill you and any other bastard that tries to touch her!"

"Including Bran Donovan?" the man taunted.

"Anyone," Shelby snapped, and then he stalked off to try to speak with his older brother.

The tent flap opened and Cornsby stepped inside. "Get up," he ordered Molly after he'd untied her ankle ropes. "We're moving out of here."

"Moving?" she asked. "Where?"

But Cornsby just smiled evenly and grabbed hold of her arm. Squeezing cruelly, he propelled Molly out of the opening before him. Molly stumbled as the blood flowed to her sleeping limbs, making her feet throb with pain. Cornsby reached down and yanked her up by her tunic.

"Move, bitch!" he ordered, shoving her ahead.

Molly tripped forward and hit something hard. A man's body, she realized as that something—someone—grunted. She righted herself and mum-

338

bled an apology without looking. She glared at Cornsby, silently condemning the storekeeper to hell.

"Molly!" a voice behind her gasped.

She turned. "Patrick!"

The air grew tense and angry. Molly and Patrick stared at one another.

"Move!" someone ordered. Patrick and Molly fell into step with the other two prisoners—Pat's men, who'd been forced in the lead of the traveling group.

Patrick peered at the woman beside him. His face changed as he noticed Molly's tied hands. "What?" he began.

"Patrick?" Molly's eyes had widened as she noted the ropes about Patrick's own wrists.

They chuckled softly, smiling simultaneously as they realized that they each had falsely condemned the other.

Molly's smile faded. "Where's Bran?" she asked anxiously.

"Safe on his ship."

"Thank God." Closing her eyes, Molly sighed.

"Not for long, though, I imagine," Pat said, gazing at her with concern. "He sent me to bring you back. When neither I nor my men return . . ."

Molly's heart thumped. "Bran sent you to find me? He knows I'm here?"

Patrick looked away. "He knows you're somewhere . . . with Darren." His eyes swung back, narrowing. "Your brother." His tone sounded half accusing, half confused.

"My half brother," Molly said. Her eyes held sadness. "He always hated me. Only I never realized just how much . . ." She blinked, recalling Pat's flushed face, his look of guilt. She drew in a ragged breath. Pain hit her hard, twisting her stomach.

"How does Bran know I'm with Darren?" she asked quietly. "No, no, don't bother telling me. I can see it in your eyes. He had me followed, didn't he?" The knot in her stomach encompassed her breast. *Bran didn't trust me.*

"You don't understand."

Her expression went blank, but her voice was but a choked whisper, "I don't want to talk about it." She averted her glance to stare at the surrounding woods. "Do you know where they're taking us?"

Pat shook his head. "No. But perhaps if we stay together, or convince them to keep us together, between the two of us we'll be able to think of a way to escape." He stared at her, troubled.

Molly met his gaze. "You got a knife?"

Pat shook his head.

She glanced back toward the wagon of goods. "I know where we can get one."

Chapter Twenty-five

"Knots!" Bran called, climbing up onto the main deck. "Any sign of MacDuff?"

"Afraid not, Captain," the sailmaster said, bending his head over the edge of yardage that was draped across the main deck. He seemed oblivious to the leashed tension in his commander as he plied his needle through the piece of cloth.

Without shipyard or sailmaker's loft, it was an awkward arrangement with the sheets across the deck, but with many of the men gone, Bran thought that the time waiting should be put to good use. One should always be prepared for the danger of a torn sail, especially in time of war.

"How's the new 'suit' coming?" Bran asked, coming around the sailcloth to stand behind the man's shoulder.

Joseph Knot paused in his even stitching. Raising the hand with his leather seamer palm, he scratched his head. "Fine, Capt'n, fine." The sailmaster ran an expert eye over the expanse of cloth before he went back to work.

Sighing irritably, Bran turned to the rail, searching the shoreline. He was anxious, restless with the urge to abandon his ship in order to find Molly.

What was happening out there? he wondered. Why hadn't he heard from MacDuff, Dickon, or any of the others? Something couldn't have gone wrong with every one of them!

He thought he'd be long on his way through the Pines, toward Manville, to join Patrick and his men by now. Had Pat found and rescued Molly? Had they been mistaken? What if Molly hadn't needed rescuing at all? What if it was all a trap to lure Rebel smugglers?

The sweet vision of her face haunted his mind. Her tear-filled eyes, her pain when he'd accused her of betrayal. *She loves you,* the memory seemed to say. *She didn't betray you.*

He needed to do something to help, but his hands were tied. His feeling of helplessness had increased with every passing hour until he wanted to bellow with the pain of it.

It'd been a day and a half since Pat had left, over two days for Angus MacDuff. If anything happened to any of them . . . Bran's frame tightened with rage at the thought. If MacDuff or one of the others didn't come back soon . . .

He felt the desire to do violence spiral inside him until he was afraid he would explode at any second. He was tired of waiting! Something was wrong! It must be! He had men enough to accompany him, but he needed someone he could trust, someone to take charge of the ship.

Bran went below. "Tommie," he bellowed in his

search for the cabin boy.

Tommie peeked his head out of the galley, instantly wary. "Aye, Capt'n?"

The captain's lips twisted as he saw the tension in the boy. He'd been like a bear during this waiting, he knew. A bear likely to bite the head off any one of his poor crew. "Sailor, can you get to Clamtown?"

His face brightening, the youth stepped forward. "Why, of course, Capt'n!"

"Good," Bran said. "I want you to go to Falkinburg's. Find Josiah Morse. Tell him I need him at the ship." He hesitated, his eyes watchful. "Can you do that, boy?"

Tommie straightened. "Aye!"

"Fine. Then get moving."

Next Bran went about the ship selecting men to accompany him on his journey through the Pine Barrens. By the time he had picked five of the crew, issued instructions for those remaining, and prepared a satchel of supplies, Josiah Morse was boarding the *Bloody Mary.*

"What's wrong?" The innkeeper looked concerned when he entered Bran's cabin. "Something happen? Have you heard from Pat?"

"No," Bran said. "Not from Pat, Dickon, or any one of my men. Not even MacDuff."

The older man seemed puzzled. "That's funny. I saw the Scot only yesterday. We talked briefly. Caught up on what's happening. Told him about Molly. I remember you saying how he liked the girl. He said he was heading toward Hugh Woberney's to check with his wife to see if he'd returned.

343

Then he would return to the ship."

Josiah became alarmed. "You don't think his concern for Molly sent him to join Pat?"

Bran frowned. "I hope not. Well, in any case, I'll find out myself soon enough." He stared at the old man as if daring him to argue with his next words. "I'm going, Josiah. If Pat needs help . . ."

Josiah blinked. "Do you think that's wise?"

"Hell! I don't give a damn if it is or not! I'm going and that's final."

Bran's look suddenly turned sheepish. "Will you stay on board, Josiah? Will you watch *Mary* for me?"

Josiah felt honored. He smiled. "Bran Donovan," he scolded with affection. "Need you ask?"

The Tories made camp in the Shamong, an area of the New Jersey Pine Barrens not far from the Atsion ironworks. Familiar with landmarks, Molly recognized these woods immediately. It was the Delaware hunting ground, and she was bothered by the fact that the Pine Robbers were invading Lenape territory. And they were bringing war with them. War and trouble.

Since the time of the white man's arrival in the early part of the century, the Lenapes had been driven from their homes by the woodcutters, who'd destroyed their woods for the sawmills they built. Wasn't it enough, Molly thought, that the Indians were no longer able to roam freely? Was it any wonder that there were so few left of her mother's people?

Molly feared for her grandfather. Wood Owl was among those who had chosen to stay in the New Jersey area. If the white people continued to come into their woods, would he too pick up and move his people west or south?

Molly glared at Darren from across the campsite. This was his doing! It wouldn't be Shelby's, she insisted to herself. Shelby, a frequent visitor to Wood Owl's village, had great respect for the Lenapes. He and Molly had often talked of the sad fate of the Delaware Indians. Surely he didn't lead Darren's men here intentionally!

Her gaze darted around the camp. One part of her wished that the Delaware, having discovered the Tories' presence, would come and rescue her so she could find Bran. But another part of her hoped that the Indians remained oblivious to the white men, because Molly feared there'd be blood shed.

She had to get free. So many lives were at risk: Bran and his men, the Delaware, Pat and the other prisoners. And herself.

Unfortunately, she and Patrick had been separated as soon as they'd reached the new site. If she was going to escape, then it would be by her own cunning. Pat would be unable to help her.

Molly decided that one thing, at least, was in her favor. She hadn't seen Reginald Cornsby lately. The man must have gone back to his store in Manville. She was exceedingly thankful that her new prison guard was George Merriweather. She recognized the man from her spying and thought perhaps she could use his cautious nature to her advantage.

"You!" Molly hissed.

345

George Merriweather turned. He had been standing within twenty feet of her, his back toward her, his eyes on Pat and the other Rebel prisoners. Molly thought Merriweather might be upset with what was happening within the Tory band. The prisoners. The threats.

Merriweather stared at her. "What is it?"

He approached when, with a jerk of her head, Molly beckoned him closer. "What do you want?" he said, frowning.

"Could you untie me? I have to . . ." She glanced toward the bushes and back, and then bent her head, pretending to be too embarrassed to discuss such an intimate function.

The man seemed flustered. "Oh, I see." She gazed at him in time to see him struggling with indecision.

"It won't take long, I promise."

"Well, maybe I'd better check with—"

"No, please," she pleaded, panicking when he flashed Darren a glance. "My brother . . . ah . . . I'm sure it'll be all right."

But he seemed skeptical as he eyed her bonds.

"Ask Shelby then," she suggested. "I know he'll do it, if you won't."

That seemed to convince him. Merriweather sighed with resignation. "All right, I'll do it," he said. He bent down to undo her ropes. "You can go, but I'll be watching you."

"Mr. Merriweather," she gasped, horrified.

The man flushed scarlet. "I didn't mean . . . um . . . what I meant was . . ." He composed himself as he stood up. "No funny business!" He patted the handle of the gun stuck into the waistband of his trousers.

She nodded and struggled to her feet. "Over there?" she asked pointing toward a clump of bushes.

Merriweather agreed, and he followed closely as she went. Molly did, in fact, have to relieve herself, and she wasn't about to allow the old man to watch. "Please," she said, "can I have some privacy?"

The Tory scowled. "I guess so. But I want you to keep moving so I can hear you." He pulled out his pistol and waved it in the air. "I wouldn't try escaping. This thing's loaded and I'm a crack shot."

Molly released a shaky breath and then silently slipped away so she could answer nature's call. She started humming softly, making as much noise as possible, so that Merriweather wouldn't become suspicious or feel the need to come investigate. Her mind raced quickly as she planned her escape route.

She needed to get George Merriweather to relax his guard.

Fortunately, they were well enough away from the eyes in camp for her to have a chance to make a break. Unfortunately, if she didn't take that chance soon, then someone, most probably Darren, would realize she was absent and come looking.

"Girl!" Merriweather called.

"Coming!" *It's now or never,* Molly thought. With a last glance past toward the old man, she took off running, dodging trees and any other obstacles in her path.

Suddenly she heard a harsh masculine cry. George Merriweather. He must have been distracted by something, she thought, because it had taken him well over three minutes to sound the alarm.

The forest came alive with activity and shouts as the word of her escape filtered through the Tory camp.

I'm going to make it, she thought. *I'm going to make it.*

Once away, well out of sight, Molly paused to catch her breath and get her bearings. She struggled with the decision of whether or not she should head toward her grandfather's village. She decided against it. There she would find refuge, but at the risk of danger to the Lenape people.

"Lass!" she heard a gruff cry.

Startled, Molly froze. "MacDuff?" she whispered. Could it really be the Scot?

The call came again. She turned toward the sound just as a man broke through the brush about twenty feet to the left of her. It was the big, burly Scotsman from Bran's ship!

"Molly?"

"MacDuff!" she exclaimed, running. Overjoyed at finding a friend to help her, she flung herself into his arms. She felt the man's arm tighten about her, and she pulled back to grin at him.

"How? What?" she gasped, laughing. "I'm so glad you're here," she rushed on. "Where's Bran? MacDuff, he's in trouble! They're going to kill him. Pat and the others, they got captured by the Pine Robbers! We've got to do something. You — *we've* got to be careful; they mustn't find out we're here!"

She hurried to explain what had happened. About her spying. About her capture and the capture of Pat and the other Rebels. About Darren and the Pine Robbers. About the traitors — Woberney and that other one — the man she suspected was someone close to Bran. By the time she was done her eyes were sparkling and she was out of breath.

Angus MacDuff had listened carefully, his face changing with each new revelation. "Their camp, lass, where is it?" he asked.

"It's over there," she said, pointing. "Oh, no, Angus!" she exclaimed when he pulled out his gun, "There are too many of them. You can't do this alone!"

"I've no intention of doing anything," MacDuff said, using a strange tone. He pointed the gun at her.

Molly stiffened. "You!" she gasped. "Oh, no, Angus, it can't be you!"

"Afraid so, lassie." His eyes turned hard. "Now, I want ye to turn around slowly. We're going back to camp. Do ye understand?"

"But why, Angus?" she cried.

"Money. And I'm tired of this war." He used his gun to nudge her in the right direction. "Do ye really think the Continentals have a hell's chance in winning?"

Molly was sick. "But the captain's your friend!"

The Scot didn't answer her. Glaring, he told her to get moving back to camp.

Chapter Twenty-six

It was the ninth day of September when Bran and his men reached the outskirts of the Pine Robbers' camp. They had caught up with Nate Redding and his men outside of Manville. They were under orders, given by Pat, to return to the *Bloody Mary* in the event of trouble. For several hours Redding and his cohorts had hung about not far from the McCormick cabin, waiting for word from the rescuers. When none came, he and his men searched the area. Luck had eluded them until they'd stumbled onto a recently vacated campsite. The Pine Robbers had moved. There'd been no sign of anyone.

"Do you see her, Capt'n?" Talbot whispered as he hunkered down beside Bran in the thicket. "Or the others?"

Bran glanced at the young seaman. " 'Fraid not," he replied, his low voice gruff with worry.

It was dark. Night had fallen, bringing with it a mist. They had found the new camp by tracking.

Careful examination of the soil had shown wheel tracks in some places, while in other sections of the woods a broken twig or a bent blade of grass was the only indication that the Tory band had passed through that stretch of woods.

Bran had first realized they'd been successful in their tracking when he detected the soft glow of a campfire through the damp haze. The Americans had crept in for a closer look and were able to detect a wagon, but just barely. The humid haze that protected the Rebels' cover made it difficult for them to see into the Tory camp.

"What of the others?" Bran asked when the young seaman moved, drawing Bran's attention. "Any luck?"

Talbot's head bobbed in the darkness. "Aye. There's a man on watch to your left, sir. We think, but we're not certain, that there are three men sleeping on the far side."

"Any idea how many they total?" Bran asked, his gut twisting at the thought of Molly and his men in the hands of the Tories.

"Nate thinks ten, Capt'n."

"Ten to our six," Bran murmured thoughtfully. "Hope he's right." Nate, he knew, would have calculated the number from what he could see of the position and size of the camp. Bran flashed Talbot a grin. "Not bad odds, eh, Mike?"

"Aye." The youth returned the grin, pleased with the note of camaraderie.

Bran rose up slightly to peer over the patch of briars. "Sailor," he said, "I'm going to circle around to the other side to check by that wagon.

351

You can stay here or return to Nate." He spared Talbot a glance. "If you decide to stay and you hear or see anything strange, think carefully, son. Don't be too hasty with that gun."

The seaman nodded, his face grave.

The vehicle was a fuzzy but recognizable blur that became more distinct as Bran neared where the wagon stood along the western fringe of the camp. It was slow going for the captain, who had to be careful that each footfall was noiseless.

Bran knew Nate and the others were scattered about the perimeter of the encampment, their gazes watchful, their hands clasped on their flintlocks.

Ordinarily, with these odds he would have attempted a rush on the camp. But he had the safety of the prisoners to consider—Molly, and perhaps his brother Pat and Pat's men. Although it was late and in all probability all but the Tory watch was sleeping, Bran couldn't risk injury to those he cared about. They could be hurt or killed in the fracas.

He crept close to the wagon without mishap and took a hiding position behind a cluster of short pines and other wood brush. Leaning forward, Bran received a better view of the Tory camp. The mist didn't seem as thick from this angle. He saw the smoldering remains of their campfire, the three sleeping men that Talbot had spoken about, and two others lying on the ground directly before him.

He moved from the copse closer to the wagon. There was a horse hitched to the vehicle. As Bran came near, the animal snorted and then settled down quietly once again. Eyes narrowing, Bran peered through the darkness and was rewarded with sight of the Tory prisoners at the far end of the wagon.

A man suddenly moved into the line of Bran's vision—a fat bloke with thinning hair. His gaze darting about the surrounding woods; the Tory robber carried his rifle awkwardly.

The watch, Bran realized. Was he the only one? His mind worked quickly while he debated his next move.

Bran was jerked from his thoughts by the ominous click of a gun hammer from directly behind him.

"Freeze," a deep voice growled menacingly.

Bran stilled, his hands cradling his flintlock.

"Now I want you to stand up slowly," the man said. "Drop the gun first. *Now!*"

Sighing heavily, Bran dropped his gun and rose slowly.

"Cornsby!" the man suddenly shouted. Bran saw the watch jerk with surprise. "Get the hell over here! Damn it, you fat arse, don't ya know how to keep watch?"

Cornsby blustered. "But, Darren—"

"Sonavabitch! I give you one damn stinking job to do!" Darren McCormick exclaimed. He waved his gun in the storekeeper's direction. "I ought to—"

"McCormick!" someone cried from the other side of the camp. "We've found us a couple more!"

"How many?"

"Three."

During the exchange, Bran had turned carefully.

353

He fixed his stare on the Tory leader. Darren Mc-Cormick. So this was Molly's brother. He could see no resemblance between the woman he loved and the man before him.

"Three?" McCormick echoed, frowning. "How many of you are there?" he said to Bran. "Answer me! Who are you? And what are you doing here?" He shoved his gun hard into Bran's stomach when Bran refused to answer, making Bran gasp with pain.

"I know who he is," someone said, stepping closer from inside the camp. It was Hugh Woberney.

"Woberney," Bran gasped, clutching his belly. "You bastard!"

Woberney flinched, but spoke evenly. "It's Donovan."

"Bran Donovan?" Darren looked astonished. Then his mouth curved into a smile of satisfaction. "Molly's lover."

He spoke his sister's name with a loathing that didn't escape Bran's notice. Darren's eyes gleamed. "Well, well, well, how very convenient." He calmly took the captain's measure and was clearly amazed by Bran's polished appearance. Traipsing about the woods, Darren thought, and not a strand of the captain's queue was out of place.

He was startled by the man's commanding presence and power. It stunned him to see how tautly his adversary's muscular frame stretched his fine linen shirt and dark knee breeches. Even his boots seemed impressive and out of ordinary, Darren mused, for they'd retained the high gloss of a recent shine despite the captain's trek through the Pine Barren woods.

Darren dragged his gaze from the captain's face to Reginald Cornsby. "My sister—she didn't—"

"She and the others are still here. They haven't escaped," Cornsby reassured him.

Darren McCormick's gloating grin flashed in the darkness. "Good. This rounds up matters nicely." He paused. "I'm in your debt, Captain Donovan. You've just saved me the trouble of laying a trap for you."

He directed Bran to the clearing with a wave of his gun. "So nice of you to visit us this way, Donovan. I'm sure the dear British general will be delighted at your capture."

Bran was startled to hear of the British army's involvement with the band, because he'd heard of no recent evidence of Redcoats in the area.

Seeing the captain's expression, Darren laughed. "Robinson's been giving me the devil about you— you and your nest of Rebel pirates."

"Me?" Bran asked, frowning now.

"Ah," Darren said. "I imagine you're wondering how General Robinson knows of you specifically? Well, the simple matter is that—"

"I told him," a voice called. A man stepped out from the other side of the wagon.

Bran felt a shock. "Angus?" He drew a ragged breath as the Scot nodded.

The traitor was Angus MacDuff.

Molly had fallen into a light doze when a commotion in the camp woke her.

"What's going on?" Patrick asked from beside her. Since Molly's attempt at escape, the Tories had kept their prisoners close together, where it would be easier to keep them under watchful eyes.

"I don't know," she murmured, stretching her neck to see. She heard men's voices, but couldn't discern what they were saying.

Darren approached the prisoners. "Dear sister," he said in a scathing tone, "I have a little surprise for you."

His look of glittering triumph made Molly's heart flutter with fear. "Father's come, and you're going to let me go," she joked grimly, half hoping it were true.

Her brother tensed. "Now why would you think that? The last time I saw him he was too soused to remember he has a daughter, never mind to realize you're gone. Sorry, squaw, but if you're expecting help there, you can forget it."

Molly's eyes flashed fire. "Even tied up I'm a threat to you," she taunted.

"Threat?" Darren's laughter was false. "You? A savage *breed*? Hardly," He signaled to one of his men. "Bring the captain here."

Her heart thumping, Molly stared at her brother's hardened face. "Captain?"

"That's right."

"Bran!" she cried with mingled gladness and horror as he was tossed onto the ground beside her.

"Molly!" Bran whispered joyfully. His large hands tenderly cupping her face, he devoured her with his concerned gaze. "Are you all right? They

356

didn't hurt you?"

Tears filled Molly's eyes as she shook her head. "No, no, I'm fine. And you?" She felt warmed by his look; it told of love and desire and was full of promises.

Bran's lips twisted. "I'm all right," he said, his face becoming a study in frustration at being caught by the Tory band. Suddenly his expression softened. "Molly," he breathed. "I've died a thousand times these past few days, wondering about you, worrying."

His touch felt like heaven as he caressed her cheeks. Molly's lashes feathered her silken cheeks as he stroked her hair gently from her flushed face. "I know," she said huskily. "I've—"

"How touching," Darren interrupted mockingly. He'd been watching the scene with strained forbearance, but his impatience had finally snapped.

Bran's gaze hardened like blue steel. "Let her go, McCormick. It's me you want, not her."

"Really?" Darren looked amused by this display of protectiveness on the captain's part. It confirmed he had a tool with which to torment and manipulate both Bran Donovan and the squaw.

"It appears, Donovan, that you know little of my relationship with my *dear half sister.*" Molly's brother's eyes gleamed with hatred. "I've as much love for her as I do you."

Darren chuckled. "Actually, I find I like you better." He walked away several paces and turned to regard the two with a thoughtful look that brought the hairs up at the back of Molly's neck.

"Unlike my brother, Shelby," he said, "I've never

once been fooled into caring for the savage bastard!"

"For God's sake, she's your sister." Patrick Donovan piped up from Molly's other side. He was too angry to see Bran's reaction, to hear his brother cry out at his discovery of Pat's presence.

Darren had shrugged his shoulders. "Maybe to some she'd be considered a beloved sister, but not to me." He stared at the woman in question and saw the way the captain had drawn Molly against his side.

With an evil smile, the Tory leader gestured to two of his men. "Get him up," he ordered, his gaze glittering. "Tie him between those two trees over there."

"No," Molly cried, struggling against her bonds. "No, please! Let him be!"

Her half brother laughed maliciously. "So you really love him, do you?" He watched with satisfaction as his men reached down to heft the captain to his feet.

"Molly, don't cry, love. It'll be all right—" Bran's unfinished sentence became a gasp as he was punched in the stomach by one of McCormick's brutes.

"Yes, dear Molly, it'll be all right," Darren mocked, chuckling wickedly.

Bran was incensed. As soon as he caught his breath, he began to fight the Tories' hold, struggling against their arms, kicking them with his booted feet. One man grunted when Bran's boot hit his shin, but Bran's satisfaction faded when someone's fist connected with the right side of his jaw, and he reeled under the impact. He gathered his senses to renew the fight, but found that two others had joined in to restrain him.

Bran was forced to give up. He realized that if he didn't he'd be too weak and injured to think clearly, to help Molly and the others, including himself, escape. He hung between two of Darren McCormick's ruffians, caught by his arms stretched to full span. His jaw throbbed. His head ached from repeated blows to his face and temple. He felt nauseated from the stomach punch, and he knew a sharp pain in his arms from the way the robbers restrained him, with limbs twisted and pulled out so tautly that he felt the wrenching of his arm sockets.

His senses blurred; a wave of blackness threatened him. Bran heard Molly's harsh sobbing pleas for her brother to let him go, and he felt the strongest urge to comfort her.

"Molly," he gasped, struggling to see past heavy eyelids. "Don't, love—" He didn't see Darren's approach, but he felt the blow to his gut where Darren kicked him. His breath whooshed out at the pain, and he had trouble breathing again.

"Darren!" Molly screamed. "No!"

Bran's head snapped back with the force of another blow. The last thing Bran was aware of before he was rendered unconsciousness was the new note in Molly's tone as she cried, "Shelby!"

Shelby had returned to the Tory encampment after a trip home to check on his father. He wore a stunned expression as he entered the clearing and saw the brutal beating of a restrained man. Molly's heartfelt cry brought him up short as he stared at her tear-ravaged face. She was pleading—no, begging!—for him to help the prisoner, Shelby realized through a daze. He blinked, and his senses cleared enough to try to assess the situation accurately.

Tension within the camp ran high. He could hear the harsh breathing of several members of the band, but what gained his attention most was the sound of Molly sobbing and calling his name.

His glance landed on his brother, Darren. "What's going on here?"

Darren seemed startled, and Shelby wondered if it was a look of guilt that he saw briefly in his brother's eyes. "Shelby," Darren said, "you're back."

Shelby's gaze narrowed. "I asked you a question, brother. What's going on here?"

Darren grinned. "While you were gone, we got us a Rebel sea captain."

Taken aback, Shelby transferred his gaze to the unconsciousness man being held up by the Tory men. "I see," he murmured. But he didn't. He eyed his sister with a worried frown. "What's the matter with her?"

"Our Rebel is *hers,*" Darren said with thinly veiled disgust. "He's Bran Donovan, Molly's lover."

Shelby experienced a jolt. "Donovan?" He moved to where Molly sat sobbing, her tears running down her pale cheeks in dirty streaks. "Is that true?" he asked, his voice even. "Is he the one? Your lover?" He tensed, waiting for her answer.

"Shelby . . ." she pleaded.

"Damn, it's true, isn't it?"

Straightening her spine, Molly sniffed back her

360

tears. "If you're asking whether I love him," she said quietly, "then the answer is yes. I do."

The simple, soft declaration of love had a profound impact on the younger of her two half brothers. "I see," he said, fighting mixed feelings of betrayal and relief.

Shelby turned to his brother. "What are you going to do with him?" Meeting Darren's gaze, he displayed none of his inner turmoil.

Darren smiled at his brother's cool, unemotional tone. "The captain? Kill him, of course."

Molly gasped. "But I thought you said that Robinson wanted him!" Although she couldn't be sure that being taken prisoner by a British general would be a fate kinder than death.

His brother scowled. "I've changed my mind. Dead or alive, Robinson won't care as long as the man's been stopped." He ordered his men to throw Bran's body down at his sister's feet. "No sense in tying him up there now," he said, gesturing toward the two trees. "It'll be easier tomorrow when he's awake and less of a burden."

With a murmur of agreement, his men obeyed.

"What about Molly?" Shelby was careful not to allow Darren to see his concern for their sister.

Darren stiffened. "What of her?" He relaxed when Shelby didn't appear to blink a eye.

"Just wondering." Shelby paused. "I was thinking of Father. What are you going to tell him about *her?* You can't tell him the truth," he pointed out. "He wouldn't believe the truth about her and the captain. He'll only hate us for telling him."

The leader's face contorted with pain. It was a

sore spot—his father's love for Molly. And Darren hated Molly as much as he hated her mother, Shi'ki-Xkwe, for replacing his dead mother in his father's affections. Through the years, Darren's only source of comfort had been the fact that Tully McCormick and the Indian squaw had never been able to marry legally. It would have been more than Darren was able to bear if Molly had been his father's legitimate child.

Darren stared at Shelby, recalling his brother's question. "We can't let her go. Surely you can see that. And Father?" His lips curled. "If he's ever sober enough to ask after his daughter, we'll lie and convince him that her death was an accident." Grinning, he slapped Shelby on the back. "There, does that answer your questions?"

Shelby nodded, concealing his horror behind schooled features. He didn't know what to do. His brother, he realized, had slipped beyond the bounds of sanity. That he could speak so easily of their sister's murder!

Somehow I must help Molly. He'd never be able to forgive Darren, or himself, if because of them their sister died.

Shelby's first chance to speak with his sister privately came a short time later, in the early morning hours.

He jostled her shoulder. "Molly," he whispered.

She jolted to full alertness. "Shelby!"

"Sh-sh!" he cautioned.

Tears filled her eyes as the memory of the night came back to haunt her. Still unconscious, Bran was lying near her feet. Molly had tried several

362

times to maneuver herself so that she could lie alongside of him, but her bonds were such that every movement caused her great pain. And Bran's awkward position, she realized, would have made it impossible anyway.

She beseeched her brother with a tear-brightened gaze. "Please," she begged. "Please help us."

Shelby's mouth firmed at the *us.* "He's a Rebel."

"And what have they done to you?" Molly challenged.

He seemed taken aback. "He's the enemy. Darren —"

"My God!" Molly exclaimed in a whisper. "Is Darren thinking for you now?" She felt his immediate withdrawal, and she apologized. "I'm sorry, Shelby."

Shelby softened. "You really love him." He sounded surprised, awed by the depths of such love.

She nodded. "With all my heart."

"But he took you prisoner."

Molly smiled. "He treated me kindly." She paused. "He's a good man."

"He's a Rebel."

"He's a man fighting for his freedom," Molly defended. "Can you condemn him for that?"

Reluctantly, Shelby shook his head.

"Darren's going to kill us." Molly drew a ragged breath and then released it. "I don't want to die, Shel."

Shelby froze, shuddering. "You won't die, Molly, not if I can help it."

"And Bran and the others?" Molly questioned,

363

hope rising within her breast.

"Them, I can't promise."

Molly's face fell. "Then forget about me. I love Bran; I won't live without him."

Shelby gasped. "Surely you don't mean that!"

"My mother loved Father, gave up her people for him," she reminded him.

"And you're your mother's daughter," Shelby murmured. He couldn't help smiling as he remembered the Indian woman he'd loved as a child adores his own mother.

Molly nodded.

"Very well," Shelby said, rising from his hunkered-down position near Molly's side. "I'll see what I can do."

"Bran," she said, begging him again with her midnight gaze. "Could you move him closer?"

"I don't know—"

"Please?"

Shelby glanced around to see if anyone was watching. Everyone else was sleeping, except for the one other guard on the other side of the camp.

Grumbling beneath his breath, Shelby gave in to his sister's wishes, grunting as he hefted Bran's body to rest full length at Molly's side.

"He's hurt," Molly said. "I saw blankets in the wagon."

Shelby scowled. "Next, you'll be asking me to untie your hands so you can stroke the bastard's brow." He inhaled sharply at his sister's expression. "All right. All right," he muttered, bending to uncut the ropes binding Molly's wrists. "I don't suppose there's any need for this with your lover

364

senseless."

Molly beamed, her eyes filling with tears of gratitude. She touched her brother's arm. "Thanks." The tears overflowed to trickle down Molly's cheeks.

Shelby nodded, his throat suddenly feeling too tight to swallow. "I'll get that blanket," he said hoarsely.

Chapter Twenty-seven

Bran felt the tender touch of Molly's hands and thought he was dreaming. "Molly?" he asked.

The fingers against his cheek stopped. His eyes fluttered open, and he saw her sweet face above him, the loving look in her glistening dark eyes.

"Bran, oh, Bran, I love you," she cried softly.

He felt a drop on his cheek — a tear. Hers? The realization came that what was happening was real. Molly was real, and she was stroking him, tending him as a woman cares for the one she loves.

Bran moved, and pain brought back his last memory with sharp clarity. "Are you all right?" he asked huskily. "Where are we? Have we escaped?"

Molly bit her lip. "I'm sorry." She gave a sob. "Oh, God, I'm sorry! I didn't mean for this to happen!"

"Molly."

She blinked, startled by his tone.

He smiled. "Come here, love. I need to kiss you."

"Oh, Bran . . ." She bent forward and pressed her lips lightly against his mouth, and then gasped when Bran reached up and caught her head in his hand. Holding her to him, he slipped his tongue between her lips, plundering her mouth as a man who was starved for intimacy.

"Take him up!" a harsh voice commanded suddenly.

Startled, Molly and Bran broke apart.

"No, Darren!" Molly saw the evil intent in Darren's eyes and she was afraid.

Several men converged on Bran, pulling him up by his shirt. "Who untied her?" Darren bellowed to the group.

"I did." Shelby said, stepping forward.

Darren flinched, turning white. *"You did?"*

The brother nodded. "I didn't see the harm since he was out like a light anyway." He lowered his eyelids. "Might as well let them know what they'll be missing."

Color flooded back to Darren's face. He chuckled. "Yes, yes, I see what you mean." He turned his attention to the glaring sea captain. "Well, Captain, it looks as if you're feeling better this morning." He didn't wait for Bran to comment. "Adams, Woberney! String him between those trees!"

The men started to drag the captain off. Bran struggled briefly, but his injuries from the day before gave him strength for only a token resistance.

Molly, who'd used her free hands to undo her leg robes, scrambled to her feet. She lunged at her brother Darren, beating him with both fists. "You

367

bastard!" she cried. "You can't do this!"

Darren cursed, hitting her with one mighty blow against the side of her head. Stunned, Molly slid to the ground unconscious.

Bran's heart stopped as Molly fell. "You slimy scum!" he snarled, breaking free from his captors' hold with a bodily strength born of fear. He launched himself at Darren's head, and the two crashed to the dirt, the solid impact of their fall making a dull thud that echoed about the clearing.

Cursing, Bran rained punches upon Molly's brother with his closed fists. Darren tried to fight back, but Bran's attack was vicious, out of control. The captain managed several smashing blows to the Tory's nose and mouth before the robbers recaptured him, dragging him off Darren McCormick's inert body.

His nose bleeding, his mouth split, Darren rose to his elbows. He looked dazed, and then his eyes cleared, making his gaze deadly.

The Tory leader struggled to his feet and stood, swaying. "Tie him up," he ordered, wiping away the blood from his cut lip with the sleeve of his muslin shirt. "Tie the captain up and then teach the bloody bastard a lesson he won't forget."

When she came to, the first thing Molly did was look for Bran. She gasped with sick remorse when she spied him. He was suspended by his arms between two trees.

Bran's head hung down, his chin sunk against his chest. He'd been stripped of his shirt and

368

beaten cruelly, and there was blood dripping down his hard chest. Whether it was from cuts to his chest or from his injured face, Molly had no idea. Nor did she care at this point. Her only thought was to cut him down and see to his comfort.

"Oh, my God!" she choked out in a horrified whisper. "What have they done to you?"

"Molly."

"Pat," she cried, turning to Bran's brother. "I'm so sorry. This is my fault!"

"Damn it, girl! 'Tis not your fault! 'Tis plain to me you love that brother of mine."

"Molly," a quiet voice drew their attention. Shelby had come upon them quietly. His eyes were dark with concern, his expression worried.

"Look what you've done!" she accused with tears in her eyes. "Look at him! They've almost killed him."

"I believe that's their intent," Pat interjected.

"No." Molly shook her head. "I won't let them."

"Molly, we're leaving," Shelby said. "On a raid. Rebel wagons have been spotted over by Dog's Run."

"So?" She glared at him, startled to realize that the activity within the camp suggested a preparation of some sort. She was angered to learn that the robbers were getting ready for another raid. "Why tell me? Have you come to gloat?"

"I've come to give you a chance, if you'll let me." Shelby's gaze went to Patrick Donovan, whose gaze suddenly narrowed at the hint of escape. Bran's brother was propped up next to Molly against a large tree, his hands tied, his legs bound.

"Donovan," Molly's brother said, "if I help you escape, will you promise to take Molly and the others away from here? Not come back?"

Patrick stared at him. "You don't want us to retaliate."

Shelby nodded.

"Don't promise him anything," Molly said. "He can't be trusted!"

"Molly!" Shelby was deeply wounded.

"You could have helped Bran—us!" Molly said. "How do I know this isn't some sort of trap to make it look like an accident?"

"You don't know." Shelby's expression had turned hard. "I guess you'll have to trust me."

Pat spoke up. "Molly, I think he means it." He addressed Molly's brother. "What kind of a chance?"

Shelby shifted, looking uncomfortable. "Do you swear you'll leave?" He checked to see if anyone within the camp was watching.

Pat nodded. "I swear it."

Shelby appeared relieved. "Here." A thud drew Molly and Pat's attention to a small knife Shelby had tossed to the dirt. "We'll be gone for at least an hour."

"That's all you're going to do?" Pat gaped at the man and then the knife.

"That's all I can do." Shelby paused for a long moment, his eyes sad. "Darren McCormick is my brother."

"I understand," Pat said, and he did.

Shelby left with the other Tories, leaving only two men behind to guard the Rebel prisoners—Reginald Cornsby and a youth by the name of Peabody.

Molly and Pat exchanged glances. And then conferring on tactics, they began to maneuver themselves across the hard-packed earth.

"Bran."

Bran forced his head up. "MacDuff," he mumbled. "You bastard."

Angus MacDuff felt a surge of guilt. "Believe me, I had no idea."

The captain snorted. "You took the papers." He saw the Scot nod. Of course, Bran thought. Angus had easy access to the cabin; it was he who threw the box on Molly's bunk, hoping no doubt to implicate Molly as the thief.

"What did they offer you, Angus?" Bran asked. "It couldn't be money. You had a fair share of *Mary's* profits."

"Aye, it wasn't the money. It was a ship." The Scot's voice was quiet.

All Bran's injuries seemed to throb with pain. "The *Bloody Mary*."

"No, Bran. Not *Mary*, I swear it!" In his eagerness to be understood, MacDuff grabbed Bran's arm, withdrawing his hand abruptly when Bran tensed with pain. " 'Tis the *Nancy* I was after."

"The *Nancy?*" Bran's brow crinkled. "The English brig?"

"Aye. McCormick, Robinson, they've got connections."

Bran glowered at him "You should have told me

371

you wanted a command, Angus. You could have captained the *Bloody Mary*."

"But . . ." MacDuff clearly didn't understand.

And Bran chose not to enlighten him. "Get the hell out of my sight, you Scottish swine."

Angus grew deathly pale.

"Take a good look at me, Angus. Look at Molly and the others. You're responsible for these cuts, you bastard. And if any of us die, you'll be responsible for our deaths, too. Go, Angus MacDuff. Go on your Tory raid. I don't give a damn. But may you rot in the hell, you traitor!"

"Did you get it?" Molly asked after Pat had been struggling for a time to cut her wrist ropes free.

"Not yet," Pat grumbled. "Will you hold still?"

"Just cut it, damn it! We don't have much time left." Molly gritted her teeth impatiently. "Nate!" she asked the man next to Pat. "If we move around, could you help Pat by telling him where to cut?"

"Molly, I can do it!"

"Then for God's sake, do it!"

"There!" Pat murmured triumphantly. Molly winced. The knife blade had caught the edge of her hand as Bran's brother sawed her ropes free. "Now hurry and undo me!" he urged as Molly rubbed her hands to restore circulation.

"But Bran—"

"Damn it, Molly. Cut me free! It'll take the two of us to rush the guards! You can help him while I release the others."

When she was sure that she wasn't being watched, Molly cut off her leg ropes and then helped Patrick.

"See the guard over there," Pat said, nodding toward Reginald Cornsby. "I'll go after him. Think you can handle the other one?"

"Peabody?" she asked. "Of course." Isaac Peabody was a slim youth; Molly was sure she'd have little difficulty pinning the man down.

Pat reached into the back of the wagon, withdrawing what looked to be a large wooden club. "Here." He handed the weapon to Molly. "Use this to take him out."

"I don't need that."

"Take it, damn it!" Pat growled.

"All right! All right!" Accepting the wooden club, Molly skirted the edge of the camp toward where Isaac Peabody held watch.

Silently Molly crept up behind him. "Isaac," she whispered. He turned and she brought the club crashing down upon the youth's head. "Sorry, Isaac," she murmured as he dropped.

Satisfied, Molly spun back toward the encampment in time to see Reginald Cornsby fall under the butt of an English musket.

She and Patrick exchanged triumphant grins. Then Molly hurried to Bran's side, and Pat hastened to release the Rebel prisoners.

"Bran!" She tried to rouse him. "Bran." Her heart lodged in her throat when she saw the injuries to her beloved's face and body.

Bran blinked up at her through bleary eyes. "Molly?"

373

"Yes, it's me, Molly." Relief made her dizzy. She felt like crying at the knowledge of Bran's pain. "I'm going to cut you down," she told him gently. "Will you be able to stand?"

"Molly? Is it really you?"

Tears filled her eyes as she cradled his face. "Oh, Bran, I'm so sorry. They've hurt you badly and it's my fault."

Bran came to his senses. "Cut me down," he said firmly.

"Of course, love." She sawed at the rope holding his right arm. The hemp frayed and then snapped, and Molly grabbed Bran's arm so he wouldn't fall. "Are you all right?" she asked, her voice husky.

He nodded. "Hurry up and do the other one."

She did so, and Bran would have stumbled when he was free if not for Molly's shoulder beneath his left arm, supporting his weight. "We have to leave before they return," she said.

"What about Pat?" Bran tried to focus his gaze, but his eyes felt heavy. His limbs hung like dead weight.

"He's coming. He's releasing the others." She began dragging him toward the woods. "Pat!" she called, "hurry up!"

"I'm coming!" Pat answered as he released the last of the Rebel prisoners. "Is Bran all right?" When Molly answered in the affirmative, Pat said, "Go on ahead. We'll be right with you. I know I promised not to kill the sorry bastards, but I didn't promise not to raid their supplies!"

Molly leaned her head forward to kiss her beloved's cheek. "We have to go, Bran. Can you make it?"

Bran flashed her a grin. "With you by my side, I can do anything."

Molly caught her breath. His words, the flame of desire in his blue gaze, made her feel warm and tingly inside. "Let's go!"

" 'Fraid not, *little sister,*" a dark voice drawled.

She froze. "Darren!"

"Thought you'd make it, eh? Sorry to disappoint you."

"We're leaving, Darren." Her bravery was a false show of bravado.

"I think not." Darren trained his pistol on Bran's head. "Turn around and head back to camp."

Molly decided to try to stall him. She and Bran couldn't get away, she thought, but at least she could ensure that the others had time to flee!

"Just a minute, Darren." Molly seemed composed, but inside she was shaking. "If it's money you want, Bran can help you. His ship—the *Bloody Mary*—there are riches on board. Let Bran and I go free and you'll be rewarded."

Bran had slumped against her, unconscious again, and his weight against Molly's shoulder was staggering, bearing down on her painfully.

"You must think me an idiot," Darren snarled, fingering his gun. "Do you really believe I'll let you go? That it's money I want and not revenge?"

"Revenge for what?" Molly asked. Her eyes widened with disbelief. "Surely not that!" It couldn't be because he believed that Father had slighted him by sharing his love with his only daughter. Surely it wasn't jealousy that had driven Darren on a quest for revenge.

"You're just like *her*," he said, his jaw tensing. "And I hated her. God, he never loved Mother like he loved his squaw!" His eyes glistened with emotion. "It wasn't fair. Mother was dead only a few months before he brought *her* home."

Gaping, Molly knew who the *her* was; it was her mother, Shi'ki-Xkwe.

"Father loves you," she insisted.

"Then why did he start drinking after *she* died? Why did he fall apart then when by rights it was Mother's death that should've destroyed him?"

"My mother raised you!" Molly exclaimed. "Cared for you!"

"But she *loved* you. You were her precious baby. You and Shelby."

"She would have loved you, but you wouldn't let her! She wanted to!"

Darren's smile was menacing. "That's right. I didn't let her. And I didn't want a sister, but then you were there." He raised the gun with the intent to shoot. "But not for long, by Jesus, not for long!"

"Molly!" Pat cried.

"Darren, no!" someone shouted.

A shot rang into the air. Molly watched with horror as Darren's mouth gaped in an expression of surprise, his eyes glazing over as he dropped his gun and clutched at the red stain spreading across his shirtfront.

"Oh, God!" It was Shelby. He ran to his brother, his face pained. "I'm sorry," he cried, cradling Darren's head, "I didn't want to shoot you, but you gave me no choice! I couldn't let you do it! She's my sister. I love her!" His rasping sobs filtered through the camp, stunning all who had gathered near the two brothers. "I couldn't let you hurt her!"

"Molly?" Bran whispered, opening his eyes.

"Bran, he's dead. Darren's dead." Her voice caught. "Shelby —"

"Go!" Shelby cried, looking up. "Hurry, before the others return!"

Pat and another man rushed forward to relieve Molly of the burden of Bran's weight. "Yes, let's go," Pat said.

Then they became aware that the Tories had already returned, having discovered that they'd been called away falsely, there were no Rebel wagons at Dog's Run. Someone had purposely led the Tories away from camp.

George Merriweather looked shocked as he regarded Darren's felled body and the Rebel prisoners who stood with rifles aimed high and ready to fight. "Well," he blustered, surveying the camp and the odds against him. "I'd say we're about finished here."

"Damn right you're finished!" Mark Dickon stepped into the clearing, backed up by a gang of American seamen. He had Tully McCormick with him, and Talbot and Smith, the two men who had escaped capture. And to everyone's astonishment, Angus MacDuff.

"I couldna allow 'im to 'urt ye," MacDuff said, his face reddening, giving away the identity of the man who'd tricked the Tories into leaving camp.

Molly gave the Scot a wry smile before her attention was drawn to her father, who had suddenly appeared in the camp. Tully was cold sober at present. He saw his two sons and fell to their side with a wild cry.

"Darren!" he wailed, stricken with grief.

Her heart twisting, Molly looked away from her weeping family, her gaze blinded by her own tears. That they had come to this. Brother threatening sister. Brother killing brother. Would it ever end? It wasn't just the war that destroyed families, it was jealousy, misunderstanding, and greed.

"Molly," Bran said. Seeing Molly's distress, he'd found the strength to leave his brother's arms. He wanted to offer his woman comfort.

A gentle touch on her shoulder. A warm hand against the side of Molly's neck.

"Bran," she sobbed. With a cry of pain, Molly burrowed within her beloved's arms. "Darren's dead."

The hand caressing her back stilled. "I know, love." His fingers started to move again as understanding took the place of Bran's momentary anger.

"Sh-sh, love," he soothed, stroking her hair. "Don't cry. It's all over now." He kissed the top of his head, and she shuddered, rubbing her cheek against the warm hard muscles of Bran's bare chest.

Her head lifted. "Oh, Bran, your bruises!" She met his gaze, and Bran caught his breath at the pain in her expression.

He smiled. "I love you, Molly. I'll always love

378

you."

"But the war? What are we going to do?"

Bran sighed. The war was far from over, but he'd decided Molly would remain by his side, war or not. He wasn't about to let her go a second time. He sure as hell wasn't going to wait for the end of this bloody war. "Molly, love, somehow we'll manage."

"If you go back to sea, I'm going with you," Molly stated, pulling from his embrace to gaze at him with dark, defiant eyes.

Bran raised an eyebrow. "Oh, you are, are you?"

She jerked her head. "I am."

Stifling his amusement, Bran opened his mouth to respond. But then his eyes widened and his mouth suddenly fell open, speechless.

"Molly," he said carefully after he'd gathered his wits. "Tell me, love, do you know of any Indians in these woods?"

"Indians?" Molly turned and saw the half-naked figure in the brush. She broke from Bran's hold, stepping forward to meet the fierce-looking warrior as he emerged from the line of trees. Worried, Bran silently followed her.

"He! N'ox!" she greeted the Lenape.

"O'ho! Aluum, n'dah-nes!"

"Molly, what did he say?" Bran whispered anxiously. "Is he alone? Is he friendly?" He frowned, placing a hand on Molly's shoulder.

The warrior suddenly spoke, his eyes narrowing on Bran's hand.

Molly laughed, a series of high tinkling notes that resembled music. Bran stared at her, puzzled but delighted with the singing sound.

"Well?" Bran asked. "What did you tell him?"

"I greeted him, saying, 'Hello, grandfather,' and he answered, 'Hello, Dove, my daughter.

"Grandfather?" Nodding, Molly grinned at her beloved sea captain, before introducing the two men.

Epilogue

"Captain!" Dickon cried, entering the captain's cabin. "We just got word. Cornwallis has surrendered! At Yorktown!"

Molly stirred from the bottom bunk. "Surrendered?"

"It means, love," Bran said, rising from behind his desk, "that the tide may have finally turned in our favor."

"That's right." Dickon smiled at Molly as she rose to her elbows. "The war will be at end any day now, I'll wager."

"Thank God!" Molly murmured. She placed a hand on her flat stomach. *Our baby will be born in a time of peace!* She had yet to tell Bran about the child. She didn't want to worry him. It wasn't her first pregnancy. Two years ago, Molly had miscarried during her eighth month. It had been a painful time, but one that had drawn husband and wife closer.

Molly reflected on their marriage. Starting a new life together hadn't been easy for them. The horror and pain of her brother's death, the terror brought by the continuing war about them, had been too real. That fateful day of the Pine Robbers' capture, she and Bran had gone with Tahuun Kukuus to his village. Shelby, her father, Pat, Dickon, and a few of their other Patriot friends had gone, too. Even the Scot. The Tories were handed over to the nearest branch of the Continental Army.

Bran and Molly had married while among the Delaware. Later, they'd taken their vows again before a preacher in Cooper's Ferry. "So that no one would ever question that you're mine," Bran had said.

Poor Angus, she thought, remembering the Scot. He'd made a terrible mistake, which he'd tried to rectify, but in the end he'd paid for it dearly—with his life. Last year, Angus MacDuff was killed during a battle between the *Bloody Mary* and an English ketch. Bran had forgiven his friend, but the Scot had apparently never forgiven himself. In his need for penance, Angus had courted danger and death—and had lost.

Closing her eyes, Molly sighed. She would never regret her marriage to Bran. The times they were together were filled to overflowing with love and a joy that knew no bounds. When Bran was at sea, Molly's days became empty and worrisome, and she sought comfort in the Lenape village with her Delaware family—and with Shelby and Tully, who'd elected to stay at the settlement at Wood Owl's invitation. Whenever the threat of danger was low,

Bran chanced to take his wife on the ship with him. But Molly found these runs to be too infrequent and all too short.

She thought of the war and what the end would mean to all of them. During her time with Bran, Molly had come to understand the war. Freedom and liberty were worth fighting for, she realized. Should she dare hope that freedom was won?

"Bran, can it be true?" she asked as he sat down beside her on the berth. "Think of it! No more fighting! Will freedom finally be ours. Ours and—"

"Our children's?" Bran finished for her. Drawing her into his arms, he nuzzled his face in the silky dark strands of her hair.

"You know." Snuggling against him, Molly felt a surge of desire.

She felt Bran stiffen. "Know what?" Setting her back, he stared at her warily. Then his beautiful blue gaze widened with discovery. "Your illness! You haven't been seasick, have you?"

Molly shook her head. "As much as I hate being below, have you ever known me to be sick?"

"No." His voice sounded choked.

Molly's eyes took on a gleam of amusement. Recalling the first mate's presence, she said, "Dickon, would you leave us?"

"I'm on my way," the mate said, grinning.

"Molly," her husband whispered, his face pale. His fingers trembled as he cupped her jaw. "Is it? Are you?" When she nodded, he gasped, "A babe?"

"Yes, love," she said, reaching up to trace his

383

lips with a caressing finger.

Bran frowned with worry. "Molly . . ."

Her dark eyes flashed. "Don't you be looking at me that way, Captain Donovan! I'm fine; our babe's going to fine." She stopped and smiled. His brow had cleared at her display of spirit, and laughter lurked in the back of his blue eyes. She felt her breasts tingle at his flaming look. Her pulse quickened, and a sudden warmth invaded her being.

"Bran?" she said shakily.

"Yes, love?"

"Kiss me, Taande Wee-lan-o, before this child grows too big between us."

"Our child will never stop me from kissing you, dear heart," he promised. And then Bran kissed her.

And she burned.